NO BROKEN BEAST

NICOLE SNOW

ICE LIPS PRESS

ABOUT THE BOOK

Fierce. Scarred. Ginormous grump.
   And I get to tell him he's a father...

Brilliant life decisions—falling for the bad guy.
   Leo damn Regis. Hated scourge of Heart's Edge.
   A wall with arms and legs. Hercules dipped in ink. Incandescent eyes.
   The legend, the outcast, the boy I loved.

But the man they call "Nine" isn't the villain they think.
   He saved my life and seared my heart once upon a messed up time.
   We planned our great escape. He made promises in diamond.
   Then a sucker punch of fate said *Nope* to our fairy tale.

I'm not here to kiss and make up. I'm looking for my missing sister.
   Only one hulking, gravel-voiced man has the clues.
   Ugh. I so don't need Leo's protection.
   Don't even get me started on his oh-so-secret past.

The best part? He doesn't have a clue what *I'm* hiding.

It's got ten little fingers and ten little toes and eyes just like his.

I'm no beauty. He's too beast. Fun times ahead.

They say you can't run forever. Sometimes you stand. Sometimes you fight.

And sometimes an unbroken hero barges back in to lay down the law...

I: IT'S NOT THE BEGINNING
(CLARISSA)

I always thought déjà vu would be like the books and movies.

Seasick, blurring vision, sound coming down a wind tunnel of slow, sleepy voices.

Everything swaying back and forth.

On TV, déjà vu is this slow thing that whirls you around like a merry-go-round grinding to a halt with your stomach left somewhere far behind your bobbing horse.

But in reality, déjà vu comes quick.

Harsh.

It's a slap to the face, a gut punch, a falling elevator.

And right now it's hitting hard enough to leave me breathless as I stand in the ruins of my once proud candy store.

Can I even call it *my* store?

My *stores* are back in Spokane, where I started this chain. Sweeter Things shops pepper Eastern Washington and branch west to Seattle.

Technically, I co-own the Heart's Edge branch, too, but I haven't even seen it until now. Not beyond a few photos when my sister Deanna first bought the property to bring our franchise to Montana.

I've never needed to *see* it before. I trusted my baby sister to keep the business running just fine.

Especially when seeing it means returning to this cursed town, after I swore I'd never, ever come back again.

Last time I was here, I stood in the ruins of a life, watching everything I love burn down around me.

There's no fire here in the candy shop.

Just displays tipped over, supplies strewn everywhere, glass and dishes and cookware smashed and thrown across the room.

But I can smell phantom smoke anyway. It makes my chest so tight I feel like I'm choking on memories, the worst night of my life.

"—iss Bell? *Ms. Bell.* You listenin' to me?"

I blink, shaking myself.

There it is. The *wah-wah* voice, that Charlie Brown's teacher trombone thing, and I realize Sheriff Langley has been talking to me through his thick handlebar mustache, looking at me quizzically with his pad held awkwardly in his hand while I just stare numbly at the shop's carnage.

For his sake, I nod, never taking my eyes off the scene.

All the pieces are still here, just broken. Everything except my sister.

She's *missing.*

That's part of the sucker punch, too. Remembering that awful night, trying to find her, trying to save her, to be the big sister she needs and protect her, only I was so much younger then.

I'm older now.

Old enough to realize, far too late, that I should've *been* here in Heart's Edge to help watch over her, instead of running away while she meddled with things better left alone.

I press my fingers to my mouth, closing my eyes, taking a shaky breath as I remember our last phone call, how excited and yet frantic she sounded as she said, *I think I'm onto something,*

Rissa. Something big. Something that'll finally let us take back our lives and move on.

Don't, I'd told her. *Our lives were never taken, sis. We're alive, and I'm grateful for that every day. I don't need anything else. I'm happy now.*

She'd been so angry with me for saying that.

Called me passive, scared, a liar, said she was going to—

I don't even know.

The phone cut off with an ominous crackle. I thought she'd hit her limit for tough sisterly love and ended the call.

Then the next time it rang twenty-four hours later, it was this small-eyed sheriff with his peculiar way of squinting and his familiar drawl, telling me somebody broke into the shop, and Deanna's nowhere to be found.

"Ms. Bell?" Langley whispers again. "You don't look so good. You sure you don't just wanna–"

"No." I take a deep breath, open my eyes, force myself to focus on him with my head swimming and my heart so heavy it crushes everything inside me into a massive ball of pain. "I'm listening. I'm sorry. I...you're sure she's not at home?"

"I searched up and down, ma'am. Even know where she keeps the spare key. Them fake rocks don't fool nobody." He tries to smile, but it's a sad thing, a confused line, like he wants to try to make me feel better but knows he can't. "I looked all over her apartment, Ms. Bell. Everything's all neat and tidy. If anybody's been in there, they weren't looking for loot. And it doesn't look like she left in a hurry. And..."

He clears his throat and looks out the front display window.

The *shattered* front display window, open to the slowly cooling air of early autumn whisking inside. Not far from my sister's car, an Easter-candy-pink vintage VW bug, sitting in the lot.

It's surrounded by the shards of glass from the broken windows. They're mixed with the broken window pieces of the shop that used to say Sweeter Things in curly gold letters

3

garnished with pink and green flowers made to look like they were sculpted out of fondant.

Jesus, is that blood?

Is that glinting red edge along one glassy fragment *blood*?

Or just the sandy red earth of the rolling landscape? Mountains and valleys and forest beyond the main road, reflecting back in the broken pieces?

I can't ask myself that.

I can't, or I'll hyperventilate and pass out right here, and then I'm no good to anyone.

Langley clears his throat again. He can't say it.

So I take a deep breath and finish his sentence. "...and you think if she was kidnapped, it had to be here?"

"Uh, yup." He frowns down at his pad. The page is blank, but I don't think he realizes I notice that. "Look, I'm gonna be straight with you, ma'am. This doesn't make a lick of sense."

"Do senseless acts of violence ever make sense, Sheriff?"

"No, but...dammit."

He squints, looking out across the sunny afternoon, slow and thoughtful. Sheriff Langley's not cut out for this kind of sleuthing.

Heart's Edge shouldn't be cut out for this kind of crime at all, if you take the town at face value.

On the surface, it's Pleasantville.

Small-town values, small-town goodness, small-town charm.

Beautiful vistas.

Quaint local legends.

All the heart and warmth and welcome of a place off the beaten path, where no one's a stranger and everyone's a friend.

But underneath, it's totally Stepford town.

Vicious secrets with a smile, and every last one of them could kill you.

I just hope those secrets haven't gotten Deanna.

"I just don't get it. Why the kidnapping?" he finally finishes, like his mouth caught up to whatever his brain was turning over.

Probably trying to figure out how to handle a crime scene investigation that isn't cow tipping or someone getting a little too wasted at Brody's and trying to drive home. "I mean, we got ourselves a pretty standard smash and grab here. Break in, get the cash in the register, get out. Why they gonna go and take your sister?"

I have a thousand answers to that, but none I can give him.

Some things are better left buried. The less people know, the better.

Some things I wish *I* didn't know. But there's something I can do, at least.

Stepping through the shop front gingerly, the glass crunching and crackling under my heeled boots, I pull the sleeve of my thin knit sweater over my hand as I round the shattered display counter. I don't want to mess up any fingerprints with my own, if Langley ever manages to get around to taking them.

But when I punch in the override code, the cash drawer pops out.

I stare down at the stacks of bills and coins inside.

"It's full," I say, my lips numb. "They didn't take the money."

They just took Deanna.

"Shit. Huh," Langley says, scratching his pen into his thinning hair, frowning. "Like I said...don't make sense."

"No," I answer slowly, dread turning my mouth bone-dry. "No, it doesn't."

There's a long, awkward silence.

Langley clears his throat, stops, then starts again, making a confused sandpaper sound before he sighs and hitches his belt up. "Listen, I'm gonna have to call in an investigative unit from Missoula. We just don't have the resources out here."

I nod slowly. *Good.*

Missoula means more people with more experience with crimes above petty theft, who might be able to *do* something. "How long do you think that'll take?"

"Don't know." He looks uneasy. "You planning on staying here in town?"

"*Yes*," I snap. How could I not with my sister just *gone?*

It's not his fault, I remind myself. *Rein it in.*

I know why he's looking at me so funny. Uncomfortably, nervously, like he can't believe I'm back here at all.

Small towns have long memories.

So do I.

Wentworth Langley was there that night so many years ago, same as me. I only wish I couldn't feel the pity party dripping out of his eyes.

Everyone sees me as the sad, tragic girl who lost her illustrious father. The human symbol of a small-town tragedy.

They have no flipping clue what I truly lost that night.

Langley makes an odd scratchy sound in the back of his throat and looks away, embarrassment scrunching on his forehead in ridges. "Well...you wanna lay low, keep it hush-hush, I won't say a thing. If...you know, if you don't want to draw too much attention to yourself, Ms. Bell."

Dear God. I'd rather be invisible.

I hate the way people look at me.

I hate that every time someone looks at me, they aren't seeing Clarissa Bell.

They're either seeing my father...or *him*.

The man they blame for everything. The monster. The outlaw. The demon of Heart's Edge.

And I can tell, when their eyes go just a little blank, their smiles just a little too plastic, they're thinking about what a poor victim I am. Or maybe *what a fool* to have ever loved a madman.

But I'm not a victim.

I haven't even seen him in so long. Who knows if he's alive.

Still, as long as I'm here, I can't escape how deep we're intertwined.

At least when I'm away from this town, the one sweet reminder I let myself keep only brings joy.

Until a resounding metallic *crash* comes through the double doors leading back into the kitchen, and I groan. There's my sweet little joy. *Right.*

I know that sound.

It's not a kidnapper. It's not trouble.

It's *my son,* refusing to sit still when I ask him to.

Sure as the sky is blue, when I glance into the parking lot, there's no little crop of chestnut-brown hair poking up in the passenger seat of my car, where I *told* him to stay.

Rather, the instant I push the kitchen doors open, there's a shame-faced seven-year-old boy covered in flour, surrounded by the huge industrial mixer bowls he's just knocked over.

Deanna must've been right in the middle of prepping tomorrow's batch when she was interrupted.

The thought is sobering enough that I can't even be mad at Zach.

I don't have room to be pissed at the people I love. Not when I'm so scared for the only other flesh and blood family I have left besides this beautiful—and dusty—little boy staring nervously down at his feet right now.

"I don't even know what to ask first," I say, folding my arms over my chest. "Do I want to know why, or how?"

Zach winces. "It was an accident, Mom."

"That explains the how. Now how about the why?"

"I just...I wanted to see if it was sugar or flour!" he confesses meekly, and I sigh.

What he means is, he was hoping it was sugar he could steal for his insatiable sweet tooth.

He gets that from his father.

I know from experience. But I push that thought aside before those memories, those idyllic nights, can rise up to make me hurt with the memory of what could've been.

There's no room in my life for could-have-beens.

Only for the present.

7

And it's a life I've made all my own. Piece by painstaking piece, all for a son I love more than anything.

Sighing, I reach out to draw him closer, ruffling his hair, making it snow flour down the shoulders of his already-dusty jacket. "Come on, ZZ-boy," I say. "There's really nothing else we can do here. Let's get you cleaned up."

* * *

I ALMOST DON'T RECOGNIZE the man behind the counter at the Charming Inn.

Half a lifetime ago, I remember playing with Warren Ford as a kid.

I remember him being taller than the other boys, and any time someone got it in their head to be a bully, Warren would be there, making a human wall out of himself.

I remember how he'd play and tussle with Blake and his brother, Holt, and that strange boy we all called Tiger. Usually Deedee and I just watched and laughed and braided flower crowns, Warren's sister Jenna bouncing around between us and the boys until she was a dirty mess with flowers in her hair and new rips in her jeans.

Now, standing here with all six foot something of his thirty-something self, he's a memory of my childhood, of boys with dusty knees and crooked smiles and sunshine-freckles and messy thatches of dark hair.

In my head, he's not the owner of Charming Inn, so it's just...weird.

It's *jarring* to see him here and not Ms. Wilma Ford, his grandma. Instead, he's with a short, curvy, green-eyed woman who must be his wife. She's tucked against his side, a little boy with bright-blue eyes and a gurgling laugh bouncing on his hip.

When I look at Warren, I still see that gangly boy with hands and feet too big for his body.

But there's a bearded man looking back at me, a man who's

clearly been through things judging by the scars and tattoos on his body, and the old shadows haunting clear eyes.

Things I've missed, because I ran away from home and all my old friends. It's just a reminder how much time has passed.

I've been staring wide-eyed ever since I stepped into the lobby of the main house of the sprawling Charming Inn. The place is much like I remember, at least, a mix of rental suites surrounding the big plantation-style mansion and cozier private guest cottages.

My floury son hides behind my back, but Warren stares at me with the same stricken look that must be on my face.

Then he smiles—rueful, but warm, with a kind of accepting shrug, as if to say *what can you do?*

I shrug back, offering the same wistful smile. *Not much.*

"Hey, Rissa Bell," he murmurs. "Welcome home."

The woman—she must be Haley, I spoke with her on the phone on the frantic drive out here, and she confirms it when I recognize the warmth of her voice—brightens. "Oh! Clarissa Bell, right? Are you ready to check in?" She grins, leaning to peer past me at Zach. "And I see somebody needs a shower."

"Sorry," I offer sheepishly, glancing at my boy. "Go wait on the porch, baby. You're getting flour on the carpet."

"Aw, don't worry about it," Haley says, and leans up to kiss Warren's cheek before peeling away from him and fishing through the ring of keys on her belt. "Here, I'll take you out to your cabin. It's one of our new additions in the woods, and I don't want you getting lost. They haven't quite finished grading the paths yet, so it's more of a..." She wrinkles her nose. "I don't even want to call it a trail. It's a suggestion. But once you get oriented, you won't get turned around, I promise."

"Thanks," I say faintly and let her bustle me and Zach outside.

I can feel Warren watching me curiously. Probably wondering what the hell brought me back to Heart's Edge.

He wasn't here that night. I heard he spent years as a stranger to this town himself after Jenna was killed overseas.

But I'm sure he's heard things about me, too.

All the rumors, the lies, the things that might be true, but I can't stand to know.

And there are things he can't know, either.

Things I won't answer, if he ever decides to have a friendly chitchat with a childhood friend.

Things I *can't* answer, when the one person who might be able to fill in those gaps is just a ghost, a shadow haunting this town.

I hear they're calling him Nine now. The legend in the hills. A monster man who's become so infamous the tall tales are almost turning supernatural.

To me, he'll just be Leo.

The cabin Haley shows us to is new. It's set off from the rest of the others dotting the slope leading down to the half-heart cliff that shapes Heart's Edge. She said something about privacy suites and new construction when we'd spoken on the phone. I'd mentioned wanting to keep a low profile and stay out of sight.

Which means there's a screening wall of trees separating the rustic but modern cabin from the rest of the property. I can barely see the white columns of the main house through the fat trunks.

We pick our way up the wooded slope angling deeper into the mountains and the lush green acres of untouched forest. That's what always makes the air smell like this. Crisp, cool pine, no matter the time of year.

The other cabins are nearly invisible from the wooden deck encircling ours.

Perfect.

We don't belong here. *I* don't belong here. So this will do.

I certainly don't plan on staying long enough for anyone to start painting me back into this landscape, getting silly ideas in their heads.

As if I could ever be part of Heart's Edge again.

As if I'd ever spend an extra minute in this town.

Yeah. If only Deanna's life didn't depend on it.

* * *

IT TAKES an hour to help get Zach clean, when water just turns the flour in his hair into dough.

He wriggles like a puppy while I stroke his head, scrub and rinse, until he's no longer a human cookie. Just my sweet boy, laughing and squirming. I hug him tight and blow raspberries in his wet hair, then shoo him off to finish washing up proper and change for bed, even though it's barely time for dinner.

I leave him curled up happily on the couch, half watching TV, half browsing takeout menus. I'm not up for a grocery trip tonight.

Maybe not any night.

Shopping feels too much like settling in.

Like killing time, when all I can do is wait for the detectives from Missoula to try to make sense of the crime scene and pick up Deanna's trail.

God, I hate waiting.

Knowing the statistics on kidnapping recovery rates doesn't help a bit.

People only come home with clear motives. When things like ransoms are involved, and the kidnappers want something tangible, when they leave more demands than icy silence.

I swallow something thick in my throat. The best way to silence someone is to make sure they never breathe another word, and after what happened to drive me out of Heart's Edge...

If she was here, I could smack her. Because if Deanna's been digging around old graves, maybe our friends at Galentron finally decided having her running around as a loose cannon was too risky.

My eyes sting. I'm trying not to panic.

Excusing myself from the living room, I head into the kitchen before Zach sees me close to a nervous breakdown.

I can't expose my son to this crap.

He's too sensitive as it is. He picks up on things far too easily.

I couldn't leave him behind in Spokane, no, but I'll be damned if I let the darkness here touch him.

It would only scare him, and scare me. After I failed to protect Deanna...I have to protect my sweet, bright boy, in all his soft, shy innocence.

Sighing, I want to start unpacking to distract myself, but the second I open the suitcase, a little black box comes tumbling out of the inside pocket.

Deep breath. I'm so *not* breaking down over this stupid thing. Again.

What was I even thinking, bringing it along for the ride? Bringing it *here?*

It's the stress, I tell myself, sinking down on the edge of the bed. I curl forward with my arms pressed hard against my stomach and my head low.

Stress, confusion, fear for Deanna, and all the hard, angry, lonely emotions wrapped up in that dusty little black velvet box that's so old the soft outer surface has started wearing off.

I can't even stand to open it, to look at the gleam of silver and diamond inside, to remember the broken promise that ring represents.

Swearing under my breath, I fight back my tears with all the stubborn strength I've built as a single mom raising a little boy for seven damn years all by myself.

Then I snatch up the box and shove it back into the suitcase, out of sight.

Out of mind? I wish.

* * *

Eight Years Ago

I WONDER if this is what dying feels like.

Pain bursting everywhere, the smell of my own blood, the metallic taste in my mouth.

And Leo cradling me so tight when I can't hold myself up, when all my strength is gone and bleeding out of me all over the floor, but he's grasping me like he can hold me together in one piece if he just loves me hard enough.

"You'll be all right," he growls, staring down at me with so much faith, desperation, and a million conflicting emotions in his eyes.

His eyes are the strangest shade I've ever seen, but that's just another thing I love about him.

If you look at them dead-on, they're dark, almost mocha. But when the light catches them, then there's hints of violet, crystal and luminous, like an amethyst on a moonless night.

Those eyes anchor me in place now. Those arms keep me alive.

I think if he wasn't holding on to me, I'd just slip away and maybe never wake up.

Part of me isn't sure I want to.

Not when my father's dead body lies only five feet away, his feet protruding at this sickening angle. And the blood on Leo's hands is only partly mine.

The other blood...it's spattered across Leo's cheek, the front of his shirt, the hands he holds me with so gently as he swallows tight. He presses his forehead to mine, resolve firming in his gaze, in the tight line of his jaw.

I don't know how to feel.

Just three minutes ago, my father's hands were around my throat, choking me until I couldn't breathe and stars burst across my vision, and I realized the man who's always controlled my entire life was about to end it.

My head keeps ringing from the vase he smashed against my skull.

And the worst part is, Leo needs to leave.

I know it even before he brushes my hair back, easing me against his chest.

"Hold on for me, Rissa," he murmurs, that thunder voice gentle, pleading.

I try to nod. He's so handsome even now, racked with guilt and purpose, his face cut in square regal lines and his hair a dark sweep across his brow, raw strength in every line of him. "I love you—I'll always love you. Hold on. Wait for me. I have to stop this shit. I have to..."

"N-no." I can barely get the words out. I'm weak, but I manage to lift a shaking hand, reaching for him. "It's...th-the risk...it's too much. L-Leo, if...if they find out...they'll...th-they'll..."

I can't say it. I don't need to. I think he knows.

His smile is sad yet brave, so brave, and I realize he's already accepted his fate.

That's one thing I love about him, and it's the same thing I hate about him.

He's a noble man.

So noble he'll sacrifice himself, if it means doing what he thinks is right to save me, to save this town.

He cups a large, weathered hand to my cheek. He's such a beast, my gentle giant, full of so much passion I never thought he could hurt anyone. Even though security is kinda his job.

But after tonight...

He looks at the maid behind me, helping hold me up, his eyes pure violet-black fire. "Get her out of town," he says. "Out of Heart's Edge. You, too. Get as far away as you can."

"Leo, Leo, come with us..." I whimper.

He protests softly at first, says a few things that just wash over me, tries to tear himself away. But I'll never, ever forget his last words as he comes back and holds me again so, so tight.

"I'm already damned," he says. "Already going to jail. Let me do one last thing right before they find me and throw away the key. I have to, Rissa. For the town. But if you'll wait for me, I'll come back. Somehow, some fucking way, I swear I will. I'll *always* come back for you, woman, no matter how much hell it takes."

I try to clutch at him with my blood-streaked, shaking fingers.

But he's already pulling away, already gone, even as the maid standing nearby gestures and hisses for him to hurry, even as I hear my father's secretary in the hall, even as the howl of ambulances coming to save my life moves in and it's already too late to save my father's.

And too late to save Leo.

No matter his promises, no matter if I believe them...

He's leaving me now.

I have no way of knowing, in that moment, what's to come, but I feel it.

It's deep in my shivering, hurting bones and the fading sweet heat of his Hercules bear hug.

I'll never see Leo Regis again.

* * *

Present

"Mom?"

I jerk up from staring blankly at the webbing of the suitcase's inside pocket, my hand still tucked inside, the velvet box clutched against my palm. I suck in a harsh breath, my chest tight, as my vision re-focuses.

Zach stands in the doorway, clutching the stack of takeout

menus that were tucked in the utensil drawer of the cabin's kitchen.

I force a smile, holding out both hands for him.

"What's popping, ZZ Top? Need something?"

He wrinkles his nose.

"Don't call me that," he says, but it's a halfhearted protest as he bounces over to settle down next to me and tuck against my side, fitting himself into my arms. "Can we order pizza tonight?"

"Sure. But no olives."

He sticks his tongue out at me. "Olives are the best part."

"Which is why you get your own pizza, and I'll just have to live without the best part." I pluck the top menu from the stack, looking down at the prices and flipping it over to check the phone number.

Zach watches me curiously. He's got round, inquisitive eyes. Someday, he'll grow into them, but right now, when he's this small, they only make him look even more like a puppy. Though I've never seen any puppy with his unique shade.

Mocha in the dark.

Brilliant amethyst in the light.

A legacy he'll never know.

I'm just glad most of the time his glasses hide them, keeping the color murky and unclear. If anyone in Heart's Edge ever got a good, solid look at him...dear God, the things they'd say.

Would some angry people even pin the sins of his father on my sweet boy?

It's like he senses my thoughts. He puts his pint-sized hand against my arm and murmurs, "Mom? Why are you so sad? Is it Auntie Deanna?"

I stiffen, trying not to let him feel it when it might upset him.

Instead, I plaster on a motherly smile for him, finding it in me somewhere because I always find *something* buried deep in my heart for him. That's what happens when someone calls you mom.

"Yeah," I answer faintly. "I'm just worried about her, but you shouldn't be. We'll find her sooner or later and she'll be okay. Soon we'll have a whole team of pros helping track her down, don't you worry."

"I know," he says. I hear the conviction in his tone only the very young can have. "But Mom, if she's going to be okay...why are you so sad? Isn't this like coming home?"

I flinch. This time, I can't hide it from him, and he makes a soft, apologetic sound and snuggles closer to me.

Heart's Edge hasn't been home for almost a freaking decade.

I don't know what he overheard, how he knows it was home once a long lost time ago. Some little thing I said to Deedee on the phone, maybe.

Zach's a smart boy. Crazy observant. I just hadn't realized he'd figured it out.

This isn't just visiting a weird little mountain town where his aunt lives.

This is a homecoming I never wanted.

But I press a kiss to the top of his head, wrap my arm around his shoulders, and pull him into a hug. "It's not home, sweetie," I murmur. "But we can try to have some fun while we're here, once your Auntie Deanna's back safe."

And we *will* find her safe, I tell myself. Galentron's already taken too much from me.

It won't devour my sister, too.

I swear, I won't let it dismember my happy little family.

II: IT'S JUST THE END (NINE)

*H*eart's Edge has a pulse.

And I know when that pulse is agitated. It's like I have my fingers pressed against the throat of the town constantly, feeling its heartbeat racing. Tonight, it's pounding with adrenaline and fear and keyed-up tension.

Something's happened, and I can almost smell it in the air like ozone.

Death's come back to this town.

It's prowling the streets, looking for an unsuspecting victim. Or has it found one already?

I crouch on a small bluff overlooking the town's twinkling lights, hiding myself in the shadows of the trees. Not that anyone would think to look up and see me here. They never do.

Every day, every night, this place goes about its business so complacently, never aware I'm always here. Always watching. Always waiting.

What I'm waiting for, I don't even fucking know anymore.

But I think there's a piece of it here.

I watch Sheriff Wentworth Langley's small silhouette trundling around the wreckage of Deanna Bell's candy store, stringing up bumblebee-yellow crime scene tape around the building and its parking lot in the fading twilight glow.

What's strange is that he's the only person there.

It's too early for reinforcements from Missoula and Spokane. I know damn well Langley and his part-time deputies can't handle whatever ill wind is blowing into Heart's Edge—and the good news is they have the sense to know it, too.

But he shouldn't be getting into his patrol car and driving away.

Someone—Hawthorne or Sanchez, one of his usual guys—should be on patrol tonight.

So I wait.

I wait till nightfall sinks deeper, and no one will notice me. I also wait to see if another pair of headlights will pull up in one of the town's rare police cruisers.

Nothing.

Something's off.

And considering Sweeter Things has only been open for three weeks, and considering who runs it...fuck.

Yeah, I'm worried.

I'm just glad that whatever trouble's surfacing, *she's* not here to get caught between a wrecking ball and a hard place. That's my job.

Once I'm sure no one's coming, I move, taking a second to make sure my hood's pulled up, my face covered.

I take the short way, dropping down the side of the bluff and catching protruding roots and crags to slow my fall, swinging down in short leaps. I know these mountains and forests and bluffs like the back of my hand. Never fail to find my way even in the night.

I fit in better out here than I ever would in town.

Even if it means turning into an animal that prowls around in the dark.

Hell, maybe I *am* an animal, after all this time. Just another beast, drawn by the faint whiff of blood on the air.

Gone feral, back to the wild, out here alone.

I hit the ground in a thicket of trees at the foot of the bluff and linger there while a truck sweeps along the highway, headlights leading it, then vanishing only to turn in at Brody's. Probably one of the pub's usual evening guests.

The moment the light disappears, I'm vaulting the guardrail and sprinting across the street, then ducking around the side of the building out of sight. I pause just past the perimeter of the crime scene tape.

I can't let anyone see me.

Sure, a few people glimpsed me now and then over the years. But as long as it's just flashes, they can treat me like an urban legend. The twisted myth, the monster in the woods, all scars and arcane tattoos.

But if anyone sees me long enough to be sure, to report it, that's when I'm boned. That's when the cuffs come out.

I can't go back to fucking prison.

Never again.

If I'm a beast, I was never meant to be caged.

From the shadows, I take in the destruction out front. The storefront window looks shattered, glass shards winking like a mirror image of the sky, bright points on black. A pink Beetle that I know belongs to Deanna Bell is roped off in its own pointless circle of crime scene tape, the passenger window broken out.

Shit.

I know Deanna lives alone, ever since she moved back here and got herself an apartment. Not much choice when the old mansion—her father's place—was turned into the local Heart's Edge History Museum.

Besides a couple part-time teenagers and supply runners from Spokane, she runs the shop by herself.

Why smash the passenger window?

If you were going after Deanna, you'd hit the driver's side.

Unless it was meant to intimidate. Random, crude vandalism.

I wonder, taking in the chaos visible through the broken shop window.

Whoever came here tried to scare Deanna. Stop her from even thinking about making a break for her car and escaping.

They must've snatched her here, using another vehicle. It's the reason her car would still be in the lot. The only reason for this chill down my spine, this thing some might call premonition, but I label *instinct*.

The only other logical explanation in the scattered evidence and echoes of violence is that someone broke into the shop and Deanna fled, then lost herself in the woods trying to escape.

My brows furrow.

There's *one* last option, but I already know Langley and the search teams from out of town won't turn up with Deanna's body in a day or two, a victim of random violence.

Bull. Nothing in Heart's Edge is *ever* that random.

When someone dies, there's a reason.

And Deanna's not dead, I tell myself firmly.

Maybe because I couldn't stand it if she was.

She's like the little sister I should've had, and after I failed to protect Clarissa...

Dammit, no. I can't stand that the girl might've been murdered in cold blood on my watch.

Deanna's my responsibility.

This entire town is my responsibility.

Even if I haven't seen her face-to-face in years, I know Deanna Bell. Know how well she knows Heart's Edge and its wicked secrets.

She grew up here, just like me.

Just like Warren, and Blake, and Holt, and Jenna.

Just like Clarissa.

Deanna's more likely to get lost between her own living room and kitchen when she knows these woods almost as well as I do. She'd spent years in Spokane, yeah, but you never forget your old childhood stomping grounds.

So if she's not here, not home, not dead, isn't it obvious what happened?

Taken.

Possibly taken hostage by someone who's going to regret it dearly.

The shop might give me answers. A hidden clue, a coded message, more details left in crumbs of evidence that Langley likely isn't qualified to nibble.

I slip around the back of the shop. The front is too visible, and there's still some part of me hard-coded to law and order that says not to cross that bright-yellow crime scene tape.

Still, I'm perfectly okay with picking locks.

Reaching into my coat pocket, I fish around till I find something I can use. It's a slender awl, long and almost needle-like, used for wood etching, but it'll do—though I'll be pissed if I wind up snapping it.

Tools like this are hard to come by when you live off rare cash and can't set foot in a single store in a fifty-mile radius.

I don't get a chance to try the lock. A sudden noise from the far side of the building has me bolting up, retreating back into the darkest shadows against the wall.

Is that...?

Someone retching, I realize.

Loud, hoarse, and most definitely not happy about their guts, judging by the swearing coming from the mouth of the alley.

I should go.

Make myself invisible again and leave this crap to the police. Missoula will send someone sharp. They'll get to the bottom of it. For all I know, in a week Deanna will be home, and this will all be forgotten save for a brief headline splash.

But whoever I'm hearing sounds like they're gagging. Possibly choking.

A rough sigh scrapes out my lungs. *The shit I do for this town...*

Whatever. I'll make sure they're okay, and then disappear.

I make just enough noise as I round the corner of the

building that they'll hear me coming, scuffing my boots so they'll pick up on my footsteps without being scared out of their skin.

Still, when I stop at the end of the alleyway and realize who it is, I'm not sure who flinches more.

Me—or Blake's sixteen-year-old daughter.

Andrea Silverton.

I can smell moonshine on her. *Strong.* Overwhelming. Stinging my nose.

It's that clear rocket fuel some of the local kids brew, though they think their parents have no idea.

She's not old enough to be drinking.

But I'm sure she's figuring that out awful fast, considering the mess she's left and the way she wipes at her mouth sourly as she eyes me with wary eyes from beneath her crop of half-shaved, defiantly rainbow-dyed hair.

"Go away, you creep," she slurs.

For a second I cock my head. Do I really look so hideous in the open like this?

Usually, though, when people meet the infamous monster of Heart's Edge, there's wild screaming.

She's just tipsy, but that doesn't stop her from fumbling her keys from the pocket of her patch-covered jean jacket and clutching them between her knuckles, thrusting them at me like a kitten and staggering a step back. Her breath clouds gently in the cooling evening air. "I don't h-have any...sch...m-money."

I hold up both hands.

"I'm not here for your money, Andrea." I shouldn't have let her name slip, to most people in this town I'm a stranger. It's out now, and I continue calmly. "Just want to make sure you're okay. Where's your old man?"

I'm lucky she's drunk enough—and upset enough—to take the question at face value and not even think to ask how I know her name, or her father.

Her face screws up into a sullen scowl.

She's flushed with anger, not just booze.

23

"He's at the stupid radio station again," she mutters, letting her keys drop to dangle limply from her fingers. "Like he thinks he's some kind of hotshot shock jock or something and he's like..." Her shoulders sag. "He's making us look stupid. With his dumb advice line. I mean, *advice?* He's so dumb. *So dumb.* Nobody should be asking him anything." She lets out a moan. "Everybody at school laughs at him..."

I get it now.

Blake's embarrassing his daughter, and she doesn't know if she wants to defend him or be furious with him.

So all she can do is rebel, act out the way teenagers usually do. Nothing says teen spirit more than getting drunk and doing things you shouldn't.

I let my hands drop. "He's gonna be upset if he gets home and you're not there."

"I don't *care!*" she yells. "Clark...Clark Patten dared me...he dared me *and* Lucy Ardent, and Lucy was a big fat *cluck-cluck* chicken but I'm *not.* I'm gonna get photos of the crime scene and the dead body. Just you wait."

My eyes widen. My heart stops. My blood rages.

"Dead body?" I repeat, and Andrea slumps against the wall. "What're you talking–"

"There's gotta be one, right?" She glowers at me, her eyes dilated and hazy. I wonder if she can even make me out, or if I'm just a huge blur to her, one she doesn't match up with all the local legends about Nine. "They wouldn't put this much crime scene tape up if there wasn't a stiff in there!"

I breathe out a sigh of relief as my heart remembers how to beat again.

Fuck, she's just guessing. I should've known.

Kids' rumors always grow in the telling.

If there was a body, *Deanna's* dead body, Langley wouldn't have left the crime scene unguarded.

I've got to figure out what happened, though, before those rumors spiral out of control and turn from idle speculation into small-town gossip. That crap has a way of bending the truth and jumping well beyond Heart's Edge.

And I can't have anything scaring Clarissa into coming back here. Not after the way she ran. She must have a happy life somewhere, a peace she never found with me, and I won't be the reason it goes up in smoke.

I won't be her ruin again.

I've already brought enough destruction.

And after the dustup over Gray a few months ago nearly turned this town into a hotbed of death and destruction, the whole place is still on edge—especially with no real explanations. At least nothing anyone believes about why the old theater burned down.

I'd bet if you told anyone I had something to do with it, they'd believe you.

And, of course, I did have something to do with that, but not the way most people think.

But I'm not talking, and the hero of the day, Doc—Gray Caldwell—has kept his mouth shut for good reason.

No one here needs to know how close Heart's Edge came to experiencing disaster again.

For the second time in less than ten years.

I'm still worried Galentron will try for number three.

And if those fucks succeed, I'll be the only one left alive because I'm the only one immune to their shit.

That company has infected this town like poison. Deanna's disappearance is just another sign of how deep the rot could spread.

I have to bring her home alive. I *will*.

But first I need to get Andrea off the street.

Or else Blake will shit kittens and a few low-grade explosives when he finds out his underage daughter was stumbling around alone after dark, shitfaced on rotgut moonshine and trying to find a corpse that I *hope* with every part of me doesn't exist.

"Hey," I coax. "There's no dead body. It was just a smash and grab. I already checked. Boring, right? So maybe you should just go home."

She pouts. "I can't go home. Clark, he'll...he'll think I don't have any fucking stones at all."

"He doesn't need to know. Where the hell is this kid, anyway? He couldn't come down here himself? Seems like you've already earned your street cred. Plus you look like you really want to brush your teeth."

"Oh my God." Andrea grimaces and swipes the back of one hand across her mouth. "Yuck!"

"Exactly."

She looks up and stares at me then. I'm thankful she's drunk enough not to question who I am, or why I'm dressed in black from head to toe, my face shrouded in a hoodie that's way over-done for keeping warm.

The girl isn't stupid. I've watched Andrea grow up from afar, and she's tough and fearless and smart, but maybe she could learn to worry a little more about being alone in a dark alley, drunk, with a very large, very spooky man looming over her.

Heart's Edge isn't usually the kind of place where you have to be afraid of things like that.

But you can never be too safe.

And I damn sure can't leave the daughter of a man who used to be one of my closest friends out here to fend for herself.

"C'mon, little badass," I growl, offering her my gloved hand. "I'll walk you home, and we'll figure out how to make Clark jealous you came out here tonight when he didn't."

* * *

Years Ago

"HEY! HEY, TIGER!"

26

I look up, stopping the scritch-scratch of my pocket knife over the branch I'm whittling.

I don't know what it'll be yet. Haven't decided because I want it to be something small and pretty, but I'm real clumsy and sometimes Dr. Ross gets mad at me for having a knife so I can't practice as much I'd like.

He'd be furious if he knew I was outside, too.

He doesn't like it when I go out on my own where people can see me, sneaking through the cellar door that I always manage to open no matter how he locks it.

Wandering around where I might say the wrong things.

But I'll be a good boy today. I'll keep my mouth shut.

I just want to be in the sun.

And I just want to see them again, as Blake and Warren and Jenna and Deanna and Clarissa come barreling down the scrubby hill to the creek, all full of laughter and smiles.

They're beaming at me like I'm some big, exciting secret. I need that so much I don't even care if Ross will hurt me later, if he catches me when I sneak back in.

I don't care that Blake messes up my nickname because he thinks Leo means Tiger instead of Lion.

I just care that it's warm and bright outside, and they're here, crashing into me. Out here, it's all giggles and play and the only time I ever get to feel like I have a family.

Warren's our ringleader. He's already taller than everyone else, brave and fierce even if he's so skinny he'll snap in a strong wind. He hooks an arm around my neck and noogies me lightly, grinning.

"Whatcha working on there, dude?"

"I don't know yet," I say, but as I see Clarissa hanging back behind the others, watching me shyly, pretty in her floaty yellow sundress with her hair pulled up in a messy twist like she's trying to look grown-up...I get ideas.

I think I know.

I want to carve a flower. Yeah, yeah, it's silly, I know, but it's

27

not for me.

I'll give it a stem so delicate it weighs nothing, petals as thin and soft as paper.

I'll make it super real, except it won't ever wilt and die.

And when it's done, I can give it to Clarissa Bell.

* * *

Present

WITH A BITTERSWEET ACHE in my bones, I stand across the street from Blake's sprawling ranch style house. The windows are dark, and the porch light isn't strong enough to reach over and pierce the shadows beneath the trees concealing me.

Still, as she climbs groggily up the porch steps, Andrea pauses, looking back, searching the night to see if I'm more than a figment of her drunk brain.

"God, you're *him*, aren't you?" she calls out softly.

She's more sober now, after the slow stumbling walk home through back streets where I wouldn't be seen—and after nervously asking me *You won't tell my dad?* only to nod quickly when I said *As long as you promise not to do this again.*

Yeah, no, she told me. *Like...somehow the booze tasted* worse *than puking.*

I'd just laughed at her.

Her eyes are wide now, though, her voice a bit awed. "Holy crap. You're...you're the monster," she says. "You're Nine."

I don't say anything. I can't confirm it. No use in whipping her into a frenzy.

But I won't deny it, either.

"Oh my God," she strangles out. "That's so *cool*. Clark will never believe this!"

I smile faintly and slip my hand into my pocket.

28

There's a half-finished carving I was working on, one with a design that makes it easy to carry around to keep me busy on long nights.

It's a coin, a carved wooden medallion, barely bigger than a quarter.

On the back, there's the start of an etching, a blooming tree with gnarled branches, small and detailed, barely an outline for what I want the finished piece to look like.

On the other side, though, is a 3D relief of a dragon with looping coils, seeming to rise out of the wood as if it's clawing free to become flesh, every scale and whisker and curving tooth carved out one tiny splinter at a time.

To me, it's the beast that's choking Heart's Edge. The secrets. *The truth.*

To Andrea, it'll be her proof that she saw me.

Hell, maybe it'll make her the popular girl at school. I know how flippant high school pecking orders can be.

So I bend, set the wooden coin on the ground, exaggerating my movements enough to make sure she sees it.

She gasps, darting off the porch toward me.

But by the time she's dashed across the street to where I stood, I'm gone.

I retreat into the thicker trees that lead up into the foothills, watching as she stares left, then right—then notices the little pale circlet of pine wood against the grass and dark earth, glowing in the moonlight.

Smiling, she bends and picks it up, her eyes widening, her lips parting as she turns the coin over with a breathless sound.

She grins, and just like her old man, her smile looks wide and lopsided.

"*Cool,*" she breathes.

She'll be okay.

I stay just long enough to make sure she gets inside and locks the door. Blake should be home from whatever stupid shit he's doing at the radio station soon. I'll have to see if I can get a signal and tune in from my lair, because I've *got* to hear this. It's hard not to laugh.

Blake? An oversized human Labrador, giving people *advice?*

That big dummy.

Smiling fondly, I shake my head and turn to make my way through the trees, running parallel to the main road through town. I can't linger here. Andrea's fine, and it's time to focus on what I really came here for.

As much as I've enjoyed this trip down memory lane, it's not why I'm here.

There's still work to be done tonight.

* * *

I'M SURPRISED I don't find the man everybody still calls "Doc" and his wife Ember at The Menagerie. To me, he'll always be Gray, the friend who saved my life two times and counting.

Hell, I thought I knew what *workaholic* meant back when Doc opened his vet practice in town and did damn near nothing else for the better part of a decade.

But it's nothing compared to the way the two of them are *together,* and ever since Doc and Ember got married, I don't even know when they stop to have time to *live.*

But I guess with Ember pregnant—though she's not showing yet, and I only know because Gray broke his stoic silence and texted *everyone*—they're finally slowing down and checking out before midnight.

So when I find the office locked up and the windows dark, I track them back to their house.

I haven't been here in a while. But I remember it as a spartan place, grey and utilitarian.

It's completely changed.

Their lawn has wildflowers everywhere, though they're beginning to wilt as autumn settles in, and the trees along the edge of the yard light up brilliant orange. Cozy patio furniture draped in bright-colored but slightly lumpy quilts dots the porch.

There are actual *curtains* hanging in the windows, replacing the militant simplicity of Gray's old blinds. There's a blindingly neon plastic playset already set up on one side of the yard, even though Ember can't be more than two or three months along, and they won't need it for years.

Can't blame Doc for being overenthusiastic.

And I can't blame him for finally moving on, either.

I'm fucking glad he did.

I guess this is what married life does to a man. And I'm happy at least one of us gets to pick up, start over, and leave the bad memories behind to have a real life.

But although Gray is one of the only people in Heart's Edge I can speak to safely, one of the only people who doesn't think I'm a murderous, disfigured monster, I'm still edgy, tense, as I step up on the porch and knock.

The door opens a minute later.

Not Gray, but Ember, sleepy-eyed in an oversized, faded sweatshirt and a pair of cozy pajama shorts, a fuzzy black cat twined between her legs and looking up at me with curious golden eyes that seem to recognize me.

Baxter.

That damn well takes me back a few months. Makes me think of people I don't want to remember.

Like Fuchsia Delaney, the cat's original owner. Just thinking the witch's name makes my skin crawl. I hope thinking damn well can't summon her, too.

So instead I offer a smile at a squinting Ember, even if I know it's not visible behind the hood pulled up over my head. "Hey, Ember. It's–"

Ember blinks, her eyes widening as she snaps awake with a gasp.

"*Leo?!*" she says, and from inside the living room there's an echoing *What?* before she reaches out to grasp my arm and tug me inside. "Oh my God, get inside. The neighbors might...just come on!"

It's both heartwarming and sad that my best friend's wife actually touches me without disgust and immediately jumps to thinking about my safety, if I'm seen, instead of flinching back from the giant, scarred beast in front of her.

There's that old echo of family again.

In another life, Doc and Ember could be my brother and sister.

It's not something I've ever had, not really. That doesn't stop me from wanting it.

Also doesn't stop me from basking in the warmth of their home, shuffling into a living room that crackles with the crisp fire burning in the hearth. I find him in the living room, perched in an overstuffed chair.

Though there's tension now, as Gray stands, emerald-green eyes watching me intently behind his glasses, the battle-readiness of a former soldier already flowing through him. "Leo? Are you all right? Is everything—"

I hold up one hand, hovering near the door.

I don't want to intrude, and I don't intend to stay.

I'm not taking him away from his hard-won family.

"I'm fine," I say. "Nothing to worry about. I just wanted to know if you've heard anything about the break-in at Sweeter Things. From what I've got, somebody took Deanna Bell."

Ember's eyes widen, her fingers clutching at her chest—while Gray's brows lower. He sinks back down in his chair again, steepling his hands. "Damn, it always amazes me how you know things like this before anyone."

"I have eyes and ears. The evidence is pretty clear." I frown. "What? Is it being kept secret?"

"From what Langley let slip...yes." But Gray's evading something; I can tell. He sighs, avoiding my eyes, raking his hands through his thick, dark hair, looking at the fire instead. "I'm guessing you'd like me to be your ear to the ground and relay back anything I find?"

"If you can. Obviously without drawing attention. Don't get in too deep, Gray. Not the hell again."

"I'm already in, man. I've been 'in' this for most of my adult life, same as you, and just because we cleaned things up a few months ago doesn't mean it's over. Not with the company still intact."

Those piercing eyes of his slide back to me. Gray has this way of looking at you like he knows all the things you hide from yourself, and he does it to me far too damned often.

Because he cares, I guess, as hard as that is to accept.

And that caring resonates in his voice, warming from its usual cold precision as he says, "It won't be over until you don't have to hide anymore. Until we clear your name, Leo. If I just—"

"No!" I can't help the harshness as I cut him off, retreating back a step till the doorknob hits my back. "It's not time for that yet."

"That's what you said months ago." Gray just watches me quietly, while Ember settles in on the arm of his chair, her pale-blue eyes so worried. It's like she actually knows me enough to give a damn.

No one knows me *that* well anymore.

I've kept enough distance to make sure of it.

Turned into the monster in the hills, prowling the darkness, forbidden to ever step into the light.

"Will it ever be time?" Gray asks softly, and I growl, looking away.

"This isn't about me," I snarl. "I just want to make sure Deanna's found. You know Clarissa. She'll never get over it if something happens to her last surviving family. I don't want anything to force her here, dragging her back to this hell."

The silence that descends is hushed, terrible.

A warning or an omen or some fuckery I can't even put into words.

Raw instinct pricks my skin again, and I retreat another step. I can't go any farther when the door bumps my shoulder.

"What? What is it?" I can barely choke out the question.

Gray eyeballs me somberly. Some twist of my stomach and the painful beat of my heart tells me what he's going to say even before it comes out.

"She's already here, Leo," he says, and my mouth goes dry. "Clarissa Bell has returned to Heart's Edge."

III: STUCK IN THE MIDDLE
(CLARISSA)

There's something I'm missing.

It's been two days of torture.

The cops from Missoula have been all over the crime scene, but wouldn't tell me anything besides *disturb nothing.*

In my own freaking candy store.

Okay, so technically it's Deanna's shop, but it's mine, too. I started this company. And now I'm not allowed to touch anything there because I might damage some tiny, overlooked clue.

I can't even clean up the bonbons smeared across the shop floor, nothing but chocolate puddles now over two days of melting in the sun and then cooling and hardening at night.

It's going to be pure hell to get out of the grout between the tiles.

Or maybe I'm just hyper-fixating on the little things so I don't panic.

But I'm also hoping one of those little things will finally point me to something the cops missed.

They haven't been back to the crime scene since the first day. I don't even know if the relief team is still in town.

It's like they don't care at all. Too swept up in 'just doing their jobs.'

Like they've already given up on finding Deedee alive.

I can't accept that. I won't.

So pardon my French, but *screw* don't disturb. If they won't look harder, turn over every last thing for my sister, I will.

I pick my way slowly through the front of the shop, careful not to touch anything or even kick aside a shard of glass. I can't make sense out of this chaos.

My sister's hand is everywhere. I see it in all the little flourishes like the pink plastic cocktail swords stuck in the truffles and the little blue ribbons sealing toffee wrappers closed.

But her hand isn't in this violence or this mess.

I don't want to think about the person who'd do this, or why.

Honestly, I don't want to think about this kind of force inflicted on my sister at all.

So I swallow the lump lodged in my throat and *focus*.

Nothing in the front of the shop, nothing in the kitchen, so I duck into the back office, dipping under the crime scene tape stretched across the door.

It's been tossed, too. File cabinets tipped over, the desk toppled, papers strewn everywhere. The desktop computer's monitor is totally smashed.

Then I see the tower's been ripped open. There's no hard drive inside.

Hmm. I'm no computer genius, but I know what a hard drive looks like, and it's missing from the slot where it belongs inside the machine's dusty black case.

Frowning, I crouch down in front of it, peering inside.

Just why?

There's nothing special about this basic computer. Should just be for accounting, inventory, and order tracking, and for updating the shop's website. Maybe Deanna played Minecraft on it or something, but...

But it tells me what they came here for. Even though there shouldn't be any info on that hard drive to provoke *this.*

There's something Deanna knows that she shouldn't.

Something they want.

Even if it's senseless and grim, that gives me hope.

Because as long as she doesn't tell them what they want to know, they can't kill her.

I start to turn away—only to pause as something else catches my eye, something that got lost in the general chaos, half-hidden behind a tall file cabinet that's been shoved aside.

A hidden wall safe.

Its door hangs open, practically blasted off, dangling by one hinge.

I frown, drifting closer to the wall. I signed off on every bit of the construction plans for this shop, even if I never actually set foot here in person.

There was no flipping wall safe in the initial design.

Especially not one this heavy duty, made from what looks like six solid inches of steel.

Jeez. I don't even use a safe like this at the main branch in Spokane. All I've ever needed is a cubic foot-wide strongbox. We're not a bank. Just a candy store.

When did my sister install this thing? And what was inside that was so devilishly *important?*

Whatever it was...it wasn't the money. A few zippered cash bags sit in the back of the safe, their sides bulging with rectangular bills.

Just like the untouched register.

Ugh. There's nothing else damning inside the safe.

Nothing that'd warrant this kind of protection. Either the intruder didn't find what they wanted...

Or they did.

And they took it.

But there *is* something else, pushed up haphazardly, half-crushed against the cash bags.

A bouquet of flowers, so wilted their scent is barely a ghost.

White lilies, gone yellow as they died—mixed in with the pink and blue wildflowers that grow all around Heart's Edge.

I can't stop frowning. It just keeps getting weirder.

Though I know I'm not supposed to touch anything, my curiosity gets the best of me. I reach inside and open the little folded card tied to the bouquet by a slender, shining blue satin ribbon.

I'm sorry, Clarissa.

Um, what? My heart stops. My breath, too, and my entire chest aches.

These flowers were for me? *From who?*

I have one good guess and no—no, it *can't* be.

So I shake my head, backing away numbly, swallowing, instantly nauseous.

Not him.

It must be a sick joke by the kidnapper. Someone connected with Galentron, *mocking* me after taking my sister.

Oh, God. Not *him!*

Violent shivers rush through me, and I fold my arms tight, desperately trying to hold myself together.

This is vile. Frightening. Brutal.

If only Deanna could've just walked away.

If only she *ran*, got the hell away from Heart's Edge, just like I did.

Some things in life are better left behind. Nothing good ever comes from clinging to the past, much less shoving your nose in it.

But then, Deanna didn't see what I did that night. She was so young...

To her, it's just one more memory of fear, of loss, of sadness. Frightening men doing frightening things.

It wasn't her bleeding out on the floor after her own father tried to kill her.

She didn't watch the man she loved do the unspeakable to save her life.

And she didn't *have* to let the man she loved walk away from her and never come back, all because he had to be a big dumb hero and save the world.

I won't cry. I *won't*. I—

The sound of a footstep scuffs behind me.

I spin around sharply, reaching out for something, anything I can use as a weapon.

I come up with a stapler. *Awesome.*

A pair of cool grey eyes stares back with condescending amusement. They're attached to a tall, statuesque older woman in a sleek black sheath dress.

I can tell with one look she's not from Heart's Edge.

She's too cosmopolitan, too elegant, her face sharp and harshly flawless, her ink-black bob haircut too severe, her clothing too expensive.

Her eyes are hard, cold, knowing; the twist of her deeply mauve lips one step above a sneer.

Jesus, I *know* her.

A rush of cold familiarity tells me I know her, that I should be afraid of her, and I clutch the stapler tighter like some kid ready to chase an imaginary monster back under the bed. Except this monster's *real*.

I can't remember her name. Just vague impressions buried in lost memories.

But I know she can't be trusted.

She arches a sculpted brow, looking me over, that sour twist of her lips turning into a smirk.

"Really now, Clarissa," she says. "Are you going to put that thing down, or do you want to try to staple me to death first?"

I tense, sinking down a little. Maybe I can bolt past her, get the drop on her, make it out the door. "I was thinking more of using it as a blunt object first," I say breathlessly, tightening my grip. "How do you know my name?"

"Oh, I've known you since you were very young, Clarissa Bell."

Just hearing my full name turns my stomach. It's a cursed name, and no one in this town would say it out loud.

But she just holds my eyes like she's trying to *tell* me something and dips her hand into the pocket of her dramatically long black coat. I stiffen, bracing for a knife, a gun.

It's...a ball of hard candy, wrapped in clear cellophane. Violently pink.

And then the memory comes crashing down on me like a ton of bricks as she purrs, "Hello, little girl. Would you like a piece of candy?"

* * *

Years Ago

PAPA TOLD me to stay in my room—or else.

He always tells me to stay in my room when his people come to visit late at night.

I'm supposed to be asleep anyway, and Deanna's curled up hugging her stuffed Elly and snoring like a big bear.

But I can never sleep when Papa's people are in the house.

There's something scary about them.

I think it's because, when I watch from the upstairs walkway, peeking through the bars of the banister...their shadows always come first.

Long, marching black things, too thin to be human in my imagination, hollow and scary.

I've convinced myself the shadows are what they really are, and the ordinary-looking humans in dark suits who come after are just costumes. It's kinda like that old horror movie, *Invasion of the Body Snatchers.*

They're monsters wearing human makeup, and I'm scared they're slowly making Papa into one of them until he'll go away somewhere, and there'll just be a monster with a cruel smile in his place, looking down at me and calling me Clarissa and smiling like he knows me when he doesn't anymore because he's turned into a stranger wearing human skin.

My real Papa went away after Mommy died. Maybe before when they fought so much.

And I don't think he's ever coming back.

It's just the ice-cold monster-Papa now, and the shadow-people he talks to every night.

I have to stay away, out of sight.

Or they might just take me away and replace me with a monster-Clarissa, and throw me down in a deep, dark pit.

I'm so focused watching those shadows move across the thick rug in the front entryway that I don't realize someone's behind me.

Not until the woman speaks at my back, her voice sharp and weirdly rolling.

"Hello, little girl," she purrs as I tumble back with a muffled scream and get myself tangled up in my nightgown, staring up at her jet-black hair. And she gazes back with empty grey eyes, her smile full of teeth as she offers me a ball of pink candy wrapped in plastic. "Would you like a piece of candy?"

Present

OH, crap.

I remember that candy now.

How I took it because I was scared not to, and the first time I made myself eat it because she was watching and I thought, back then, that she was another shadow-thing in a human costume who'd hurt me if I didn't.

The stuff tasted gross and cloying, full of artificial flavors that gave it this nasty powdery aftertaste.

The eight-year-old little girl that I was feared the candy was really some kind of scary magic to turn me into a shadow-monster.

It hadn't.

But because I'd eaten the first one, she brought me one every time she came to the house after that, and I took them and squirreled them away so the monster lady wouldn't get angry.

Back then, I'd thought if someone was bad, they were actually monsters who pretended to be humans to fool the people around them.

I know better now.

Humans *are* the monsters. Always.

They don't care about fooling anyone, just as long as they get what they want.

And I'm afraid to know what Fuchsia Delaney wants now. The last time I saw her in Heart's Edge was right before my entire life was ripped out from under me.

"*You*," I hiss, taking a step back, putting more distance between us. "What do you want? Did Galentron send you here?"

"Ah—hush, hush." She clucks her tongue, shaking her head, her eyes glittering. "We don't say *that* name around these parts. Ears everywhere, you know." Her lips purse, her chin lifting. "I suppose you haven't heard the news, ever since you missed the latest mess. I'm more of a free agent these days."

I narrow my eyes. "So what? They used you up and threw you away, too? Big surprise."

"More like a voluntary separation. My choice. And you should be glad I chose, little Miss Clarissa." She cocks her head, watching me like a snake that sees a particularly small, juicy mouse waiting to be devoured. "Because I think I can help you find your sister."

My heart drums faster.

"The fact that you know my sister's missing tells me not to trust you," I bite off, clutching the stapler tighter. Maybe I can throw it at her. My other hand creeps to my pocket, and my phone. "Give me one good reason why I shouldn't call the cops on you right now."

"Because that bumbling Mayberry reject wouldn't know what to do with me. Do you honestly think Wentworth Langley knows the truth about this town?" God, she's so *smug* I want to hate her even more, but I don't know if that's possible. "If you tried to explain what you're so upset about, you'll just sound like the stress and fear are getting to you. Poor, delusional Clarissa having a hysterical fit. I'm just passing through, after all. A tourist. And you went all crazy and threatened to bludgeon a poor little lady with a stapler."

She flutters her lashes with mock innocence, and I sigh, closing my eyes.

Yep, I remember her, all right.

If there's one thing you find out fast about Fuchsia Delaney, it's how insufferable she can be.

Always ten words where two will do, and that smarmy attitude that makes everything she says sound like lilting, condescending mockery.

"Just get out," I mutter. "I can't deal with you right now. Not with everything else."

"Aw, and here I thought you'd be happy to see me," she taunts. "Or would you rather see someone else? I'm sure your dashing beau has just been *dying* for a reunion. Or is that just dying, period?"

"*Stop*," I force out raggedly. "Just stop. Leo's not dead."

"Would you even know if he was? Considering the way you packed up and abandoned town, well..."

"I'd know, bitch. Trust me."

I'd feel it deep down in my heart.

Like one day there'd be some light inside me snuffed out, left in constant darkness.

But I can't let this woman get to me. That's what Fuchsia Delaney does best.

Her weapons are her words, and she uses them to peel people open and leave them vulnerable to her wicked ways.

Not today.

Not when I have a son to think of, and I won't let her anywhere near him. She may claim to not be with Galentron anymore, but it doesn't matter.

Everything they touch turns to darkness, and if she's here, then she must be connected somehow.

I won't let her claim Zach with her black and terrible touch.

I won't let her taint him.

And I clench my jaw, glaring at her, hefting the stapler in what's probably a useless threat. "I told you before to get out," I say. "I don't want to hear anything you have to say. Just go to hell, Delaney."

"Been there, done that." The way Fuchsia looks at me is odd, almost bitter, before she tosses her head with a disdainful sniff and turns to strut out. "But whether you realize it or not, I'm trying to get us both *out*."

Then she's gone.

Gone, and when I break my frozen stillness and bolt out after her, it's too late.

She's nowhere in sight. But I'm not alone, either.

There's another tall figure in the doorway—so hulkingly large he barely fits in the doorframe, poised stock-still just outside.

He's covered from head to toe in black, wrapped up in a thick coat like some desert nomad, hood drawn up, a scarf or mask drawn over his mouth and nose.

But I can see his eyes.

They're shaded beneath the hood, just barely catching

enough light for a single tiny amethyst spark to glimmer in the shadows.

My heart nearly bursts. I start running forward, reaching out a hand, a name on my lips, but my voice dries up and I can only let out an anguished cry.

He says nothing.

I clutch my hand to my chest, curling forward, closing my eyes, trying to keep my heart from breaking out through my rib cage. *Is this even real?*

I look away for a split second.

But when I open my eyes again, there's no one there.

And when I race out into the parking lot, crunching over glass and ripping through crime scene tape, a desperate name on my lips...

There's nothing.

Nothing but the hollow ache inside me, a jolt of recognition and longing and hurt so deep I wonder if I'm actually losing my mind.

Going crazy, wanting to see him so bad I just imagined him, standing there looking at me with his entire soul etched in those deep, dark amethyst eyes.

* * *

I HURT SO MUCH by the time I finish my business in town and head back.

I can't stop thinking about him. And I still can't forget that bitter parting look Fuchsia gave me.

Even as I pull up outside Charming Inn, I'm dwelling on it. So freaking rattled I had my hands clenched on the wheel the whole drive back.

Silly, I scold myself. *You should know better by now.*

Both Leo and Fuchsia Delaney are nothing but ghosts of the past.

45

The first ones I've seen in almost a decade. I've tried so hard to leave it all behind and start fresh.

I *had* to, I remind myself. It wasn't cowardly fear that sent me running. Not for myself.

I'd been very pregnant back then.

No room for anything else on my mind besides getting my unborn baby as far away as possible from the death and rumors swallowing Heart's Edge.

Said now-very-born child is nowhere to be found, though, when I pick my way along the thin trail back to the cabin and let myself in.

His books are all over the sofa, the Discovery Channel blares through the TV's speakers...

But I can't find Zach.

For the second time in just as many hours, my heart stops.

Not him too.

Not him too!

If someone took my boy the way they kidnapped Deanna, I swear to God I'll tear Montana apart to get them both back.

But there's no good reason to take my son. There's *not*.

I don't know anything. They can't use him for leverage against me.

Then again, they can use him for leverage against Deanna, can't they?

"Crud," I hiss sharply.

Okay, so I'm overreacting. That's why I hurl myself out in the hazy afternoon light, taking in breaths of razor-sharp chill autumn air that knife my throat as I cup my hands over my mouth and scream, "Zach!"

Please. Please just let this be a prank, let me find him playing outside somewhere. Down by the heart-shaped cliff, or exploring the woods.

Tearing through the trees, I break into a run, pulse pounding, crying out his name over and over. "Zach? *Zach!*"

There's no answer. No laughing. No shouting back.

I don't hear him anywhere.

My eyes burn. Terror thickens my blood. Jesus, if I lose him, I'll–

"Clarissa?" a familiar, softly cultured voice calls from the main house. "Clarissa Bell, is that you?"

I know that voice, and this time it's not one that makes me sick with its familiarity.

Ms. Wilma Ford. Pretty much the wise old owl around here.

If anyone knows what to do to help me find my boy, it's her.

I go bolting through the trees, tearing toward the main house, ignoring the twigs and bushes scratching at my hands as I shove my way through them. Warren's grandmother, Ms. Wilma, stands on the back porch between two tall ivory columns, ladylike as always, even if her once-black hair is now much greyer than I remember, almost snowy silver.

She watches me with a kind of thoughtful calm, her hands folded together, a small smile on her lips.

"I knew that was you," she says, watching me break from the trees onto the lawn. "Whatever's the matter?"

"Zach," I pant out. "My son. Have you...have you seen him? I can't find him anywhere."

"Taking in strays is one of my many talents," she says, her eyes gleaming with gentle warmth and amusement. "Yes, dearie, I think you're in luck."

Luck? I cock my head, just staring, not daring to get my hopes up until she speaks again.

She beckons toward me, turning to the door. "Come see your darling boy."

For a moment, rather than follow her, I sag, dragging a hand over my face, my bones going loose with relief.

Thank *God*.

So maybe Fuchsia was right about one thing in a broken clock sort of way.

I really *am* losing my shit.

Fear and worry and terrible memories are eating me alive, until I'm nothing but ragged pieces of a woman.

I straighten up and trail Ms. Wilma into the main house. I've not seen much of it besides the front reception desk, but she takes me through carpeted hallways with little warm odds and ends here and there, leading me deeper into the interior...and something I'd have never suspected.

An open-air atrium, surrounded by shaded colonnades and trees and summer's last flowers. So much bright sunlight cascades down, shining off the jeweled wings of a hummingbird straggler who hasn't migrated south yet.

The sun also gleams off my son's messy hair. He's curled up on a little white-painted bench, looking happy as a clam with an orange cat half as big as he is weighing down his lap.

Oh my God.

If I wasn't so relieved, I'd scream.

"Zach!" I start forward, my voice rising, then dropping as I just...deflate.

I can't be angry. I just can't. He's everything that's precious in this world, and as he looks up at me, blinking quizzically, I drop down to settle in on the bench next to him. Looking down, I rest my hand on the top of his head, while he tries to wrestle away, petting the enormous cat. "Why didn't you stay in the cabin like I told you?"

He flushes. At least he has the grace to look chagrined.

But he always *does* look genuinely sorry after he's gotten himself in over his head. He's a good kid.

One more way he takes after his father, too.

"Sorry, Mom," he whispers. "It was just kinda creepy out there by myself, and the cat came stumbling up on our porch. He looked lost."

"Old Mozart's never really lost," Ms. Wilma says kindly, leaning over the back of the chair and scratching behind the purring tabby's ears. "He's just looking for someone new to spoil him, and today this lucky boy found your Zachary."

I offer her a faint, grateful smile.

This could've gone down a lot worse. I'm lucky kind old Ms. Wilma truly doesn't mind keeping an eye on my son.

But that brings up another dilemma.

I don't have real childcare here. I shouldn't be leaving a seven-year-old alone for anything, even if it's just a brief run into town. I asked Haley to keep an eye on him while I was gone, but I'm sure she had to step out if someone needed something in one of the other units.

Heck, I know there's more truth to those old rumors about abducted children than almost anybody.

Even though I've raised Zach alone, I've done my best to make sure he's not a latchkey kid. There's always someone close by to watch over him when I'm working, keeping him entertained, engaging his sharp little mind.

He's the reason I worked so hard to make Sweeter Things successful.

All so I could afford to give him the good life. A happy life. A life any mother would want to deliver.

A *safe* life, which is more than I can say my father ever gave me.

He tried to justify all the horrible things he did, the people he hurt, the crimes, swearing it was all for me and Deanna.

But that's the thing when people turn into monsters.

Their excuses get flimsier.

He'd shown who he really was the night he struck me across the face with a priceless Ming vase, then wrapped his arms around my throat and tried to squeeze the life out of me.

Sighing, I catch my fingers drifting to the scar on my cheek. It's a habit whenever I let myself sink into the past, but the moment I feel the sensation of ridged scar tissue, I stop myself.

Ms. Wilma's still watching me, her eyes kind but knowing.

I can't stand this.

Can't stand being here, with these people who see a tragic past every time they look at me.

So I take a deep breath, standing and offering Zach my hand. "This big ol' kitty will be around later, I'm sure. Want to come with me for some ice cream and a few errands, kiddo? And then we'll figure out what to do about that spooky cabin."

Zach perks at hearing 'ice cream,' rubbing his eyes, trying and failing to hide his smile.

I know my boy. The easiest way to keep him out of trouble is through his stomach.

"Yeah, okay." He gently sets Mozart aside with one last scratch, and slips his hand into mine. "Huckleberry swirl, Mom?"

"If they've got it." I toss my head with a tired smile. "C'mon."

He slides off the bench and trails in my wake happily.

As I pass Ms. Wilma, though, I mouth her a huge *thank you*.

She just smiles, her eyes glittering. Thank God Almighty there's still somebody here who, even if she knows me, even if she brings up memories like everyone else...I can trust her not to judge.

Out in the bright sunlight, I pile Zach into the car, make sure his seat belt fastens, and try to calculate how fast I can get him in and out with ice cream. I've got a meeting at the local café and bakery, The Nest.

As much as I hate being practical right now, I need to keep myself busy or I might do something drastic. Something that could screw up the ongoing investigation worse than my little stumble this morning, and if I get in the cops' way, it might slow down bringing Deedee home.

So I'm focusing on Zach right now, and on business, keeping Sweeter Things viable here. It's what Deanna would want.

I just hope The Nest's owner, Felicity Randall, will give me a few display cases for our candy. It'll be a win-win. They won't have to spend inventory and time preparing treats for their coffee. I know even after two days in town the café is struggling and understaffed.

And I get to keep cash flow and branding going, and maybe

attract a few new customers who'll come by the reopened shop to satisfy their sweet tooth once everything's settled again.

Lucky for me, Zach doesn't mind a quick dip in and out of the ice cream shop. They've got his huckleberry swirl, and he happily licks away at a waffle cone topped with a purple lump as I drive to my meeting.

I find him a chair with a window view and leave him with a stack of his Animorphs books—he's already reading well above his grade level—and his ice cream with a warning that's half plea to behave, stay put, and I'll be right back.

"Welcome back to town, Ms. Bell." Felicity's waiting behind the counter, all warm smiles and grasping hands. She's younger than me, not by much, but young enough that she wasn't in the thick of the mess eight years ago. Young enough that the rumors and scandal the adults were talking about probably went over her head.

It makes it easier for me to relax, to breathe, as she squeezes my hands and welcomes me back to town.

I don't have the heart to tell her I'm not staying.

We talk over cappuccinos, me perched at the coffee bar while she cleans an espresso machine.

I get it, really—it's the same thing I'd do.

The work never ends when you're a small business owner, and even if I hate the circumstances, it's still nice to support another woman running her own shop.

And I think we've come to a good deal by the time I've finished my drink.

It's something.

Something positive to focus on in the middle of this mess.

"Awesome. I'll have the first batch over by next week." I shake her hand with a warm smile, sliding off the stool, and turn to collect my huckleberry-sticky son.

Only to find him gone again.

Ughhh.

Seriously. I'm about to put him on a leash, collar and bell included.

Thankfully, this time he's still in my line of sight, and my freak-out lasts approximately half a second.

He's outside, talking to a strange blonde woman in the parking lot—but I don't think I have to worry about this one. She's young and slim with a bright, sweet smile and soft blue eyes, and she's leaning down, talking to him on his level.

She's also practically glowing in this way that tells me she's pregnant, even if she's not quite showing yet. Sometimes you can *just tell.*

Just like you can tell people who are good with kids. Who *get* kids. And I know this lady wouldn't harm a hair on Zach's little head.

Still, I glance over my shoulder at Felicity. "Who's that? She's not from around here?"

"Technically, she is by proxy." Felicity laughs, wiping her hands on a rag, and I get why that girl seems familiar when Felicity says, "That's my cousin, Ember. She came out here to take a job at the vet practice and ended up marrying our local Instagram hottie, Doc."

Oh, I can see the resemblance now.

It shouldn't make me ache so much.

But, you know. It's almost like seeing sisters.

And it reminds me that Deanna's out there somewhere, waiting for me to find her.

It's starting to feel like if I don't, no one will.

She's the only piece of the normal family I always thought I'd have. A husband, kids, and Auntie Deanna always over spoiling them rotten.

But all that vanished in a flash. Just like *him* vanishing this morning.

Was it even real? Why didn't he stay? Say *something?*

After all these years, doesn't he have a single word for me?

Then again, it's not like my words would come easily, either.

How in the holy hell do you tell a man in exile, who's suffered *so much*, the truth?

How do I ever tell Leo freaking Regis he has a son?

* * *

I STILL HAVEN'T ANSWERED that question by the time I've introduced myself to Ember, retrieved Zach, and headed toward home.

Well, more like home-for-now.

I think one reason it was so easy to walk away from Heart's Edge is because nowhere really feels like home anymore.

The mansion I grew up in belongs to the town now. I guess Deanna and I could've claimed inheritance rights after my father's death, but honestly? Neither of us considered living in that house of shadows again for a split second.

I couldn't stand the idea of bringing new life into those halls where violence, anger, and sadness stalked for so many years.

It's a museum today. In some ways, that makes it a lie. The history it chronicles is only part of the story, but I think I like how it's been repurposed that way.

It's a vision of a better Heart's Edge. One that never existed. I'd rather people see that than know the truth.

I drive past it on our way to the inn, barely slowing. I'm more focused on making sure Zach gets himself clean with the wet wipes I keep in the car.

Sigh. No one told me I'd practically be buying them by the pound, but they've been lifesavers.

But as we follow the highway to Charming, I pause at the intersection. I'm caught up in the deep blue autumn sky and how the cliffs above look like strange cutouts against the vivid, rich blue.

One cliff curves behind the inn with its half-heart shape and the steep drop down into the meadows, and then the slow rolling slope to the valley below...

Of course, I still remember the old legend.

The one about the star-crossed lovers, the farm boy and the mayor's daughter, who were kept apart by fate until they decided to make their own.

How they threw flowers over the edge and ran into the hills to hide away and live happily ever after. It probably happened a century ago, if it ever did at all.

But there's another story about that cliff.

Another mayor's daughter, and the strange, sweet, hulking noble man who said he'd always love her. Who swore he'd come back. Who once stood on that cliff and promised to marry her.

To make everything right.

My chest hurts. Feels like it'll burst open and just spill this pain out everywhere, and I can't stand it. It's awful, but I'm frozen with the car idling and my breaths rattling and my fingers digging into the steering wheel.

"Mom? Hey, what's wrong?"

Zach's quiet, curious voice reminds me why I keep moving. Why I don't stay stuck in the past. My sweet boy loves me, and I love him right back, and I'm grateful to him for reminding me what's real.

What matters.

I reach over and squeeze his shoulder, offering him a smile.

"Nothing, kiddo," I say, pressing down on the pedal and making that last short turnoff to the inn. "Nothing anymore."

IV: PROMISE ME IN TRUFFLES
(NINE)

I must be out of my fucking mind.

I can't believe I was right there in broad daylight. And there *she* was.

Older, more tempered, more graceful, more dignified, but still so damn beautiful she tore my breath away. Clarissa Bell made me reckless.

So reckless I almost spoke to her.

So reckless I almost *went* to her.

So goddamn reckless I almost forgot she's never meant to see me again.

I'd been trailing Fuchsia Delaney. When I'd seen her coffin-black SUV cruising through town and heading for Sweeter Things, I knew she was up to no good. Also knew I never should've even thought her name and summoned that witch.

Now she's here, crawling out of the woodwork, making things ten times more complicated.

But then, right there, through the shattered shop window...I saw Clarissa.

Tall, lithe, graceful as a dancer in her stylish cropped fall jacket, tight jeans, and nimble brown leather boots. That unforgettable tumble of glossy, dark-brown hair. Always windswept and a little wild, gleaming with a shine and just a touch of reddish chestnut highlights.

That serene, elegant face I once savored. Her curves, the same I once roamed. The stubbornness of her jaw. The new scar that marks our fateful night, just like mine.

And those forest-green eyes, vivid as a deep clear lake, looking right back at me with total shock.

Despite my hood, my mask, she recognized me.

Even though I've changed so much. I'm not the Leo she knew.

I'm a fucked up mess of poison thoughts and scars and three times the mad ink I had the last time we were naked.

Still, one look, and she *knew*.

I feel like I've been punched in the chest. Snarling, I settle down on a rickety old chair next to the fire pit in what I've come to call my lair. It's not a proper home for anyone.

It's an old Galentron bunker, carved from the mountainside a good ways away from the remodeled silver mine that once housed a lab before I set it all on fire.

The bug-out shelter was meant to be an emergency defense station in the event something happened that required us to defend the facility.

Well, something did happen.

I fucking happened.

And after the inferno, this cave is one of the only surviving sections left.

It's a natural depression in the rock, smoothed into a four-walled room, barely accessible down a slight slope and then a short drop down a ladder. For most of the day, natural light filters in, but the subtle solar collectors disguised as black mica crystals around the mouth do for me in the evenings, and power the few electronics I keep around.

Going nomad beats prison by a long shot. The only time I truly thought I'd snap was the weeks I spent caged up under lock and key.

This place has it all.

Fire, bed made of stacked-up pallets, and even a little plumbing built-in and sourced by a clear, cool underground stream that bubbles up through the rock. I mostly hunt my own food. The hides of elk and rabbits I've kept and cured help me keep warm in the winter and patch my clothes when it's too risky to go into town for new ones.

Hunting helps patch *me*. More than once, I've cleaned an injury with dried herbs and stitched it up with a needle carved from bone looped with dried sinew for thread.

Damn good thing I read *Clan of the Cave Bear* like sixty times when I was a kid.

This place isn't home, but as far as Batcaves go, it's not bad.

Even if the leftovers here and there, Galentron's legacy in the wires molded along the walls and the logos on the pallets and blankets, remind me why this is less my cozy little hideout and more like my purgatory.

It's the place where I deserve to rot.

* * *

Eight Years Ago

I CAN'T BELIEVE I'm here again.

It's been years since Dr. Ross took me away from Heart's Edge.

Years since he realized it was too easy for me and the other kids in the Nighthawk program to get out, to possibly escape into the hills and never be seen again.

It was *my* fault.

My fault we were all taken away, and our lives changed from the strange, deep hallways in the mansion's basement to the cold white-walled facility. I remember the scrubs, the needles, the blinding lights, the frigid metal tables under us. And the way everything went numb after our "treatments" made us all feel so strange, like we didn't own our wits anymore.

All because of the damn flower I carved.

All thanks to the day he caught me curled up on my cot with my little knife and a twig of pine, slowly shaving it down into a flower with a stem as fragile as a glass pipe and petals that curled like paper.

"What's this, boy?" he snapped.

I still remember how hard his eyes were behind his thick glasses. Ross looked down at me with his mouth curled into a sneer in his curly, greying beard, and slowly crushed the sole of his shoe down on the flower until it was sawdust.

He was just a man, a monster, doing his job.

Despite the pain, despite the tests, despite the way he liked to wiggle his voice inside my brain and pull all my strings, I still hadn't hated him yet.

Not till that day.

That was the day a deep, visceral loathing sprouted inside me. I'd nurtured it from the eight-year-old prisoner boy I was then to the twenty-two-year-old man I am now.

It's a patient thing. A quiet thing. A fucked up thing I've learned to mask for survival.

And when Dr. Maximilian Ross stops outside the door of the mayor's office inside the sprawling mansion that was once the beating heart of my first torment, I force it.

I manage to smile. Ross gives me an acidic look back and reminds me to stay out of trouble.

He's older now, the thin skim of hair clinging to his skull almost fully silver, but there's still a cold, commanding menace in his voice, a darkness, a distrust.

I let it roll off me like water off a duck's back.

Because I'm older now, too. I don't fear him anymore.

And I know exactly where I'm going the instant he shuts himself in that office and I'm left to my patrols.

I doubt she'll remember me.

I haven't seen her since the day I never knew would be the last when Blake came running across the creek, laughing and tackling me and calling me Tiger.

But I slip my hand into the pocket of my Galentron uniform coat and gently touch the delicate carving waiting there, and I hold Ross' eyes till he makes a disdainful sound and lets himself into the mayor's office.

Then it's just us Nighthawks out here on guard duty.

It's almost ironic.

Spend billions of dollars turning orphaned children into mentally warped, psychologically conditioned supersoldiers and assassins. Ship us off to missions in war zones so secret the historians in a dozen flash point countries will never find a shred of evidence we ever existed.

Then bring us home and use us as glorified guard dogs.

Bad timing, I guess.

By the time we were all grown up and ready to deploy, the Feds who contracted Galentron mercenaries only needed us for a few years before the government shifted focus. A few too many wars and little interest in spending more on soldiers who were there to escalate and destroy and kill from the shadows.

Guess we've got to earn our keep somehow, though. We're practically company property.

It beats being snuffed out, but I think the Galentron execs are too proud for that, when it's essentially throwing money out the window.

Plus, I'm not sure they could pull it off if they wanted.

They made us too efficient, too tough, too smart, too lethal. Pushed beyond normal human bounds.

How do mere mortals destroy the monsters they've created?

They don't.

I exchange glances with the others, but they're already moving, laughing and shoving at each other just a little too hard.

What looks like idle horseplay among young men and women is actually a dominance game.

They're ignoring me as usual.

I've never fit in.

Never really played at their bullshit wolf-pack hierarchy of constant aggression.

Maybe it's because Ross' conditioning never quite took hold on me.

Or maybe it's because I'm just angry enough, cruel enough, that I don't need their ugly little games to make my dick feel bigger.

I *know* I can still grind every last one of them into the dirt, if needed. But I don't want to think about that now.

There's a reason I volunteered for this boring-ass guard duty here instead of the lab today.

Clarissa.

I still remember her wide green eyes, her shining brown hair, the way she'd watch me with such frank and fearless curiosity.

The little girl she'd been is just a childhood memory, a secret buried in my heart.

I just want to see the woman she's become. And maybe, if I'm lucky, introduce her to the man I've turned into.

I owe her that gift, after all, since Ross ruined it the first time. Even if I'm late.

This place is damn huge. I only saw the underground remnants of the fort it was built on before. The mansion's massive arching hallways and winding staircases are new to me.

There are so many rooms to get lost in, and I could cause an uproar if any of the servants catch me poking around places I shouldn't, but fuck it.

This place is like walking through one big shadow.

Devoid of warmth and love.

Did Clarissa really grow up here the whole time?

All those years, never knowing I was several floors below her, writhing in agony?

Did she sleep cold nights in these loveless rooms, wondering at the strangers creeping in and out of her old man's house?

I wander the halls, lingering on those thoughts, idly fingering the carved wooden flower in my pocket very carefully.

It's the spitting image of the one I meant to finish years ago. A perfect replica of an evening rose with its subtle layers and broad petals like crinkled tissue paper.

Fuck, man, what are you doing? I really wonder.

I'm almost ready to give up on finding her.

She'd be over eighteen now. For all I know she's probably off at college or just...out. Away from her father. Away from this house.

Maybe out with a boy who's not as tainted and damaged and strange as me.

Even if I've never forgotten her.

Even if I've held on for so damn long.

Even if her shy little smile was all that kept me sane while Ross flayed my mind and tried to remake me in his warped image...

Shit, I can't forget.

Maybe it's best that I can't find her.

I'm about to give up and head outside to see where I can sneak a good beer in this town when a soft murmur catches my attention just as I'm passing the kitchen. There's a light on under swinging double doors down the hallway, almost out of sight.

My pulse slows.

Considering how late it is, I hadn't expected anybody in the mansion's service areas. And I almost walk past without checking, but some hunch, some tugging, some awareness tells me, *look, damn you!*

Fine. Just one peek, and then I'll accept it's not meant to be.

Or is it?

Because when I nudge the door open, she's there.

Clarissa damn Bell spears my heart from a thousand angles, and even the pain she gives me feels exquisite.

61

That lightning-shock of instant recognition hits hard.

Even after so many years, I'd know her anywhere. That tumble of mahogany hair flowing down her back, that slim figure encased in an apron, that elegant face that used to look like a china doll but now resembles royalty.

Yeah, there's a touch of wicked sensuality in the fullness of her lips and the way her liquid-hot green eyes are half-lidded thoughtfully, her thick lashes making them glow.

Fuck.

Worse, she's got her tongue caught between her teeth while she murmurs to herself, bent over a tray of truffles that look picture-perfect and gourmet ready.

Every piece looks different. Chocolate hues from white to black, others dipped in some kind of pink or blue or orange glaze, topped with everything from little green-leaf swirls of icing to bits of candied rind.

She tastes each one in a delicate nip, her tongue flicking out to catch a crumb from the heavy fullness of her upper lip.

It makes my gut clench. I fight to keep my pulse from surging under my belt.

Oh, hell.

It's bad enough that I'm already standing here like a Peeping Tom, watching her take those truffles like it's an X-rated flick. I'm not gonna be caught leering at her with my cock ready to bust through my trousers like a wild animal the second she turns around.

So I rein myself in and watch as she pulls a notepad from the neat black apron belted over her full chest and hips, murmuring to herself about measurements and something about texture as she jots down notes.

I don't know how much time passes.

I just feel like I've been starved for something human all these years with the Nighthawks and Galentron. Something to make me a man, and not just this beast.

And if I've been starved, then she's a *feast*. I could watch this chick for hours.

She turns away, back to a pot of something chocolaty and aromatic simmering on the stove, only to catch sight of me and freeze mid-step.

Shit.

Her eyes widen. She gasps.

Then her elbow bumps the pot handle, sending it spinning off the stove. It hits the floor with a sharp clatter, gooey brown liquid flying everywhere.

"Oh!" she gasps, disappearing behind the kitchen island, grabbing a roll of paper towels with a quickness so efficient you'd think she was a SWAT girl going for her tactical kit.

I lurch forward, rounding the island, dropping down next to the largest puddle. It's a massive mess, it's my fault, and I should help her clean it up.

But as I reach for the roll of paper towels to take a wad, she freezes, eyeballing me warily, pulling the roll back out of reach like she's guarding it from a thief.

It almost hurts to see.

I don't remember her being so tense. There's something different about her than just being ambushed by a stranger.

She's not scared of me, no.

Her eyes shine bright and fearless.

Then comes the sting that might as well be a slap to my face, "Who...who're you?"

She doesn't recognize me.

Well, fuck. I'm hardly surprised, but it still stabs me.

She's grown into a woman, yeah, but there's a hint of the same airy fresh-faced thing I remember. *But me?*

I've gone from a skinny boy who's all elbows and angles into the fucking Hulk.

Maybe it's for the best.

If she recognized me as Tiger, she might ask where I disappeared to all those years ago.

Those kinds of questions are dangerous.

The answers, even more so.

I can't risk letting anything slip that could make Galentron turn its eyes on her. People have disappeared for less.

Taking a rough breath, I offer her an apologetic smile. "Sorry. I'm Leo."

"Right. And who's Leo again?" she asks. I remember her voice as a soft, shy thing, but now it's just liquid silk and melted chocolate. "I mean, nice name, but it doesn't really tell me why you're in my house."

"I didn't break in, if that's what you're thinking." I toss my head toward the door. "I work for those assholes meeting with the mayor."

She snorts. Something glimmers in her eyes, a touch of amusement. "Wouldn't that make *you* one of those assholes, too?"

"Probably, but I try to limit my douchebag quotient to the mandatory minimum when I'm on duty."

That actually gets a laugh from her, the tight set of her shoulders relaxing. "Okay, Leo. I'm Clarissa. So why are you skulking around my kitchen?"

"They let the guard detail off the hook while they talk, and I didn't want to go drinking with everybody else." I shrug sheepishly. "I was just exploring. And making a mess, apparently." I hold out my hand for the paper towels. "We should probably get this cleaned up before it starts to dry. I hear chocolate's hell to clean out of grout."

"Yep. Words of wisdom."

But she smiles even while rolling her eyes at me. I'm grinning like a damn fool as she rips off a sheaf of paper towels and passes it over.

It takes us nearly half an hour to get the mess wiped up.

Fun fact: fondue just smears more when you use dry paper towels.

By the time we've managed to get it spotless with wet

kitchen towels and wet paper towels, there's more chocolate on us than on the towels. She's downright adorable with several smudges on her cheeks and one down the bridge of her nose.

I can't help myself.

Reaching out, I trace my fingertip over that little chocolate streak, skimming between her eyes to the tip of her nose. "Here's your next big idea: Clarissa truffles."

Her shiny green eyes briefly cross before she laughs shyly—and blushes. Her cheeks fire rosy pink against skin as soft and smooth and pale as lilies.

Goddamn, this woman.

"Yeah," she whispers, a throaty edge to her voice. "But who'd want to eat me?"

I almost bite my tongue in half. It's too tempting. Especially when she realizes what she said and ducks her head, tucking her hair behind one ear, sucking at her lip.

I could say something truly terrible right now.

Something hungry and hot.

Something as crude as my hard-on digging at my belt.

But I don't want to scare her away. Not after the way she'd looked at me for that first split second.

She'll feel safe with me because she is, and I'll make damn sure of it.

So I just smile, pull my hand back, and lick the bit of chocolate off my thumb. "I can see it."

"Huh?" She looks at me, tilting her head.

"Half the town of Heart's Edge lined up around the block, if everything you make is even half as good as this."

"Really?" She lights up a bit breathlessly. "I usually don't let other people try my experiments, but..."

"But?"

"Well, I...I'm trying to develop a signature taste profile." She stands up, unfolding gracefully and brushing her hands off on her apron. I stand, too, watching as she continues shyly. "I want everything to be delicious, but I also want people knowing the second they taste something that I'm the one who made it."

There's something dazzling, something hopeful in her voice. It makes her even more breathtaking, and I can't peel my eyes off her.

"You thinking about going pro, Clarissa?"

"I want more than that." She turns those glittering eyes and that entrancing smile on me. "I want my own shop someday. The best candy company in the Pacific Northwest."

"Ambitious. You're off to a good start." I lean over and eye a truffle that has a white chocolate shell on the outside and a little bit of candied orange peel on the top. "May I?"

She bites her lip. "I'm not sure about *that* one. I used this orange liqueur in it, and with the rind it might be too rich."

"Let me taste test."

"If...if you really want to..."

"Woman, after being covered in melted chocolate, I'm so hungry I can't help myself."

I grin at her, popping the truffle in my mouth with all the grace of an elephant, and bite down.

Holy fuck.

It kicks my tongue. A fierce citrus tartness and glazed sweetness, then the delicate white chocolate, and a liquid burst of potent orange booze.

Taste profile? *Bullshit.*

It's like a metal concert in my mouth.

I stop just short of grunting like a boar.

"Goddamn," I growl, swallowing it down. "Now we've got a problem."

Clarissa fusses with her apron, a worried knot appearing between her brows. "What's wrong?"

"I was thinking about asking a pretty girl out, but I think I just tasted something divine...and now I don't know which one I want more." I love how her breath catches, that hot blush coming back in full force. "Might need to try both to see which one's really better."

"Leo!" she gasps softly, but there's this breath of laughter behind it. She covers her mouth with her fingers, turning her face away, then peeking back, watching me through her curly lashes. "You're totally not...are you? Are you trying to ask me out?"

"Maybe," I tease. "Unless you'd rather just leave me with the whole tray of truffles. You might want to leave, though. This could get pretty pornographic."

Her laughter comes out startled but warm, and she steals another look at me, her lips parting to answer.

Only for her face to go pale as a deep, harsh voice belts out behind us.

"Just what do you think you're doing?"

I snap to attention immediately—thinking it must be directed at me.

Rest in Peace. I'm caught, just a lowly soldier, a security guard, in here flirting very inappropriately with the mayor's daughter.

I'll probably pay for this later.

Possibly in blood.

But when I turn, it's not Dr. Ross or anyone I expect standing there. It's worse.

Mayor Edgar Bell.

Fuck!

Weirdly, he's not staring at me, but Clarissa, his darker green eyes hard with contempt and disdain and disbelief.

He's an imposing figure in his three-piece suit and his iron-grey hair swept back, his thick beard cropped close. He's broad-shouldered, even if he's not nearly as tall or as muscular as me.

He looks like a man who's used to owning things. Owning people, maybe, and ordering them around.

At my side, Clarissa goes stock-still, save for the slow fumble of her lips and throat as she swallows.

It's not a hard picture to understand.

It's not hard to figure out her old man's the real reason why she tensed up when she saw me.

For a second, I just eye him and wonder.

While I was tormented in the rooms hidden under this place, was she in her own hell? Suffering alone several floors above?

Especially when he bites off coldly, "Did I give you permission to bother our guests, Clarissa Bell?"

Permission? Is he joking?

She's a young woman. An adult. Maybe not old enough to drink, but legal to vote, legal to drive, and even if she lives under his roof, she shouldn't have to ask his permission just to talk to someone, and—

"No, Papa." She bows her head, speaking softly, submissively—but behind the kitchen island, where only I can see, her fists clench slowly, the tendons in her wrists and arms straining.

Her jaw is tight, half-hidden past her mane of hair. "I'm sorry."

He sweeps her with a cutting up-and-down look, ignoring me like I'm not even there. "Clean this crap up and go to your room. On second thought, no—" A hard look slides toward me, finally acknowledging me. "You'll just make a bigger mess. Just go. I'll have the maids take care of it."

She flinches at the criticism.

Like Mayor Fuck thinks she can't even do something so simple on her own...

Who talks to his own daughter this way?

Clarissa flicks me a quick, almost apologetic glance from under her lashes. Then she turns and nearly flees the room, shoving past her father to leave the double doors swinging while he just makes a soft, annoyed hissy sound under his breath, brushing off his suit like she just dirtied it.

Then he, too, turns and walks out, sparing not even another glance for me.

I might as well be damn near invisible. Rather than standing here frozen and seething, wishing I hadn't been too startled to say anything.

I'd probably have made things worse, though.

Still, it fucking hurt, watching her stand there like she's seen the Medusa and turned to stone. Like she's been conditioned to just accept it.

I know that feeling, too.

I hate it.

Maybe that's why I feel this protective rage boiling my blood. This blinding need to get her away from this.

Damn. I just want her to be happy. And I meant it earlier when I thought about keeping her safe.

That's what I'm here for, isn't it? To protect Galentron assets and partners, including the Bell family. From anyone and everyone.

I wait in the kitchen for a small eternity, trying to get my temper under control, but excuse myself when a sleepy-looking older woman comes shuffling in, yawning, still in her pajamas with a pair of yellow rubber gloves and an apron.

I mutter an apology to her, then slip out.

There's no sign of Dr. Ross, and the mayor's long gone. I've got a few moments.

So I head upstairs to the bedrooms I'd passed before in my wanderings. One's still open, a younger girl sleeping inside, tucked up inside a ruffled yellow bedspread, peaceful and quiet.

But the other door, the one that was open before, looks closed now.

I fish the carved flower out of my pocket and lay it down in front of the door where she'll see it when she opens up before she has a chance to step on it.

I'd wanted to give it to her directly, but not like this.

Right now, she needs space.

So I'll leave her a promise, and I'll also leave behind every last fuck I have to give.

Don't care that it's insane. Don't care that it's wrong. Don't

NICOLE SNOW

care that I'm making plans for a girl who might as well be a princess to my pauper, and who I only really met after an eternity apart less than an hour ago.

Don't call me crazy.

Because I'll come back for Clarissa Bell. It's what I'm meant for.

And if she wants me to, I'll fight like hell for her.

Somehow, some way, I'll take us both away from the fucked up life Galentron and Mayor Bell have planned for us.

* * *

Present

"My, you're really going soft these days, aren't you?"

A raw, sarcastic voice jolts me out of my memories, dragging me back to the present with the sharpness of a gunshot.

That's where my brain goes the moment I realize I'm not alone. Someone's crept up on me while I was lost in my thoughts.

Not anymore. My brain snaps to guns and violence, defending myself the way I was trained to.

I'm diving for my sidearm between the layers of pallets on my bed before I even register who's here.

I swipe the Glock out, rolling to one knee, snapping the clip into place and taking aim at the thin figure silhouetted against the fading twilight at the mouth of the cave, next to the ladder.

A second later, my vision clears, and I want to smack my head. Or hers.

Fuchsia goddamn Delaney.

Hardly reason to lower my weapon.

I keep my finger on the trigger, narrowing my eyes at her. "What do you want now?"

I still haven't forgotten what she did the last time she was in town. Nor have I forgiven her.

That little ruse about needing my blood—blood immune to the virus Galentron once intended to unleash on Heart's Edge in a test—led to a mess that nearly got people killed.

And with too many loose ends hanging, I don't doubt that Galentron wants to do cleanup.

Maybe even sweep little old Heart's Edge right off the map.

Scrub any and all evidence they were ever here, and silence anyone who might know what they've been doing.

Like the daughters of the man who sold the town out for profit.

Like yours truly, the escaped freak in their fucked-up super-soldier program.

Last time, Fuchsia swore she wasn't with Galentron anymore, right before everything went to hell in a handbasket.

I didn't believe her then. Probably won't believe anything she has to say now, either.

Especially when she just sighs, fully relaxed like she doesn't have a gun pointed at her.

She tilts her head to the side, her razor-sharp salt-and-pepper bob kissing her equally razor-sharp jaw. "Why don't you come up here so we can talk?" She taps the toe of one of her red-soled black spike heels on the metal walkway. "You aren't going to make a lady use a ladder in *heels,* are you?"

"I'm not coming, and you're no lady. You can talk to me from there, or come on down."

Rolling her eyes, she folds her arms over her chest. "Really? I'm the only friend you have left, Leo. You might want to be a teensy bit nicer to me."

"You're no friend of mine. I know who my real friends are." I stare her down over the barrel of the Glock. "I'm gonna ask you again what the fuck you want. Last courtesy."

"That's a statement, not a question."

"Okay. You can be pedantic, or I can put a bullet in you for every time you refuse to answer me."

"That's hardly a way to treat a girl," she mock-pouts.

I snort. "Bull. You've probably got six guns inside your dress, and if I blink for too long, you'll murder me in cold blood."

"Aw, come on. That's the *old* Fuchsia. I've turned over a new leaf!" She raises both black-gloved hands, fluttering her lashes. "I only have *two* guns, Leo. I'm here to finish the job, not finish *you*."

I frown. "What damn job?"

"Exposing Galentron." She smirks slowly. "Lots of rumblings that they're trying to wipe the slate clean again. We already wasted our first window of opportunity. The other ones are closing far too fast. If we're going to do this, we need to do it now."

"Stop saying 'we' like I'm a part of this shit." I shake my head. "I'm not interested in exposing Galentron. Any attempt will just make those pukes come down harder on innocents."

"*You're* an innocent. As much as you can be, I mean. And yet you keep denying any efforts to exonerate you." She watches me shrewdly, her lips pursed. "Why?"

"Because I'm not that innocent. There's still blood on my hands, even if it's not as much as yours. I'll take my penance." My jaw clenches. "So, kindly fuck off out of town, and take your cronies with you."

"Wow. You really do think I'm still working with them?" Fuchsia shakes her head and slips her hand inside her tight cropped black coat. When I tense, shifting my aim, she sighs. "Oh, stop. I'm just getting these."

She draws out an envelope, thick and manila, then bends and lets it drop.

It falls down, landing on the floor of my little lair. I eye her, then edge closer, keeping the gun on her with one hand while I bend to pick it up with the other.

Sinking down on the crate I use for a chair next to my fire pit, I stretch my gun arm out toward Fuchsia, keeping one eye on her while I shake the contents of the envelope out across my thighs.

Photos.

Large, high-quality eight-by-ten glossies.

All of them are Clarissa, picking her way through the wreckage of the candy shop.

My heart nearly stops. It's that same painful jolt of recognition as the first time I saw her so many years ago, but there's nothing sweet about it this time.

Just a hard, hurting rush of longing, of loss, of worry. What the fuck is this? A threat?

My throat aches, but I grind out the words. "I already saw her. Know she's back in town. This isn't news. Leave her the hell alone."

"Keeeeep looking." Fuchsia sounds horridly triumphant.

I dart a hard look up at her, then flip through the photos more slowly.

Clarissa at Charming Inn. Clarissa at The Nest. Clarissa buying groceries, her eyes pensive, that scar on her cheek another bad memory of the last time I saw her, only it makes her look both fiercer and more vulnerable than ever.

Clarissa with a little boy.

A kid with her dark-chestnut hair and straight, slim nose, his expression shy behind a pair of thick glasses.

Her son, I realize.

Her *son.*

Fuck. My stomach bottoms out.

He looks like he can't be more than six or seven years old; hard to tell when he seems small for his age, but hell.

Did she move on that fast?

Did she just leave Heart's Edge—and me—in her rear-view mirror, and forget me as soon as she could?

Have I been the only idiot holding on for *dear life* all these years, aching with losing her?

I swallow hard, trying to shove down the sick feeling inside me. "Why're you showing me this?"

"Because, you thick dummy," Fuchsia says. "Both her and that kid are going to be in a whole mess of trouble if they don't get out of here. Her sister's already gone. Missing. So what are *you* going to do about it?"

Something about the way she says *already gone* sends a chill down my spine, and I lift my head, glaring at her. She's so *smug*, like she's enjoying the way my heart cracks.

"You know something about Deanna's disappearance?" I'm almost roaring.

"I know she's alive," Fuchsia whispers, and some of my hard, awful tension unravels, even if I still feel like I've been socked square in the chest. "Not much more."

"So I was right. Galentron took her. Why?"

"*Ah-ah.* You still seem to think I have some special inside connection. Well, I don't. I have my eyes, my skills, and what I can find out through a little sleuthin' and more common sense than you or your ex-girlfriend have." She arches a brow. "I just know you'd better move fast if you want to get that girly back in one piece."

"Why?" I shoot to my feet. My finger tightens on the trigger again.

I have to fight to keep aiming at her throat. "Why, Fuchsia? What's going to happen?"

She only smirks that shitty, insufferable smirk I hate so much and reaches inside her coat again.

What she pulls out this time is a newspaper, folded into quarters.

Without a word, she lets it fall, spinning to the floor.

She turns and walks away, her silhouette melting into the night. I keep the gun trained on her till I can't see her anymore, and even then I'm slow to lower it.

I roll my shoulders, suppressing a shudder.

Damn.

I've always had my suspicions that Fuchsia was one of the

first experiments in what became the Nighthawks program. Even now when she's middle aged, she's still as lethal as someone half her age, hiding a borderline supernatural talent for stealth and subterfuge. Not to mention she could drop a grown man with a ball point pen from fifty feet away.

Yeah.

She's *that* kind of femme fatale.

Annoying as she is real. And I'm not giving her the chance to get the drop on me as I set the photos aside and edge closer to the folded newspaper.

The front page story doesn't make sense.

It's about *me*.

I don't understand why till I see the name on it.

It's Tara Brenley, Warren and Haley's niece.

I still remember finding her lost in the dark woods months ago, this scared little thing I guided back to town. She figured out I was the town's infamous Nine.

Guess she decided to write a story about how I'm not such a savage hell-monster after all, and it ended up winning a contest in Seattle and being featured in a local newspaper.

It'd be heartwarming, if I wasn't so confused.

This can't be what Fuchsia's talking about. A kid writing a story about a local legend wouldn't bring down Galentron on Heart's Edge, even if there's a grain of truth to the story.

With another suspicious glance up, I shake the paper open, flipping through it for anything relevant.

On the fourth page, there's a short little block column about Deanna Bell.

It's frustratingly brief, terse, as if the info was censored.

It probably was. I know how Galentron works. Their tentacles are everywhere, including the media.

But if it's not that...*what am I missing?*

I flip another page.

A note flutters out, written on a piece of blindingly pink stationery.

She's even got handwriting like a knife. I know it as well as I know my own, remembering the times I've seen those sharp, slashing letters giving me orders or sharing company secrets.

I KNEW you'd be difficult. You always are.

But I don't really need you, not really.

I just need your story.

You can cooperate and be part of this, Leo, or you can sit back and watch.

But one way or another...

The whole town will get the truth.

Today.

The town plaza.

Six-shooters at high noon, cowboy.

Giddy-up.

OH, God.

Oh, fucking *hell*.

What's *wrong* with her?

Even if the people of Heart's Edge will listen to her instead of dismissing her as a batshit crazy lady ranting in the town plaza about conspiracies with government contractors, it's a guaranteed disaster.

If she goes public with that info, it's a death sentence for everyone here.

Galentron will torch this place to the ground and exterminate everyone. They might even get a chance to test SP-73, and then pay the news to write it off as a freak outbreak in an isolated small town.

Either way, Fuchsia's little plan spells *slaughter*.

Shit. I've got to find a way to stop her before she destroys this town.

Especially before she kills my Rissa and her son.

V: A FEW STEPS DOWN THE ROAD (CLARISSA)

I hate newspapers.

Loathe reporters, in general.

They always seem to swing between one of two extremes: either they make mountains out of molehills, sensationalizing the smallest things for clicks and page views. Or they take serious life-or-death issues and brush them under the rug.

Like my sister's disappearance.

I stare down at my iPad, my mouth pulled into a tight line that I can't seem to unbend. I haven't touched my brunch since I decided to check the news. The waitress asked me twice if there was something wrong with my food, and even now watches me across the diner like she's worried I'm terminally ill, ready to collapse into my cold, rubbery eggs and sausage.

No.

I'm just a very scared sister, looking down at a sterile, emotionless block of text that reads more like an obituary than a missing persons report. So this is what it's like to lose my mind in slow motion.

Sighing, I flick through a few more pages of the Seattle paper online, then scroll back to the beginning.

I tried so hard to ignore that story on the cover page. But now I can't seem to look away from the large, lurid headline.

MONSTER HAUNTING THE SMALL-TOWN HILLS?

There's more—apparently some girl related to one of the locals—I think she's Haley's niece, actually—wrote some kind of school project about "The Legend of Nine."

Nine.

Is that what they're calling Leo now? Naming him after what sounds like his prison number?

The write-up starts like the usual crap. A legend about a brutal outlaw who burned down the Paradise Hotel and murdered the mayor. They tried to put him away, but he broke out of a Montana prison and ran away to hide in the hills around Heart's Edge, turning into some kind of beast.

Now, that monster stalks the hills at night, howling at the moon and standing watch over the town, living in a kind of purgatory where he's cursed to stand guard over Heart's Edge as an odd sort of penance, protecting the town he once menaced.

There's an odd shade of truth there, but I don't know what to think about it. Or about whatever's happened to Leo in the last eight years to make him a legend.

But I linger on the girl's story of how she got lost in the woods, and how the magical Nine appeared to rescue her.

He was carrying flowers, she said. My heart clutches as I remember the crumbling flowers in the safe, real ones too much like a single wooden flower he laid outside my bedroom door a lifetime ago.

He was carrying flowers...and apparently this little girl doesn't think he's a monster at all.

Not when he was so kind to her and walked her home.

God. It sounds too much like the Leo I know.

The way he tried to protect me from everything–even my own father.

How he supported my desperate need to escape from Papa's crushing grip; how he never minded when I'd go off for hours about making candy, big plans for my shop, the life we should've had.

I'll taste everything for you, sweetheart, he'd tease, those strange dark-amethyst eyes glimmering in the sunlight cascading over his naked body as we stretched out in my bed, whispering to keep our little affair super secret. *Gonna get so fat you'll have to roll me down the hall.*

Now that hard line of my mouth relaxes—yep, I'm smiling, but I feel like crying, too, my entire body racked with tight, sweet pain.

"Hey, Mom?"

I breathe in sharply.

Zach.

The kiddo pulls me from my reverie with a hand on my arm, leaning in to squint at my tablet. His face is sticky again with pancake syrup. He's so beautifully untouched by all of this, so content, and I want him to stay this way forever.

Maybe that's why I flinch when I realize he's reading the story about Nine. About *Leo.* About his freaking father.

"Whoa, is that for real?" There's a spark of excitement in his eyes, eager and curious. He's a little information sponge, always hungry to learn new things and go on adventures. "Is there really a *monster* here?"

"I..."

I stop.

I don't even know what to say. My tongue suddenly feels like it weighs a hundred pounds.

Ugh. I swore from the moment Zach was born that I'd never lie to him, but right now I don't know how to be honest. If I tell him *yes,* that's calling Leo a monster.

He's not.

But if I say no, it's denying Leo's real. And doesn't Zach deserve to know something, now that I'm here?

I don't know. No clue what's right or what to say. I guess I could circle around it by saying there's no such thing as monsters, but that would be another lie.

My father proved monsters are real.

My hand drifts up to that scar on my cheek, then my throat.

There's that feeling again. Vicious fingers closing around my neck, cutting off my air, the light fading into darkness as my father's wild, insane eyes bore into me with raw hatred.

I shudder. I hate that I can still feel the faint echo of fear, the memory of the moment when I realized the man who raised me didn't care the slightest for my life. Maybe even *hated* me.

You don't know true terror until you look into the eyes of someone who hates you enough to kill his own flesh and blood.

"Mom, you okay?"

My eyes snap back to Zach. My sensitive boy. And when I look down at him, he smiles up at me with that quiet, nervous smile that makes him seem too old for his years, but that always seems to say I'm making things too complicated when he can just tell that everything's going to be *okay*.

I hope to God he's right.

I smile, my throat tight, curling my hand against the back of his head.

"I'm fine. Clean yourself up, Zim." I'm full of Z nicknames, and he hates them all. Call it special mom privileges. "You want to know about monsters, let's read *Frankenstein* tonight. It's a bit grown-up, but I think your reading level's high enough."

He grimaces and reaches for a napkin, before I pluck it out of his hand and wet it on the side of my glass of water before handing it back. With an aggrieved sigh, he says, "I've already *read* that one. You know the monster's name isn't Frankenstein, right?"

"My little honor student," I tease, but mentally make a note to keep a sharper eye on my little imp's library.

When the hell had he snuck *Frankenstein* in there? Has he read *Dracula* too? Is he already reading Anne freaking Rice?

Little things like that are the only problems he ever causes, though.

It's always about that insatiable need to satisfy his curiosity, without the adult rules that warn him when certain things might blow up in his face like a tipped-over bowl of flour. He's in advanced placement classes at school, but he's so smart he gets bored, goes looking for entertainment and sometimes stumbles into things that are a little above his emotional maturity level even if he can handle them intellectually.

He's almost scary intelligent.

Leo was, too.

He had this odd way of assessing situations and then making these bizarre jumps of reasoning he could never explain beyond *instinct.* But they almost always turned out to be true. Like his brain just moved too fast to keep up with words.

Honestly, there was always something a little off about the man I loved.

It's part of what drew me to him. He was strange and fascinating and not like anyone I'd ever met. He even *thought* differently.

And his son might just be the same kind of different, in ways I'm afraid I won't understand unless I talk to Leo himself about just what Zach might've inherited from him.

I don't think there's anything wrong with our son, necessarily.

But I'm starting to think there are certain things he needs that only his father can give him.

I take a shallow breath, trying to calm my twisting insides as I watch Zach meticulously wipe his mouth.

God, what am I thinking, right now?

Am I seriously thinking about trying to reconnect with that haunted man I swear I'd glimpsed?

How do I even *find* him?

I get my answer sooner than I expect.

81

The diner's door slams open hard enough to make the glass reverberate, the bell attached to the handle jangling wildly.

I tense, jerking, ready to bolt, my hand on Zach's arm and my fight or flight instinct already telling me to grab my son and get the hell out of dodge before everything goes south.

But the man who dives in—I vaguely remember him as the owner of the new garage—is wild-eyed, but unarmed, his face flushed.

"He's here." He gasps. "Nine—he's right...right here in town!"

"What?" a waitress pipes up from behind the counter, frowning. "No way. That's not possible, Mitch. He's not even real—"

"He *is*," the man insists, and that's when my confused numbness snaps into something like mixed dread and excitement, my pulse slamming as he gestures wildly toward the door, the street. "He's in the plaza—he's *there*, with some weird lady dressed in black, he—"

There's no chance to finish.

Whatever he was going to say gets drowned out by a babble of excited, breathless noise.

Everyone in the busy diner floods the door. I'd bet some of them are even skipping out on their checks, but I don't think anyone even cares since the waitresses and cook are right there in the rampaging throng, squeezing through the door.

The only people holding still are me and Zach.

What even?

But my heart's pounding too, and Zach looks at me with his eyes bugged out, nearly bouncing. "Mom, Mom, I want to see too!"

I groan, swiping a hand across my face.

Dear Lord, if I wasn't dealing with little ears that pick up every single thing they hear, I'd probably be swearing myself blue right now.

My son doesn't even realize he's begging me to see his father for the first time in his life.

This is such a *mess*.

But...but I want to see him, too.

That sore place in my heart that's still branded with his touch *needs* to see him.

I need to see what he's become, why everyone calls him the monster of Heart's Edge.

And it's like the universe is trying to tell me something, delivering an answer to my question right at my feet.

"Okay, sure," I murmur, already feeling like my chest crushes into a little knot at the thought. I stand, slipping my wallet out and leaving some cash on the table, then hold out my hand for my son's. "Let's go see this monster."

* * *

Oh.

Oh, boy, this was an *awful* idea.

I know it even before I see him.

I know it when we pull up to the plaza and see it packed to the gills. I think everyone in town is here, and it's a strange sense of nostalgia to pick out so many familiar faces that have aged over the years, from Tandy Thatcher who runs the tack and feed store to the kids I went to school with, all grown up now with babies of their own, holding their kids up on their shoulders so they can see.

Everyone faces the platform, the podium on the far end of the plaza.

I don't think it's been used in years. There's another memory.

My father, standing there giving stump speeches with the low brick building of the town's single school at his back, even though he ran unopposed for years because there's just no one interested in running a town this small. Hardly enough political controversy and drama for anyone to feel like they needed to step in and *change things* for the better.

Papa was the mayor because he was the only one who *wanted* to be mayor.

It's horrifying to think about *why*, in hindsight.

Back then the podium and platform were covered in bunting and political signs, ticker-tape showering down at the end of Dad's speeches like he thought he was Richard Nixon or JFK or something.

Now it's bare, save for some old stone planters that have probably been there since the podium was built decades ago, overflowing with flowers that have gone wild since it's not really anyone's job to tend them these days.

It's empty, until Fuchsia Delaney steps out from behind a pillar and climbs the podium. And then she gestures for someone behind her, a tall, bulky form that not even the thick stone pillar can hide.

My throat dries. My tongue goes stiff, wooden, and yet the taste of a name tingles on the tip.

Leo!

Even wrapped from head to toe as he is, this tattered shadow, I *know* him.

I know him in the breadth of those shoulders I used to dig my nails into.

I know him in the bulk of muscle that once pressed me so close, holding me in the protective circle of his ginormous, corded arms. They bulge against the fabric like he'll split right through the black cloth hiding his skin.

I know him in that slow way he moves. Like he knows just how strong he is and he's holding back so he won't break the world with that Redwood body.

And I know him in those eyes, the only naked thing I can see past the thick wrappings and hood over his face and head.

The noonday light falls down, turning darkness into brilliant amethysts, shades of crystal violet. His eyes nearly glow from the shadows.

Then those eyes lock onto me, and I forget how to breathe.

Sweet Jesus. If I'd ever doubted it was him, standing in the doorway of Sweeter Things, all doubts are obliterated now.

His eyes burn through me. I kinda get now why people call him a monster. He's a predator, a carnivore, and right now...I feel like prey.

But there's no malice on his face. Leo just looks *hungry*.

Hungry in the most anguished, tortured way a man can be.

Hungry like he's somehow satisfying some deep, wild craving with every spare moment our gazes fuse and I'm frozen in place. My body spins through hot flashes and cold chills, numb to Fuchsia starting to talk at the podium or Zach tugging my hand and asking me to lift him up.

Numb to everything but the cruel, vivid trembling I feel to the bone. I stare into Leo's eyes and realize it then.

I've *missed* him so effing much.

I've tried so hard not to think about him all these years. I couldn't deal with the conflict and confusion of figuring out how to feel when he saved my life.

He killed the man I hated to love and loved to hate, because even when your father treats you like an afterthought and dominates your life, even when he belittles you and then tries to sweep you aside in a murderous rage, you still love him because he's all you ever had, and you don't know any better.

I'm older now. I know better and I've been on my own for so long, trying to be the parent my father never was.

But that knot of emotion comes undone inside me. The stormy conflict that comes from not knowing how to feel, it's still there. Still trapped in that moment eight years ago, and I never knew how to deal with it, so I just *didn't*.

Well, I might not have a choice anymore.

Not when Leo's gaze flicks from me and down to the little boy holding my hand, something darkening in what little I can see of his expression. My chest nearly explodes with *wanting*.

God.

No matter what he did, no matter why I ran away...

There's something deep inside me that's just as hungry as him.

Just as tortured. These feelings rip out of me so raw and hot it's like we just tumbled into bed together yesterday, full of laughter and promises and tomorrows.

And a crazy part of me wants my son to have a father.

I've got to figure something out. I've got to...

"—this man isn't the monster you're looking for, when the real monsters at Galentron—"

Maybe it's that dreaded m-word that pulls my focus back to Fuchsia like some kind of terrible curse, a trigger word dragging my attention away from Leo. She's in full public speaker mode, projecting her voice, and I realize she's telling everyone about...

Oh *crap*.

This sixth sense hits me.

Before I even hear the tell-tale *zing* of a speeding bullet, I'm diving for Zach, dragging him to the ground.

A split second later, that bullet smashes into the stone column right behind Fuchsia's head.

One inch to the right, and that would be her skull exploding. Not the pulverizing cloud of grey dust as the bullet disappears inside a new hole in the stone, cracks radiating all around it.

For a second, Fuchsia blinks and goes oddly still with that eerie calm she has.

Then the entire plaza erupts into chaos.

People screaming everywhere, people running, people forming a stampede.

We've got to get out of here *now*.

I don't think anyone's going to shoot at me, but I can't risk Zach getting trampled to death. So I bundle him up in my arms and stand in a half hunch, keeping low as I push against the crowd, ducking and bobbing and weaving through the shouting masses.

There's barely time to see Leo charging toward us.

I don't even think.

The instinct to see him as *safe* is too strong, and I adjust direction, shoving us through flailing arms and churning bodies toward the juggernaut parting the sea of flesh to get to us. Zach clings to me, eerily silent, but that's what he does—shuts down and goes completely quiet when he's afraid.

I think he got that from me.

Making himself so small the bad things can't find him.

I *won't* let them hurt him. I just clutch him protectively close, as Leo and I finally crash together.

Time freezes.

There's one lost second where the world falls away, and we just stare at each other up close.

"Nine, get *back* here!" Fuchsia snaps, descending the podium.

There's a growl from behind his mask. I just stare at him with this breathless, wordless understanding, as easy as if we haven't been apart for almost a decade.

Then his hand is on my arm, hot through his gloves, gentle.

He steers me and Zach away, just as screaming sirens erupt over the plaza.

Leo lets out a low snarl in the back of his throat. "Hurry," he rasps.

I realize his voice is different.

It's always been deep, husky, but there's something nearly scorched about it now. Ragged. Gravelly.

Leo, what happened *to you?*

But I bite my tongue so we can break through the crowd and duck around the side of the school. I recognize the bright blue double doors set into the ground—the storm shelter, the big one we used as a town evacuation space for natural disasters.

Leo lets go of my arm long enough to wrench the double doors open in a massive heaving of strength, his entire body straining and shoulders bunching.

Then his hand falls on the small of my back—massive, heavy, long fingers spread so wide they touch nearly both sides of my waist, blazing hot.

As the screams fade and Sheriff Langley's voice rises over a bullhorn, the beast they call Nine ushers me down the steps into the darkness.

It's not long before I bump up against a locked door—the entrance underground. But it's already too late to turn back. Leo draws the doors shut again, blocking out the light from outside and casting us into pitch blackness.

We're trapped in the stairwell, so close there's no room to move.

Leo's body crushes against mine, with Zach wedged in the small space between us.

My heart pounds so hard I can barely hear anything but that and the soft, shallow sound of Zach's panicked breaths.

Outside, there's still so much noise, but the double doors and the walls around us mute it until it's just us in the pitch blackness, and the raw living heat of Leo.

Even when I can't see him, I *feel* him.

He's so tall, so massive, takes up so much space.

Against my shoulder, I sense the flex and pull of his abs in tight, moving ridges as he breathes.

I don't know what to say.

My tongue is tied in knots, and God he even still *smells* the same, this wilderness scent that makes me think of the bursting forests and earth and pine needles.

"Clarissa," he grates out.

"Leo—"

We both stop, and he goes more tense against me.

Okay, this is killing me.

I don't know if I want to cry or just throw myself against him, wrap us all up together and hold on *tight*.

But after a moment he takes a slow, audible breath and says, "The kid all right?"

"My name's Zach," my son pipes up softly before I can answer, his voice barely a whisper, but steady, and I can't help but smile.

"He's tougher than he looks," I murmur. "He'll be fine."

Nothing. That's what Leo gives back.

In the silence, a crazy part of me wants to scream *of course he'll be okay, he takes after you, he's yours!* but I'm not that reckless. Not that brave.

So all I say is, "What were you thinking, going out there like that? And trying to—"

"Stop Fuchsia." He cuts me off. "She was trying to put on her little expose like a piece of bad performance art. I tried to stop her before it happened. I didn't want anybody getting hurt."

I shake my head. "Who was shooting at her, though?"

He pauses. "I don't know. I've got one guess, and it's the same as yours."

Galentron. Or someone they'd hired. Everything begins and ends with them.

But there's something about the way he says it that makes me think he knows more.

And if he does, then he might know how and why Deedee got herself tangled up in this.

"Look," I whisper. "I didn't mean to come back, I just..."

I can't finish. It feels too much like an apology.

Like I'm saying sorry for intruding in his life again, dragging him out in the open, even if it's not my fault and it's just the way things happened.

Or maybe I'm apologizing for *running away.*

For leaving him behind, for being too scared to face my feelings.

Too afraid that I'd turned into a monster, too, being *grateful* to him for killing my father.

I swallow, holding Zach tighter. "It's just that Deanna—"

"I know," Leo says softly, some of that harsh, burning edge to his voice soothing. "I've already been on it. Rissa, I swear—"

"Don't," I whisper, almost too quick. "Don't make any promises. We don't do very well with those."

The silence tastes like hurt.

Bitter.

I don't know why I said that. I'm reeling, probably in shock, falling apart, and I don't know what I'm thinking, what I'm saying. That wasn't fair of me.

I was the one who left.

But I don't know what else to say now, and I bite my lip, searching for something, anything.

Until the doors over us rattle, parting just enough for a sliver of light. It bursts in, illuminating one amethyst eye. His gaze is locked on my face and cuts me so *deep*.

But Zach whimpers, burying his face in my throat, clutching close. "*Mom*," he squeaks, obviously scared.

Someone's getting in.

I don't know what to do. Where to run. What to even think except it's all bad.

What if it's the person who fired the gun?

What if they know I'm Deanna's sister, and they're here to take me away from my son and leave him alone with no one to love him and no idea he's with his father *right now?*

It can't just end like this...can it?

"Leo," I strain out, only for his massive bulk to shoulder me gently out of the way.

He stops, positioning himself at the foot of the stairs, right in front of the doors. Between us and danger. It's incredible how some things never change.

"Stay put!" he growls. "Stay quiet. It'll be all right."

It won't. I know it won't.

But right now, I have no one I can trust.

No one except Leo Regis.

VI: A JOURNEY OF A THOUSAND MILES (NINE)

I'm pretty sure we're hosed.

More precisely, I'm pretty sure *I'm* fucking hosed.

Clarissa and the kid will be fine, whenever the cops break down the door to rescue them from the big bad wolf of Heart's Edge. It won't be Galentron, not a skeletal strike team in broad daylight where half the town might see them.

Me, though? Confronted by Langley and his boys or maybe some backup from the rest of the county?

I know what'll happen.

I know what I'll do. Even if I don't have a clue about how.

I won't go back to jail.

I fucking *can't*.

I'll lose my mind, locked up in a six by eight cage again, pacing like a lion in a zoo, slowly suffocating.

But if I resist, even old Langley just might give the shoot-to-kill order.

I don't think he'd honestly mean to.

He'd just lose it in a fit of nerves, and accidentally pull the trigger, or have one of his bumbling deputies do the same.

I turn for a second, staring at the boy. Even if he's Clarissa's son by whoever took my place in her life, I can't.

Can't force him to watch a man get gunned down in front of him.

So I close my eyes, take a deep breath, and raise my hands.

Prison or not, I'm going to surrender, and figure out the logistics of getting loose and disappearing again when I don't have to worry about scarring a kid for life.

I'm ready. Waiting to be told to come out with my hands up, when the cop on the other side finally manages to pop the tricky latch on the doors and yanks them open.

"Are you coming, or are you putting on a mime show?" A familiar voice bites off coolly.

Gray Caldwell.

He stands tensely in the doorway, a tall shadow with the sun at his back, the light reflecting off his glasses as he glances over his shoulder sharply. It's still pretty wild outside, judging by the background noise.

Shit.

No time like the present, then.

I glance back at her.

Rissa, who's staring at me with haunted eyes, so many questions swirling in her irises.

I can't believe she even recognizes me. I'm wrapped up like a damn mummy, covered from head to toe, but hell. If anyone would know me, it's her.

Just never wanted her to see me like this.

Give it a day. I'll be out of her life as soon as I can.

Then she won't have to see that the monster I've become is worse than the monster the town thinks I am.

Taking a deep breath, I toss my head at her. "Come on. Let's get the hell out of here."

"*Move!*" Gray snaps in that authoritarian tone he has. "Our annoying friend is keeping the police *quite* busy, but once the code for a sniper in downtown Heart's Edge spreads, we'll have uniforms swarming in from ten towns over. Not even Fuchsia can delay that."

He's right, and I can't risk that shit.

Rissa seems to understand, finally. After a second of hesitation, she nods and steps forward. I hang back, waiting, letting her and the boy go ahead, before I bring up the rear, keeping them safely hidden between me and Gray.

From there it's a frantic run to the back of his shiny new truck. He's parked it skewed across the mouth of the street leading down the side of the school, giving us enough cover so we're able to move mostly out of sight.

I catch one last glimpse of Fuchsia. She's eerily calm, looking like she's saying something cutting even as Langley maneuvers her into handcuffs. Then I've got Clarissa around the waist and I'm lifting her into the back of his truck with the boy still in her arms.

She's so damn light I'd almost forgotten how small she was, next to me.

She's a tall woman, yeah, but I'm something else.

And I remember how she always used to tell me, *You make me feel fragile, Leo. But you also make me feel safe. And I kinda like it.*

I like feeling protected.

For a moment, as she flashes past in a wild swirl of mahogany hair, our eyes fuse together again.

And I know she remembers those times, too. I know they hold her prisoner, same as me.

She's breathless, flushed, and swept away with me back to that moment.

* * *

Eight Years Ago

SHE'S WITH ME, dammit.

That's all that truly matters right now.

I hurt all the fuck over.

Hurt everywhere in ways I haven't in so long. Not when I've been good about toeing the line like a good little soldier, pretending to be obedient. Pretending the conditioning *works* on me.

Pretending I'm one of the Nighthawks pack.

Too bad I'm not.

For some reason, Dr. Ross was in my room in the barracks today, deep in the Galentron facility buried inside the abandoned silver mine. He found the new carving I'd been working on.

The little figurine of a woman with her hair pinned up in a messy twist, her hands in the middle of crafting some invisible thing.

It didn't matter what.

I just wanted to capture Rissa's essence as this creative, beautiful soul, her hands always shaping sweetness from the smallest things.

But I still remember that sadistic piece of shit stomping down on the flower I'd carved as a boy. On damn near everything I'd made in the following years.

Dr. Ross sees rebellion. A sign of my individuality, maybe, when that's not allowed in the Nighthawks.

The bastard always thought I stopped misbehaving like a good boy. He never realized I just learned to hide it better.

Now, he knows.

Somehow, the punishment feels worse as a combat hardened mercenary than it did as a kid.

My entire face throbs from the beating I took, deep in a back storage room where no one would hear the sounds of ten fists hitting my body.

The other Nighthawks didn't even question their orders.

Hell, I'm not sure they were even aware they were doing it. Their eyes were blank, expressions focused, completely controlled by the fucked up shrink and his commands.

But at least I didn't scream.

I didn't yell once, though I hiss as Rissa touches her fingertips to my cheek with a worried noise, turning my face from side to side to see the damage.

"Leo," she murmurs, looking up at me with her eyes dark. "Who did this? *Why* would anyone do this to you?"

I smile, though it makes my lower lip hurt, still swollen and split. "I insulted the galley cook's mac and cheese. Sue me."

She smiles faintly, sadly, and leans over to rummage around in the hastily thrown-together bag of first aid stuff she'd dug out. I'd shown up under her window in the dead of night, tossing sticks and pebbles softly at the glass till she peered out, caught sight of me in the light spilling from her window, and let out a soft, hurting gasp before disappearing.

She came back minutes later, a bulging satchel thrown over her shoulder, and her hand already in mine as she dragged me off into the woods.

We're sitting in the clearing by the creek now, resting on a log, looking at each other in the moonlight.

It's the same place we used to play as kids and she doesn't even know it.

Through the trees here, not far away, there's an old set of doors buried in the earth, covered in honeysuckle vines.

That's the door where I'd escape into the trees to be with friends, before vanishing again.

I wonder if she even knows about it.

Then I wonder how one soft touch can hurt so fucking much. Rissa presses an alcohol-covered gauze pad to my jaw, wiping gently at my skin.

"Hold still," she whispers.

"Fuck," I hiss through my teeth, swearing softly under my breath.

Her smile strengthens, turns teasing.

"You big baby," she murmurs, but there's no sting to it. Just the warmth I crave so much while her fingers carefully tend my face. But her smile fades as she studies me, her eyes so clear in the moonlight. "Leo, be honest...is this because of *me?*"

The look she gives me tears my heart out; hook, line, and sinker.

"No." I hate lying to her, even if it's necessary. "Fuck no. Why would you even think that?"

She smiles weakly and sets the gauze down, replacing it with a tube of cream so cold it stings like frozen hell as she rubs it into my skin. "You work for a very powerful company that's involved with my father. I'm his daughter, you're a security guard, soooo...not exactly rocket science putting the pieces together."

"The princess and the pauper." I shrug, catching her wrist to stop her from playing nurse, and turn my head to kiss the heel of her palm. "It's not that, sweetheart. I promise."

There, at least, I'm telling the truth. Even if I can't tell her I'm no *ordinary* security guard.

It's not her fault. None of this shit. Not even what happens to me, seeing how she has zero influence over Galentron or her own vicious father.

I stop there. Can't tell her anything else. The pain in my gut just churns, worse than the damage in my body.

And I tell myself it's just to avoid more questions. That's why I do something stupid.

I fucking kiss her.

I kiss her like mad, trying to lie to myself the entire time, but that frantic collision of lips and teeth and tongue speaks a thousand truths.

I kiss Rissa Bell because she's balm on my soul.

There's no pain my body can take that her touch can't fix. The way she kisses back, all fire melted into a soft moan, might be magic.

There's no one here but us and the stars and this psycho longing that's been building inside me like an angry volcano for weeks. Every almost-kiss and every hasty touch that breaks off too soon, whenever we hear the creak of footsteps or realize just how little time we have left before we have to part, to keep our secret, to hide, has just made it *worse.*

I've wanted to claim every inch of her, starting with her mouth, consequences be damned. Out here, it's the first time we're truly alone.

There's no one to hide from under the lush green canopy of the trees and open sky.

No one to get in the goddamned way.

No one to eavesdrop but the moon and stars.

Half-sighing, half-growling, I weave my fingers through her hair and coax her head back, begging her without words to open, to let me in, to melt real sweet for me.

My kiss stakes a claim I don't quite have a right to.

For all the promises I've made, we haven't been able to escape just yet. There's one piece holding her back.

We need to get Deanna, too. Take her some place where no one will fault us and search up and down for stealing away her little sis.

It's too soon to figure that out.

But here, now, my lips don't care.

They need her bad.

And that animal need builds more and more with every whisper of her breaths, every hitching sound in the back of her throat, every hot little whimper as I tease my way deeper inside her and attack her tongue the same way I want to have the rest of her: with slow thrusts, slipping into the depths of her mouth to explore and fill and ask her if she'll have me, if she'll take me, if she could *ever* see herself with me in the most intimate, hungry, perfect way possible.

Good thing there's an answer.

It comes in the seething clutch of her hands on my arms, "Leo" whispering against my lips. My name's a question, an answer, and a plea.

Her perfect tits crush against my chest and abs as she digs

herself into me, her nipples hard points against my shirt. I shudder with a hot bolt of desire that rips through me like a raging lion, roaring in my blood, nearly overwhelming this gentle moment with a demanding burst of pure lust.

I tear back from her lips, looking down at her with a growl hovering in the back of my throat.

Fuck.

She's so tempting it's painful, her lips still rose-red from my kiss and swollen. Her eyes are gleaming smoky and dark, her breaths panting, making the soft, pale curves of her tits push up against the sweeping neck of her blouse.

My dick is almost nuclear.

Feeling her pulse through her throat makes me want terrible things.

And that flush in her cheeks is an invitation.

I want this girl to blush for me, and only for me. Wear my jealous mark *forever.*

Clearly, I'm not thinking straight. But how the fuck could I when Clarissa torments my dick so hard it could pound nails?

"Rissa." My fingers burn as I stroke her hair back, snarling at her warmth, the smoothness of her skin, the softness of her hair.

I don't think she gets how someone so delicate, so beautiful, so terribly sweet sets me on fire. I want to fuck this girl into oblivion, take her cherry, and ruin her for any other man. I want her fucking *mine.*

She's my opposite.

Where I'm rough and crude and masculine, she's this gorgeous thing dripping with a sexuality I don't think she even notices. It's innocent and knowing, wise and untried, inviting and unconscious.

It's also wreaking hell on my cock and my common sense.

I swallow another growl, twining her hair around my fingers. "I need you," I rasp out, lust making my voice thick. "Need to be with you, Rissa, if you want me. If you'll have me."

There's not even a flicker of doubt. No hesitation.

Just her fingers in my scruff, tracing my jaw, slim and hot and nimble.

"Leo," she whispers again, gasping my name as she pushes herself up and seals her mouth to mine, then slips her plush, delicious body into my lap.

Any ideas I had about control are gone in a flash.

I can't control shit.

Not when her dress is so short and her thighs are so full and lush, and she's straddling me.

Not when I can feel just how *thin* her little panties are as she comes down against me, pressing our bodies together till we're just burning flesh and fabric that might as well not be there.

Not when it's her wetness and heat so naked against my skin.

She wants me.

This beautiful fucking woman wants me, and I'll explode if I can't have her right the hell now.

You'd think our first time would be gentle and slow.

But there's this passion in Rissa, this wild animalism I never expected. She bites my mouth with heat so fierce I have to bite her back, tumbling her down into the grass and leaves, ripping at her dress. The fabric shreds under me and all that delectable pale flesh spills out for my greedy eyes and mauling touch.

I've never seen a woman like her.

The way her hips curve out, so thick and lush, from a high, tiny waist that swells out into breasts that fill my hands to over-flowing.

Her thick, pink nipples are begging for my mouth. I nip and suck and bite and toy till they're swollen, nearly red, and she's fisting her fingers in my hair, moaning my name and squirming under me like she can't stand another minute of it.

She's like this primordial goddess, naked against the leaves with her mahogany hair everywhere in tangles and her eyes this vivid jade green.

It's like she was made to give life.

And she brings my soul to heaven as I grip her soft, yielding thighs, spread her legs, and bury my face in her pussy with a ravenous hunger.

She's so wet. Fuck, it's hot, in the moonlight I can see her glistening, and when I rake my tongue over her sweet cunt she nearly screams.

Her fingers fist my hair as I lap at her like mad and she's still dripping, still pouring, still turning me on so much I'm about to bust through my jeans.

She tastes so damn good I can't stand it. I shudder as I probe my tongue deeper inside her.

I need her ready. I need her willing. I need her open and soft and ready to take me.

Because I'm not a small man.

What I'm packing will make her *scream.*

And while there's a wicked part of me burning with the thought of completely tearing her open and making her mine, I want her to enjoy every second.

I want her to want it—and me—again. I want her addicted when she comes.

Yeah, there'll be pain. I can't help that. Not when I am what I am; not when it's her first time.

But I can at least make the pain sweet, leave her so sensitive she can't sort it from pleasure.

So I use my tongue. I use my fingers. I explore her depths, and she's so *molten* inside I can already tell how good she'll feel wrapped around my cock, writhing all over.

I play with her pussy till she's wrung out, arching and convulsing and practically struggling, spilling more sweet wetness into my palm as I slip my fingers in and out of her again and again and again.

Every time I think I should stop, she clamps her knees shut, her thighs folding around my hand and wrist, trapping me inside her.

Fuck, she's so sensuous.

So needy.

So completely given over to the wild abandon of sex without shame, without hesitation.

It's beautiful. Fucking intoxicating to be wanted by this woman this much.

Can't stand it anymore.

I go still, breathing hard, staring down at her through narrowed eyes. She's such a perfect mess, her thighs streaked and gleaming, her folds pink and swollen from my thrusting fingers and sucking lips, her expression so blissfully *tortured*.

I want too much: to ravage her, ruin her, keep her, cherish her, protect her, break her.

No one ever said I wasn't an animal.

The beast in me has full control now as I drag my jeans open and bare my cock. It hurts when I fist it, my lust throbbing hot and painful, the cool night air against my skin, the tip beaded wet with pre-come.

It makes me hiss through my teeth. I catch its weight in my hand to steady its hungry pulse, my own palm almost too much to bear.

I half expect her to flinch when she sees me.

When she remembers I'm over six and a half feet tall and the rest of me matches, and she's not a tiny woman but next to me?

She's small. Delicate.

I need to ease her into this.

But Rissa doesn't hesitate.

Not even for a second as she reaches out to touch me with soft fingers that feather over my cock and nearly undo me then and there. My balls burn.

Falling forward with a groan, I brace my hands on her sides, my hips jerking as she explores me, electrifies me, traces fire over my skin with slow, sweet touches. They shape my cock to the print of her palm, sensitive and so fucking hot.

She guides me down to her. Spreads her thighs around my hips, and presses the head of my cock to her slick, swollen folds.

"Fuck!" I gasp.

And it's the last coherent word I've got in me before I *snap*.

My kiss comes like wildfire with teeth.

I dig my fingers into her hips, pulling her into me.

And I just *barely* remember to fumble for the condom I've kept hopefully in my back pocket for weeks before heat meets heat and I give in to the irresistible gravity of Rissa.

There's a frozen second as I poise there, caught on the edge, the tip of my cock just barely inside her.

Then she cries out, arches her back, wraps her arms around me, locks her thighs around my hips again, and pulls me in.

She's. Fucking. Tight.

Hotter than sin. And clutching at me like she never wants to let go. Pleasure hits so deep in every wild, shaking thrust, it leaves me dizzy.

My hips piston-slam hers, fucking her right through the discomfort, kindling her pleasure and crashing her headfirst into orgasm.

I love how she whimpers. How my name becomes like music and a curse, the raw insanity of an angel losing herself on every churning inch of my dick owning her depths.

She finds my rhythm after she comes, lifts herself up to crash into me, to meet me with a wildness that's purely us.

Our kisses turn savage. Our sex, even more so, and I'm no longer worried about hurting her when her nails scratch my neck and her heels dig into my ass.

Shit, I'm no longer scared of *anything*.

Rissa accepts me like no other human being I've met, welcoming me with her body, her voice, her begging, grasping hands.

And as I surge deeper, harder, riding the high of a pleasure so stark it's pure, sugar rush agony, *I fucking know*. I know right before the fire in my balls rips up my cock and electrifies my spine, bathing my brain in pure caveman heat.

She's with me. She's already mine. And I'm so hers, I can't imagine being anything else.

* * *

Present

THE MEMORY LEAVES my mouth dry, my head spinning, as the noise of someone screaming from the plaza drags me back to the present.

Back to reality, where I find Rissa still staring at me.

Shit. I realize I'm gawking at her, too, and holding on tight. We need to get out of here.

I swallow, starting to murmur an apology, but I can't read her expression anymore.

So I shut up.

Then I let her go, feeling the sensation of her warm flesh soaking through her clothing and into my palms, before I grip the edge of the truck bed and vault over it. When I land, the truck bounces hard on its tires, dipping, and Gray gives me the evil eye.

"Would you mind going easy on my suspension? I already lost one truck this year," he says, moving past with the speed that's as much Gray as his icy wit, letting himself into the driver seat.

"Down," he orders, slamming the door and starting the engine.

I oblige, dropping to lie flat in the truck bed, even though it's almost not long enough for me.

Clarissa does, too. I want to tell her she doesn't have to.

She's safe.

It's me they'd come after. Me they'd hunt us for. But my damn lips won't move.

Not when it's been so long since we laid together, face-to-face, eye to eye. Even if it's nothing like before, a strange part of me wants to hold on to this as long as I can.

So I let silence do the talking.

I drink my fill of Clarissa Bell quietly, taking her in with a greedy gaze, while Doc's truck goes rolling out of the plaza and away from Fuchsia's storm.

* * *

No QUESTION, The Menagerie is the safest place for us right now.

At Gray's vet practice we're barely out in the open for two seconds before he ushers us in through the back entrance, and then into a room that's overflowing with spacious kennels, the scent of clean fur, the quiet sounds of curious dogs and cats and a few other things that probably aren't legal to keep as pets.

I don't expect him to leave us alone for long.

It's just me, her, and a little boy who's already over his fear. He's crouched in front of a kennel, poking his fingers in to let a ragdoll cat with smoky-colored fur sniff and nuzzle at his fingers.

Meaning it's really just me and Clarissa right now.

Staring. I can't stop myself from looking at the scar on her cheek.

I remember it as a blood-wound scratched down her face, right after that hateful demon of a man rammed a vase against her skull hard enough to shatter the ceramic.

I don't realize my hand is moving till I feel the softness of her skin, warm and smooth even through the insulating layers of my gloves. She's so damn alive.

So *real*.

I still feel like a ghost, a phantom haunting these hills, a life written in rumors.

The instant we come into contact, though, her eyes widen, her gasp slips out, and she stares at me, holding still, trembling.

But she doesn't pull back, even as I slowly draw my finger down the line of the scar, tracing the way it cuts a ferocious mark into her skin, a single small blemish that only makes her beauty more goddamn radiant. It's the contrast, I think.

If only my scars were the same.

When she starts to reach for me, a whisper of "Leo" on her lips, her fingers skating dangerously close to my face mask, I come back to earth.

"Don't." I jerk back, growling harsher than I intend, breathing ragged.

I can't help myself.

I can't let her *see* how fucking disfigured I am.

Watching me with stricken eyes, she lets her hand fall.

That terrible silence builds between us again, a silence made up of years and distance and so many unanswered questions. I want to ask all the shit I've got no right to.

Ask her about the boy.

Ask her why she *ran*.

Ask her if what we had was ever real.

If she really loved me, if she held on to that feeling the way I've held on to her.

But I don't get the chance when the door flies open.

Even though we're standing more than a foot apart, we both break away, putting more distance between us, retreating to opposite sides of the room as Doc and Ember step in.

They both look at us oddly, Gray tiredly knowing. Ember just seems puzzled as the kid looks up and smiles. "Hi, Ms. Ember."

Ember offers a nervous, sunshine smile, leaning on Gray. "Hi, Zach."

Yeah, that's his name. He'd told me in the cellar.

Zach.

And as he lifts his head, waving at Ember with a friendly, gap-toothed smile, for just a moment the light pierces his glasses instead of reflecting off them.

His eyes are dark till the light hits them. But when it shines right into his irises, they turn a faint shade of clear, translucent purple.

My heart drops down to my goddamned knees and then slams back up in my throat.

What. The. Fuck?

I stare at the kid. *My* kid?

Holy shit. It can't be. But I've never, ever seen anyone with eyes like mine.

Trust me, I've looked.

Any time I could get anywhere with internet access, I've *looked*, tried to figure out where I came from, who I was before Dr. Ross took me out of my foster home and turned me into *this*.

I wanted to find out who gave birth to me. Who gave me up.

Instead, all I found was a blank, terrible emptiness. Next to sterile facts like how rare violet eyes are, and sometimes how prized.

There's a reason Liz Taylor made such a splash.

Yeah. It could be a coincidence, but the odds, his age, my time with Rissa...

Fuck.

Fuck my life, I have a kid.

A son Clarissa never told me about.

Jaw so tight it might break, my gaze darts to her. I'm almost choking, trying to process this behind my mask, my entire brain and body just shutting the fuck down while I try to make myself grasp what's happening.

It's not all her fault. Even if she'd been able to find me, I wouldn't have wanted her to.

Doesn't change the present. I want to bark questions: *how, why, when?*

But now's not the time.

While I stand there fucking dumbstruck, looking between Rissa and Zach, Gray starts off matter-of-factly, "So, we should probably make sure everyone's on the same page."

Ember smiles faintly. "I think, as the newcomer, I'm the only one really in the dark. Right?"

Not quite.

I think some of us have been in the damn *dark* about some very important shit.

Snarling, I take a deep breath, trying to pull myself together. Clarissa must've had her reasons. Everything that happened when she fled Heart's Edge, I know it had to be hard on her.

Shit. Should I even bring it up? Or just wait till she's ready to tell me herself?

Will she ever *be* ready?

Goddamn. Now that I look at Zach, I can *see* myself in him.

That same crooked gap in his teeth...mine straightened out as I grew and my jawbones realigned. Something about the set of his jaw, too, and his smile. He's got her pale skin, her mahogany hair, her little nose, but my eyes.

His features are a blend of hers and mine. It's as unmistakable as it is uncanny.

Breathe, dammit, I tell myself. *Focus.*

Dragging my attention back to Gray, I listen as he tells Ember, "To keep this brief, Firefly, it would take the equivalent of a natural disaster to bring Ms. Bell back to Heart's Edge. It started years ago. Before the incident with Galentron that led to my recent dustup with Peters and his crew, Leo was forced to intervene to save Ms. Bell from her own father. In the fighting, Mayor Bell died. Leo's been vilified for that ever since as the monster they call Nine, especially after escaping prison. But the rumors around that incident have marked the Bell family. It's not a name many say around these parts anymore."

I could fucking kill Gray.

As far as I know—and from the way she's staring at me—Clarissa has no clue I'd been in prison.

That's something I'd rather have told her myself, on my own terms.

Still, we don't have time to be delicate.

Ember gasps, sucking a breath, staring between us. "Oh, Clarissa, I had no idea! I'm so sorry."

Clarissa just smiles tightly. "There's a reason I try to keep a low profile here. Honestly, the rumors aren't as bad as the truth, considering everything my father was involved in with Galentron. I'd rather have people making up tall tales than be hurt, knowing what really happened."

"But that's likely why Deanna was taken," I say, struggling to keep my mind on the present. "For knowing the truth. And now we've got ourselves a real problem. Didn't take that sniper long at all to pop up in the middle of town. Tells me they're watching us. And they know someone's up to something."

"But who?" Gray asks, a touch of frustration in his voice. "Is this about Fuchsia's little games with going public? Or about something else with Deanna?"

Everyone looks at Rissa like she might have an answer, but she shakes her head sharply. "I don't *know*. I told her to just let things lie and move on. I thought she'd done that when she focused her attention on the store." She makes a frustrated sound, raking her hair back from her face. "God, I never should've let her open a store back here, let alone left her to manage it. I should've sent her off to Bellingham like we planned."

"It's not fair that you have to hide," I growl. "I manage in the shadows. No one else should have to." I shake my head. "We need Fuchsia. She taunted me into making an appearance today. She knows more than she lets on."

"The problem," Gray points out, "is that she's been arrested. Somehow, I don't think Langley will grant our interview request lightly."

"Fu—" I catch myself, glancing at the kid. *My* kid. I still can't stop thinking that, my mind rabbiting in circles around it. "...fudge."

That actually gets a little laugh from Rissa. It's tired, with an edge of fear and frustration, but it's there. Damn, I'm drawn to her, lingering on the curve of her lips, wishing I could give her more reason to smile.

But Haley and Warren stomping into the back room gives me a good reason to look away and try to focus myself again.

They get the same run down, mostly for Haley's benefit, before Warren shakes his head. "Listen, clearly Clarissa's a target. I'll go get her car from—where did you leave it?"

"The diner," Clarissa tells him. "Zach and I walked to the plaza from there."

"No worries. I'll grab it. Let 'em target me for a bit, while Hay takes you and Zach back to the inn," Warren says. "Since you're in one of the new cabins, I think you should be fine—it's isolated there. Hell, most folks don't even know any of the new construction's been finished."

I don't like it. I should be the one protecting Rissa and her belongings.

Before I can stop myself, I bite off, "Isolation's a problem."

Gray frowns. "How so?"

"Can't see those cabins from the inn. Out there alone, Clarissa and Zach could disappear and no one would know it for days. No one to see her being taken. Nobody to hear her crying for help." When her face goes pale, I grunt, lowering my eyes. "Sorry. I'm not trying to make you freak. Just saying you need security."

Suddenly, everyone's looking at me.

Everyone *except* Rissa. And it dawns on me what I've just volunteered myself for.

Shit.

If I've been in purgatory, I think I just crashed down to a lower, personal level of hell.

Standing watch over the woman I couldn't let go, with the kid she never told me about, when she's glaring down at the floor like she can't even stand to look me in the eye.

God *damn* it.

I'm the only one who can do it without drawing suspicion,

though. If Gray, Warren, or Blake skip out on their jobs to stand watch, they'll lead anyone watching straight to her.

Me, I'm already a ghost.

Nowhere for me to disappear from. Nowhere to disappear to.

I start to speak, then stop. Because there's something strange about how Warren looks at me. Like he's seeing me for the first time.

He knows I'm not the danger, the beast everyone thinks I am. He *knows*.

He was there with us when we joined Gray to save Ember and her family not so long ago. Warren might not know everything, but he knows enough.

He just doesn't know we met long before that.

He doesn't know the scarred, broken man standing in front of him is the Tiger from his childhood.

But the odd, questioning way he's looking at me says he's getting a hint of an inkling.

I look away, avoiding his eyes, grinding my teeth with a nod.

Right. Stick to the present.

"I'm on it. Should be me, anyway," I say.

No denying it. I made this mess.

It's only right that I should do everything I can to clean it up.

But when Clarissa snaps her head up, fixing me with a fierce look, her lips trembling, I wonder if there's anything I can ever do to truly fix this.

Or am I just damned forever?

VII: BEGINS WITH A SINGLE STEP
(CLARISSA)

*E*verything's happening too fast.

One second, I'm having brunch with my son.

The next, I'm running from a sniper, locked away with my outlaw ex, then somehow, *I'm* a target when we still don't know how to find Deanna, and I hate the idea of being shuttled away, cooped up and passive and just *waiting around.* Even worse, the insanity at the plaza will probably shuffle Deedee's case even further down the cops' priorities.

I need to *do* something.

Instead, I'm standing at the cabin's window, looking out over the dark silhouettes of the trees. A second later, I see the faint orange glimmer about a dozen yards out, and the glimpses of movement that tell me Leo's out there somewhere.

Watching. Waiting.

I let out a sigh. *One thing's for sure, this has been a long damn day.*

After what happened, I don't even know if I'm dealing with Leo at all.

Has this masked madman thing called Nine taken him over? Has he become someone and something I no longer understand?

He's been in *prison*. The little girl's article tipped me off, but his friend Doc confirmed it.

Why? For my father's death? For something else, some secret with Galentron I don't even know?

Is that why he covers himself so no one sees his face? So he can't be identified? Is there something else hiding behind the mask?

"Mom?" Zach comes up to my side, looking outside with me. "Is the monster out there in the woods?"

"He's not a monster, baby," I murmur absently.

He's your father.

Jesus. It's right on the tip of my tongue. It's been there ever since Leo looked at me today with so many questions swirling in his eyes.

Zach curls his hand in the crook of my arm and leans his head against my side. "It's okay if he's a monster, Mom. I think he's a nice one."

I smile faintly. "Yeah? Where'd you get that idea?"

"He protected us today, didn't he?"

"Well. Yeah, he did." I rest my hand gently on top of Zach's head. "He's protecting us right now. That's why he's around. He will be for a while."

Zach frowns. "How long is a while?"

"I don't know, baby."

"But...I have to go back to school Monday."

Crap.

He's right.

But I can't leave Heart's Edge. I *can't* leave without finding Deanna.

I love my son more than life itself, but I love my sister, too. Even so, I can't neglect his education.

I bite at my thumbnail, turning that over, staring at the orange flame flickering in the distance. "We'll get you a tutor, ZZ-boy," I say after a minute. "Honestly? I don't know how long we'll be here."

Zach frowns, looking puzzled. "Are we moving here?"

"*No*," I say vehemently.

Then a growling voice at my back says, "You shouldn't."

I nearly fly right out of my skin, whirling—and instinctively grasp Zach and push him behind me, making him squeak.

Breathing hard, I stare up at Leo.

Sweet Jesus. How does a man this large move so quietly?

He's as stealthy as the lion he's named for. Silent and powerful, but there's something *different* about the way he moves now. He was always strong, lithe, handling his bulk with an easy grace, but now he *prowls*, like the animal inside him has taken over and lent him a sort of beastly sensuality.

Something I shouldn't be thinking about. Especially when those deep, dark amethyst eyes look down, flicking between me and Zach, asking what I really think he'll do to my son.

Asking if I trust him that little.

No. It's not that at all.

It's just that, after losing Deanna, of course I'm on edge. Truly terrified of anyone taking my son away from me.

But after I manage to catch my breath, calm my racing heart, and straighten up, loosening my grip on Zach, I finally ask, "What do you mean, *shouldn't*?"

There's movement behind the mask that makes me think Leo's arching his brows. "Are you saying you want to? Settle down here in town again?"

"*No*," I say, almost spitting it back.

No flipping way. There are far too many bad memories here.

But, there are good ones, too.

That's why this place feels like a torture chamber. Worse, it feels like the better parts still live inside those eyes watching me so strangely and steadily.

His eyes shutter as he looks away. Distant, quiet, before he growls, "If you want a tutor, they'll have to be cleared. Full background check, credentials, the works. Start looking for someone tomorrow."

I bristle. I've never liked anyone giving me orders, especially since my father.

"Um, that's not your decision," I snap.

"You—" He stops, closes his eyes, takes a deep breath. "I'm sorry. I know. Screw it. I'm just on edge, same as everybody."

"Yeah, well...me too." Now it's my turn to look away, swallowing thickly, tucking my hair behind my ear. "I'm just worried there's no one qualified in Heart's Edge. Zach's reading at more than twice his age level. He's real smart."

Zach grins and bounces on his toes.

Smart like you, I want to say. *Those same weird intuitive leaps you make.*

And there's a rigid tension in Leo's shoulders as he stretches, thinking. "Bring in somebody from Missoula. I wouldn't recommend a local. Tales grow in the telling. Would someone tutoring at the high school level do?"

"Probably. As long as they get that he's got a brain like a high school freshman, but the emotional IQ of a seven-year-old."

Zach lets out an exasperated sigh, propping his hands on his hips, then pushes his glasses up with one finger. "*He's* right here, Mom, you know."

"I know, kidlet, but *you* can't fall behind. It's already going to be tricky explaining to your school and getting them to let you make up tests and homework."

Wrinkling his nose, Zach says, "Aw, seriously? I have to do homework on vacation?"

"It's not really a vacation," I say, wincing.

Leo's face shifts behind the mask again, and from the glitter in his eyes I'd swear he was *smiling*. "Listen. I hated homework when I was a kid, too. If I find you a tutor you like, will you do your work if I help you?"

Zach's eyes go wide with delight. It's exactly the right bait.

To Zach, Leo's like this mythical monster-man. A legend standing right here in front of him, offering to help with his freaking homework.

If that's not enticing to a little boy, I don't know what is. It's like he's got his own personal Sully.

"Yeah!" he says breathlessly, bouncing on his toes. "That's great, Mr. Nine!"

A raspy sound rises from the back of Leo's throat, a deep chuckle. "You can just call me Nine."

He should be calling you Dad, I think bitterly, and ugh it's on the tip of my tongue. Again.

Something about seeing them like this. The way Leo just *gets* Zach on such an instinctive level.

If things were different, he'd make a great father.

Would he even want to be, though?

It's been so many years, and they haven't been kind to him. I don't even know what's happened to change him into the huge, dark slab of bundled muscle standing in front of me.

My eyes pinch shut as a memory hits me square between the eyes.

Hey, he'd whispered in my ear, tucking my hair back with his fingertips and caressing my earlobe with warm lips. *What do you want to name our first six kids?*

Six?! I'd laughed, shoving a hand into his face, pushing him away. *Um, my vagina isn't a clown car. We're having three, and then I'm retiring from baby duty.*

Three? That's station wagon numbers, not a clown car.

I used to laugh so much with him. Even when I wanted to shove a pillow in his mouth to make him shut up. Leo always had the *worst* jokes.

And now, he doesn't seem like he laughs much.

His gaze shifts from Zach to me. I realize I've been staring at him with my heart in my throat, lost in memories. Clearing my throat, I tear my gaze from that penetrating stare and lower my eyes.

"You cool with that?" he rumbles.

"Sure." I nod. "How soon do you think you can bring someone in?"

"I'll get you a few people by the end of day tomorrow. Vetted and cleared. You pick the one you think is best."

Fair.

I like that even if he's trying to look out for us, he's still stepping out of the way so I can make the right call for Zach on my own.

But he should have a say, too, that guilty voice whispers in the back of my mind. *Zach is his son.*

Whatever. Soon. I'll tell him, some way.

I just can't blurt it out right now, in front of Zach, while Leo lives like a wild man and probably has a dozen warrants out for his arrest.

Ugh.

It's complicated doesn't even touch this mess.

There's a long silence, and then I catch the faintest creak of a floorboard. I look up sharply to see Leo's back. He's treading toward the door with that lion-like stalking lope.

"Hey," I say, my voice weak, catching against the tightness in my throat.

He stops but doesn't look back at me.

I gather my courage. It's never deserted me before, and I won't let it now. "Are you sleeping outside? Isn't it cold?"

He shrugs tightly. "I'm used to it."

"Well, you could just...I don't know, sleep in here?" I offer.

A strange stillness passes through him like he turns to stone. Then he throws this piercing look over his shoulder, a single eye watching me with that predator's gaze.

"No," he growls softly. "I can't."

Then he pushes the door open and steps outside, disappearing into the deepening night.

Leaving me alone with Zach and the wild, frantic beat of my racing heart.

* * *

I END up picking a recent college grad named Derek.

He's warm, friendly, with a Master's in Education but no job in a depressed local market, and he talks to Zach in tune with what he is: an extremely smart little boy who still has the maturity of someone who doesn't know how to regulate his own feelings just yet.

He's good with my son. I can see that from the first day.

He's good with me, too, making me feel a little less lonely cooped up in here and involving me in some of Zach's more active lessons. They're designed to keep his hyperactive mind focused and occupied.

Derek doesn't stay with us past evenings, though. His boyfriend expects him back every night and he's already grumbling about the long-distance job, but it's almost a relief to have someone to fret with over how *frustrating* men can be when we take a coffee break while Zach heads outside for "recess."

And I watch through the window with my heart breaking one little piece at a time.

Zach and Leo playfully chase each other through the trees, only for Leo to lift Zach on his shoulders, raising him up high so the kidlet can gather acorns. The trees are all heavy with nuts tucked in their blazing orange leaves.

When Leo gently shifts Zach's loose scarf back into place, I almost *die.*

Derek watches me across the kitchen island, his blue eyes glittering with warmth and sly amusement. "So you and the iron giant out there have history, huh?"

I catch myself, face flushing hot, and look down into my coffee cup. "Is it that obvious?"

"I mean, you're looking at him like you'd climb him given half the chance, sweetie."

"I—*no!*"

Oh my God, but he's not wrong.

I can't forget the delicious way Leo used to touch me—coaxing my arms up over my head, stroking down them, gripping my wrists just so I could struggle against the pleasure he gave. His grip tethered me, left me writhing at the end of my leash while he teased me with slow touches and long, deep licks of his tongue.

I feel too hot even thinking about it.

My breaths come a little too short, and I set my coffee down and fold my arms over my chest, tucking into myself and warning my body to calm the heck down.

I have company, damn it.

But...it's been a while.

I never thought about dating. My whole life was taken up with a newborn and launching a business. There wasn't time for romance.

Actually, I didn't *want* romance.

I'd been burned by men too much already.

And if I couldn't have him, I didn't want anyone at all.

I guess I still feel the same way. So does a body that remembers his touch, and with him so close, it's brutal.

Like waking up from a long winter sleep, the heat of summer rushing through me.

"Clarissa." Derek smirks, but it's full of sympathy. "You look like a woman who's *pining*, darling."

"Shhh." I drag a finger over my lips. "Next thing you know, he'll be standing over your shoulder and you won't have even heard him, but he'll have heard *you*."

With a little laugh, Derek winks, holding a finger to his lips. "Your secret's safe with me. I'm not here to get up in anybody's business, just teach the kid."

He gives me a wink. He's hinting he knows this isn't normal, and neither is Leo. I'm grateful we don't have somebody who'd try reporting him, but I imagine Leo already asked him about that during vetting.

I offer a weak smile, then pause as my phone vibrates in my back pocket.

My whole body goes cold when I pull it out and see the number for the Heart's Edge sheriff's department. *Crap.*

"Sorry!" I tell Derek. "I have to take this."

I rush off to the bedroom and swipe the call. "Hello? Sheriff Langley?"

"Yes, ma'am, Ms. Bell." He sounds uncomfortable. I sink down on the edge of the bed as my legs go weak, already anticipating bad news. "Er, listen, I..."

I close my eyes. Pain lances through me. Please, no, not this. Not now.

Please.

"Just say it," I whisper, shaking, already picturing the worst.

I can already see the morgue, the cold table, the white light, someone asking me to identify my little sister's body. *I can't.*

"It's been more than forty-eight hours," he straggles out. "I dunno if you know the statistics about leads going cold on missing persons cases, but..."

"I do."

"Well, ma'am, we haven't found anything. The Spokane and Missoula teams haven't either, and they've been diverted to other business. We can't keep them here indefinitely. They've got responsibilities in their home precincts and some follow up work to help us with thanks to the ruckus in town the other day. Right now, they can't even confirm it was a kidnapping. It's just as likely your sister and an accomplice staged a break-in and left with—"

"With what?" I demand, hot anger rushing through my blood. "That's crazy. She wouldn't. And all the cash was left in the register and the safe. You saw it, Sheriff. They weren't there for money. They came for *her.*"

"I'm sorry. My hands are tied. I just don't have the authority to make them stay on this case."

"So what, then?" I hiss, unintentionally harsh, but it's either hiss, snarl, scream, or sob. "Everyone just gives up and moves on with their lives like she never existed?"

"N-now, we'll keep looking locally, but we've got that incident with the shooting to investigate, I'm afraid, and—"

"And a single gunshot with no victim takes precedence over my *missing sister.*"

"It could be a federal matter of terrorism—"

"And this is a personal matter of my sister's *life!*" I'm shouting now.

I think I've heard enough.

So I fling the phone away, barely remembering to cut it off on yet another stammering excuse before it goes skittering across the bed.

Jesus. I only sit there for a few miserable moments, hugging my arms to my stomach, before I jump to my feet and fling the bedroom patio door open.

I go spilling out into the afternoon light, taking in deep breaths of cool, crisp air, clenching my fists. There's a scream building up in my chest, and I'm ready to lose it.

What now?

What do I do now?

I'm not a cop. I have no flipping clue how to hunt down a missing woman properly.

But I can't just leave and forget her. Never.

Our father swept us under the rug so often. He forgot we existed, acting like we didn't matter at all, whenever he wasn't beating us and chewing us out by our teen years.

I *won't* abandon her the way he abandoned us. Acting like she's dead when she's still alive.

I won't cry, either.

Tears are for grieving. You only mourn the dead.

Somehow, I effing *know* my sister's alive.

"What's wrong?"

I nearly shriek at the gravelly voice at my shoulder, even though I should be used to this. Leo moves like a ghost, appearing out of nowhere. With a startled squeak, heart thumping, I jerk back, turning to face him, breathing hard—then groan, hanging my head.

"Swear to God, I'm going to put a *bell* on you."

That twitch of his mask hints he might be smiling. "I could try to make more noise."

"Yeah, and I'd probably still jump out of my skin." There's no denying I'm on edge. I sigh, straightening, pushing my hair back as I scan toward the house, watching as Zach goes tumbling up the front steps to meet Derek. "Recess over?"

"He found an old seed pod he couldn't identify and wanted to look it up." There's an odd way his voice softens when he talks about Zach, and it does twisty things to my insides.

But Leo's still watching me, not Zach, as he murmurs, "You're upset."

"Yeah." I can't meet his eyes for long.

Every time I do, the memories swamp me. So do the questions.

So I tilt my head back, looking up at the sun dappling light through the orange leaves, making them glow like flame. "Langley called. Said the out of town teams can't spend more time on this, and his two-bit team needs to focus on the shooting."

"So Deanna's officially a cold case."

"Forty-eight hours." I smile bitterly. "That's as long as they're obligated to care."

"Don't worry. We'll just make up their slack."

I frown, glancing at him. "What do you mean?"

"They quit. We don't have to." He shakes his head. "I don't know where to start yet. Will you give me time?"

A hurting, harsh laugh escapes before I can stop it. "Time is all I've got." There's a knot in my throat, and I swallow, but it won't go away. "I don't know what to *do*, Leo."

"You can start by thinking of everything you know about Deanna."

Those sharp, amethyst eyes are locked on, holding me in place with his magnetic, totally Leo Regis warmth.

"You're the key to saving her, Rissa," he says softly. The way his gritty voice rolls my name feels like fingers on naked skin. "You know her better than anybody. You know her patterns, her habits. You'll know where to find the missing thread to unravel all of this. Once you've got a scent, I'll be your bloodhound."

He steps closer to me and my heart nearly pounds out of my chest. Even through the layers wrapped around him, even in the deepening autumn cold, he's a burning force of nature.

Almost more than I can handle. I swallow roughly, looking up at him as he nearly whispers.

"I'll do anything to bring her back to you." But as fervent and heartfelt as he sounds, there's something dark and almost ominous, too. "*Anything*," he says again.

Then he's pressing something into my palm. I'm so shocked by the sudden contact, the strength of his fingers, their warmth through his gloves, that I don't pause to wrap my hand around something cool and round and textured before I realize what I'm doing.

Confusion swirls through me as I look down, unfolding my fingers.

There's a wooden coin in my palm, barely larger than a silver dollar. It's wafer-thin, but delicately carved on both sides, with a detail most people couldn't master with a fine-point pen on paper. Yet Leo manages with simple knives and etching tools.

"Turn it over," he tells me.

On one side, I see a crescent moon, surrounded by glittering stars.

On the other, there's a woman in a Greek half-shoulder robe, hair flowing behind her, expression fierce as she draws back a longbow, readying an arrow to take aim.

I frown—until it clicks.

"Deanna!" I murmur, sucking in a gasp, lifting my head. "From Diana, goddess of the—"

But he's gone.

Leo vanished into the woods, leaving behind nothing but the

warmth of his body soaking into my palm as I clutch the little coin.

It might be a small thing to some.

To me, it warms my heart like a bonfire, easing the ache.

It's a symbol of hope.

* * *

THE NEXT MORNING, I set out on my own.

I feel safe leaving Zach with Derek for a few hours. Zach doesn't even notice I'm leaving because today Derek brought him a college biology textbook, turning him into an overexcited bundle of *What's this word mean? And this one?*

My kid.

If you think he's a handful now, just wait until he gets older and the hormones kick in.

I'm so tired even coffee isn't helping in the slightest. I barely slept last night, honestly, racking my brain for any clues I could find in Deanna's life that might give Leo something to work with.

And the entire time, I couldn't stop myself from staring out the window at that glimmer of light burning in the darkness; that orange fire-glow that told me Leo was there.

So close to my lonely bed, yet so far away.

I hate this.

I've been *fine* for years.

Before, every day I'd just collapse in bed, so tired I never noticed how empty it was. I've done pretty well with this *single mom* thing. The only plus-one I needed was Zach.

But there were long, dark nights, now and then, when I wondered.

Why didn't Leo try to find me?

Back then I'd told myself that wasn't a fair question. It's not like I was looking for him, either. He probably stayed away for the same reasons. Too much confusion, too much chaos, too much *everything.*

But now, I wonder.

Where was he all these years? What turned Leo into *Nine?*

Those questions kept me up as much as the quiet ache that made me remember how it felt when he'd pull me in close, tangling our bodies together. Every single part of me used to lock with him. There wasn't even a breath between us; just sweat-slick skin and gasps and shaking limbs.

We'd throw the covers over our heads and shut the world out, pretending nothing was waiting to drag us back to reality.

Not my father. Not Galentron. Not that mega-creep Dr. Ross, who always freaked me out whenever I saw him skulking around the house.

Just us.

Just me and Leo, with his strange eyes glowing in the dark like two gorgeous gems dug from the earth.

Last night, curled up in the sheets, I'd pressed my hand over my stomach. Years ago, I'd known I was pregnant, before everything ended with my father dead and the fire at the Paradise Hotel.

Leo obviously hadn't.

I'd been trying to figure out how to tell him, hoping he'd be happy, but worried it would be a problem. And night after night, once he'd fallen asleep, I'd lie there with my hand pressed over my stomach just like that, trying to find the words.

He still doesn't know. When he saved my life, he also saved Zach's.

My father nearly snuffed out two lives that fateful night.

But I can't think about it right now. I'm almost at Deedee's apartment, hoping something there will jog my memory. Maybe she left me a message.

We used to leave each other secret messages all the time. We had our own language, in a way. A really simple language, but one people wouldn't think of.

We called it mirror code. We'd write in alternating letters.

The first letter of a word was the right one, but the second one would be an upside down version of what we called the letter's mirror. If the right letter was five letters from the beginning of the alphabet, like the letter E, then we'd write the letter that was four letters from the end of the alphabet. V.

But always there'd be a few random tricks to throw people off. Like if there was a dot next to the letter, then it meant add one when counting. So if there was a V, the right letter was actually F.

Yeah, I know. It's not exactly genius cryptography.

It was the kind of silly little thing our father never bothered noticing, let alone decrypting to figure out we were warning each other when he was in one of his moods, telling each other where we'd hide when he wanted someone to take his temper out on.

So we'd leave each other notes tucked into diaries, behind picture frames, underneath vases.

In the secret passages behind the walls in the house, where we'd creep around in the darkness to hide, huddled together and listening to the shouts echoing through the house.

The crashing.

The rage.

Even if he couldn't find us, he'd find *something* to hurt.

We were just easy targets that gave him the reactions he wanted.

Fear and pain. Raw, hurt human agony that might distract him from his own.

I'm sick with the memories by the time I pull up outside Deanna's apartment complex—one of only a few in the entire town. There are only twelve units and two floors. I probably look entirely out of place pulling up and climbing the steps to her door.

Although everyone who sees me probably knows who I am.

Even if the townsfolk don't know the truth, I know the older ones blame my father for the Paradise Hotel burning down, killing the local economy. People lost their jobs, their livelihoods.

But since he's dead...it's easy to transfer that hate to me and Deanna.

Thankfully, no one bothers me while I fish around under the mat and then check the inner corners of the window until I find the spare key.

I let myself into a space decorated in shades of light and dark teal, patterns that are *so* Deanna—fresh, lively, like she trails spring wherever she goes. I fight back a smile.

The apartment looks like she left just this morning. Even though the police have been through here, they didn't disturb much. There's still a shirt tossed on the linen easy chair, a book sitting on the sofa with a bookmark in it.

Leo Tolstoy.

I smile to myself. Deanna always loved the classics, and I thought her double majoring in Russian lit was one of the most ridiculous things ever.

I set the book down, then move slowly through the apartment, looking for places where she could've hidden a note. Some clue what she was working on, what she was getting into.

Checking behind picture frames, I open the kitchen cabinets and look between stacked plates and bowls, even peep inside the freezer. I find her spare checkbooks—who keeps checks in the freezer?—but no note.

Nothing in her bedroom, either.

Not under her pillows or the tangled covers or under the mattress. Nothing in the nightstand drawer except her reading glasses and a few battery-operated things I could do without knowing my sister owns.

The closet just has empty shoes and a few lonely dresses. God, I even turn the pockets of every garment in there inside out.

Nothing.

Standing in the bathroom after ransacking the medicine cabinet in a fit of frustration, I stare at my tired, hollow-eyed expression in the mirror and blow out a sigh.

My angry breath mists up the surface.

And that's where I see my *something* in the condensation.

Holy hell. It looks like someone drew on the mirror with a finger, but I can't quite tell what when there's only the swirly curve of a letter and the leg of another.

Did Deanna do it while it was steamed up from the shower?

I'd seen something like this in the movie *Constantine*. Twin sisters who used to leave messages for each other "in breath and light," drawing messages in dew and frost on windows.

My heart thumps with a touch of hopeful, breathless excitement.

Did she really?

Bracing my hands on the sink, I lean in closer, blowing gently across the entire mirror. My breath steams it up, revealing more letters.

A Confession, it says.

I blink, pulling back, just staring at it.

Confession? A confession of what?

I don't understand. I don't—

Wait. The book.

Leo Tolstoy's *A Confession*, with the bookmark tucked inside.

I bolt back to the living room, grabbing the book off the couch and flipping through it, searching for a piece of paper, a note written on the inside covers, anything.

But there's nothing. Just the bookmark, and—

And something on the back of the bookmark, slashed there in Deanna's familiar handwriting, the same swirly, slightly awkward caps as the letters on the bathroom mirror.

NRGT.TSADKG.

I'm so used to our code that I translate it in seconds.

Nighthawks.

I...what the hell does that mean?

Nighthawks?

I don't understand. Was she taken because of something to do with this Nighthawks thing? What would they want with her?

Frowning, I sink down on the edge of the sofa, staring down at the blue ink bled into the white cardboard.

"Find something?" a voice rumbles behind me.

I leap off the couch like a cat with its tail being pulled, the back of my neck prickling as I nearly trip over the coffee table, the book and bookmark dropping from my fingers. "GAH!"

Leo stands behind the couch, blinking at me calmly.

"Sorry," he whispers.

It takes several messy breaths before I can speak, pressing a hand to my chest, trying to calm my pulse, staring at him. "What are you *doing* here?"

"You left without telling me where you were going," he replies, like it's the most natural thing in the world. "So I followed."

I scowl. "I never asked you to stalk me, Leo."

"I'm not stalking *me.*" He holds my gaze, eyes steady above his mask. "I'm protecting *you,* Rissa." His voice drops, quiet and heartfelt with a touch of edge. "What if Deanna's kidnapper decides you're next?"

Crap, he's right.

He's right, and I hate it.

Until we get to the bottom of this, I'm a possible target. Just because I walked away from everything to do with Heart's Edge and Galentron doesn't mean Deanna's kidnapper knows that.

I lower my eyes. "Okay, fine. Sorry."

"Don't go off without letting me know," Leo growls, but it's a concerned one. "Or with Zach. Always take somebody else with you, even in town."

"But we—"

"Always, Rissa. You heard me." There's that thunder again in his voice. Like I've got a prayer of arguing with it.

I almost hate how calm he is. How steady.

He's always been fierce like that, though. Quiet, kind, gentle, calm, and sharp as a dagger.

It always took the worst to rile up his temper. He's a slow burn kinda guy, but when his anger or his passion finally hits its limit...talk about *explosive*.

Maybe that's why this edge-of-the-storm calm he carries bothers me. He's all ice, when just being in the same room with him tears me to itty bitty pieces.

It feels like he's indifferent to me. Numb. Like time sanded away all the sharpness of *us* for him, while it's still cutting me apart.

Avoiding his eyes, I bend to pick up the book and its lost bookmark, setting them on the table. "Sorry. I can't expect someone else to babysit me."

"It's not babysitting," he rumbles. "Especially not if it's me."

"Oh? And just how're you supposed to look for Deanna if you're shadowing my every step?"

Again, I hate that I never hear him moving, and it's a mistake looking away for even a second—because suddenly I *feel* him so close, his boots and close-wrapped fatigue pants in my peripheral vision, the scent of him like something wild.

"Believe me, I'll find a way," he snarls, so low and deep and *close* that I practically feel the vibrations of his voice stroking my skin.

I shiver, wrapping my arms tight.

"Ah, yes, Mr. Invincible," I tease softly. An old joke, but one that makes neither of us laugh. I try to smile in the silence between us and lift my head, looking up at him, taking in the lines of strain around those bright, tortured eyes that are all I have of the man I used to know, right now. "When was the last time you even slept, hero-man?"

He shakes his head. "Doesn't matter."

"It does." *It matters to me.* "You look dog-tired."

His mouth moves in a slight upward smirk. "How can you tell?"

"I know," I whisper, staring at his mask. "I can see you even when I can't see all of you."

The ache inside me is a full body throb.

I just want to see the man who once promised me forever, with all his heart and soul. So I reach up, running my fingers along the edge of his hood, before reaching for his mask.

"Leo, let me? *Please?*"

His hand shoots up and catches my wrist so fast, so hard, I gasp.

He takes a loud breath, eyes widening, going completely still, but there's a tiny flinch as he turns his head to one side. "*No.*"

"Why?"

Damn, I can't stop myself. I'm in for a penny, in for a pound, and I slip my fingers into his hood as he pretends to fight back, cradling his face in my palms. It's still fabric, but it's the closest we've come to a real touch in so long that I'm ready to break down sobbing and ask him to just flipping *hold me.*

Hold me, and we'll figure out how to make everything right.

"Why?" I beg him. "What happened to you?" Gently, I search for the edges of the mask with my fingers, and he doesn't pull away, but he won't look at me. "It's me, Leo. I won't hurt you. I'd never..."

"Rissa," he growls. Ragged, tortured. "Quit being cute. Don't you get it? You're the only fucking person who *can* hurt me now."

I take a deep breath, shifting my eyes to his, losing myself in mocha fire and mystic amethyst.

"I won't," I promise softly, and he slowly turns his face back to me.

It's still just those deep, aching eyes, but they seem to say everything without words.

As if he's telling me, *you already did.*

But he doesn't pull away as I find the bit of cloth that tucks the mask in place and gently begin to pull, unwrapping it.

And that's when I realize, Leo is trembling.

He's an entire mountain *trembling* while I peel his mask away, gently stroking his hood back to reveal what he's become.

I gasp, but I don't stagger back.

Because even though he's been scorched by flame, forged and tempered, I recognize the man staring back at me. His gorgeous, chiseled face is mostly untouched by the ravaging scars going down one side of his neck.

His hair falls over his face in a wild mess of brown, a shade lighter than I remember, almost like the fire sucked the color from him. Or maybe it's just from spending so much time in the shadows. My hands tuck into his fabric, pulling, and my eyes trace his damage.

The scars make fierce crags that border on chaos in his skin, where they blur into ink. The edge of a few tattoos I remember, plus some newer, deeper, darker ink he'd added to hide what the fire did to him.

He's become fierce and harsh and animalistic.

Something ferocious, bestial, predatory. But he's the same beautiful man with the same face I adored, the same strong soul behind the flame, the hurt, the torture.

He's still Leo.

Swallowing a growl, he shifts, pushing his hood down lower. "Look, goddammit. Is this what you want to see? What kind of freak I've become?"

Slowly, I shake my head. "Hardly. You're the man I remember."

He opens his mouth to bark something back, but closes it instead, like he's shocked by my words.

How can I blame him? I just smile, grateful he's let me in, if only for a split second.

He's not a monster. He's elemental now. Kissed by the flame, this fire-scarred golem of raw strength and endless muscle.

Sure, he's different, there's no denying that. So different, this thing gone feral with his humanity stripped away. But he's also truly *beautiful*.

This is where any sane person probably wants to smack me across the head.

No, I can't explain it.

Can't explain how the sight of him like this, transformed and yet still so *Leo*, makes my pulse skip and my heart race faster. There's something dangerous about this new man, something scary.

But it's the kind of fear that ignites all your senses and makes the beating pulse of the forbidden that much hotter. It's the fear that could leave me almost as savaged and wounded as this unbelievably rare beast-man standing in front of me.

Maybe what's in front of me is more animal than man.

I don't care. This beast pulls on me just as deeply as the man ever did.

If only I knew what happened. What made him like this, if it happened during the hotel fire, or some other way?

But more than anything, I want to know *him*.

I want to meet the new Leo as he is now, instead of grasping at who he used to be.

Because even if he's a wild thing now, even if he's this prowling carnivore, this ferocious stranger who still looks at me like he can't believe I find any part of him sexy or sweet or redeemable...

I still *know* the same heart hammers away inside his wall of a body.

And this man wears his heart in his eyes as he stares at me, waiting for me to reject him, to shove him away like poison.

He never expects what I actually do.

I shouldn't, but sometimes a girl has to let instinct win.

Pushing myself up on my toes, I rest my hand on his chest. Then, with a soft whisper of "*Leo*" on my lips, I let it happen.

I kiss Leo freaking Regis so hard I give him a better reason to burn.

VIII: ONE STEP FORWARD (NINE)

Somebody pinch me. Wake me the fuck up.

The last sixty seconds can't be real life.

I'd never wanted Clarissa to see me like this. I'm a monster. I'm the crazy outlaw killer everyone in town calls me, burned into this disfigured mutant.

I'm barely even human anymore.

Hell, maybe I wasn't before the fire, ever since the Nighthawks program scrambled my brain and ran more medical experiments on me than I could ever guess. *Did* shit to me that I can't describe.

But at least I looked like a man then, and not a beast.

At least I was something a woman could still love, not this hideous husk of muscle and ink and scars. When she'd tugged at my mask, everything inside me broke.

I hadn't realized till then that deep down, some not-quite-dead part of me was *hoping*. Wanting. Wishing that we could pick up where we left off and start all over again with our son.

The moment she'd yanked off my mask, my hope vaporized once she saw what a fucking monstrosity I am.

Or so I'd thought.

I waited for the scream, the gasp, her sweet face twisting in sick revulsion.

But she'd just rested those slim hands on my chest, pushed herself up as high as she could reach, and still barely found me. She'd pressed her soft, intoxicatingly red mouth to mine. She'd given me her tongue, and I'd taken it like a man wandering the desert raids water when he finally stumbles across an oasis.

Fuck, I'd nearly gone paralyzed for a second, letting out this deep, searing groan that was more like a bear than a man.

I haven't felt anything like her lips in almost eight goddamned years.

Sure, I've remembered it every day, every night, her kiss branded on my psyche, but it's nothing compared to the reality of her body so close to mine and the lush sweetness of her mouth under my lips.

I'm damn near frozen.

Then some deeper part of me takes over, and I sweep her closer with a snarl, wrapping my arms around her, clutching her tightly, jealously, angrily.

It's not her I'm pissed at, no. I just hate the demonic twist of fate that stole away this kiss for almost a decade.

Rissa moans, wrapping her arms around my neck, digging her fingers into my hair with something like desperation. Like I've infected her and made her a starving animal, too.

We kiss like tigers, savaging and breathless and biting, licking and tasting with the desperation of years apart. Motherfucking *years.*

I need her—I need her so much, my entire body blazes with neglected desires. Almost like the fire that transformed me still lives inside me and now it's crackling back to life.

Rissa feels so perfect.

Still tastes like the gourmet sweetness she creates.

The same sublime, mad perfection and softness and tartness that explodes into rich, heady, intoxicating sweetness.

She's burning up against me. Her curves mold perfectly to

my muscle, another thing the years haven't changed. Her waist feels so slim in my hands, her breasts so plush and heavy and soft against my chest. *I'm dying.*

For just a second, I let my tongue delve past her slick lips, drowning myself in her taste.

All growls, I start turning, dragging her down to the couch and bringing her closer to me, and my eyes open for half a second to take in my surroundings.

That's when I see the bookmark on the coffee table.

NRGT.TSADKG.

A code. A message. I remember once she told me about her and Deanna sending each other notes, and in a flash, I've worked through the pattern to figure out what it says.

Nighthawks.

My blood goes cold.

A dirty word I've always been careful to never say to her. A secret I've always tried to keep.

Shit. It's like my past is coming back full force, reminding me why I can't have her, why I'm too dangerous for this beautiful woman in my arms and her scent teasing my nostrils.

I pull back from her sharply, sucking in a deep breath. She curls her fingers tight in my top, looking up at me blankly.

"Leo?"

I draw back, out of her reach, and snatch up the bookmark.

"What's this?" I ask harshly.

She stares at me, hurt coloring her eyes. "I think Deanna left it for me. I found a message in the bathroom telling me to look in the book." She bites her lips, giving me a long, haunted stare, before looking away, folding her arms around her shoulders. "Do you know what it means?"

I can't answer that. Won't lie to her, but I can't stand dragging her into this bullshit.

"We have to go," I say.

"Huh?" She lifts her head, eyes snapping. "Just like that?"

"*Yes*," I growl. "If the Nighthawks are involved, this apartment's being watched. We'll be lucky if we aren't tailed back to the cabin."

"By who?" she asks with a little whimper of frustration. "Leo, what does 'Nighthawks' mean?"

"It means," I answer grimly, "that your sister's probably alive —but Galentron definitely has her."

* * *

THE DRIVE back to the cabin is tense, silent.

I'd come on foot—I walk everywhere, and Heart's Edge isn't large—and now I feel like a giant crammed into a pea pod in the passenger seat of Clarissa's compact car.

She's glaring straight ahead, eyes on the road, while I'm watching the rear-view mirror.

No cars on the highway behind us. So far, so good.

Still, it doesn't mean we aren't being watched via long-distance scope, but at least there's nothing obvious.

Rissa's nearly steaming up the windows, her jaw clenched, eyes snapping like bright-green fire. She keeps opening her mouth, then shutting it.

I get it.

She's pissed.

I let her kiss me, then pushed her away, bundled myself back up behind my hood, and dragged her out of there with no explanation.

Call me an asshole. I deserve her anger, but I'm trying to save her life. When I said *anything*, I meant it—even if it means protecting her from me.

We're almost back to Charming Inn when she finally snaps, smacking the heel of her palm against the bottom of the steering wheel.

"Leo, goddammit, you owe me some answers!"

"What?" I answer, trying to keep my voice neutral.

"*Everything,*" she hisses. "Where have you been all these years?"

"You think you get to ask me that when you left?" I fire back before I can stop myself.

She falters, glancing at me, some of her scowl easing to an almost lost expression before she fixes her gaze on the road again. "I didn't mean it like that. Jeez," she murmurs. "Just...what happened? Who hurt you? Why can't we make this Nine stuff go away? There must be some way to clear your name. Were...were you really in prison over it?"

I take a slow breath, staring out the window. "None of that shit matters. Won't help us find your sis."

"It matters to *me.*" She takes a harsh breath too. When she speaks again, it's calmer. "Fine. Whatever. If you won't tell me what happened, at least explain this Nighthawks thing?"

"They're very fucking dangerous people, Rissa. That's all you need to know."

And I'm one of them.

I can't tell her that part. She huffs a breath, probably ready to pull over and push me out of the car, if she could move me an inch.

I shake my head, keeping one eye on the mirror, one on the landscape rolling by, all hills and cliffs and blazing orange trees. "Look, if anybody ever says that word to you, don't start asking questions. Just *run.*"

There's a long silence. I glance over to see her with her lower lip caught between her teeth, expression worried, aching. It's a fresh kind of hell, trying to save her from the shit I know.

Clarissa takes the last turn for the inn. "So why was Deanna involved with it?"

My jaw tightens. That's the part I don't have a quip ready for.

"Sweetheart, you'll have to tell me."

She's quiet a little longer, then sighs, slowing as she eases onto the shady lane running alongside the inn. "Deanna wouldn't let it go. She was convinced Galentron isn't done with Heart's Edge. After the things we saw when we were kids...mostly, she just wanted answers, I think. Answers she wasn't going to get with Dad dead."

I wince, but bite my tongue. She shoots a guilty glance at me. "Sorry."

"I don't think you're the one who needs to apologize," I grit through my teeth. "What else?"

"She just kept digging. Looking through old things that got cleared out of the old house and tossed into storage when they turned it into a museum. Searching for clues in Papa's belongings."

"Sniffing around the ruins of the Paradise Hotel," I add.

Her breath catches. "You saw her? What was she doing out there?"

"A few days before she disappeared," I tell her. "Your sis didn't find anything. The facility is deep past the old mine's entrance. There's no access now with the elevators shut down and the ruins left to rot."

Rissa slams on the brakes, jolting the car to a halt and punching me back in the seat belt. "*What* facility?"

She stares at me, her eyes cutting, demanding.

Fuck. I wince again, closing my eyes, rubbing my temples.

"Look, you know more than most about Galentron," I say, "but you don't know the truth of what happened at the hotel." I push the door of the car open and step outside. "I'll tell you later. This isn't the time or the place."

She follows me, rising out of the car and slamming the door, frowning. "Later when?"

"Tonight," I promise. "After Zach's asleep. Meet me by the fire."

* * *

I must've been crowned king of terrible fucking ideas today.

Kissing Clarissa back.

Letting her see my face.

Agreeing to tell her more than I should about the truth surrounding the hotel.

And now, letting myself be alone with her, out here in the dark.

I drop down on a stump to one side of the fire pit I dug, slowly turning the rabbit I'm roasting over the flames for my dinner. It's been a long afternoon of thinking, planning, regretting.

And I hate how thin my options are. I really fucking hate the fact that I may just need to talk to Fuchsia again.

She's here for a reason. Not just coincidence. Something to do with Deanna.

My guess? Deanna's snooping turned up something she wasn't supposed to know; something that could be dangerous to Galentron interests if it ever leaks publicly.

That shit would catch Fuchsia's attention like a mouse draws an owl. Her whole agenda revolves around hurting her old employer by dumping as much confidential info as possible. Too bad fate keeps cockblocking her on that and undermining her best efforts.

It must've tipped someone off at Galentron, too. And if they've sent someone out here to take care of their latest woes, no doubt it's a Nighthawk.

The question is whether or not neutralizing that problem just involves killing Deanna Bell, or do they think she knows more?

It's worth keeping her alive to find out, so they can destroy any and all evidence she might be keeping.

I hope to hell that's it.

Because even if it means the unspeakable, torturing her to try to force her secrets out, it means they'll keep her alive. It buys us time to find her.

Dealing with another Nighthawk should bring more clues. They'd have the same training. The same experiments and modifications. They'd *think* the same way I do in a tactical situation.

So I just have to ask myself what I'd do.

Except...something's already off.

I sure as hell wouldn't make such a heaping mess, smashing up Sweeter Things. That's enough to draw attention and make a kidnapping obvious, rather than just let it look like Deanna disappeared into the ether for any old reason.

If I were the one running this mission, I'd get in, get out, and leave without a trace. I wouldn't come charging in like a bull in a china shop.

It can't be recklessness. The kidnapper must have an ulterior motive, to draw out either me or Fuchsia. Possibly both of us.

We're more loose ends for Galentron.

Hell, I've avoided retaliation all these years by staying hidden. They can't find me, and the fact that I'm basically a fugitive has made me a low-priority risk.

Fuchsia's a bit worse, though that woman's as slippery as an eel. She's probably enjoyed leading them on a wild fucking goose chase.

Still, get us both here, together, hot on the trail of the same woman?

I know a damn setup when I see it.

They get us in the open, they can take us out in one coordinated swoop.

Silence us and Deanna and maybe Clarissa too, all the last dregs of their epic clusterfuck in Heart's Edge.

They could even come after Gray. Though I'm not sure they've got the balls.

One woman disappears and it's just local news. But Deanna and Gray, simultaneously, that'd get people digging. Get them panicked.

So they leave Gray alone, take me out when I'm a ghost and no one would miss me, and Fuchsia's a stranger nobody would miss?

I smile grimly. It's almost fucking elegant, in its own twisted way.

Better than their older methods, wiping an entire town clean off the map. Not the kind of thing you can do anymore in the age of instant social media backed by live video streams.

So if that's the plan...the next step is getting Deanna's info. Considering she's come back for brief visits from Spokane over the years, before moving here for Sweeter Things' latest branch, any intel stashes she has would either be hidden around town or else uploaded somewhere safe and secure.

If she's smart, she's got multiple digital copies, plus physical proof scattered around so there's *always* backups on backups.

So what would I do if I had a woman captive, holding onto info I wanted?

I'd make her *take me* to the locations.

I'd need a hostage to make her cooperate, someone she cares about. Obviously, I wouldn't trust her to send me to the right place unless she was with me and I had a gun to her back.

No leaving her alone. No falling into traps.

But in a small town, you can't hardly move to the next block without somebody noticing.

Unless you're moving at night...

Shit.

If I'm gonna track them, that's where I need to start. Watching for signs of unusual movements at night, within the town radius.

Now I just have to figure out how to do it without leaving Rissa and Zach unguarded.

It's like my thoughts summon her.

I hear the faint sound of Rissa's heeled boots on dry leaves and twigs a second later. She's moving hesitantly, shyly, between the thick trees.

Goddamn, she's vibrant in the firelight. Bright sparks shine in her eyes, making them burn green-gold. The glowing flames accent the chestnut highlights in her dark hair till she's more like a phoenix than a woman.

I smile at my own warped thoughts.

Am I just drunk on this girl, or personifying the flame that tore me apart? Merging both wildfires that won't stop upending my life?

She pauses, watching me with haunted eyes, then ventures a faint smile. "Hey, Captain Broody."

I smile slightly. "I'm not brooding."

"Oh, okay. Sunshine and roses, then. We'll have it your way tonight, Leo."

My palm twitches as I bite back a smile, remembering the times when that sass would buy her a crisp spanking later on.

She picks her way through the clearing I've made for my camp and pulls over a metal trunk—my weapons cache—and sits down delicately on it, long legs folded. She watches me, then nods. "Is that really still necessary?"

It takes me a second to realize she means my mask, my hood.

I reach up, touching the edge of the cloth.

"It's practical this time of year," I mutter. "Damn cold out here tonight."

"Well, you're right about that." She shivers, all bundled up in her fitted leather jacket. Her gaze flits to my bedroll and tent. "I wish you'd just sleep inside. What's the harm?"

"I wouldn't be able to see or hear someone coming from inside." My glance tells her I'm serious.

"I mean...you can't see or hear anybody lurking around if you're frozen to death, either."

I chuckle. "It's October, Rissa. Not January in the Arctic."

"I just worry." She shrugs, self-deprecating, managing a little smile that makes my heart thump harder.

It isn't fair, the way she still worries about me, like we have any shot at a normal life. But her smile fades, and she lingers on me, eyes searching. "So, remember how you said you'd tell me about the facility?"

"Yeah." I sigh. "Guessing you don't know everything about what your old man was working on with the company, do you?"

She shakes her head, hesitates, then ventures, "No. I just know there were Galentron staff staying in the hotel, and they were working on bad stuff so close that it was a danger to the town. Weapons or something. And...and Papa cared more about money than the fact he was endangering everyone's lives."

My brows furrow. "I'd say that's a start, but it's worse."

Fuck, I shouldn't be telling her this, but I don't know how she can think anything worse about her father after she lived with him. After he tried to *kill* her.

Still, I've tried to protect her from the truth. Even *knowing* about Galentron's top secret projects is dangerous. Trouble is, right now, ignorance could be fatal.

"The hotel was just a front," I say, starting slowly. "An old cozy place for the top brass to stay, and the specialists who'd need to come into town without being noticed. The real work happened underground in this place built in the old silver mine next to the hotel. Highly secure, access-controlled, multiple levels deep underground."

Her eyes widen, reflecting the light in green-gold discs. "Wow. I never knew."

"You were never meant to."

"How big was this place? How many people were down there?"

"At any one time, maybe two or three hundred. After the place was built, I was stationed there on guard duty. They pulled me and the rest of my group home from overseas for this. Guarding the facility and the odd covert ops were most of my job during the..." I swallow. "During the time when I'd visit you."

She's quiet a little longer, biting her lip, before she asks, "So the fire in the hotel spread to the facility, or what?"

"Other way around." I take a deep breath, every burned bit of my skin aching at the memory. "The fire started in the facility and caught the hotel. I started it, trying to stop a lethal virus from escaping. But the damn safety system flipped, worked too well, and then shorted. It started an inferno that killed almost everyone."

"And burned you," she whispers, awareness dawning.

I nod reluctantly, staring into the fire. I can't look at her right now.

"Gray—Doc Caldwell—he used to work at the facility, too. He was my friend, a researcher there. He tried to stop me from doing something reckless when I wasn't in my right mind, after shit went down with your old man...he saved my life. I was trapped in the flames. If Gray hadn't come for me, hadn't waited, I'd have lost more than my career as an underwear model."

She gives me a shocked look and then manages a laugh like heaven. "Oh my God, don't do that."

"What?" I cock my head, looking at her.

"Be so...*Leo.*"

I glance at her from under my hood, my smile fading. She's staring into the fire like she can see the horror I tried to sweeten —the bursting flames reaching up, engulfing me, trying to kill everybody trapped down there.

No question. Without Gray, we would've died, and the scars on his fingers are proof.

Rissa rubs at her face. "God. I just...I knew Dad knew they were working with bad stuff, but viruses?"

"I'm not done. Still not the whole story," I growl, and she flinches.

"How bad, Leo? Be honest. How twisted was my father, really?"

"Considering what he got paid for...think he was an eleven on the grand scale of fuckery. He was ready to sell lives for a few million bucks and a guaranteed seat in Congress." I take a deep breath. "If things went according to plan, you and Deanna and your old man would've been virtually the only survivors of Heart's Edge."

She sucks in a breath, going pale. "Wait, wait, wait. You mean...they were going to release that stuff on *purpose?*"

I nod like my head weighs a ton.

Nod and wait, giving her time to hash the full horror.

Her gaze flicks back and forth, and she actually wavers in her seat for a moment, before she braces hands on both her sides and clutches hard, taking several shallow breaths. I'm on the edge of my seat, ready to bolt across and save her if she goes into a full panic attack.

"My dad...my fucking dad took money to let them *kill* everyone in town?" Her face goes violent red.

It's so soft, so shaky, so disbelieving, she almost sounds like the sheltered girl she was when I first met her.

This is *fucked.*

Everything in me aches to comfort her, but I can't cross that distance. I can't hurt her more than I'm doing now, driving the truth into her like a stake, even if she asked for it.

Not when she's probably still upset with how I thrust her away today.

Not when I'm the bastard shaking her entire world apart, tearing open old wounds.

"They called it a controlled test release," I say quietly. "The virus was first developed by a rival overseas, but the CIA confiscated a sample and gave it to Galentron to reverse engineer to figure out how to fight it in the event of a bio-attack. They just weren't specific about how that had to be done...and Galentron thought a small town was an acceptable loss to understand how the virus works in the wild, to chart disease vectors and survival rates. They expected single digits, Rissa. A handful of people out of hundreds."

"Jesus!" She presses her hand over her chest, swallowing tightly. "Deedee figured that out, didn't she? And she...she wouldn't let it go even after I ran away. She couldn't."

"Right. That's probably what got Galentron's attention," I say.

"No." She shakes her head sharply, clapping her hands over her mouth and nose, her eyes welling. "No, they couldn't have—"

Her voice goes thick with tears.

Before I can stop myself, I'm up—rounding the fire to her, sinking down to sit on the trunk next to her, even if my bulk nearly crowds her off it, resting a hand against her back.

"Hey," I say softly. "*Hey*. I've been thinking this through, and they've got to keep her alive. She's going to be okay. She *is*."

"How do you know?" she chokes. "Why wouldn't they just kill her?"

"Because Deanna's smart. She'd have kept whatever she found out, made backups—and for all they know, they're with you. Deanna's the only way to get to you. She's no damn good as a hostage if she's dead."

"But I don't *know* anything!" Clarissa explodes. "This is all too much, Leo. I..."

I know before she does that she's going to break. Maybe it's the scent of tears, but she curls forward, fighting her own gag reflex. I curse myself even as I wrap an arm around her shoulders and pull her in *tight*.

She comes willingly, burying herself against my side, hiding her face in my chest. Her shoulders are shaking, her breaths hitched, but she's not crying.

I rub her back slowly, my own throat tight with rage.

"It's okay," I whisper. "It's okay if you need to cry."

"No," she mumbles, muffled against my chest. "I won't. I promised her. I promised Deanna. Crying's for grieving, and I won't grieve when she's not dead. I want to believe you."

I can't help but smile.

It's so like her, thinking this way.

Determined. Fierce. Holding out hope against plane crash, lightning strike odds.

It's my job to make sure those odds even out.

"Hey," I say. "I won't let them get near you. Just rest, think of anything you can about where Deanna might've hidden anything she had on Galentron."

"I don't have a clue," she says softly, taking a deep, shaky breath. "I've been gone for so long...I haven't lived here in ages."

"But you can still think like her. And I can think like *them*." I touch a fingertip under her chin, lifting her face up gently to look down into glimmering eyes that still stubbornly refuse to break into full tears, even if her nose is pink and her lips are trembling. "So between us, we'll mirror their movements. We'll figure them out. We'll *find* them, Rissa, and then we'll bring Deanna *home*."

Clarissa bites her lip, and fuck, I hate myself for how even now, all it takes is *that* to make my desire tighten into a steel core in the pit of my stomach. Her mouth pure sin.

Sweet fuck.

She's got the kind of mouth that makes a man want to devour her whole.

That first time I saw her at the mansion, in the kitchen, her lips playing sensuously over her chocolate, my mind went straight south.

And it's already there now, my pulse throbbing wild. I remember too well how those butterfly lips feel on my skin, wrapped around me, taking me deep and letting her tongue flutter against my—

She speaks again and might as well have punched me in the face.

I blink. "What?"

"How could you?" she asks, her voice breaking. "How could you ever work for a company like that, knowing what they were doing?"

Fucking hell.

Just like that, she knocks the wind out of me, and I pull back, letting her go and looking away, glaring into the darkness.

"It's not that simple," I growl. "It's just not."

"How isn't it?"

"I was practically a fucking prisoner. You'd know," I mutter. "You'd know exactly what it's like when horrible is all you have. The only family you have. The only *life*...till one day you can't take it anymore and you snap." I work my jaw, every inch of my body tense to the point of pain. "What your father was to you, Nighthawks was to me."

She's quiet, her warmth drawing away. It's like our little universe just experienced its own heat death. I hear the faint motions of her standing, denim rasping as her thighs slide together.

"Yeah," she whispers. "I'm sorry. I guess...yeah, I do get that. I shouldn't have asked."

I look up—unsure whether I'm pissed or just so fucking sorry for everything—but she's turning away. She moves in that controlled way she has, where she wraps her arms around herself, trying to hold everything together.

There are no more words as she walks away.

Nothing but one last murmur, her voice drifting back.

"Good night, Leo."

Good night, I think, but my voice stays trapped in my throat.

Because if I say anything, I'll beg her to stay, and I can't fucking do it.

She's more than I deserve, alone in this darkness.

IX: TEN STEPS BACK (CLARISSA)

I'm even more confused than before, and two days of pacing around in this cabin hasn't really helped.

There's so much spinning through my head.

The truth about my father, about Heart's Edge, about Galentron.

Hints of things I never knew about Leo. Things that make me wonder if I ever really knew the man I fell in love with at all.

Sure, I have to believe that what he showed me was the truth of who he was, a truth he had to hide to stop the company. An organization I know now was abusing him as much as my father abused me.

I feel like a coward. This is the justice Deanna's after, isn't it?

She wants to redeem our names.

Maybe deep down, she'd wanted Papa to be innocent, but there's no clearing him. No forgiving him. He was straight up vile, abusive *scum.*

He's also dead. And ironically, it's Leo who's alive and who's taken the fall.

He suffered, burned for it, only for this clueless town to vilify him.

That's the man I know.

The Leo I watch from a distance as the days drag on, my heart so heavy, wishing I could just reach out to him and close the chasm he opened between us. We'd been so *close* in that frantic, painful, beautiful kiss.

But I can't distract him, either. This can't go on forever, and he's my best shot at stopping it.

I can't spend my life in limbo, wondering if my sister is dead or alive.

Neither can Zach. Every day, I watch him run outside to play with Leo, smiling and laughing. It's like he *senses* the connection between them.

He calls him Mr. Monster, Mr. Nine, and Leo lets him, hiding his subtle, smirky smile behind his mask, and every time I see Leo smile at our son? I'm so effing close to breaking my promise my eyes sting red.

He's such a good father, and *he doesn't even know it.*

He's nowhere in sight right now, though—at least not by daylight. When I can't see his glowing fire, he seems to melt away in the trees and magically reappears when Zach calls his name.

I hope he's resting.

He may try to hide it, but I know he's running himself ragged, watching over us.

Last night, I caught a glimpse of him moving, slipping into the shadows.

I know where he went.

He's out there, looking for Deanna, scouring the land to find so much as a footprint or an empty canteen that might say she was there with her kidnapper for even a moment.

I've been staring at my laptop for the last half hour, trying to focus on the emails my assistant manager's been sending me from Sweeter Things HQ in Spokane. Just ordinary stuff like inventory orders, budgeting, a customer claiming she found a stray hair in a bonbon and the manager having security video of her plucking the hair off her own head and shoving it into the chocolate.

People, right?

But I look up as Zach tumbles over to the kitchen table, folding his arms and resting his chin on them while he looks up at me with that eager smile and those bright eyes that say he's about to ask me a question that's pure trouble.

Usually it's something age-inappropriate, but this time...

This time, when he chirps at me, I feel the blood drain from my face.

"Derek's teaching me town history," he says. "I didn't know you used to live in the big museum place, Mom! Why didn't you ever tell me?"

My tongue turns to wood. I shoot Derek a helpless look, and he winces, mouthing *sorry* over Zach's head.

Ugh.

I force a crooked smile. "Um, sure did. It wasn't always a museum, though. It used to be my house, but after your grandfather" —*tried to murder me*, I cough, pausing bitterly— "passed away, your Auntie Deanna and I didn't want to stay in the house anymore. So we donated it to the town and they made it a museum."

His eyes go round and wide. "What was Grandpa like?"

Oh, crap.

Some things, I can't.

He's smart, but he never needs to know some facts.

So I just smile faintly, painfully, and search for a careful answer. "Well, he was mayor for most of our lives. He was always busy. Career focused. *Tall.*"

Yeah, okay, my father's towering height scared me too, but it's also the most mundane fact I can give him without turning into a sobbing mess.

Zach giggles. "Big people don't have to be scary. Mr. Nine is huge and he's not scary."

"Mr. Nine is a nice guy." I sigh, resting my chin in my hand.

"Do you want to see the museum, ZZ-man? I can even show you my old bedroom."

I might as well have just offered to let him live on ice cream for a week. *Awesome.*

He lights up, nodding quickly.

"Yeah!" Then he turns back, giving Derek wide eyes. "Can I, Mr. Derek?"

"Hey," I say, laughing. "I'm the mom here."

"But Mr. Derek's my teacher." Zach pouts. "And I need his permission to miss lessons, don't I?"

"The boy's got a point," Derek teases lightly, then laughs. "We'll count it as today's history lesson. I'd meant to ask if I could head out a little early anyway, honestly."

I tilt my head. "Big plans?"

"Sort of?" He wrinkles his nose. "I'm, uh...meeting my boyfriend's parents."

"You don't sound very happy about that."

"Would you?"

"I really don't know." I smile, shrugging. "I only ever had one boyfriend, and as far as I know, his parents don't even exist."

"Ah, *mysterious.*" Derek wiggles his fingers, then laughs and ruffles Zach's hair. "Be good for your mom, munchkin. It's a field trip, but try to actually *learn* something."

"I will," Zach promises with utter solemnity, prompting us both to laugh.

Derek bundles himself up and heads out, while I stand to change into something a bit warmer.

What have I done? The very notion of going back to the museum, to that *house*, makes me feel sick.

But I'd rather show Zach my childhood home in my own words, before he hears something awful around town.

And who knows, maybe looking around the house, I might find a clue.

Maybe Deanna left something behind, something I can use to help Leo *find her* before it's too late.

I hate feeling so helpless I'm depending on total luck.

I couldn't help Leo back then. I hadn't even known what he was going through. But I need to be Deanna's hero *now*.

I shrug Zach into his jacket, then slip out to Leo's campsite.

I know how exhausted he must be. He doesn't come on the alert the second I set foot anywhere near him.

He's sound asleep, stretched out on his bedroll with a thin blanket pulled over him.

Even with the weak autumn sun filtering through the trees, brassy with late afternoon threatening to turn into evening, that can't be warm enough.

So I slip back indoors as quietly as I can, dig around in the chest at the foot of the bed, and tug out several huge quilts that might've been put together by Ms. Wilma years ago. Then I creep back out to the campsite and shake them over Leo, tucking them around him as gently as I can.

Before I tiptoe away, even though I know I shouldn't...I lean down and kiss his cheek.

* * *

BY THE TIME we drive up to the museum, I'm ready to throw up.

Even with the plaque over the door and the printed banners down the sides, the tall, blocky, square mansion is *home*. And for me, that's a curse.

Home means raised voices, pain, stalking, fear.

It means being small and powerless.

It means living surrounded by secrets more terrible than I'd even known at the time, making myself invisible while terrible shadow men moved through the halls, always whispering their schemes.

I don't want to be here.

But I can't let Zach see how uncomfortable this place makes me, so I plaster on a smile as we park and head up to the entrance. It's nearly closing time per the hours posted outside the door, so there aren't many people around.

Just a few staff members and a couple elderly folks who don't pay us the slightest bit of attention. I pay for our tickets—paying to get inside *my own house*—and lead Zach inside.

At least no one seems to recognize me. Even if there's an absolutely *terrible* painted portrait of younger me mounted over one of the display cases. It's next to my father's stern, forbidding portrait, with Deanna's on the other side.

Zach stares up at it. "Mom, is that...you?"

I grimace. The painting looks like it's making the same face, only half-melted.

"Supposedly," I whisper.

He tilts his head to the side, scrunching his little nose up with a skeptical look, then looks back at the painting, then at me, a smile teasing his lips, promising suppressed laughter. I snort—and he bursts into giggles.

"I'll draw you a better picture, Mom."

"It'll be the best one ever, kidlet." I draw him in to kiss the top of his head. "Come on."

I lead him through the rooms, wandering from display to display.

I'm thankful the other exhibits aren't about *us*. They're just town artifacts like a lump of old silver ore, which used to be the lifeblood of Heart's Edge. There's a diorama of the famous cliff, and a plaque about the legendary lovers who ran away. Some info on the local Native tribes. Details on recent forest conservation efforts, too.

It would almost be relaxing, if not for the feeling that I'm walking around on haunted ground.

There are too many security cameras for me to really go digging around, too.

I wonder if the museum staff know about the secret passageways...

I didn't tell them when I ceded the deed to the town, but

Deedee might have. Or they may have stumbled down there themselves, even though it's hard to find the entryways unless you know exactly where to look.

There's an old dumbwaiter lift in my old room that would go all the way down to a sub-basement, with doors leading into so many strange little rooms. I don't think I could fit in it anymore, but I could try. The paneling is concealed in the room's wood trim, and as Zach and I step inside, I can't help how it draws my gaze.

It's open.

Just a tiny crack, just enough to see the difference in the paneling, but it's *open*.

Someone's been inside recently. Kinda freaky, though I doubt it was more ominous than some museum staffer.

My lungs hitch. Zach's tugging on my hand, wrinkling his nose as he quietly asks another question.

"You really used to *sleep* in here?"

I blink, taking in the room around me. It's not quite how I remember.

It's been turned into an installation about early settlers and their fur trapping. Rusty bear traps and pelts hang on the walls next to old guns and the remains of wooden animal cages. A huge stuffed bear stands in one corner, paws raised and jaws open.

I laugh. "It was different when it was my room, kiddo. No bears then. Just white lace everywhere, and shelves and shelves of cookbooks."

"Oh." He looks thoughtful, then asks, "So did you like living here? It's just really *big*."

I want to say *no*, to scream it, but that would be a lie. Even with my father's vicious words and his hand crashing across my face, there were happy times, too.

Deanna and I chasing each other through the secret corridors, finding our joy where we could. The games we'd make up, pretending to be spies or ghost hunters, the thrill of it halfway real when sometimes we'd feel cold drafts from nowhere or hear sounds we'd swear were voices.

That's the thing about sisters. We always had each other through thick and thin.

Then when I got older, the hours in the kitchen, losing myself in creating one confection after another. That counted for happier times too.

Oh my God, and *Leo*.

Leo sneaking in to lock my door and tumble me into bed, teasing me with his body until I bit his hand to keep from crying out in ecstasy...

Sneaking me out with him, too. A memory pulls a smile on my lips.

He was the first man who proved there was a whole wide world outside of my father's kingdom.

* * *

Eight Years Ago

THE ANNUAL HEART'S Edge summer festival.

No one even remembers what it's meant to celebrate, but it's such a tradition that every summer solstice the town spills out with sparklers in their hands and flip-flops on their feet and coins in their pockets to trade for candy popcorn and frozen slushies and silly fair games that you never win but get a consolation stuffed animal for anyway.

The night smells like sweet, sticky sweat and candied apples. There's even a petting zoo this year, one of the ranchers from the town's outskirts brought in half a dozen of his cute little Shetland ponies, and kids are lining up to feel their soft, velvety noses.

There are glowing paper lanterns everywhere, electric lights on strings, making a second galaxy of lights beneath the night sky.

It's a risk being here.

I know my father's roving around somewhere, kissing babies and shaking hands for the next election that's already a foregone conclusion. He can't see me holding hands with Leo and looking at him like he hung the moon.

But Papa's not the reason why I'm so nervous, my stomach so jittery.

It's the folding table under Leo's arm, and the stacks of little white boxes hanging from my hands in plastic bags.

I've never let anyone but Deedee and Leo taste my candy.

But when this man has so much faith in me, when he believes I can *make* people love the things I create, and that someday I can have my dream, my own shop...I have to freaking try.

Have to. The faith just shines in his violet eyes when he looks down at me with an easy smile softening the roughness of his features. That smile still makes my knees weak because it feels like he can't see anything in the world but me.

My little booth isn't much after it's set up.

It's not even a booth at all, really.

It's a plastic folding table with a bunch of cheap aluminum serving trays set out with paper doilies and my bonbons and truffles and petit fours laid out in arrangements I hope look enticing.

God. I shouldn't be so scared, but this isn't just the people I've known my whole life.

Every year, people come here from several towns over for our little festival. Heart's Edge may be small, but sometimes it's the only entertainment for the next fifty miles.

At least I'll get some honesty. Strangers have no reason to be nice to me, if my candies just plain suck.

So I set myself up behind the table in my apron and a breezy summer sundress, with Leo hulking at my side.

Yep, he's also got an apron on. A big black manly one.

Just what I need to see, right?

He's so huge he can't even tie it in the back. I hide a giggle behind my hand as I watch him struggle with it, grunting as he tries to stretch it to fit.

When he catches me laughing, he mock-glowers at me, and I burst into laughter. "It's not a rubber band! It won't get longer if you stretch it."

He makes a playful *harrumph* sound. "So, what? I'm just supposed to let it dangle here?"

"Here." Still laughing, I catch one of the strings I'd used to close the confectionery boxes, then slip around behind him and tie the string up with little loops to hold the apron together.

He's a wall with arms and legs. I can't see anything but him— so I'm startled when a pleasant woman's voice says, "Oh, my— these look heavenly! And they're only ninety-nine cents?"

Flushing, I peek out shyly. An older woman with blue-washed hair and a floral cardigan hovers over the table, peering at the trays with a curious smile.

"W-why yes!" I make myself creep out from behind Leo, but his hand on the small of my back gives me courage, warm and reassuring. I manage a smile, smoothing my hands over my apron. "If you're curious, you can have the first one free."

"Really now?" she says, reaching for one of my pink and white strawberry petit fours.

And that's how I sell a little box of a half-dozen petit fours after she takes one bite, before she calls her friends over to fuss over the chocolates.

It's a whirlwind.

One moment, I'm hiding behind Leo, and the next I'm selling candies so fast I'm worried I'll run out. We're drawing a crowd, and I'm flushed and flustered and don't know what to say when people ask me what shop I work for and if they can find me online.

I'm trying to stammer out that this is all homemade, but maybe one day...

The warm delight overwhelming my nervousness goes cold when I see a familiar broad figure moving through the crowd, a familiar head of silvered hair.

My father.

And while I don't think he's noticed me yet, from the hard set of his face, I don't think he approves of the ruckus, no matter the source.

"Oh, crap," I whisper, shoving at Leo's arm. "Hide!"

He stares at me. "How am I supposed to hide, I'm the size of a tru—" Then he follows my line of sight and swears sharply. "Shit."

He's gone just in time, like he just wisped away on the wind.

I catch sight of him then, behind the long caravan that brought the ponies in. I don't know how he moves so fast, making it seem like he can turn invisible, but I'm grateful.

Especially when my father's eyes land on me, and a hard glint darkens his eyes.

Please, I beg silently, sending a desperate prayer to the universe. *Please don't let him make a scene.*

I want to believe he wouldn't hit me in public, in front of all these people.

But I'm really not sure.

He shoulders his way to the front of the crowd, stopping at the table, looking down his nose at the trays that only have a few truffles left, next to a few crumbs against the white paper doilies.

"Clarissa, what's the meaning of this?" he demands coolly.

Because I don't want people to worry—I hate how *keeping up appearances* is drilled into me—I smile. "Hi, Papa," I say a bit weakly. "I thought, you know, I'd try selling some of my candy."

There's a thunderhead building on his brow—then he pauses.

There are still people all around us, and those folks are trading bites of my sweets and exclaiming enthusiastically, and as my father sweeps his gaze over the small crowd, his expression changes.

When he looks back to me, he smiles.

It's his politician's smile, his fake smile, and it creeps me out. But it's better than seeing the cold, hard face of the monster underneath.

"Well now," he says, in that particular way that tells me he's trying to sound gracious. "I just wish you'd told me you wanted to run a campaign fundraiser. I'd have provided you with signage and a nicer booth, dear. Keep it up. You're doing great."

The praise does nothing for me.

It just makes me ice-cold.

Of course, he'll let me do this. He thinks it benefits him.

He just had to take something I did for myself and make it about him.

I think this is the first time I've ever really been able to quantify what I feel toward him as hate, instead of this nebulous scared thing where he's all I have besides Deanna.

And my smile feels like poison as I bare my teeth. "Thanks, Papa."

Sick.

I'm just glad when he turns around and walks away.

But I'm even happier when the coast is clear, and as people lose interest and wander off with nothing else to eat, I'm free to collapse into Leo's arms.

He's so strong, so solid, holding me up without the slightest hesitation. I bury my face in his warmth, struggling to hold back tears.

"One day, Leo," I whisper. "One day, we *have* to get out of here. You're my salvation."

I believe it with all my heart.

For the whole beautiful summer, I believe it.

That this man, this strange and passionate beast who's both so sweetly open and an utter mystery, will love me forever and we'll run away together like the legend of Heart's Edge and find our happy ending.

But that was before I knew.

Before the night that painted my world in blood and flame.

* * *

Present

IT'S SO easy getting lost inside the past in this house.

I've been staring at the fearsome bear the whole time while I wandered down memory lane.

I shake myself, lifting my head and turning to search for Zach, a habit I've formed ever since he was born. I need to know where my kid is at all times.

And my gut lurches as I see him standing in the doorway, cheerfully chatting with a man I've never seen before.

He's so large I almost mistake him for Leo. I've never seen anyone else like Leo in my life.

But no—this man isn't a masked behemoth.

He's tall, trim, very muscular, almost too sleek and graceful in jeans and a black button-down, open at the throat and sleeves cuffed to his elbows. He's got this casual, serpentine body language and grey eyes that don't quite match the warm, encouraging smile he's giving my son. His sandy hair is swept back from a handsome, too-chiseled face.

And as pretty as he'd be to most red-blooded women...I already don't like him.

I can't quite put my finger on it. There's just something about him that makes me uncomfortable, and it's two steps before I'm catching Zach by the shoulders, nudging him behind me.

Zach makes a startled squeak, but that stuffed bear isn't the only grizzly in the room. I'm in protective Mama Bear mode. I draw myself up tall and stare the man down firmly.

"Something I can help you with?" I ask.

His smile doesn't waver, but he studies me. "You seemed to be thinking, that's all," he murmurs pleasantly. "I didn't want to interrupt. Your son's a lovely talker, Ms. Bell. Real smart boy."

He cocks his head, looking at me in the strangest way. "You know, now that I see you up close, your portrait downstairs doesn't do you justice. You *do* have lovely hair."

My entire body bristles.

He knows me.

And he's not anyone I remember from around town.

I eye the sliver of space left between him and the door, wondering if I can shove Zach through and follow if we have to risk it. "Sorry, do I know you?"

"Not...necessarily. But I'm here to help you, Ms. Bell. A friend."

I'm prickling all over.

Something's *so* not right.

"And what could you possibly help me with?" I ask coolly.

"Your poor missing sister, for one thing." He steps back, bowing cordially, offering a clear line to the door. "Maybe if you'd like to chat somewhere a little more private?"

Oh, no.

Hell no. I'm not going to fall for the oldest trick in the book.

Even if he knows something about Deanna, I'm not going anywhere with this man.

This stranger who addresses me by name. Who *knows* I'm looking for my sister.

Every instinct tells me to take my son, get away, maybe scream so any staffers still milling around will hear me before they close this place up.

I have to get to Leo.

I can't find Deanna if I end up abducted, too.

Jesus, no, this isn't happening.

Taking that opening between him and the door, I pull Zach with me firmly and turn so I'm always facing the stranger, moving quickly.

"Thanks," I strain out. "But if you've got any tips, report them to the police."

Then I grab Zach's hand and practically *run*.

I feel those empty grey eyes on me the entire time, and the distinct feeling this man could stop me any second, but he's *letting* me get away.

Especially when he calls after me, his voice chilling and low.

"Enjoy your evening," he says. "I'll be seeing you real soon."

X: STEP UP (NINE)

I'm starting to feel a little violent.

Especially after Clarissa came rushing back to the cabin the other day, just as I was waking up to find out she'd tucked me under several quilts and then slipped out.

Alone.

After I'd nearly begged her not to leave my sight. And trouble had found her, in the form of a man with grey eyes and light hair.

The way she described him told me everything I needed to know.

Everything I needed to worry about.

Big, she said. Almost impossibly, inhumanly huge.

Just like me.

And smooth in the way he moved. Confident. Powerful. *Deadly.*

Another fucking Nighthawk, showing up here with Deanna's name on his lips, trying to entice Rissa away.

I'm just damn glad she was smart enough to see through it. Still, I've had to keep my distance for a few days.

Otherwise, I'll do something insane, like slam her up against the wall and kiss her till we both suffocate in sheer relief that she didn't wind up abducted, too.

So I've bowed away while trying to stay as close to the cabin as possible, save for short naps and brief trips searching for any hint of this grey-eyed stranger.

I'm even more convinced that Deanna is still somewhere in Heart's Edge. And that the grey-eyed freak knows something about where.

There's something nagging at my memory.

Something that says I should *know* him, should remember, but fuck.

There's too much blanketed in fog.

So many gaps in my memory. After Dr. Ross took me out of Heart's Edge and shut me away with the other kids in that awful white-walled facility in the middle of God knows where, the rest is just a blur.

Worse, it's been days, and I still haven't unearthed what that weird familiarity might be. Shit itches under my skin like needles.

But I do know I don't want to be here, separated from Rissa for even half a minute while I stare down Fuchsia Delaney and tell myself I won't cross that last line into inhumanity by *wringing this fucking woman's neck.*

I don't even know how the hell she's busted out of jail, let alone how she made it to Gray's vet practice without getting caught and thrown back behind bars where she belongs.

She sits on Gray's desk in his office, her legs crossed, one heel tapping lazily against the side of the desk—sleek as ever, leaning on one hand and eyeing us slyly.

She's like Cruella de Vil, if Cruella had discovered Botox.

And I can't stand that even now, when she claims we're on the same side. She's still fucking toying with us.

"Come now," she taunts, her horrid little smirk curling the corners of her mouth. "Surely you don't think I respond to threats?"

Gray arches a brow. "I think you know me well enough to know I don't make idle threats."

"I know you well enough to know you've gone soft, Caldwell. You don't want blood on your hands when you're staring impending fatherhood in the face. So." Her cunning gaze slides to me. "That leaves you. And since you're *already* a father, I'm guessing the only thing that could make you shed blood is if that kid is threatened."

My fucking lungs seize up.

Gray blinks, staring at me. "Leo? What does she mean, already a father?"

I growl. Of course. Of goddamn *course* she's figured it out.

Ducking my head, I grab at my hood, shifting it angrily. "Clarissa's son. Zach. He's mine." Then I glower at them both. "Keep your fucking mouths shut. She hasn't told me yet. She will when she's ready."

Gray just nods slowly, while Fuchsia holds both hands up in mock-surrender. "Yes, *sir*," she lilts.

"Shut it, Fuchsia. Last warning. I had to leave them with the damn *tutor* to come play at your whim. So start talking or I'll make sure we end up cellmates for life. I'll get myself locked up in ultra-max, if it means shoving you down a dark hole where you'll never see another Chanel store again."

She flicks her fingers disdainfully. "I'll pass. Have you seen that hideous shade of institutional blue they use in women's prisons? I'd look *terrible* in a jumpsuit." With an exaggerated sigh, she crosses her legs. "Be patient. I'm still rattled, you know. I didn't expect Galentron to be ready for me, though I suppose they expected I'd come back to the scene of the crime. I still thought I'd have a little more time before they tried to feed me a diet of lead and gunpowder."

"A little more time for *what?*" I bark.

"The favor I was asked to do." She arches both brows as if I should know what she's talking about. I have no fucking clue, and I just stare at her flatly till she sighs again, her shoulders slumping. "Neither of you are ever any fun. Fine. Does the name Marianne Jonas ring a bell?"

Gray cocks his head. "...parakeet."

Fuchsia's upper lip curls. "Excuse me?"

"She had a parakeet. I treated it for molting issues." He strokes his chin, eyes narrowing. "Didn't she pass a few months ago?"

"And wasn't she Edgar Bell's secretary?" I add, my breath clogging my throat.

Yeah, I remember her.

She was *there* that night.

A trim older woman, spectacles, hair drawn back in a tight greying knot, slim pencil skirt.

She'd caught me in the hall just as I'd gone bolting out of the room, intent on stopping Galentron and tearing that whole facility apart with my bare hands before coming back for Rissa and taking whatever punishment was meted out to me.

Marianne had looked into the room. Her jaw tightened and she gave me a hard look.

She said almost nothing but, *I'll take care of her. You need to run.*

Those words told me everything I needed to know about whose side she was really on.

Everything there was to know about the legacy of a man so cruel that the sight of his dead body raised no questions. Not from Marianne, or the maid who found me hunched over his body.

We'd looked at each other for a long time. I'd nodded and ran like hell to set the wheels of fate in motion.

"What was her cause of death?" I ask.

Fuchsia shrugs a shoulder. "Who knows. Her obituary said 'natural causes.'"

"Which means she was probably eliminated."

"Now you're catching on." Fuchsia cocks her head knowingly. "But before her unnaturally natural death, she practically begged me to come back here and keep an eye on poor Deanna. Keep her safe. The problem is...Galentron beat me to it, after the last incident. Quite unfortunate, really. A serendipitous intersection of Deanna's curiosity with Galentron's renewed interest in this lovely little hamlet."

I growl, pacing restlessly. "What're they after? What could Deanna *possibly* have that would interest them so much?"

"Evidence that would hold up in court," Fuchsia replies, yawning.

Gray sucks in a gasp. I go still.

For a moment, Gray and I just stare at each other before looking back at that smiling Cheshire cat of a woman.

"Gonna need you to be a hell of a lot clearer," I say slowly.

"Ask me nicely then."

"*No.*"

"I had to try." With a sigh, Fuchsia kicks her feet, heels tapping, then stands, smoothing her skirt. "To put it briefly, records from the mayor's office. Marianne kept backups of everything, and shared it with Deanna. Between them, they could likely sink the whole company. So if they were smart..."

"They bought themselves life insurance by hiding the data," Gray finishes.

"Bingo!" Fuchsia says smugly, clapping her hands together in the most annoying way ever.

"Then Deanna's still alive. There's still a chance," I say.

"A slim one," Fuchsia says. "Galentron is extremely effective at *efficiently* extracting information. If she broke under torture, they might already have what they want, and she may have been disposed of."

"No." I say it firmly—because I have to believe it's true. I can't even consider another possibility. "If they had the info, we'd have seen more coordinated action. It's possible they'd even run a paramilitary operation in the town. They're being covert, which means they're trying to keep everything under wraps. They still have something to lose."

"Such a clever boy. I hope your son takes after your side of the family."

I growl. "Don't talk about him. Don't go near him, witch."

"Down, big daddy. I have no interest in brats." She waves a hand. "Run back to your little pseudo-family unit. That's all you're getting out of me."

I eyeball her. "Implying there's more to know."

"On a need to know basis, and you don't need to know." She saunters to the door with a toss of her hair. "I'll fill you in if you end up being useful."

A snarl bubbles in the back of my throat, but I stay silent.

I've lost interest in fencing words with this woman.

Don't trust her to tell the truth anyway. She probably found being *honest* about Marianne and Deanna physically painful.

But as Fuchsia slips out, Doc calls after her. "Stay low. You'll get arrested again, and probably bring down hell on the entire town."

"No worries, I have no desire to get shot again," she hisses over her shoulder as she breezes through the door. "Your bedside manner was *terrible* last time. I'll behave."

Then she's gone, leaving us alone.

And leaving Doc giving me the strangest look. "So. That boy is your son? You're sure?"

"Positive," I say. "And I have to make sure nothing ever happens to him or his ma."

* * *

I'M STILL BROODING over that on the walk back to Charming Inn and the cabin.

Fuchsia confirmed what I'd guessed but brought an entirely new clue into play with Marianne Jonas.

Making my way through the trees, I pull up a search on my

phone to find her obituary. It's short, with no other news—no reports about anything suspicious, and the obituary cites her cause of death as heart failure.

Something that could be passed off as nothing in an older woman.

Something that could easily be induced with any hidden substances that wouldn't be detected by a county medical examiner who wasn't looking for foul play.

That tells me who they think is more dangerous, though. And more useful.

Marianne was disposable, but they think Deanna's the key to hunting down all rogue data that could incriminate Galentron and the late Mayor Bell.

Unease knifes through me as I draw close to the path that turns off into the woods. Next to Clarissa and Derek's cars, there's a vehicle I don't recognize, a sleek black BMW.

No one in Heart's Edge drives a car like that. And no one from out of town would bring their six-figure car out to this backwater to clog its engine up with road dust.

Something isn't right.

I go bolting through the trees, not even bothering with stealth. I don't care if whoever's in there hears me coming like a charging rhino. I hope it scares them into getting the fuck away from my girl and my son.

But I slow down, bursting through the woods, into the clearing around the cabin.

I can see everything through the floor-to-ceiling windows.

Derek and Zach at the table, flipping through one of his textbooks.

Clarissa in the kitchen, pouring tea with a strained expression on her face, staring into the living room.

She's looking at a tall man I've never seen before. Who I feel like I *know* as well as I know myself, even if I can't place him. He's thick and bulky and utterly calm as he watches my Rissa with a smile that turns my bones cold.

I don't know who the fuck he is, but I'd bet he's the grey-eyed stranger who cornered her at the museum.

He's trouble waiting to happen.

XI: OUT OF STEP (CLARISSA)

*N*ow I know how a mouse feels being cornered by a big, lazy snake.

His name is Nash.

I know that now, and the only reason I haven't bolted for the phone and called the police is because Derek is here, and I'm trying to keep up appearances and not tip Nash off that I don't trust him.

I really don't.

Chances are he's with Galentron. I'm convinced that if there wasn't a surprise witness here, he'd have snapped my neck. He wouldn't have bothered inviting himself into the living room, nearly taunting me with little tidbits of information.

Something about my dad's old secretary, Marianne. I'd heard about her death from Deanna, but now Nash says she shared stuff with my sister?

How? Why?

But when I ask how he knows that, who his connections are, anything I can try without even *saying* the word Galentron...

He dances around it, mentioning concerned friends, knowing Marianne from a long time back.

Right. I don't believe a word of it.

I've got to get him out of the house, and then I've got to get Zach somewhere safe.

Somewhere Nash can't find us. Something about him sends chills down my spine, all the way to the tips of my toes, and I'm barely able to breathe.

Call it a mother's instincts.

But there's something horribly tempting, too. If he knows where my sister is, maybe I can tease it out of him. Talk him into slipping up.

So I put on my best smile, finish pouring tea, and bring it out to him, setting it down on a coaster on the coffee table. "You know, when I saw you at the museum, I thought you seemed familiar," I say. "Did you ever come to the house to visit Marianne?"

"I was by the mayor's mansion many times," he says obliquely, lifting his brows and watching me mildly.

It's a careful answer. One that says he *was* there, without confirming he came to see Marianne.

I sink down onto the sofa across from him, folding my hands in my lap. "Are you related to her, by any chance?"

"We have connections." Again, evasive, answering without answering. He smiles against the rim of his glass. "I was real sad to hear about her passing. Same as Deanna."

Something twinges inside me.

I watch him keenly. "You talked to Deanna after Marianne died?"

He raises his glass in an almost mocking salute. "Sure did. In fact—"

He doesn't get the chance to finish.

The door flies open sharply. Derek yelps and grabs at the textbook. Zach squeaks, and I jump, gasping.

Only Nash remains icy calm as Leo storms into the room, completely filling it with his bristling rage his presence, and a silent, protective menace.

For a long minute, he and Nash simply look at each other—

173

Nash smiling and cool, Nine stony and silent—before Nash raises his glass again.

"It looks like I've worn out my welcome," he says blankly.

Then he stands and sets the glass down on the coffee table with this weird precision before sweeping me a mocking bow.

"Ms. Bell," he says. "It was a pleasure. I sure hope you find your sister soon."

Then he turns to sweep toward the door, but pauses, shoulder to shoulder with Nine. There's too much pent-up, howling anger for me to call him Leo right now.

There's a charged energy between them.

Like two magnets of the same polarity, pushing back at each other with invisible force.

Nash's eyes narrow, and he cocks his head.

"*Interesting,*" he snarls softly, right before a sly smile flits across his lips and he raises his hand, slipping around Leo and through the door. "Good night, folks."

I slump into the chair as the door closes. Leo holds furiously still for a moment and then shoots Derek a look.

"Lesson's done for the day," he growls, his voice deepening to quiet command. "Zach, go wash up for dinner."

I'm too drained to snap at Leo for telling my son what to do.

Our son.

Ours.

Crap.

Derek looks uncomfortable but nods and pushes to his feet, gathering up his things, excusing himself with a polite murmur. "See you guys soon."

Zach is oddly quiet, but he rises obediently and slips into the bathroom in the back, leaving me alone with Leo.

I press my face into my hands, exhaling tiredly. "You have really bad timing."

He rounds on me, glowering past his mask. "I'd say my timing's pretty damn good. What were you thinking, letting him in?"

"Um, maybe I could get something out of him?" I bite off. "I couldn't exactly stop him."

"You didn't have to invite him past the threshold."

"He's not a vampire. Jeez. If he wanted to get in, he was coming, with or without an invitation."

Leo swears, dragging a hand over his masked face. "Rissa, do you have any sense of tactical awareness? He could've fucking *murdered* you and I wouldn't have been here to do shit about it!"

"What was I supposed to *do?*" I flare, shooting to my feet and fixing him with a glare. "I can't just sit here and do nothing all day, and I had a chance with someone who might know something about Deanna. I couldn't keep him out—this entire place is nothing but windows! So I could either play along and see if he'd slip, or I could leave him no choice but to get violent. And I wasn't letting that happen in front of our—"

I stop, my heart freezing over.

Jesus. I'd almost said *our son.*

And Leo glares at me like he *knows* what I was about to say.

God. I breathe in shakily, ruffling my hair. "Look, I was cornered. And he told me something about my dad's old secretary—"

"Marianne Jonas," he growls. "I know." He stalks closer, glowering fiercely, just a pair of bright violet spots and the outline of a beard under the shadow of his hood. "You can't trust anything that man says. He's probably telling you just enough truth to make you believe his lies."

That's enough to steal my breath away.

"How's that any better than you?" I ask, a hot rush of anger and hurt running through me. "I have no idea what's been happening to you the last eight years, Leo. You've been in *prison,* and I...you won't tell me *anything* unless it's just enough to make me be a good girl so I'll sit here and twiddle my thumbs and *wait!*"

He goes still, looking at me strangely. "Not fair, Clarissa."

The worst part is, he's right.

It's not fair of me, especially with the things I've been keeping from *him*.

But I'm hurt and angry and scared and desperate, and maybe I don't want to be fair right now.

I want to be *safe.*

That weirdo showing up here where I'm supposed to be tucked away like Rapunzel in her tower tells me I'm not truly safe anywhere.

And neither is Zach.

Staring at Leo, I press my lips together, words clotting in my throat. Another horrible memory churns in my head.

So I just turn away, trying to shake it, and walk out of the room before I say something I'll regret.

* * *

Eight Years Ago

I STILL CAN'T GET USED to the house being so full.

In some ways, it's a blessing in disguise.

Because ever since Galentron has practically moved in, that means Leo has more reasons to be here.

He's even got a room here, one that he's only in about a quarter of the time while he shuttles between the house and some secret company lair half the time.

And the rest of it?

Well, it's kinda hard for him to be in his bed when he's in *mine.*

But even with that little bit of happy serendipity, the house is freaking stifling. Ominous-looking men and women pace around everywhere. It's constant meetings, endless secrets, smothering security.

Places in my own house I'm not allowed to go anymore, like the library.

And Papa keeps getting worse by the day.

It's like whatever he's doing with Galentron is bringing out his truest self.

He's had a nasty temper ever since our mother died. I never know when that hand will fly down and leave my cheek throbbing. Or when he'll grip my arm hard enough to leave bruises that burn for days.

Just another grim reminder that it could be worse. And it probably will be, sooner or later.

I just haven't pissed him off enough recently.

Mostly because he's been distracted, preparing for his big congressional campaign next year.

It makes me shiver with disgust and fear—the idea of him with even *more* power. Even more ability to hurt people.

I can feel his iron fist squeezing my throat right now, while I try to keep my hands steady to pour a fresh pan of toffee.

Papa's voice shakes the house, rattling the walls, as he roars at Deanna upstairs.

I can't effing stand it.

She hasn't done anything.

She's never done anything, but then neither do I.

We creep around here as meek as mice in the walls. We've learned the hard way that if we try to rescue each other, if we try to intervene when he starts up, he'll make us both pay.

He always finds ways to make us bleed where no one will see the marks.

Something crashes upstairs, and I wince. The pot jitters in my hand, and the toffee piles up too high in one spot. I slow my pour, letting the thick caramel-colored goo slowly smooth itself out, holding my breath and telling myself it'll be okay.

Will it, though? She only stayed out five minutes past curfew.

As long as he's sober, he won't hurt her. Just scare her. I hope.

I can't go up there and...I don't even know. Fling the entire pan of scalding hot toffee over his head?

He'd kill us both and have us buried somewhere no one would ever find us.

I'll only make it worse for her, fighting back.

I have to remind myself again and again, biting the inside of my cheek, my eyes stinging, while I force myself to stay put. It's like some messed up metaphor for my life.

All the things I do, trying to keep our lives from getting even *worse*.

But I could leave, too.

Just like Leo wants. He's aching to get away from that horrid company. I want to get away from my father, and we could just run. Take off together one day when we're both away from the house, grab a rental vehicle, and never look back.

Run away together and be happy.

But I can't.

I can't just run and leave Deedee to suffer alone.

And I can't take her with me. I'm not even old enough to drink, and she's a flipping minor.

There's got to be another way.

Something I can do, instead of just enduring this until he either gets sick of us or a happy accident kills him. I stare down at the settling toffee, my whole body numb.

He's going to kill us one day while I'm just waiting for something to happen to him.

I can feel it.

The violence building to a head like a volcano.

Heck, he might even erupt so ferociously he can't hide what happened. And then people will say they always suspected something was off about him, *oh, why didn't someone save those poor girls?*

He might be in jail, but we'll be dead.

"You can't let it happen," I whisper to myself, angrily pacing by the stove.

Technically, he doesn't have to murder us to be guilty of a crime. What he's doing is abuse, plain and simple. Criminal assault and battery.

All I have to do is get recorded evidence of how he treats us. Leo can help me, maybe he can back me up.

And then? Then he's finished. Then we'll all be *free.*

* * *

Present

IF THERE'S one thing I miss since leaving Spokane, it's being able to get a good night's sleep.

By the time I went back out last night, Leo had vanished to his camp again.

My feelings were still too raw to try talking to him, so I'd just made dinner for Zach, picked at a bit of food myself, and dragged myself to bed to spend half the night lying awake, brooding over Deanna. Plus everything Nash said about Marianne.

Hardly a recipe for sweet dreams. I guess that's why I spent the other half of the night trembling through nightmares of my father and his abuse.

And now I'm just lying here, used up and bleary-eyed and staring up at the dawn light on the ceiling, wishing I didn't have to get up and get dressed and think of practical things like meeting with a contractor about fixing up the shop.

That's the thing people don't tell you about crises.

The whole world stops for you, but not for everyone else.

It's the strangest thing how life never stops.

Even when you wish it would.

But I force myself to get up, shower, and make breakfast for

Zach. Derek's coming in late today because of another commitment, so it's just me and the kiddo.

As I scrape eggs onto a plate, I can't help how my gaze drifts to the window again. I know he's out there. I think about telling him where we're going, but he really can't babysit us every waking minute.

And we'll be in town, in broad daylight, around other people.

We won't be alone.

I can't spend my entire life looking over my shoulder.

So maybe I was too harsh on Leo last night. And he was too harsh on me. I know he's just trying to protect us.

That's all he's ever tried to do, one way or another. And he's not wrong about Nash.

It's just too suspicious. He's not from Heart's Edge. I can tell that with a single glance, even if I can't shake this weird, uneasy sense of familiarity.

If he's with Galentron, did I see him in the house, and just never met him face-to-face?

Was he just one of the many shadows moving through the mansion, and I registered him subconsciously?

But then if he's with them...

Why would he come to me talking about Deanna, only to lead me in circles with teasing bits and half-answers?

Unless he wasn't trying to give me real information at all.

Unless he was trying to *get* information from me.

Crap. Does he think I know what Deanna knows? Or that I can give him some key to decipher my sister?

He could've just taken me, if that was the case.

I linger on Zach, nudging him into the back seat of the car and wait for him to buckle up.

Derek may have been the only thing that saved us last night before Leo showed up.

The last thing Nash wants is one too many witnesses to wipe out, after Deanna's already gone.

I shiver something fierce. Not even the heater warms the

chill going through me as I make the drive up to town and the shop.

The contractor's already waiting for me. I'm pleasantly surprised to find it's Mark Bitters, grandson of old Flynn who works up at the inn. Mark and I were in high school together. It's actually not half bad catching up with someone who doesn't say my name like it tastes bad on his tongue, and who's friendly and kind as we walk through the damage and tally up estimates over losses, materials, reconstruction.

He shows me pictures of his wife and kids, and seems surprised by how smart Zach is when my son starts asking him about the math he uses to estimate material needs.

Maybe sometimes it's not all bad that life goes on.

Right now, this little bit of normalcy keeps me from falling apart. I need more than anything to hold it together. For Deanna's sake, and for Zach's.

I can't save anyone if I'm a nervous wreck.

By the time Mark leaves, I'm calmer—until I realize I've lost sight of Zach again.

God damn it!

He's smart enough to know his talents as a little escape artist scare the bejeezus out of me. Quick as a little ferret, half the time I turn around and he's just *gone*.

Thankfully, I only have to go a few steps to find him this time. He's right around the corner of the building, a bit off from the street and talking to another contractor.

Wait.

Another contractor?

I feel my breaths stabbing me as I stare at the massive man in coveralls and a huge helmet masking his face. Oh my God, if Nash touches my son, I swear I'll—

But I only have to take two steps to realize it's not him.

Leo lifts his head. Those dark amethyst eyes catch me, glittering with warmth and amusement, gentle like last night's shouting match never happened.

The high neck of his coveralls hides half his face and the helmet does the rest, but damn, he's still too recognizable.

I could *kill* him.

Looking over my shoulder quickly, I duck into the alley, holding my words in by the barest thread until I'm close enough to hiss at him without being overheard.

"Are you crazy? There could be Feds in town after what happened in the plaza! And just because you won't tell me why you hide doesn't mean I don't *know*. Are you that fu—" I stop, cover Zach's ears, then scowl and finish. "Are you that fucking eager to get caught?"

Leo eyes me thoughtfully, then smiles—and this time I actually see the hint of his lips above the collar. His beastliness in full glory turns his smile absolutely wicked.

"What? You worried about me, Rissa?"

Ohhh, that look stirs hot things in my blood.

Makes me aware of just how large he is, how his shadow nearly blocks out the sun. His shoulders stretch from side to side of the alley, filling it completely, and the coveralls look ready to burst off him when his muscles strain against them, those powerful shoulders tapering down to a thick, rock-hard waist and those insane tree trunk thighs.

All parts I've felt caging my body, flanking me, pinning me to the bed while he makes me suffer with pleasure.

All things I totally *can't* be thinking with my kid looking up at me curiously, wondering just what dirty words I'm saying that he can't hear.

Surprise, what I'm thinking is *far* dirtier than anything I might say.

That's how I wound up with Zach in the first place.

"Of course I'm worried." Flushed down to my neck, I duck my head and clear my throat, letting my hands fall away from Zach's ears. "Zach's worried, too. People like to catch monsters and put them in cages, don't they?"

Zach bites his lip, nodding, and looking up at Leo with wide eyes. "Please don't get caught, Mr. Nine. I don't want anyone to lock you up."

Leo's eyes soften, and he rests a hand on Zach's head. "I'm not going anywhere, kid."

The way he says it feels like a promise to both of us. My heart leaps in my chest as Leo catches and holds my eyes.

"I'm planning to stay around for a good, long while," he says, soft and deep and striking to my core. "But right now, we're gonna find Deanna, come hell or high water."

I can't stop thinking about Nash.

Or the sneaking suspicion Deanna's kidnapper strutted right out from under my nose, just because he *could,* and there's fuck all we could do when you can't call the cops on someone for being a bit smarmy and strange.

The question is, *why?*

Why toy with Clarissa like that?

Why does this psycho bullshit feel familiar?

Here's the thing with serial nutjobs: they like to self-insert into their own crimes. Normally, it's with the police.

A typical serial killer—or even just a repeat murderer, there's a difference—will act like someone trying to help law enforcement. It's to keep an eye on the investigation and to get the insider scoop that lets them know how best to confuse the cops more and stay one step ahead.

A twisted fuck might be someone in authority, or he might just be playing at an average citizen with some connection to the case, acting as an informant with misleading tips.

But he enjoys it, too.

He loves the risk of standing right there next to the people looking for him.

And he enjoys seeing the frustration and dead ends cops keep running up against. It tells him he's smarter than they are. If there's anything a true psychopath relishes, it's demonstrations of his own evil intelligence.

We're not cops, no, but we're the only ones trying to find Deanna Bell.

The only ones with a real damn stake in this.

Now we're Nash's prey. He can't even think the hunter might also wind up being the hunted.

If I'm working the psycho angle, there's a definite possibility Nash is a Nighthawk. Especially with how massive he is, but mostly it's the mental clues.

After what they did to us, it's a miracle I'm not as batshit crazy as the rest of the soldiers who survived.

Or hell, maybe I am, and I just don't realize it.

I must be nuts, coming into town in broad daylight, standing on public streets like no one's going to question a tattooed giant in coveralls and a hard hat.

Rissa's worth it.

I hadn't even meant to follow her. Just wanted to check the shop for more clues.

The fact that she and Zach are here just means I can breathe easy with them in my sights.

Nothing's been touched, not really, save for some glass kicked around by stomping feet.

I pick my way through it, scanning slowly, looking for something that catches my eye. Something that seems *off,* something overlooked.

Every human action leaves a trail, makes a pattern.

Smash in a window, and glass falls down in a way that tells you how much force was applied, the angle of the blow, whether it was done with a blunt object or a closed fist. Even the shape of the shards tells a story. A crowbar strike will cause it to fracture in a different pattern and different pieces than a hand wrapped in a glove.

You can even tell the height of the person, based on the point of impact, the force, the leverage, the angle.

It's all there. You just have to be able to put the puzzle together.

And I can, assembling it in my mind, tracing backward from the scattered glass across the floor to the moment when...yes, it *was* a closed fist.

Someone punched the fucking window. Someone huge.

High angle, driving downward.

Extreme force, more than most adult men could muster.

My spine tingles.

There's no blood, no drag path, so Deanna wasn't hauled through these shards. She'd have been fighting if she was conscious, and if he'd lifted her off her feet, even at his size, her kicking and struggling would've surely caused him to leave skid marks in the glassy scatter while he forced her to heel.

So the perp smashes the glass window to catch her off guard, instead of coming through the front door. She runs in the opposite direction. She's likely behind the counter.

I sniff, my mind racing. I study a few more shards kicked out farther than they should've gone on landing, falling under the edge of the front counter. Then I see it, plain as day.

A man lunging forward, kicking glass, vaulting over the counter. The napkin dispensers are crooked, a little thing of toothpicks knocked over.

He lands, divebombs her. *Catches her.*

I circle the counter to the point just before the swinging gate where he'd have caught her.

Shit. There's a fresh dent in the plywood, a matching divot in the wall. They slammed into it together, combined weight.

No other signs of impact.

If he'd hit her head against the wall to knock her out, there'd at least be a faint smear on the paint from fear-sweat smudging it.

My nostrils flare. Yeah, there's a faint scent, but what?

"Chloroform," I mutter a second later, glancing back at Clarissa, who's watching me tensely from the doorway, letting me do my thing, holding Zach tight. "You said the office was tossed?"

"Yeah." She nods, then swallows. "What do you mean, chloroform?"

"He needed her zonked out so he was free to search around without her interfering. He used chloroform to knock her out, then searched the office and left with her." I frown. "You're *sure* nothing was taken?"

"Pretty sure, but not a hundred percent." She grips Zach's hand, then steps gingerly inside, guiding him around the glass carefully. "Come on. I'll show you."

She's looking at me oddly, though, almost warily. "What's wrong?"

"Nothing," she says, shaking her head. "It's just...strange how you do that. Almost supernatural."

I smile, realizing it's not wariness putting that expression on her face.

It's wonder.

Embarrassed, I look away, clearing my throat. "It's just math," I mutter.

"I like math!" Zach pipes up.

How am I not surprised?

A chip off my shoulder. I wonder if he sees the world the way I do.

Arcs of trajectory, paths of probability, subtle clues that tell stories in the traces people don't even realize they leave behind.

Does he feel alienated and isolated when he realizes other people don't see things that way?

They see the surface and nothing else.

For a second, I reach over, ruffling the boy's hair, before turning to follow Rissa into the back.

The office is a wreck. It's obvious this was the attacker's ground zero.

It's also clear he was frustrated from how the room's been torn apart.

Desk tipped over. Papers everywhere. File cabinets ripped open.

He did a cursory search, then got angry.

Psychos don't like to be frustrated. They don't like when their assumptions are wrong.

So they lash out, destroying everything around them, trying to force what they expect to be true.

He was damn mad when he tore this place apart. Convinced if he just destroyed enough, he'd find what he was after. And then when he didn't, he took Deanna.

She was always Plan B.

I think Plan A was kill her once he had the data.

Smart Deanna, not keeping it here.

The safe on the wall catches my attention. I frown, creeping through the mess to the far wall.

Then I see what's inside, and my stomach twists.

A crumpled bouquet. Dead flowers. Probably a few months old.

I already know what the note card attached to it says. I've written the same damn thing on every bouquet for all these years.

I'm sorry, Clarissa.

She's quiet at my shoulder, looking inside. "You left those, huh?"

"Yeah." I take a harsh breath. "I...yeah."

There's a heavy, hurting silence between us till she says, "That's new."

It actually takes me a second to realize what she's talking about. There's another note, buried among the shriveled petals, almost hidden except for a tiny corner of pink.

Bright *fuchsia* pink.

Aw, hell. I feel a groan coming on even before I fish the note out and unfold it.

You're too slow!
  This bouquet's prettier than the last, Clarissa.
  You should see all *the ones he's left you over the years.*
  Such a big sap.
  See if you can catch up to me, lovebirds.

It's Fuchsia's knife-like handwriting again, and I sigh. "She enjoys playing cat and mouse too much for someone who's supposed to be on our side."

"Hasn't she always been like that, though?" Rissa leans in, her shoulder brushing my bicep, and her maddening *scent* rises up.

It's something soft and creamy and dangerously sweet. Like she's one with her own confections. My dick going hard only adds to the confusion storming in my head.

Her gaze flicks side to side over the note, before she lifts her clear, curious green eyes to mine. "What does she mean by 'years,' Leo?"

Fuck. One soft word nearly shatters me. I clear my throat, fixing my gaze on the bouquet because it's too hard to look at her.

"Nothing," I growl, shrugging. "Maybe a small part of me kept hoping one day you'd come back and see them."

"You've been apologizing to me all these years?"

"Yeah, that."

...and loving you.

It kills me because I can't fucking say it. Not right now.

But it's rooted in me so deep it must be etched on my face as I turn my head to look at her. She's so close.

So close I feel her breath on my skin, make out every tiny curling eyelash framing those large, beautiful jade eyes. No denying I remember her fingers buried in my hair the other day.

The way she touched me without the revulsion, the disgust I'd expected. She just looked up into my unguarded face and kissed me with a light and a passion and a fever that didn't flinch in the slightest from the burn scars crisscrossing their way up my throat.

I could lean down right the fuck now and relive it. Claim her like I'm dying to.

But before I can give in to the heat tugging at me with such fierce need, a little voice pipes up between us.

"Hey, Mom? What do those numbers mean?"

We break apart, both of us gasping softly, and look down. Zach's standing on his toes, peering up into the safe and at the card where I'd written my message.

There's something else in the corner.

Something I didn't write.

Numbers. Two groups of three.

They look like degrees, minutes, maybe seconds of latitude and longitude.

Rissa cocks her head, staring at me. "What is it?"

"New. Nothing I ever wrote," I say, reaching in to snag the card and pull it free from the bouquet. "They're coordinates."

Clarissa sucks in a breath. "Leo. I think...yeah, that's Deanna's handwriting!"

"Then it looks like there's somewhere she wants us to go."

Her eyes beam like the sun. For the first time in eons, I see her gorgeous smile. "She really did leave us messages. She knows we're going to find her," Clarissa breaths, her smile practically dancing.

There's no way in hell I won't do anything to see that sunrise smile again and again.

Zach watches us intently, cocking his head too much like his ma. "Are we looking for buried treasure?"

"Not quite, little man." I ruffle his hair gently. "We're looking for something better."

I hold Rissa's eyes as I say it, and see the spark of eagerness there, rousing an answering spark inside me.

Hold on, Deanna.

We're coming, and to hell with psychos who want to play games.

The hunt is *on*.

XIII: UP THE LANE (CLARISSA)

I feel like I'm driving around with a bear in my back seat.

That's kind of what it feels like with Leo's hulking weight in my car, hunched down so he's not easily visible through the back windows.

It's about keeping a low profile, but when this is a compact car and Leo's not a compact man? He's as subtle as a big brown grizzly stuffed into a shoebox back there.

But he's enduring it with patience. Far more patience than I have when, for the tenth time, Zach twists in the back seat to stare at Leo with bright eyes.

"You really grew up here with Mom, Mr. Nine?"

I wince. I can't believe Leo let that slip, but it came out while we were sneaking him into the car—telling Zach we have to keep things quiet. Everyone here has known Mr. Nine for a long time, and not everybody likes him.

"Zach, sit *down*," I say sharply. "Seat belts don't work if you don't sit right."

He lets out a deep sigh, but obediently plunks down again, folding his arms over his chest to sulk.

Leo's deep chuckle doesn't really shake the growly man-bear thing.

"Listen to your ma," he says, and racks up a couple more Dad Points. "But yeah. I've been around these parts for a long time. Ever since I was a kid."

I frown, glancing at Leo in the rear-view mirror. "Really? I don't remember that."

Weird. I grew up with all the kids around here. I didn't meet Leo until I was out of high school, I'd always assumed he was from out of town, brought here by the hush-hush scary business.

Leo gives me a long look in the mirror. He seems to be talking to Zach, but I feel like the next words are for me.

"I lived in a sort of special foster place here," he says, long and slow, words chosen carefully. "I wasn't allowed outside much, but sometimes I'd find my way out to play with my friends down by the creek. You know Mr. Warren, don't you? He was my friend back then, and our pal Blake, and his brother Holt, and Warren's sister, Jenna. And sometimes these two sisters would come running along with 'em. Clarissa and your Aunt Deanna."

Wow. I'm so lost. So confused. Something pricks and teases inside me, some buried memory, taunting the edges of my brain.

I remember playing by the creek, watching the boys wrestle, laughing when Jenna joined in, making flower crowns with her, and a boy I used to think was so sweet. But his name wasn't Leo. He hadn't been a lion, he'd been a—*holy hell.*

"*Tiger?!*" It bursts out of me before I can stop it.

I stare up in the mirror. Under that hood, there's no mistaking the slow, feral grin that spreads across Leo's lips. "Growl," he purrs mockingly.

Holy Toledo. It's a miracle I don't spin the car right off the road.

Zach tilts his head. "I don't get it. Leo means lion, not tiger?"

Chuckling, Leo says, "Lions and tigers and bears, oh my. Tell that to my buddy Blake. He was the oldest kid there, and he still didn't know a word of Latin."

"Why didn't you tell me?" I whisper, my heart knotting up. "I mean, when you came to the house, after all those years..."

"Long story, babe," Leo says, and yet I pick up on what he's not saying.

That's not a story he can tell me in front of Zach.

I'm just floored, white-knuckling the wheel.

I knew there'd always been something strange about that Tiger boy who made my face feel too warm, only for him to disappear into thin air. And then, so many years later, this tall, handsome man with the easy smile and strange violet eyes and wild ink appears. Sometimes, maybe I even had the same feeling, this faint whisper in the back of my mind.

The same freaking boy. And I'd never known.

He'd never told me.

He's just full of too many secrets, and I don't know what to do anymore. I really don't.

But I can't say anything else right now. I'm too confused, too conflicted, so I leave Leo and Zach to their quiet chatter about old Heart's Edge.

They get on so well it's like they *understand* each other in a way that almost makes me feel left out, like they already know the big crazy thing I still haven't told them. Deep down, I'm glad, though.

A boy should get along with his father.

A man should get along with his son.

I keep quiet all the way back to our cabin. Leo carries Zach on his shoulders as we take the trail through the woods. It's more well-worn by the day, before it had just been an impression in the brush. Now it's a troubling reminder of how long we've been here already. But I'm not expecting a package waiting on the front deck.

A package in a familiar custom pink and white striped bakery box branded with the Sweeter Things logo on the side.

Strange.

I don't think I gave anyone in Spokane the address here. I'd just told my store manager I was visiting my hometown to look after my sister.

Something tells me not to pick up the box. But something else tells me I can't afford not to.

Glancing at Leo, the subtle tension making his shoulders rigid tells me he senses it, too.

Something's not right.

I unlock the door and step inside, while Leo gently swings Zach down with a little *alley-oop* that makes him laugh and lift his arms high before landing on his feet. He gives the boy a little nudge on the shoulder.

"Go wash up so you can help make dinner," Leo rumbles. "Your ma and I need to talk."

Normally, Zach would be full of questions.

But that quiet intuition he gets from Leo is so clear. He gives me a long, thoughtful look, then slips over and hugs me tight before walking out of the room without a word.

That's my dumpling. Sometimes, a kid just *knows* and listens without even being asked.

Leo and I exchange another worried look. He gives me a nod that says, *go on. Open it.*

So I set the box on the dining table and flip it open. It hasn't even been taped, the four closing panels just layered to keep it in place, and that chills me.

No way it came in the mail, then.

Someone just left it here.

"Careful," Leo whispers, and I swallow hard, nodding as I peel the cardboard back.

It's...a phone?

An old-school flip phone, apparently. The type that just barely takes grainy pictures and plays videos, something nobody uses unless they're buying the prepaid cards you get on gas station shelves and top up every thirty minutes.

"I don't understand," I say, staring down at the phone, resting there grey and steely in the bottom of the box, but Leo hisses under his breath.

"Burner phone," he bites off, his voice oddly clipped and angry.

Huh? Why's he so mad over a phone?

I lift my head, looking at him. "Do you know what this is?"

Under the hood, his eyes are flinty and dark. "Might be a message from an unknown number," he growls. "Check it."

"How do you know that?"

"Reasons. I've had to use these things before. *Check it.*"

Something about the way he says it scares me. My entire body numbs, and I bite my lip, starting to pick up the phone—then I change my mind and snag a napkin off the kitchen island, using it to pick up the phone instead. There could be finger-prints on this thing, and I don't want to wipe them off.

I flip the phone open carefully.

The screen lights up like it was waiting for me. There's a little icon in the upper left, the tiny stylized symbol of a cassette tape that says Leo's right.

There's a message. Sender listed only as **Unknown.**

Sweet Jesus. I'm terrified to think who might be leaving messages for me on an untraceable phone.

I blink hard and punch the keypad, pulling up the voicemail menu.

You have one (1) video voicemail.

Holding my breath, my throat tight and my stomach turning itself inside out, I hit Play.

And instantly wish I hadn't.

The sound of my sister screaming shrieks out.

My heart does a nasty somersault, and I shiver, clapping one hand over my mouth, the other thumb tapping frantically at the volume button to turn it down before Zach hears.

Oh my God, no.

I can't watch this.

But I have no choice. I think the only reason I don't hurl the phone away is because Leo's right there, leaning in close, his warmth and his strength holding me up while I stare at the video between panicked breaths.

It's Deanna. No mistake.

She's tied to a chair with her arms behind her back, her clothing torn. Her face is bruised on one side, like she's been struck, her mouth split open, tiny abrasive lines of red on her face.

Thin lines.

Like cuts, deliberate and cruel.

And someone has a handful of her hair, chestnut locks like mine just a shade darker. They're wrapped around a gloved fist so thick and strong it can only belong to a man, dragging her head up sharply while she screams again.

I can't see who it is! He's just a shadow behind her, cut off at mid-torso.

All I see are thick, toned arms in a sleeveless shirt.

Don't hurt her, you bastard, I want to scream, as if he can hear me. As if I can magically cross space and time and stop this.

He drags her head back until her jugular is bared, and strokes something across her throat, making her flinch and rattle and whimper. Leo's hands go so tight.

But it's not a knife like I fear.

A brush?

Yep, a flipping hairbrush, and slowly he draws the bristles up along her jaw with a touch that's almost intimate, while she cringes and leans away. The brush slowly pushes into her hair at one temple, then draws back with this slow, evil care that's intentional, controlling, and so, so sick.

"*Such lovely hair.*" The voice that comes through is garbled, distorted, deep and mechanical. "*Such a shame we had to get blood in it. Do you want me to wash it for you, Deanna-Dee? I'd love to wash your beautiful hair.*"

I'm frozen down to the bone. This is gross, and even with the strangeness to his voice, it's oily and dark and oddly *possessive*.

"Voice synthesizer," Leo growls, nearly startling me out of my skin. "He's using it to disguise his fucking voice."

"But who—"

My sister's voice cuts me off—frightened, whispering, but still so angry, so brave. *"Get away from me, you freak."*

"Can't do that. We have to say hello to Clarissa, sweet Dee." The whole time the brush strokes slowly through her hair, pulling just hard enough to make her wince. *"Now look at the damn camera and say hello. Smile real pretty."*

"You don't want her—she's not the one! Leave her alone!"

"She must be, since you won't tell me otherwise."

The awful hand snared in Deanna's hair tightens and the brush disappears.

Only to be replaced with a pair of scissors.

Deanna's eyes roll wide and wild as she jerks her head back against the point that drags against her throat, just barely pressing down enough to dent, and I whimper in the back of my throat, eyes burning, welling.

I can't stand it. I'm terrified any moment that point will dig in, and I'll see my sister's blood cascading everywhere—

"Tell Clarissa to come to me, Dee."

"I won't," Deanna spits. *"I won't!"*

"So uncooperative. You almost don't deserve to keep this."

There's a sharp *snick*, and I can't help myself—I squeeze my eyes shut.

But there's no scream, no gurgle, no wet sound. I can still hear Deanna breathing, sniffling, and slowly I peel one eye open to watch Deanna's hair go floating loose from that creep's grip.

Some of it, anyway.

He's cut off a thick hunk of it, holding the part knotted against his fist while the rest falls raggedly against her neck. He strokes his thumb along the gleaming strands in his fingers.

"Next time, I'll take more," he snarls, excited. *"More to remember*

you by. Unless your sneaky fucking *sister stops fucking around. You get one chance, Clarissa. Leave everything you have at the museum and just maybe I'll let you and your pretty sister run away from me in one piece. Or maybe..."*

This time when silver flashes, the scissors slicing a thin hole in Deanna's shirt, I know where those small abrasive cuts came from. I gasp, fingers against my mouth while she lets out a cry, twisting at her bonds, all while that leering voice mocks us both.

"Or maybe I can just send her back in pieces. Make your choice, Clarissa Bell, or I'll make it for you."

* * *

I DON'T REMEMBER PASSING out.

I just remember the video going dark, leaving a blank screen, and realizing that Leo was saying something. But I couldn't understand him. His voice was coming down a long, far-off tunnel into nothing.

Everything just faded.

Now I'm waking up on the couch, staring up at the ceiling as everything comes rushing back.

"Deanna!" I gasp, jerking up—only to wince and press my face into my palm as my head throbs.

"Careful," Leo growls. I realize he's on the edge of the couch at my feet, watching me. "You almost hit the floor. I barely caught you."

"Thanks," I murmur. "Nice of me to go full fainting damsel on you, huh?"

"Forget it, Rissa. You've been under a lot of stress, hardly taking care of yourself. All your energy goes into Zach." I can see his smile faintly under the shadow of his hood, but it's really there in his voice. "You were just overwhelmed."

"Because that creep—that *creep*—" My voice catches, nearly breaks. I swallow hard, running a hand through my hair.

Such lovely hair. His sick voice floats back to me.

199

I shudder. "Who was he, Leo? What does he want from me?"

"Got a few good guesses, but nothing concrete. Whatever it is probably has a lot to do with those coordinates."

Lightning flashes through me. "You think there's something there...and he thinks I know what it is?"

"I think," Leo speaks slowly, measured. "Maybe he didn't notice the coordinates, babe. But he thinks whatever Deanna knows, you know it, too."

"I only know what I overheard from my father. And what you told me. You're the one with all the secrets. Not me."

He stiffens. "What's that supposed to mean?"

"I mean, you never told me you were *Tiger*," I throw back. "I was just a little girl who'd lost her friend. I almost *mourned* you when you disappeared! Then you let me fall in love with you without even telling me you came back!"

"Clarissa..." He works his hands, opening and closing his fists. "There's shit you didn't know about me as a kid. Heavy fucking shit. Things were done to me. I didn't want you or the other kids dealing with that. You didn't need to know—"

"What? Didn't need to know *you*?" It's all boiling out of me and I can't stop it.

Yes, I feel like a flaming hypocrite when my biggest secret is in his room right now and can probably hear me, but my emotions are so flipping raw.

I'm glad Deanna's alive, but terrified knowing some sicko has her. "It feels like you don't want me to know *you*. Even now you hide your face. You won't tell me what you've been doing all these years, why you're Nine, why you were in *prison*—"

"You know why I was in prison!" he throws back, chest heaving with his deep, rapid breaths. "You know fucking why. You know what I did that night. To your father, for you, for the town. Nine was my prison number, Rissa. Nine-Oh-Seven. *Nine*. That's who I became."

I flinch back, staring at him, my throat tight with those tears I've been fighting off for so long. "But what you did to my father was to save me...we could've gone to the police, the FBI, Leo. We could've cleared you."

"Bull. Galentron made damn sure no one would believe it was justified homicide," he says bitterly. "They painted me as crazy. A nut who'd lost his mind, who killed the mayor and set the Paradise Hotel on fire. A maniac who wanted to kill everyone in the town. I was their patsy, their excuse, their fucking lie. Easier than admitting they meant to turn loose a deadly virus...and the only person who could've testified on my behalf fled town."

Me.

Oh God, he means *me*.

I could've saved him, could have...

Stop. I clutch my fist over the awful ache in my chest.

It's too much, I can't stand it, and I shake my head sharply. "Leo...Leo, I'm sorry, I didn't know. I was scared. I had to get Deanna out of here, and Zach..."

My ears pinch shut, hot shame weeping out.

He's deadly silent for a long moment, then he turns his head away, inhaling sharply.

"Fuck. I shouldn't have said that," he says, his voice calmer. "I don't blame you, Rissa. At all. You didn't put me in this hell and it's not your fault."

"But it *is* my—"

"No. Blame Galentron and your old man. Blame every soulless maggot who engineered this shit. The rest? We'll call it fate. And fate isn't always a kind SOB," he says firmly, like that's the end of it. "Enough bickering. Let's focus on Deanna."

I can't speak for several seconds. The guilt inside me weighs a ton, imagining the horror Leo went through in the hospital, in prison, all because I was so scared I just ran away without looking back. I was young and had Zach to think of, plus a little sister who'd suddenly had her world split in two.

And a man from Galentron paid us a visit a couple weeks after everything happened. He told us he'd watch over us, to let him know if we needed anything. But the bigger message? The one that killed me?

We're watching. That's what he laid out plain as day. And I knew our lives would just go from bad to worse if we ever tried to go to the police, the press, or...

God. I didn't know what to do.

Not when the man I love killed the man who'd abused me for most of my life.

But now that I think of it, I've always run away, haven't I?

Even when I started making candy late at night in the kitchen, I was running.

Hiding in my fantasies.

Distracting myself when it was my sister's turn to take the brunt of Papa's fury, telling myself there was nothing I could do without making it worse. And then, the one time I tried to stop it, it *did* get worse. Coward or not, I've always had a reason why I *ran*.

And Leo's about to give me another as he says, "I think we should go to the coordinates."

That snaps me out of my thoughts, everything crystallizing as I stare at him. "What? But it could be a trap!"

"Don't think so," he says. "Think about it, Rissa. If he knew about the coordinates, he'd just go, take whatever's there, and leave. He'd get what he wants and wouldn't need you or Deanna. Best way to figure out what that is, what he's after, is to get it ourselves."

"Do I even *want* to know?" I sigh. "I told Deanna to leave things alone, and now whatever she knows brought her to him. I don't want to know what she knows."

"There's no choice," Leo growls. "We can't ignore the only possible bargaining chip in our arsenal."

"*No.*" I shake my head sharply. "Leo, I can't go running around chasing coordinates when I have my *son* to think of. If we go out there and get hurt, what happens to Zach? What then?"

He just looks at me gravely. It's like I'm getting angrier and panicky while he's getting calmer and braver, and that's pissing me off more.

"So what do you think we should do?" he asks.

"Turn the phone over to the police!" I say, flinging a hand out. "It's evidence. There might be prints, they could...I don't know, they could clear up his voice and maybe identify him? The Missoula police might come back soon—"

"And they might not for months," he says. "What you're asking for could take days of tedious police work. Weeks. Deanna won't have that much time."

The hard, cold implacability of that—the reality I can't stand to face—feels like it smashes me in the guts. I stare at him, but he's hard, still, quiet. That granite courage that once made him my rock now makes him this stranger, this wall I'm dashing myself up against when I feel like I'm *breaking*.

"Get out," I whisper. "I can't believe you'd say something so cruel. Just...go!"

Leo remains silent, eyeballing me, everything in those hot amethyst eyes telling me I know he's right.

I can't stand to look at him.

That's why I turn away. So I don't have to watch as silent footsteps take him away, and the creak of the door tells me he's disappeared into the descending gloom.

* * *

I GUESS Zach picks up on my mood because he's silent and morose during dinner.

He doesn't even ask me to help him with his homework before he washes up, changes, and goes to bed on his own. He's such a grown-up little boy sometimes, and when he's so self-sufficient, there are times I feel like he's growing away from me, going somewhere I can't reach.

Once he's in bed and asleep, I settle on the edge of his bed, smooth his hair back, and press a kiss to his brow.

I feel so alone right now. But even if he feels far away...

I still have my little boy.

If only I could help wishing for more.

More than I should ever be allowed to want.

I hate that Leo's right.

I hate that the only way to save Deedee means digging myself deeper. Every new discovery horrifies me more.

Mostly, I hate feeling naïve. Sheltered.

Like everyone's tried so hard to keep me in the dark, to protect me, and I've gone along with it because I didn't want to have my illusions ripped away.

Well, there are no illusions now.

The police are too indifferent to save my sister.

Galentron wants her dead for something she knows.

And the only one who can help her is *me.* I'm the last person who knows how she thinks and can follow in her footsteps.

I've always thought I was brave enough to protect my son, but now I'm realizing something.

Sometimes, cowardice and bravery look a lot alike.

I can't hide behind Zach as an excuse to run again. To fail my sister in her darkest hour.

Those thoughts hang heavy as I drift outside to the deck, looking over the trees. There are more lights out there tonight, flashlights. Leo has company. I hear voices, recognize Warren and Blake and Doc Caldwell, but I'm only focused on one.

He lingers after they're gone, done with talking over whatever they came for. There's just the lonely hint of flame through the trees that marks Leo's campfire, and a shadow in front of it, drawing closer.

He materializes in the moonlight, standing there like some strange fairy tale beast.

And he's not hiding his face this time.

His hood is drawn back, his mask lowered, that dark hair

falling across his face and drifting against those cragged, shadowy features that are all the more beautiful. It's like someone stripped away the man and left the beast underneath, the creature too wild for this world.

When he steps close to me, onto the deck, I can't help but go to him.

It's like this moment drew us together, and my heart beats for the silence between us as I throw myself against him with a soft cry.

"*Leo*," I whimper, burying myself against his chest.

His arms close around me.

And for the first time in a long time, I feel *right* again.

Right, and maybe strong enough to do what needs to be done. Just as long as we're together.

If I have to hide, then I'll hide myself in his warmth, his courage, his faith in me.

"You're right," I whisper, skimming my arms up around his neck. "I hate it so much, but you're right. We'll go. We'll find the coordinates."

"And we'll save Deanna," he finishes, a rumble that's not just an affirmation.

It's another promise.

One I echo silently, pressing myself to his massive chest and holding on for dear life.

XIV: TO THE GRAVE (NINE)

I never thought it would be so hard to leave my own kid with someone else.

Maybe it's because, all this time, I didn't know I even *had* a kid. Talk about one hell of an eye-opener.

Makes me not want to let Zach out of my sight even for a hot minute. Still, he can't be here for this today.

I can't risk the world of shit that'd fall if we head to those coordinates and it turns out to be a trick—some crap Deanna's kidnapper planted to lure us out where he can trap us and pit us against Deanna for leverage till somebody cracks.

So Zach's with Gray and Ember for the day, with Derek tagging along to supervise a field trip to the vet clinic.

Meanwhile, I'm hunkered down in the back seat of Rissa's little car, with my knees practically folded up around my goddamn ears. This has to end.

I've either got to clear my name or get her a bigger car. Before all this hide and seek busts a disc in my back.

I should be used to pain, though.

Pain has damn near been my meaning of life. And that's what's nagging me now, listening to the GPS ticking off mile markers to the coordinates and staring blankly out the back window.

Something about that recording, that monster, seems like a pain I already know.

I never saw his face, but there's something about him teasing at those buried memories.

Sometimes I hate what the hell I've lived through does to my brain. I tried so hard to hold on to the most important things, the things I love, the things that matter most.

Not hard enough. I've still got gaps in my memory.

Gaps where I don't recall what the fuck was done to me as a kid.

Gaps where I don't remember what *I've* done, and maybe it's my brain trying to protect me.

What did I do overseas in the war? In Afghanistan and Iraq?

Maybe once, I was almost as bad as that savage puke stroking Deanna's hair and savoring her whimpers and whispering *Lovely, lovely* in that way that needles into my subconscious and rips a chill down my spine.

"Turn right in three feet," the GPS says in that girly mechanical voice, and I feel the car slowing around me. *"Continue on foot for another fourteen feet north by northwest."*

"I think we're here," Clarissa says, but she sounds puzzled.

"Is the coast clear?"

"Trust me," she says. "I don't think anyone *here* wants to turn you in."

Frowning, I push myself up, peering out the window. Only for new unease to jolt through me in a seasick roll.

We're at the cemetery on the far edge of town.

Just beyond the fence, there's another weird memory.

The crumbling ruin of a place I once called home, and the last place where I ever saw open air before my childhood fell into that yawning blackness in my mind.

There's not much left of the long, low house now.

It was falling apart then, drafty and broken-down even when

I was small. Now I realize it never was a real foster center like we'd been told.

Galentron just claimed it and stashed us away there, all the kids who became Nighthawks. We were stolen from all over this county and spirited away from parents we'd forget as our minds broke—but the townspeople's curiosity was too much to keep us bottled up in that rickety shack any longer. They took us somewhere darker, worse, yet closer to home.

Dr. Ross, his eyes cold, his beard moving around lips that shape words I can almost hear in my mind but can't remember, words that make my entire body lock up. I can only obey his command to stand, head up like a soldier, shoulders back, a puppet moving against my own free will...

Fuck, I feel paralyzed, looking at that decrepit shack.

Can't answer Rissa, even as she looks back in the rear-view mirror with her brows knit together and murmurs, "Leo?"

It's like a trigger word dragging me home to reality.

I'm Leo, dammit.

Leo, not Nine, not 907, not Agent...

What was my code name?

What did they call me in the field?

Why do I remember the smell of blood, the bang of gunshots, someone whimpering while a hard, cold voice calls me *Agent Something* in the same cold, oily inflection behind that fake voice on the phone?

I shake myself, pushing the backseat door open. "Let's go see what's waiting for us."

She only nods, watching me with silent worry. We take a minute to load up the field kit I'd packed and stashed in the trunk, a long canvas duffel bag filled with tools.

I sling it over my shoulder, and together we pick our way through headstones so old they've mostly worn off their names and dates.

We follow the voice of the phone's GPS to the far corner. It's tucked away, a spot where a fence merges with a tree that's grown over it till the trunk just fused with the iron.

I look down. Between the tree's roots, the ground looks disturbed. Fresh.

Not today, or even in the past week or two, but there are signs that someone dug up the dirt in this otherwise untouched place in the last month, then tried to cover it again. Except the grass doesn't fit quite right, the broken mat of its roots vaguely outline where it's started growing again.

Plus, there's an old grave marker planted above it, nestled against the juncture of the roots.

Flowers rest in a bouquet at the foot of the gravestone, wilted but fairly recent.

I'd pin my guess on Deanna leaving them.

"Andric Bell," Clarissa says softly, peering at the nearly invisible letters, reaching out to trace them with her fingers. "The first Bell in Heart's Edge. My great-great-great grandfather."

She bites her lip, lifting her head and glancing over her shoulder, her eyes pensive, narrowed as they move to a newer grave marker.

"There's my mom." She smiles faintly. "You know, if she was still alive, maybe none of this crap would've ever happened. My father was never a good man, exactly, but...she reigned him in."

I frown, looking away from the ground and at her. "How?"

"Papa wasn't always the way he was. The kind of person who'd do what he did." Her voice halts over the word, her lashes lowering, pensive and sad. "When Mom was alive, he was just...he was *Papa*. But then the cancer came so hard, so fast. And I don't think he ever recovered from the shock. It turned his heart black. Everything just bled out of him, and he stopped caring about anything."

"Clarissa."

I want to comfort her. I want her in my arms again, just like last night.

More than that.

But fuck, we can't.

My greedy ass can't have those things. Part of me keeps wondering what it'd be like, how it would feel to be *with* her again, to have Zach call me Dad and show them both a better father than anything Rissa ever knew.

While I'm standing there, frozen, trying to find the right words, she lifts her head with a small, broken smile, hurting but brave.

"We can't do anything for the dead," she says. "But we can do something for the living, right? So now that we're here, what do we do?"

"That part's easy," I say with a grin, slinging the kit down from my back to the grass. "We dig, baby."

* * *

I SHOULD FEEL WORSE about desecrating a grave, but someone else did it first, and I'm just following in their footsteps.

The moment I sink the shovel into the dirt, my suspicions are confirmed.

This isn't packed, dense soil that hasn't been touched for decades. This soil feels loose. Churned.

It's been dug up before, and not long ago.

Clarissa watches me from the base of the tree, perched on a thick, tall root with a troubled look on her face, her eyes dark. She doesn't say anything. There's nothing to say.

Not till we know what we're supposed to find here. We don't have to wonder for long.

Not when my next stroke digs in and the shovel strikes something with a *clang*.

Her head comes up sharply, her eyes wide and startled. I go stiff, catching a breath.

We exchange hard glances before I dig harder, flinging out scoops of dirt while she tumbles to the edge of the pit I've made.

Soon, I unearth what looks like an urn. But it's weirdly

modern, stainless steel, with stylized curls all around the edges of the lid. Rissa goes still.

"Hey, that's from the shop. What's it doing here?" she says, her voice slow. "We use them for edible arrangements."

"That's telling," I toss the shovel onto the grass and use my hands to sweep a bit more dirt away from the urn, then lift it out. "Let's pop it open."

The urn's surprisingly light. I nearly pitch it into the air when I drag it upright, but I catch it and tip the lid off into one hand before upending it over the grass.

Nothing.

I shake it, but there's zilch rattling inside. No ashes or bones.

Frowning, I tilt it so the sun shines through the opening, peering down to see if anything's stuck.

"Empty," I tell her, hot confusion curdling my blood.

"Too slow," a familiar, oily voice says at my back. "I warned you. Shouldn't have wandered back to your love nest for the night instead of trying to catch up."

I growl, gritting my teeth, my hackles instantly going up at the sound of Fuchsia's voice.

That goddamned woman. *Again.*

I drop the urn and turn, using the movement to mask my hand slipping inside my coat, falling to the hilt of my gun. I'm at a disadvantage, standing in this hole with her lording over me, looking down her nose and her stiletto heels at me, but I've also got backup.

And Rissa's the one who snaps before I can even speak, practically spitting at Fuchsia. "What the hell do you want now?"

"It's not about what I want," Fuchsia purrs and produces something from her pocket. "It's about what you—and everybody else—are looking for."

She holds something up, clasped between two fingers. It's long, slim, and black. Silver on the end.

A USB thumb drive.

I snarl, working my jaw. Clarissa stands from her crouch, her shoulders square. "I'm guessing that's the missing data Galentron kidnapped Deanna for and thinks I know about."

"Smart girl!" Fuchsia says, and my eyes narrow.

Something's off about her, but she's still playing her usual games.

She toys with the drive between her fingers. "Every last bit of data on this drive could destroy Galentron for good. Same thing we all want, don't we?" She raises her brows mockingly. "And if I happen to gain a rather lucrative book or film deal out of it, well...wouldn't I look just *dashing* on the red carpet?"

My eyes narrow. "Then why the fuck haven't you run off and done that already? Left us to deal with our own problems?"

She flutters her lashes dramatically, a hand pressed to her chest. "Out of the goodness of my heart, Leo."

"Bullshit. You used to be a better liar."

"And you used to have more skin, back before you were left to your *ever*-so-touching secret admirer bouquets for your little ex-girlfriend. Tell me, do flower arrangements come in char-broiled scent?"

Clarissa lets out a furious little sound. "That's low, Fuchsia. Stop with the playground crap and tell us what you're here for." She pauses, and I can see the sparks going off in her eyes, the clarity and comprehension. "Tell us what you *need* us for."

"My, my, Leo. While you were sitting there pounding your chest, your little baby doll figured out what your ever-so-superior enhanced brain couldn't." Fuchsia taps the drive against her lower lip, her eyes narrowing. "She's right. I *do* need you. But I also have what you want. So I think we have ourselves a mutual goal. Neither of us can get there without the other. Shame, shame."

Dammit, she's right. And that might be the sickest twist of all.

I hate how good she is at getting under my skin. I stop thinking analytically and just turn into this quiet knot of rage.

I also don't want her running her mouth about my brain and whatever they did to it in front of Clarissa, starting another argument over questions that are best left unanswered. *Maybe forever.*

So I lift myself out of this hole I've dug—figuratively and literally—making sure to keep Fuchsia's eyes on me as I hoist up and dust myself off. "So you want to profit off Galentron's downfall. Whatever. We need Deanna back. Seems like we're at a crossroads."

"What you want is so *boring.*" She folds her arms over her chest, tapping the drive against her inner elbow. "But I'm not seeing your road."

"Galentron wants what's on that drive, and they're keeping Deanna hostage as bait. Which means if you expose that info, they won't bother keeping her alive," I grind out.

"Oh, as if we can't pull off a double-cross. Turn over the information, get the girl, and then blow the roof off this fuckery." She smiles slowly. "Buuut, of course, that's assuming there's anything interesting on the drive."

Rissa shakes her head. "You don't know?"

"That, little girl, is where you come in." Fuchsia turns her drilling stare on Clarissa. "Turns out, the drive's encrypted. Either darling Nine-Oh-Seven here can crack it, or *you* just might have the insight into your sister to take a lucky guess at the password."

Clarissa starts, going tense. She looks like a deer about to bolt off in the brush.

It's a bizarre moment, the sun shining down, orange-tinted through jack-o-lantern colored leaves, and her breaths puffing on the chilly air, the dapples of light dancing through her hair. Her eyes are so wide, staring at Fuchsia mistrustfully.

"Me?" she says, shaking her head. "I can't. I don't know *anything* about this other than what I've been told. I'm so lost."

If Clarissa's the frightened deer, Fuchsia's the hunter who's got her in her sights.

I can't let her pull the trigger.

Lurching forward, I yank the drive out of her fingers before

Fuchsia can react. She makes a little grab for it, but I'm too quick, darting out of her reach.

"I'll crack it," I growl. "Don't push Rissa into this."

Fuchsia just smirks. "Oh, darling, she's already in it. And if neither of you can accept that, guess you'll end up dead and take poor Deanna to the grave with you."

XV: DEAD END (CLARISSA)

I can't get her words out of my head.
You'll end up dead and take poor Deanna to the grave with you.

I sit, curled up on the couch with my knees hugging my chest, biting at my thumb knuckle. I'm watching without really *seeing* as Leo works at my laptop with the drive plugged into one of the USB ports.

He's done something to it. Downloaded some kind of program. A lot of programs, really, and I didn't get what he was saying about secure connections and VPNs and brute force encryption, but he seems to know what he's doing.

That's another thing I never knew about Leo.

He's pretty freaking good with computers like this, understands cracking data.

Honestly, there are a lot of things I never knew about Leo. *Why?*

Was he lying to me when I fell in love with him twice? Or just trying to protect me?

I want to believe I loved the man he really was, and the secrets he hid were things I didn't need to know, some inner darkness he didn't want to keep whenever he was with me.

But now, I just don't know.

I shouldn't even be thinking about this right now.

I should be trying to think what hidden messages Deanna could've possibly left that would lead me to the password for the data.

Her face flashes in my mind—not as I want to remember her, but bloodied, bruised, frightened. I shudder, my heart hurting. Every word she said replays in my mind, but if she was hiding some clue for me in there, some phrase, some meaning...

I just can't make the connection.

"You're staring at me," Leo murmurs, his thick fingers still rattling over the keyboard, his lips moving past the shadow of the hood.

I jerk, then blink, forcing a faint smile. "You've been playing stalker in the shadows for a while. It's a little weird to see you sitting at my kitchen table instead of skulking around in the woods."

A chuckle drifts out from under his hood. "I've got a portable solar charger out at my camp, but it's not much to keep a laptop going for long."

My throat feels full, and I cough.

God, I want to say it.

I want to tell him I'm freaking *glad* he's here, glad he's inside, glad he's taking up this space in my life instead of hiding out like he thinks he's some freaky monster who can only live in the shadows.

But the words dry up on my tongue. I make myself look away.

"You look stressed," I deflect instead. "Maybe it's break time?"

"Breaks aren't a luxury we've got. What's on this drive is our only leverage, our only damn chance."

"What's on that drive could kill us," I say softly. "Once we know, we know...and giving them the drive for Deanna won't erase that. Once we see it, that's it, Leo."

"So you want me to stop?"

"No." He can't stop, not when Deanna's running out of time. "But maybe just give me a few more minutes of sweet ignorance?"

"Ah. Okay."

I'm half expecting him to brush it off and keep working.

Instead, he taps a key on the laptop and locks the screen.

Then slowly he reaches up, pushing his hood back like he's afraid for me to see him in the harsh light overhead—when I want nothing more.

He really doesn't get how amazing he is.

How nothing's changed. Not when he's so raw and primal he's magnetized, a living force of burning sexiness and dark divinity, twisted by fire into the most wicked shape yet.

In his twenties, he was divine, huge, hard as nails. But now?

Holy hell, *now* he's a giant, all hulking muscles and jagged lines and full body ink that screams, *just try, Rissa. Try to stop wanting to explore me with your tongue.*

He's pure sin.

But it's not sinful when he looks over his shoulder toward the hall.

It's nervous, almost shy.

And I smile, realizing he's worried about Zach, who's already tucked in for the night.

My heart goes soft and achy at the thought.

He doesn't even know Zach's his, and he's still worried about our son rejecting him. Fearing him, just because he's so different.

Don't you know that being different is what makes you so wild? So amazing?

I wish I could just grab him and yell it in his face.

"Leo, I—" I pause, but my brain doesn't.

I have to tell you something.

I have to tell you Zach is yours.

He needs you. I need you. So flipping bad.

It won't come out. The instant his reflective eyes lock onto me, sharp and questioning, the words knot up in my throat. I swallow, looking down at my knees.

"What about that man who came here? The one who said he knew about Deanna?" I look up.

Leo's expression blackens, and he lets out a grunt. "What was his name again?"

"Nash," I say, frowning. "Do you know him?"

"I might." He looks away, his brows lowering in thick crags. "I don't remember."

"Should you?"

"Yeah. Trouble is, forgetting some things was the only way I've survived all these years." It comes harsh, low, but it's not hard to tell that fury isn't directed at me. Not when it's full of so much pain. "Galentron *did* shit to me, Clarissa. Things that made me who and what I am. But I wasn't the only one. There are others out there like me. Like me, but still loyal to the company."

I bite my lip. "I remember when I was little...there were these stories about not going outside after dark. They said if the monsters caught you, you'd be stolen away, and even back then I knew the monsters weren't all fake because they were in our house. Shadow men who might just steal me and Deedee if we weren't good and didn't go to bed on time." I swallow, my throat tight. "You were one of the kids they took, weren't you? That's why you disappeared."

He goes oddly still. He's not looking at me, but the tension in his body says everything, hard muscles straining against his clothes.

Finally, he rasps, "Yeah. I was already under their thumb when you met me as Tiger. Everyone in the Nighthawks, they took us all. They erased who we used to be. And then they remade us into something else."

My heart thumps so hard it's a miracle my ribs don't crack. "Nighthawks? But Deanna—"

"Yeah." His eyes close, lashes lowering. "That's what that

word meant. She must've found out about it, and Galentron must've sent one of them after her."

My mind is whirling. All of these weird, scary puzzle pieces flying around, smashing against each other and trying to fit together. "Nash. He...he seemed so familiar. Reminded me of you with how big he is, the way he moves. Is he...?"

"Probably," Leo whispers. "And he's probably the demon-fuck who has Deanna."

I shudder, pressing my hand to my throat like I can grab my own pulse and slow it down. "What did they *do* to you?"

"Everything." His growl deepens. "Torture. Mind control. Psych warfare. Everything, Rissa. But I was closer to you than you ever knew. They kept us out of sight, beneath that house sometimes. *Your place*." He opens his eyes, lifting his head, looking at me with such razor-sharp pain I can't stand it. "I was always with you, even when you didn't know it. We were suffering. Together."

Oh my God.

The tears just come in this hot, explosive rush that's almost blinding.

I can't stand being so far away from him when he's hurting, spilling these vicious fragments that stab me in the soul. And before I know it I'm off the sofa, racing across the space to his chair.

He flinches as I press myself against his back. There's only the hard wood back of the chair between us, but he's so tall it barely comes up to his shoulder blades, and when I wrap my arms around him and lean my chest against his back, he gives in.

He doesn't pull away.

Thank God.

And I bury my face against his hair, lacing my hands together over his chest. Just holding him as tight as I can, breathing in his scent that's like all the wild and savage things ever made under the sky.

"I'm so, so sorry." I'm whimpering now. "I'm sorry, Leo, I never *knew.*"

"The way it should be. Did everything I could to keep you from knowing, sweetheart." His hand comes up slowly, curling against my wrists, warm and heavy and reassuring, and I ache inside with this longing that's never died. "Galentron tangled up our lives, but I never wanted those bastards to hurt you the way they hurt me."

"Did...did you really leave those flowers for me?"

There's a faint sound. Not quite a laugh, it's bitter and dark, his body jerking hard against me. "Every month. All these years. I hoped they'd find you, one way or another. Knew Deanna came back here sometimes, and I guess..." He trails off.

I'm going to break.

I'm going to freaking break myself if he keeps telling me these things, and then I don't know what I'll do.

Kiss him. Tell him everything.

Tell him Zach needs him, tell him *I* need him, tell him I don't care about the past when we have this chance to start over and create a new future.

No matter what secrets he's kept from me, I know this man.

I know who saved my life, and it's the same broken hero who's working himself to the bone to save my sister now, to save us all again.

"I don't get how you've stayed so strong," I murmur, resting my head to the back of his shoulder. "I mean, how have you even survived as a fugitive? Living in the wild?"

"A little MacGyvering never hurt a dude. I've managed, off-grid. Survival skills from the military, mostly." He turns his head, and the rough, scarred texture of his cheek, his scruff, brushes against mine. "It's been enough for me till now."

And it's not anymore? I want to ask, but my bravery keeps deserting me.

Instead I whisper, "I don't understand why you always apologized with the flowers. You have *nothing* to apologize for. Nothing, Leo."

Then I feel it. The moment I lose him.

When he goes stiff against me and his hand drops away and his amethyst stare fades.

I want to hold on tight, to never let him go, but I make myself loosen my grip as all that powerful muscle bunches and coils before he stands, stepping forward, putting distance between us. I stare at the broad, titanic shape of his back, his shoulders, as he pulls his hood up again.

"Get some rest," he murmurs. "We'll start again in the morning."

I can't speak. If I talk, I'll beg, and I'm too proud for that.

For all the raw emotion he displayed moments ago, I can't tell if he's the only one who still feels this aching pull. I can't tell if *I'm* even feeling it, or if I'm just desperate for comfort when I'm so afraid for my sister, and Leo's as familiar and safe as he is strange and frightening.

I turn away. I can't look into the storm if I'm going to find the courage to speak.

To finally ask him, "Do you think there's another way we can crack the password?"

There's no answer.

I glance over my shoulder and sigh. I should've known.

He's already gone.

Vanished into the night like a phantom, leaving me alone with better times, better memories, better wishes.

* * *

Eight Years Ago

I'VE NEVER SEEN the stars like they are tonight.

NICOLE SNOW

Maybe it's just because I've never bothered looking up, or because I've rarely been allowed outside after dark under the open sky.

It's another new thing I've learned. Another fresh, beautiful discovery, all thanks to him.

This whole summer has felt unreal.

Like a dream. Like magic.

Like every night he steals me away into our own secret fairy tale, and come morning, I don't want to return to the harsh grey light of life. The pain. The fear. The constant trauma hovering over my head like a spinning axe.

But tonight feels doubly enchanted. We stand at the base of the cliff, hand in hand, looking up at the sky.

Out here, it's just pure inky darkness and tinsel night.

The Milky Way has never looked so bright, so amazing, a sky full of billions of little pinprick lights.

And I feel every one of them burning inside me as I clasp Leo's hand, leaning into him and breathing in his scent that makes me so, so happy.

"I don't know how I'm supposed to go back in the morning," I whisper, resting my cheek to his arm. "How I'm ever supposed to let this go and return to that hell."

"Soon you won't have to." His hand covers mine, clasping it against his arm, and he looks down at me. His eyes are just two more brilliant, violet stars, gleaming in the night. "I had no idea it'd gotten that bad, Rissa. That he was fucking hurting you that way. It's coming to an end. You trust me to take care of it?"

Oh, God. I want to tell him I'd trust him with *anything*.

My life, my future, my heart.

But there's still one thing holding me back, and I bite my lip. "It's not that, Leo. It's—"

"Deanna. I know. Don't ever think I'd leave your little sis behind, woman." There's a teasing edge in his voice, but I can tell how deadly serious he is underneath it. "As far as I'm concerned,

222

the two of you are a package deal. So let's get married and adopt her as ours."

I know he's teasing, using awkward humor in that way he has to take my mind off my worries and make me laugh, but my heart still jumps at the idea.

Married?

Me and Leo, together forever, happy somewhere that isn't here.

I'm a little scared to tell him what I'm thinking.

A little scared I might chase him off, wanting too much, pushing too fast.

So since I can't say anything, I draw him down to me, rising up on my toes to kiss his cheek.

Only, he catches me before my lips find his swarthy skin and close-cropped beard, and suddenly his mouth claims mine, and I'm gasping, trembling, swept away in the ambush of his searing kiss.

I've kissed boys before. Leo may be my first real boyfriend, real lover, but in high school there were dates and a few messy pecks in the back seats of cars and clumsy hands everywhere.

Kisses that were sweet but messy, breathless and wonderful because they were the first time and still so precious and new.

But nothing—and I mean *nothing*—has ever hit me the way it does when Leo kisses.

It's like the difference between a single star and a flaming galaxy.

All this bright light warms me up and down while his arms wrap tight and he lifts me off my feet.

This is different, somehow.

Different from the stolen moments of frantic lovemaking in my bedroom, trying to be silent so we don't get caught. Different from the secretive moments in the back of his truck, in a hotel, in every stolen place where we can keep our secret, forbidden love as best we can.

Because as he lays me down against the grass, surrounded by

flowers with their petals rising up in a showering cloud around me as I fall against their soft stems, it's not so secret anymore tonight.

For the first time, I don't feel like we have to hide.

I don't feel like our love is this shameful secret. Not when we're sharing it out here under the open sky.

So I draw him lower, slipping my arms around his neck, giving back his kiss with everything in me—wholeheartedly, hungrily, wildly.

He's such a beast, dead set on devouring me, inch by trembling inch.

I barely have time to gasp. He's taken my mouth in a savage, dominating kiss, sweeping over me like a storm before I even realize what's happening.

His growling heat rains down as he delves deeper, his tongue searching and stroking and seeking like my mouth is as sensitized inside as the rest of my body. I feel every lick and caress and stroke in a phantom echo stirring between my thighs, spearing up inside me with a grasping need.

I'm already spreading myself open for him. His hand burrows under my miniskirt, dragging it up around my hips. Then with a low snarl against my mouth, Leo shreds it off, nearly splitting the seams.

Holy hell!

So this is why I'm here.

This is why I'm hungry.

This is why *horny* can't do justice to Leo freaking Regis.

He grabs my arms, raising them up so he can tear my tank top over my head and toss it aside. Exactly how I want it now.

Bare beneath the starlight.

Naked and open, with nothing to hide.

My lacy bra and panties barely last half a second before they're gone too, delicate fabric biting into my skin before shearing off.

I feel everything from the lace dragging into my flesh and scraping and tearing, to the grass blades tickling my back.

But more than anything else, I feel *him.*

His huge bulk pressing down on me, the fire in his body baking off him like he's the sun at night, soaking into my skin, turning me inside out.

I feel his strength, his roughness. Every hard muscle and those ginormous hands, his sheer size and the pressure of his body.

But I feel his gentleness, too. It's there in his fingers laced in my hair, stroking the back of my neck, in how he holds himself back just enough to make me gasp and writhe instead of crushing the breath from me.

And I feel his love in every kiss.

This man can barely breathe without me. Every single kiss is a desperate rush of air.

Sure, it's overwhelming, but I *want* to be overwhelmed.

I want this—his hands on my body, his broad, coarse palms cupping my breasts, stroking my flesh, kneading my nipples until I feel like hot clay in his hands. And Lord, I'm ready and *willing* to be molded.

Pleasure steals me away in sweet shocks.

His mouth stamps my throat and sucks at my racing pulse. His calloused palms tease my nipples and make them swell. The zipper of his jeans teases against my stomach and around my navel, the hardness of his cock pressing against me through the denim, nudging in slow, wicked friction.

I feel my thighs spread for him, baring me completely. Then the cool air caressing my wet folds, just the right quivering anticipation.

"Leo," I whisper, sinking my teeth into his lip.

He growls real slow. So slow it's like I'm melting one degree at a time as he teases me hotter.

His tongue, his mouth, his teeth trail down my throat, over my collarbones, across my breasts, only stopping to suck at my nipples, drawing each bud in deep. His fingers shape my hips, digging into my ass, grasping my thighs, spreading me wider.

Then his mouth goes *home*.

My pussy throbs as his first fiery lick gives perfect friction.

I'm losing my mind, rocking my hips in rhythm to every thrust of his tongue inside me, and he's just in his glory. Drinking me in with every soaking lick, and the breaths I'm holding come out of me in gasping, shattering cries. He teases me to the very edge and leaves my clit, my inner walls humming.

Until he stops.

Then he lifts his head and looks at me with a slow, dark smile, the moonlight gleaming in his eyes, his mouth so wet with me.

"Better," he rumbles. "No secrets, Rissa. No holding back. Let me fucking *hear* you tonight."

I flush from head to toe. It's the only warning I get, and then he gives me good reason to scream into the night, his long, thick fingers slipping deep inside me.

After this summer, after tumbling into his arms again and again and again, I should be used to him.

But somehow it's brand new every time—the sensation of those thick fingers against my soft flesh, the way he eases in and makes me aware of every tiny burst of pressure as one knuckle at a time sinks deeper, *deeper*.

It's almost a fever. How he makes me feel so deliciously dirty with something so simple.

Just one finger has me writhing, ripping at the grass, gasping out his name.

"Leo, Leo. Holy—!" My toes curl up in the flowers and the dirt as I lift my entire lower body, offering myself to him.

Next it's two fingers.

Then *three*.

And after that it's so flipping good, so deep, this intimate exploration as his fingertips curl and stroke inside me. It's almost obscene how he touches every secret place.

He pulls me into the zone, moving one knuckle against my clit. It's the one perfect place where I can't think about my father, about Deanna, about anything else right now.

Here, there's only me, Leo, and my own desperation for his body, his cock, his love.

But I break down completely for him.

He hooks my knees over his shoulders, forcing me open, and bends to flick his tongue over my clit.

Right at the exact same moment he starts thrusting and twisting his fingers inside me.

His mouth pulls on my flesh in screams of sensation. Just as his hand delves deeper, taking me over. I whimper, curling forward, burying my fingers in his hair and wrapping my legs around his shoulders.

Too much. Too explosive. Too wonderful.

I can't take it.

I can't take that hot rhythm of his fingers plunging in and out, the slow just-right suction and wetness and heat and friction of his tongue against my clit.

And there's nothing left holding me back from crying out his name to the stars as I lose it.

"Leo, I'm—"

Coming!

Oh, am I ever.

I come so hard my entire body fluxes like one big pulse, this storm churning through me in hot, shuddering waves as I spill myself all over his tongue, his beard, his fingers.

It's only the start.

Because now that I'm a shaking, liquid mess, now that I'm all sensitive and everything just blurs my vision with white-hot ecstasy...

That's when he shifts my legs from around his shoulders and wraps them around his waist.

That's when he unzips his jeans.

That's when the biggest cock I could ever imagine presses against me, naked flesh on naughty skin.

And I barely get to dig my fingers into his shoulders and hold on for dear life. He wants it too much. He drives into me in a single smooth stroke, growling the whole way.

"Leo!" I whimper out again.

I'm all soft inside. Vulnerable. The moment I feel the fire of his flesh burning me apart I can't help but scream at the top of my lungs.

He knows how to torment me so gently, how to push and pull. The lightest touch sets my body off in cascading flame, so all he has to do is stroke his cock so slowly, so sweetly inside me to turn me into a wildfire.

I'm liquid. Molten. Starved.

I'm completely wrapped up in the way he takes me, loves me, fucks me. It's so good I hardly even know up from down.

When I'm with him, I'm not the quiet, meek, good little candymaker.

I'm a wildcat in love, in lust, and I claw at his back with all my strength. I clutch Leo's shoulders and rock up to meet him, begging for the beast inside him to make me even wilder.

And he gives me everything I want. Everything I need. Everything I dare to ask for in every shaky moan.

Then he just *gives*.

He pins me to the earth with a snarl and owns me.

It's primal and perfect and wonderful.

It's frantic and hot and gasping.

We're dueling lips and tongues, grasping hands, rocking hips, and animal groans drowning out the night. We're my hands raking down his back and his balls slapping my skin, grunting as he drives in, taking what's so completely his. We're gasping breaths, and every sweet, slick sound of sliding and crashing and coming together so hard and so fast I think I'm just *ruined*.

Destroyed for any other man who isn't Leo Regis.

It hurts in all the best ways, this fabulous ache, this heat overwhelming my pussy as his thrusts come harder. So I wrap him up again as his forehead presses mine, and he pushes a low growl into me, and then we go at it so hard and so frantic our next O is lightning.

We come together.

We come raw.

We come beautiful.

It makes me want to never, ever let him go.

So I don't. Leo doesn't even pull out, too hard and too wild, he never softens, and he just keeps *going*.

And he leaves me swearing, convulsing, nearly crying as he deliberately moves himself inside me so his cock stretches me further, stirs against my inner walls, makes me clench up tight and grip him with a pinch that says, *don't you dare stop.*

He makes me feel loved and deliciously used. Two freak opposites. But maybe that's how a love like ours is meant to be.

I can't stop my thighs from gripping tight and hot and hard against his hips, the engine powering those punishing strokes that brand me *his* from the inside out.

There's a slick heat as my insides lock up, trapping him so deep, until our rocking fusion makes me feel stripped down to my soul.

It's his name on my lips when I come again, a writhing mess, all clenching muscle and dripping need.

But it'll always be his name, and only his, won't it?

He's the only man I'd even let touch me this way.

The only one I'll trust to fill me as he stiffens, snarling.

He slams in to the hilt with a roar, and I feel his cock ballooning. I bury my lips against his in a teasing kiss as his whole massive body comes apart.

Leo comes inside me. Pours himself out in a mad rush of heat and growly, primal silence. There's no mistaking the one-word signal as my pussy wrings him dry: *mine, dammit. Rissa, you're mine.*

I can't imagine being anything else.

And I cry that out secretly to the night sky as we tumble together into another kiss.

* * *

Present

SOMETIMES I LIKE to think that was the night Zach was conceived.

Bringing that beautiful little boy into this world under those beautiful stars.

Before everything went to hell.

Sitting on the edge of my bed, alone, I stare out into the night and that distant glimmer of firelight in the dark. That's when I finally let myself cry.

Not for Leo. Not for Heart's Edge. Not even for Deanna.

For myself.

Curling forward, I hug my arms around myself and choke out these shallow, hoarse gasps that feel like they hollow me out.

I only let myself cry for what's already gone, what's worth being mourned.

Mostly, I'm crying because what Leo and I had once is gone, and I still don't know if it's my fault or his or just the wretched way everything turned out. All thanks to a vile, faceless corporation and a man who cared more about money and power than he did about life.

I just wish Leo, wounded beast that he is, still knew what to do with a kind touch.

I never knew how much I wanted to reach for him until I realized how fast it could make him turn away.

XVI: FOLLOW DETOUR (NINE)

Eight Years Ago

I CAN'T BELIEVE I'm about to do this.

I'm about to ask this amazing, gorgeous, bright-eyed girl to marry me.

I don't even know what I can offer her. Not when my life belongs to Galentron as sure as Spartacus belonged to Rome. They don't let freaks like me off their payroll.

They don't let us have lives. We're not like normal agents, pretending to be ordinary people with a wife and three kids who have no idea that when we leave for work every day, we're going to do things that decide who lives and who dies.

We're ghosts. We're rumors. We're slaves.

Officially, we don't exist.

Not on paper or in any unclassified database.

I don't know what kind of life a ghost can give Clarissa Bell.

But, shit, maybe if I'm smart, maybe if she says yes, we'll figure it out.

Maybe we can both turn ourselves into another kind of ghost

and disappear somewhere we'll be safe. I'll get away from Galen-tron, from Dr. Ross, and she'll get away from that bastard piece of scum she calls a father.

I've got several leads on shady someones who can get us fake IDs, fake passports. This shady firm, Stork, Storkley, and Associates, over in some place called Finley Grove, Minnesota. This kid named Manny, fresh out of law school, talks a good game behind his old man's back. Or maybe I'll just hit up one of those biker dudes with the Grizzlies MC patches who some-times stop off at Brody's for a drink on their way through town.

They could set me up. We've got options.

I hear Thailand seems like a good place to start over.

Hell, I've already been practicing my Thai. I can learn the basics of a new language in a few weeks if I really need to. Maybe she'll let me teach her.

I let myself drift into those thoughts while I wait for her. I'm not far away from the meadow where, a few nights ago, we wrapped ourselves up in each other under the stars and went buck *wild.*

I'm standing on the cliff over the field, looking down. There's still a spot in the grass below where the flowers and dirt are all torn up.

That woman came at me so fast and hard and hot, and I gave it back in spades. That's just how it is with us.

Two hearts, always fast and hard and hot, but shit. I can't imagine not being with her *forever.*

Don't remind me I've only known her a few months.

She's the one.

The only one for me, and she always will be. A man knows these things.

Doesn't really matter where we go next.

Just as long as I get her and Deanna away from that monster.

Somehow, I always feel her coming before she appears.

I look up just as she comes down the trail, breathless, looking real sweet today in her pretty little dress, still untying herself from the apron she wears at the coffee shop. The job's a new thing, but it makes her so happy—yet it still makes me *pissed* when I think about her old man only grudgingly allowing it when she wanted to sell her sweets at the shop.

The only reason he gave her permission was because she made him look good back at that summer fair.

The wholesome, fresh-faced daughter with her homemade candies plays too well. It's perfect for a politician's load of a story about being Mr. Family Man, instead of a ruthless, conniving piece of shit.

I just want Rissa happy doing what she loves.

She looks like she couldn't be happier as she draws closer, draping her apron over her arm and looking up at me with that bright, lovely smile of hers.

"Hey," she says, stretching on her toes to try to kiss my cheek.

It doesn't work. She still can't reach though she's not short herself. So she tugs on my arm with a sort of playful begging that's become our little inside joke.

I bend so she can press her soft, lush mouth to my cheek, laughing and tucking her against my side with a familiarity that makes me ache in all the best ways. Her curves mold too well to my edges.

"Sorry if I'm late," she says. "It took a little longer than expected to clean up and close up the shop."

"Don't worry about it. I don't really have a timer as long as I'm back before they look for me in the morning."

She looks worried and curls her hand against my arm. "They're really strict with the guards, huh?"

I want to tell her I'm more than a guard.

But there's no point.

I won't be anything, soon, if she says *yes.*

I can forget everything Galentron made me. What I am now doesn't matter nearly as much as what I am to her.

So I shrug, offering a smile that I hope doesn't hint at how nervous I feel. The ring box in my pocket feels like it weighs tons. "It's like a frat house, almost. Someone's got to keep us in order."

"Because you're so dastardly. Always misbehaving."

"You make me misbehave," I growl, leaning down and nuzzling into the rich brown locks of her hair.

She smells so good, always that hint of sugary sweetness. Right now, it's touched with the hint of Arabica from the coffee shop, but underneath it, there's something that's just *her*.

Damn if I don't breathe her in again.

She laughs, pushing at me lightly. "You're always sniffing me. You really are an animal. Going to hike your leg and mark your territory next?"

"Nasty." But I can't help a chuckle, squeezing her tight. "Any more toilet humor and you'll ruin the night."

"Oh? And what would I be ruining?" She tilts her pretty face up to mine, her eyes heavy with that hint of shadow that always makes green irises glow, her lips curled in a quirk that's always too sweet and just a little bit mocking. "Planning for round two? Are we defiling more flowers?"

"Fuck. That's not why I brought you here, although I wouldn't object, depending."

"Depending on what?"

My mouth goes dry.

I'm elated, excited, hopeful, but also plain freaked.

They say there are two occasions in a man's life where he can't tell joy from fear.

The birth of his first child, and when he proposes to the girl he loves.

I take a deep breath, pulling away from her.

She watches me quizzically, tilting her head to one side right before her eyebrows shoot up.

She already knows. She watches me sink down on one knee.

I can see it in her eyes while I reach in my pocket.

A flick of my thumb opens the box on a slender silver diamond band, holding it up for her as I kneel there in the flowers and say the words that have been lodged in my throat for days.

"Depending on if you say yes," I say, clearing my throat, strengthening my voice. I don't want there to be any hint of doubt when I say, "Clarissa Leigh Bell...will you marry me?"

I'm sure she'll say yes. I think.

But there's this breathless moment when I think I might be about to get my heart crushed. She just stares at me with her eyes so wide, unblinking.

Goddamn, I know she loves me. Know she wants to run away with me.

But what if I've pushed too hard, too fast? It's honestly asking a lot after the life she's been trapped in. This much change might be terrifying and—

"Yes!" she cries, tumbling down into my arms, barely catching the ring box to clasp it between our twined hands.

Then comes *the* kiss to end all kisses. It tastes wet and salty, her tears flowing freely.

Maybe not just hers, even if I'll never admit it out loud.

Even if she'd said no, I'd still have done everything in my power to protect her.

To save her from that wretched man.

Still, the fact that she wants to leave that life behind not just as my lover, but as my wife means the whole damn universe.

It's everything. It *makes* everything I've endured to get here worth it.

The pain. The torture. The conditioning. The brainwashing that even now scares me, when I've done everything I can to fake compliance, fighting the command triggers burned into my grey matter.

She's the one reason I've been able to *hold on.*

And she doesn't even know how long she's been keeping me together.

One fine day, I'll tell her.

I'll tell her how young Tiger fought against his bonds each

and every time Dr. Ross held him down and injected him with burning shit to make him more obedient and whispered the same words to him over and over and over, engraving them deep in his brain.

I'll tell her how that boy held on to her and wouldn't let him take the memory of a pretty girl twirling a flower between her fingers under the summer sun, and the shy, sweet way she looked at him.

I'll tell her about an older kid wondering who she grew into, now and then dreaming her voice. The same voice I remembered hearing deep down in the catacombs under the mansion.

I'll tell her about carving her face into thin slips of wood, carving flowers I swore I'd give her one day, holding on to them when I felt like I'd break at the slightest provocation.

I'll tell her how sometimes the neat lines between love and obsession get so blurred, I can't even breathe anymore without picturing her.

That's why I want to save her so much.

Because Clarissa saved me.

Right now isn't the time for those words, though. Now's the time for tearful kisses, for the tight roughness in my throat, for her arms around my neck and her body against mine, and then we're hand in hand, and I'm sliding that pretty, slender engagement ring on her delicate finger.

I can't stop smiling, and my smile echoes on her lips, in her eyes.

We don't need to say a word as we stand, picking at the flowers from the edge of the cliff, hand in hand.

Yeah, it's that corny old legend, the lovers of Heart's Edge.

That old promise.

The one where they say if you toss flowers over the cliff with the person you love, maybe you'll be together forever.

So we pluck the petals with starry-eyed looks and hold them up high. And when we cast them over the edge and into the wind, sending them swirling into the night, I think I can *see* our forever.

Little do we know that our promise ends in less than a week.

Little do we know that when Rissa tries to document her old man's abuse with a secret recording, instead she captures something worse.

Little do we know that when he's shouting at someone over the toxic chemical runoff from the Galentron facility poisoning the aquifers underneath forest conservation land and eventually seeping into the town's water tables...it means something far more sinister. He says it doesn't matter, and these people won't be here long enough to notice.

Except once I hear those words played back from the little device in her shaking hand, I do know.

I know exactly what's going to happen, the way the mayor's truly sold out this town.

I don't know how to tell her.

I don't know how to tell her about SP-73 or how Galentron just might wipe out Heart's Edge on a whim.

I just know I have to stop that shit. My own happiness can't cost more than every life in this town.

Fuck, I *have* to save Clarissa.

Even if it means losing her to save Heart's Edge.

Present

WHAT WOULD my life be if one decision hadn't changed everything?

If I'd stayed complacent, I wouldn't *have* a life.

I'd have died with everyone here.

Or totally gone insane if I was extracted with other Galentron personnel and forced to watch while SP-73 ravaged everyone in this place I've come to care for.

Yeah, I could've just run away with her, but that would've meant leaving everyone else to their fate. Deanna. Gray. Warren. Blake. Ms. Wilma. *So many people.*

Couldn't have lived with that on my conscience, even if Rissa never knew the truth.

So I did what I had to—even if that, too, cost lives. Even if it destroyed any chance I might ever have at rejoining normal society.

So here the fuck I am.

The monster, scarred by flame, too tainted by my past to ever hope she could love me again.

If I'm honest with myself, that's what really has me out here in the dark, staring into the campfire. Clarissa and Zach and the cabin are just dim squares of golden light seeping through the windows.

When she'd wrapped her arms around me, when she'd leaned in close, I wondered.

How could she?

The way she kissed me the other day, is she still seeing the old Leo? The man who still knew how to smile? The man who wasn't warped into a twisted fucking caricature?

If she sees me, truly sees *me,* I don't get how.

Don't get how she could look at me and not be revolted. Not see how destroyed I am, inside and out.

I try not to think about it as I heat water for instant coffee, watching the pot with an intensity born of habit to make sure it doesn't boil over the little camp stove and douse out the flames.

Still, it's impossible to get her off my mind. Clarissa Bell's embedded so deep I'll go to my grave with her name on my lips.

A sharp sound catches my attention, puts all my senses on high alert.

A snapping twig.

It's stealthy, slow, but somebody's out there.

I'm on my feet in an instant, melting into the trees. The sound comes closer—footsteps.

Probably tracking my firelight.

Let 'em.

It'll draw them into the open, where I'll see them first.

Fuck, who am I kidding? There's no *them*.

It's probably Fuchsia, playing her little games and coming to prod me over whether or not I've done her dirty work and cracked the encryption on that drive.

Which means that snapping sound was likely a decoy.

I've never met anyone who can move so silently in stiletto heels, but she wouldn't miss this opportunity to screw with me.

Slowly, I circle to one side. I won't be where she expects. I can't trust her not to show up with a gun and demand all the data she thinks I've uncovered.

Without that info, we lose our chance at getting Deanna back.

One step at a time, I slip into the trees, listening for those hints of movement. Another footstep, another cracking twig, a rustling, and then she comes stepping boldly into the clearing.

Now, it's my turn.

I throw my entire weight forward and slam into her.

Only, Fuchsia isn't over six feet of solid muscle.

And Fuchsia wouldn't shout "Fuck!" in that deep, annoyed voice as she goes down under me.

Warren and I land hard in a tangle just as it registers that it *is* Warren Ford.

Goddammit.

As the dust clears, I push myself up, looking down at him. He glowers up at me, his blue eyes flashing. "The fuck was that for?"

Blake emerges from the trees, grinning. "Someone got lonely out here."

"You're not funny," I mutter, pushing myself to my feet, and then offering Warren a hand. "Sorry. Wasn't expecting anyone."

"Yeah, well, we thought we'd just drop in and check on

things." Grumbling, Warren takes my hand and hauls himself up, then dusts off his jeans and rakes a hand back through his crop of messy black hair. "And Grandma said you're invited to breakfast."

I blink. "Breakfast?"

"Breakfast," Warren repeats, almost grudgingly. "Look, it's Ms. Wilma...don't argue. Just eat."

"Yeah," I say, but I'm already dreading this invitation. It goes without saying it's extended to Clarissa and Zach, too.

Hell, do I even know how to act around people in the light of day? Especially the woman I love and our son?

"Breakfast," I agree, but then beckon to them, sinking down to sit on my stump. "But first, I need to show you this."

* * *

I SHOULDN'T HAVE WORRIED.

I haven't been around Ms. Wilma in a long damn time, but I remember her like yesterday. Even in her eighties, that woman's a force of nature.

She won't *let* people feel uncomfortable around her.

She's everywhere at once, plying us all with bacon, scrambled eggs, pancakes soaked in so much syrup I can smell its sweetness. Zach is already digging in, his face covered in sticky syrup; if he's not careful, he'll get it on his glasses.

I can't help watching him fondly. I want to reach over and wipe his face clean and just hug him till he squeaks, my chest filling up with this warm, wonderful feeling.

Not gonna happen. Not today.

I'm the only one here who knows he's my kid, and I'm not even supposed to know.

Plus, it'd be a little strange for a grown man to start coddling a boy who's supposed to be a stranger. But as I glance up, I catch Rissa watching me.

There's something haunted and longing in her eyes. Something I feel right down to my bones, an answer to this silent ache.

We're gathered here as a family in everything but name.

I'm not ready for the hand tugging at my hood, though, as Ms. Wilma comes sailing past and drops a plate piled high with a lion-sized meal in front of me.

She clucks her tongue. "Oh, do take that hood off, boy. You can't eat like that. You'll make a mess."

My heart goes heavy and still.

The only one I've shown my face to is Clarissa.

I've always managed to keep myself at least half-hidden in front of everyone else.

Shit. I don't want to scare my boy.

But everyone's watching me, the clank of forks against plates suddenly and strangely silent.

There's no malice in their gazes.

Just quiet curiosity, warmth.

These people used to be my friends, and it's the oddest reunion ever. Guess I can't hide forever.

Breathing shallow, I reach up and draw my mask down carefully, then pull my hood back.

There are no gasps. No nervous, flicking eyes. No muffled disgust.

Zach just grins at me, warm and approving. I'd almost think the kid seems *happy* to see my face, his eyes sparkling as he pops a messy, syrup-soggy triangle of pancake into his mouth with his bare fingers.

Then Blake lets out that goofy-ass laugh of his, tilting his head at me. "Looks more like a lion than a tiger, now, I reckon."

Tiger?

My stomach twists. I stare at him, then at Warren. "You guys knew?"

Warren grins. "Yeah. We figured it out a little while ago while we were talking." He stops then, his voice softening. "Welcome home, Leo."

It hurts.

It goddamn hurts in the most beautiful fucking way, how these people accept me like I'm one of them. Ms. Wilma's hand is on my shoulder, squeezing gently, as if to say, *I told you so.*

I look up and see Rissa watching me with that slow, shy smile. It's the same as the first time I saw her when we were kids.

It says she's happy for me.

Hell, *I'm* happy for me.

I duck my head, clearing my throat, unable to stop grinning as I dig into my food.

It's relaxed and comfortable and easy as we all settle in to eat. We pass pitchers and plates around for seconds and top-ups, murmuring to each other.

We're still short three people, but not long after, Haley comes in from putting the baby down and joins us, groaning about her one-year-old making her ravenous. Soon, the whole gang's here as Doc and Ember arrive, claiming their own spots at the table.

Gray's the one who broaches the subject first. He discreetly transfers his soaked pancakes to Ember's plate and replaces them with a stack that *aren't* disintegrating into mush in the syrup.

"So," he says. "From what I understand, we're in a bit of a stalemate."

Warren grunts, propping his chin in his hand. "I don't like it one bit. Anybody who'd kidnap and hurt a woman might start with a cellphone video, but won't take long to move on to body parts."

Clarissa goes pale. I almost wish I hadn't shown Warren and Blake that video.

I make a soft, angry sound in the back of my throat, and Warren looks sheepish.

"Sorry, Rissa," he says, and Haley smacks his arm.

"You're honestly the most insensitive lunk."

"I'm sorry!"

"He does have a point," I growl. "With the cops doing nothing, we're bogged down in a time-consuming gambit when the countdown to Deanna's kidnapper getting impatient can't be that long."

"Every second is a second too long," Clarissa whispers.

It's sweet, how Zach seems to read his mother's mood and leans over to rest his head on her arm, giving his own comfort.

Hell, we shouldn't be talking about this in front of him, but he's a smart kid. He knows something's wrong.

Doc brings everything back on track in his usual brass tacks way. "Our efforts should be twofold. One, we try to crack the encryption on the drive ASAP, so we have our bargaining chip if Galentron's really willing to try an even trade. Two, we try our damnedest to track down the kidnapper and possibly claim the upper hand by saving Deanna ourselves."

"There's one big high-heeled problem with that," I say.

Gray grimaces around a mouthful of eggs. "Don't say her name."

"I kind of have to."

"I don't want to *hear* her name. Not at this table."

"Look, man, not saying her name won't make Fuchsia Delaney go away," I tell him. "And you can bet she's watching our every move with plans of her own. I don't know why she's so dead set on exposing Galentron when she doesn't have a moral bone in her body, but she'd leave Deanna to rot if it meant getting her way. We're just tools to her. We crack the data, we risk giving her what she wants and losing our leverage."

"Then the third part of this," Blake says with a wicked gleam in his eye, "should be keeping Fuchsia busy."

Doc arches a brow. "No more fireworks, please."

"Nahhh, not this time, Doc." Blake spreads his hands with an easygoing grin. "But I bet me and War could make it look like we're onto something. Go do some scouting around, act like we're hunting for something out in the boonies. Make her curious enough to follow us around."

"It'll keep her out of our hair a little longer," I agree, stealing a second for a bite of Ms. Wilma's delicious bacon. "But we still have Nash to worry about."

There's a long silence. Then Clarissa says softly, "Nash is the man on the video. He's the one who took my sister."

I frown. "You're totally sure? He might just be working with the kidnapper."

"No. I know it." Her throat works. "He cornered me and Zach at the museum. He said something about me having lovely hair...just like he said to Deanna. I remembered. It's him."

Such lovely hair.

It hits me in the balls—the memory of Nash's face, fifteen years younger.

Dr. Ross' polished shoe grinding into my cheek, holding me down.

I've disobeyed again.

Refused to respond to my trigger word.

Shut him out.

So I get punished.

But Dr. Ross' golden boy gets a reward, and that reward is me— anything he wants to do to me.

Nash leans down, leering, his smile fucking eerie. He's warped. Kid was crazy long before Dr. Ross got his hands on him, a natural psycho or something.

I think he enjoys this.

And it's with sick pleasure that he strokes my hair back from my bruised and aching face as he growls, "You really do have nice hair."

Then his fingers tighten, digging into my scalp in this harsh grip that nearly rips my hair out, turning my skull into a crown of scorching pain.

I won't scream, but his smile only widens, his eyes gleaming with anticipation.

"It's such a shame I'll have to get it all bloody, now isn't it, Leo-Leo-Lion-boy?"

"—eo. Leo!"

It takes me a second to realize Clarissa's calling my name. I suck in a sharp, chest-scouring breath, blinking as reality resolves around me.

Everyone's staring at me.

Fuck.

Now I remember Nash.

Not everything. *Enough.*

Enough to know exactly why I blocked it all out, buried it deep inside these blank holes in my memory.

We were together in the Nighthawks program.

Kidnapped. Tortured. Conditioned.

I became the rebel.

He was everything they ever wanted.

I swallow this brutal lump in my throat, meeting everyone's eyes.

"Sorry," I bite off. "Sorry, guys. I was just remembering something about Nash. About my childhood."

Ms. Wilma watches me with sympathy. "Did you ever really have a childhood, dearie?"

"Once." I smile faintly. "I think everyone has the chance to be a kid at some point."

"But when that gets stolen away..." She makes a clucking sound, then waves a hand. "Don't mind me. Just an old woman's memories. I recall quite some time ago several families grieving the loss of their missing dumplings."

Yeah. I remember that too. I can tell she's giving me a chance to deflect, and I'll take it.

Because I was one of those missing kids.

Maybe I'll never know who my mother and father were after those memories were torn out of me.

I lock eyes with Rissa.

With the way she's watching me, maybe it's not too late to make some new memories after all.

XVII: WRONG TURN (CLARISSA)

I can't sit still.

Believe me, I'm trying.

Trying because I still want to keep this ugliness from touching Zach, from frightening him, from exposing him to the very real chance his Auntie Deanna could die.

That's why I'm settled in with Ms. Wilma in her garden, lingering with my boy long after Warren and Blake left to keep Fuchsia busy and possibly even draw Nash's attention as well. Leo's also gone, back to working on the drive's encryption, while Doc and Ember head over to The Menagerie to keep up appearances for anyone watching.

Doc said he has some contacts he could reach out to, but it'll take time.

Communications could be monitored. We can't risk creep-o Nash picking up on what we're doing to try to outmaneuver him.

I shiver with a chill that has nothing to do with the autumn air.

Here in Ms. Wilma's sunny atrium, it's still summery hot. The glass traps the heat to make a greenhouse out of her little garden.

Such lovely hair. I can't stop replaying that horrible phrase.

The way he looked at me, the fact that he knew my name...I should've trusted that prickle on the back of my neck and done something besides run.

Deep down, I think I knew.

Knew Nash was the one.

He took my sister, and then toyed with me like the gruesome psychopath he is.

I'm scared for Deedee every second she's in his clutches. He's someone truly dangerous. Someone Leo *remembers*, though he's still full of so many secrets and won't quite tell me how, or all the details of the Nighthawks program and what happened to him as a kid.

I still can't believe he was there growing up.

It shouldn't be possible. I know every freaking inch of those underground chambers, minus a few doors that were sealed up in the 1800s and never opened.

There's just no way that sweet boy I remember, that boy I played with, that boy I loved was being tortured right below where I slept every night. Him, and who knows how many other kids.

I press my knuckles to my mouth, watching Zach as he creeps through the cattails around the pond, his eyes riveted on a mayfly perched on one stalk. He's about the same age Leo was when I first met him as Tiger.

Maybe the overprotective, frightened mother in me can't stop thinking about someone snatching him away because he's so special. What if they want to use that bright, wonderful brain of his for their own nefarious purposes? Just like his father.

I can't breathe.

It's not real, I know. For now, it's just my imagination, but it was *so* real for Leo.

Even if I can't go back in time and reverse what happened to him, it hurts.

I wish I had the superpower to save the child he'd once been, but since I can't, now there's just one thing on my mind.

I want to protect him, to cherish the man he's become.

I'll come clean with him as soon as we find Deanna. I *will*.

That's my promise.

Once my little sister's home, I'll celebrate by telling Leo about Zach.

And then maybe one fine day I'll *finally* be brave enough to admit Zach's not the only one who needs this huge, snarly, hero-man in his life.

"Looks like you've got something on your mind, dear," Ms. Wilma says, sitting on the little wire park bench at my side.

Her warm, gentle voice pulls me from my thoughts.

I glance over at her, biting my lip before offering a wan smile. "Guess I'm still thinking about those kids. You know, those old rumors, the ones who went missing? It hits me harder now that I have a kid of my own."

"You don't have anything to worry about with Zach." She reaches over and squeezes my hand. She's so old I can feel the bones of her fingers through her papery skin, but there's still a strength and warmth to her touch that's comforting. "Between you, that strapping group of young lads, and me, there's no one who'd dare look at him."

"I hope so." I squeeze her hand, grateful for the reassurance. "I really do."

"I dare say young Leo wouldn't even think of letting it happen, anyway. He was such a lost child himself."

The way she says it is so offhand, so casual, it's almost too deliberate. I swallow, my mouth suddenly dry and sticky.

Does she know?

About Leo, about Zach, about everything?

There's no telling with this town's wise old owl. She's always been too keen. People always just let things slip by her without even meaning to, until somehow she knows everything and often picks up on things way before anyone else.

I don't know what to say.

I can't talk about this, about Leo, about our son to someone else before I talk to Leo himself.

So I only squeeze her hand again and smile. "I'm sure he wouldn't. But there haven't been any disappearances for years, have there?"

"No, dear." Her fingers tighten in mine. "And between us girls, we'll make sure no one's ever taken in this town again. Including your sister. My promise, Clarissa. Keep the faith and we'll find her and bring her home safe."

"I wish I could," I murmur—before something hits me like a bolt from the blue.

Wait. If Leo was hidden beneath the mansion all those years...

What else could I find there?

Maybe, just maybe something that will point me to Deanna, or breaking into that hard drive.

I have to try. I can't just sit here and do nothing.

And Ms. Wilma watches me with knowing, curious eyes as I stand up. "Would you mind keeping an eye on Zach for a few hours?" I ask, and she smiles.

"Darling, I was wondering when you'd finally ask. Take all the time you need."

* * *

GETTING into the museum is trickier this time.

Oh, it's open, but that's not the problem.

Trouble is, it's the middle of the day. There's a class of third-graders here for a school trip and way too many attendants and volunteers showing them around.

I can't exactly blend in, not when my portrait's in the main exhibit room. But I need to get belowground.

For a little bit I trail around after the kids, close enough so anyone who doesn't know the group would assume I'm with them, but far enough away so the teachers won't think I'm suspicious.

Keeping my head down to hide my too-recognizable face, I make a show of looking at the paintings, the exhibits, everything from old silver mining equipment to the broken plow that was said to belong to the very first settler who broke ground on farmland in Heart's Edge.

Then comes the presentation about the famous cliffs.

Something stings my eyes. I remember standing on that cliff, watching pale-blue petals scatter in the breeze with the weight of his ring on my finger and the warmth of his hand in mine and our perfect start laid out before us. A future broken. A life shattered. A cruel fate that—no.

I shake my head.

Right. Focus. *Focus.*

There were stairs to the subterranean level, but they're in the second floor hall, in sight of a little manned brochure stand. No way I can just sneak downstairs past the staff.

But what about that ancient dumbwaiter in my old bedroom?

That'll work, if I can fit.

I see my chance as the tour group swarms upstairs with me in their wake. They shuffle from bedroom to bedroom, and as they leave my old room now dominated with a stuffed bear, I move.

Slipping behind the open door, I hide myself between it and the wall until I'm sure the room is clear and no one's around to notice my snooping.

Then I head over to the dumbwaiter that used to be a portal to safety.

It's easier to open than I expect. Almost like it's *been* opened more than once over the years.

Probably just maintenance. Enough to keep it limbered up, the door slides up into its housing with barely a sound.

The little wooden box inside is smaller than I remember.

No, let's be real. *I'm a lot bigger.*

An adult woman, all legs and curves, and fitting in there is going to *hurt*.

Sighing, I glance over my shoulder, then bend to stoop and ease myself into the box, folding myself up one leg at a time.

I end up contorted in a weird position with my shoulders against the roof and my head between my knees, crunched up in every spare bit of space, but I manage.

Barely.

Oh crap—someone's coming.

I quickly slam the door shut.

Aaaaand accidentally hit the release with the heel of my palm.

Awesome. Next thing I know, I'm plummeting.

My stomach drops out and I scream. I bite it back, just barely.

It's really not going that fast. I just wasn't expecting it, and it scared the living crap out of me for half a second before I take a deep breath and tell myself to calm down.

It's not like the rope isn't already old.

It's not like I weigh twice as much as I did the last time I crawled in here as a girl.

It's not like the dumbwaiter isn't old as hell.

Oh God, I'm gonna die down here, aren't I? Then Leo will have to raise Zach alone.

My heart pounds a mile a minute as the thing creaks down an inch at a time. There's a terrifying jolt when the rope goes slack and drops me several inches at once.

I slam my palms into the sides and brace. But it slows a second later and then after another minute or two of creaking and fitful stops and starts...

There's a quiet *bump* under me. I feel solid ground, darkness opening up to one side of me.

I breathe in, and immediately choke on the musty, dusty scent of old places. It's faintly wet down here, mildewy, and my nose stings. I unlimber myself and crawl out into blackness, dirt and cobwebs sticking to my hands, made ten times worse by touching them in the dark.

Ew.

Staggering to my feet, I fumble for my phone and finally fish it out of my jacket and flip on flashlight mode. It lights up bright enough to hurt my eyes, but as they adjust, I turn the phone over, letting its cool white beam sweep through the space.

It's almost like I remember.

Just a little darker, a little colder, a little more run down.

I'm in a narrow hallway with wood wainscoting, old Victorian-era wallpaper peeling away from walls littered with water stains and bleeding mildew. Several old paintings molder away, tilted in their frames, while dark squares on the walls show where others used to be.

The rafters are a mess of cobwebs, feathery strings of silk.

I shudder, moving on down the hall, creeping slowly.

This place would be a haunted house nightmare to anybody else, imagining terrible hollow-eyed things in the shadows. But for me and Deanna, the monsters in our imagination were a fun thrill, a relief compared to the *real* monster hiding behind our father's fake smile.

And even now, I can't help the warm nostalgia as I step down the tattered carpet runner in the hall, sweeping my light from side to side.

This old portion of the house has two levels.

One that used to be the cramped underground servants' quarters, abandoned decades ago as seeping groundwater wrecked rooms that hadn't been used since the mining days. The other level below this is the sub-basement, the place where we used to store household stuff that's just a debris field now.

We'd mostly play in the halls of the living quarters. We never forgot Papa warning us once that the water damage undermined the foundation.

We had nightmares aplenty about hitting a support beam, making the entire building collapse.

Although sometimes, I think I wanted it to, with our father still inside.

There's no sign anyone's been down here in ages. So I make my way down the hall, peeking into the open rooms.

Nope, not even the museum staff have visited these parts. The dust is thick, choking. None of the ancient furniture or trinkets left in the bedrooms and communal bath were moved since I last saw them nearly a decade ago.

If there's a clue...I don't think it's here.

But just to be sure, I take the rickety stairs at the foot of the hall, testing each step gingerly to see if it'll hold my weight, heading deeper into the gloom.

My steps echo ominously.

I can't help how my heart shudders, even if I know I'm alone.

It's different down here alone.

This game isn't like the old hide-and-go-seek we'd play when it's Deanna's *life.*

The sub-basement is one huge space. Its walls are carved right out of deep bedrock, glistening and wet with accumulated runoff water.

I beam my light over them. A few small hallways lead off into more storage rooms and a couple of locked doors I was never able to open as a child.

Now, it's no different. The doors won't budge.

I shove at the lock plate and handle on one, trying to get the rotting wood to give way, but it *Just. Won't. Move.*

Frustrated, grunting, I smack against the door, then check the others.

No luck.

But as I check the heavy door at the end of the longest hall, there's a sudden cold draft. It wafts over my neck and face, making the thin beads of sweat forming on my skin crystallize like ice drops.

I whirl around, whipping the light back and forth, my heart slamming my ribs.

No one there.

But then where did that draft come from?

I bite my lip. I swear I felt it on my right side, just as I was turning away.

The same side facing that thick slab of a door.

I creep closer to it, squinting. It's solid oak, carefully reinforced with iron bands and bolts, no openings, and the padlock covering the latch looks rusted into an immovable lump.

Maybe the draft came from under the door?

But then there shouldn't *be* a draft coming from a fully enclosed underground room at all.

Something doesn't add up.

Frowning, I feel around the edges of the door, prying at the spot where it fits into the frame, but it's seamless, practically swollen in place from repeated waterlogging.

Annoyed, I slam my shoulder into it, showering grit and cobwebs down on my head.

Nope, not even a *fraction* of movement.

All I'm getting is a bruised shoulder.

Frowning, I step back, eyeing the wall, then decide to call out.

"Helloooo?!"

My own voice is deafening. There's no sound when the echo dies.

Nothing but a faint, far-off trickle of water, like there's a stream running underground somewhere beyond the passageway. Something about that sound prickles a memory. Long buried.

But when I try to dig deeper, it's just not there.

I've blanked out so much of my old life from before the night my father died. A clean razor cut separates the me before that night and the me after, leaving so much behind. Including these memories I can't quite *remember*.

But there's a whisper of my mom's voice, for some reason.

I don't know why.

And I can't hear anything else, straining so hard to listen.

I know no one's down here. It's unthinkable.

But some scared, hopeful, needy part of me begs Deedee to answer anyway.

"Hello?"

I jump when I hear it. My entire body prickles, sizzling, hair standing on end.

It's so faint it might be my own imagination.

Then I realize it has to be my voice. Just a faint, delayed echo coming back, falling down from the rafters.

I deflate, disappointment heavy as a stone inside me.

Ugh.

Deep down, I knew this was hopeless. But I had to *try*.

Though as I turn away, I can't help glancing back, lingering on the door. There are so many secrets I still don't know about this house. Does Leo know what's on the other side of that passage since I don't?

My pulse skips a little as I make my way back up. One step sagging under my weight sends me scurrying up faster.

But as I make my way through the hall toward the stairs, on an idle whim, I stop to check behind a painting. It's an old Monet reprint. Deanna and I used to leave notes for each other in our little code language tucked behind the paintings, a different one every time.

Maybe we forgot one?

But when I lift the painting out, what falls out isn't an old, yellowed bit of notepaper.

It's clean. It's new. It's a business letterhead from Sweeter Things.

Holy hell.

I gasp, staring in disbelief as it falls to the floor. Tremors shoot electricity down my fingertips as I dive to catch it, then flip the folded sheet open.

But I don't understand.

It's just a series of black dots. All scattered over the page, bits of ink with letters and numbers written next to them in Deanna's handwriting. One says *HR2491*, another *HR2618*, all the others the same—HR followed by four numbers.

This is something. Some kind of message.

I couldn't even guess what it means.

But maybe it's something that can help unlock that drive.

A thrill runs through me. I won't quite call it *excitement*, but it's definitely close to *hope*.

I double back and check the other paintings, but there's nothing else to find. Then dashing for the stairs, I move by the bouncing, bobbing light of my phone, and clatter up into the public areas, bursting into the brightly lit hallway without even thinking.

Only to come face-to-face with a startled-looking girl in a museum uniform t-shirt, staring at me with wide eyes set above a freckled, snub nose.

Her surprise lasts only for a second before she frowns. "Hey, Miss, you're not supposed to be in there!"

"S-sorry!" I throw back, stumbling over my words. I stuff the note into my jacket before she can see it, then offer a sheepish smile. "I was just looking for the bathroom and got lost. Can you point me in the right direction?"

She looks like she doesn't believe me.

I wouldn't believe me, either, considering I'm a frazzled mess, nearly bouncing to get out of here.

After a moment, though, she points me toward the first-floor level. "Down there, second hall, third door."

"Thanks!" I chirp, trying not to break into a *run* as I stride quickly for the stairs and, the moment I'm sure she can't see me, bolt for the door.

I've got to get to Leo.

Between us, we can figure this out. I just know it.

We can bring Deanna home.

* * *

I FIND Leo hunched over the laptop at the cabin, his hood flipped back for once.

The last few days, he tends to hide his face even around me, though he's doing it less this morning, ever since he showed his face at the table.

Is it finally happening? The dawning realization that we all love him just as he is?

It was such a beautiful moment at Ms. Wilma's.

But those eyes go wide as I come bursting in, nearly slamming the door open. He jerks his head up, on his feet in seconds.

"Clarissa?" he growls, striding toward me. "What's wrong? Are you hurt?"

"What? No—no, I—" I shake my head and fish the note from inside my jacket, flattening it against his chest with a breathless, eager noise. "I *found* something. Look at this."

His brows furrow. He looks at me oddly for a second before moving the note, his fingers grazing my hand in rough sparks before letting go as he peers down at the paper.

His mouth creases in a deep frown. He strokes his fingers over his beard and the whorls of scars lower on his neck.

"Where'd you find this?"

"The basement levels back at the old house. Remember I told you when Deanna and I were little, we'd play down there? We'd leave each other coded notes, too. I went looking for...I don't even know. This turned up."

"A clue," he whispers, soft and understanding. "Hope."

"Yeah." I smile sheepishly. "Something like that." I want to ask him about the padlocked room, too, but not yet. Not now. "Just for a nostalgia kick, I peeked behind a painting and it fell right out."

He's staring at the paper intently. I can almost see the wheels turning behind his eyes. He grunts, his frown deepening. "This was the only one?"

"Yeah. I checked the other paintings. Nothing else." Biting my lip, I scrub one hand against my other arm. "What do you think it means?"

"Not coordinates. Not this time," he muses before sucking in a breath. "*Oh*. Oh, shit."

I perk, something bright and hopeful flaring through me. "Oh?"

"These are stars. Old star designations. Hardly anyone knows the Yale Bright Star Catalog anymore, but hell." His eyes tick back and forth rapidly. He drags his free hand through his wild, shaggy hair. "I know it. This one's Sirius, the Dog Star. This one's Adhara, Wezen, Mirham, and here's Canis Major. The Greater Dog."

"Um, *how* do you know that?" I ask, blinking.

He smiles a bit grimly, almost embarrassed. "You'd be surprised at the weird shit stuffed in my head. Had to entertain myself some way growing up like I did." He shakes his head. "It's a constellation, but that doesn't lead us anywhere. You need more than just one to navigate. You need latitude or longitude, angle of degrees to the constellation..."

"So maybe it's not supposed to be a map," I say. "Maybe it's a message."

"For what?"

"The password on the drive?" Am I totally off my rocker here? I'm smart, but not the kind of uncanny genius Leo is. But I venture slowly, "Kids play word games all the time. We did. So maybe we need a word or a phrase associated with the stars."

His shoulders go stiff, and he looks at me oddly. It's like he's seeing me for the first time. Then that fierce, determined smile of his that I've always loved curls his lips. "Let's give it a shot."

We're at the laptop in seconds. Him settled in front of it, me bending over him, watching over his shoulder as he brings up the program he's been trying to use to crack the code.

"Try CanisMajor," I say, and he taps it in quickly, then hits Enter. The password field starts flashing through letters and numbers, upper and lowercase versions of the letters, plus a few numbers. I frown. "What's it doing?"

"Trying variants," he says. "If I input a phrase, in a matter of seconds, the program can test tons of variations that randomize upper and lower case, punctuation, and numbers."

Soon it's done.

Nada.

It beeps a big red error. So we try DogStar, we try Greater-Dog, we try DogConstellation, we even try BigDog and get back nothing.

Crap. It's not working.

"Maybe it's not a password," he says, huffing out a frustrated breath. "Maybe it's something else."

"No—no, she left the paper where I'd look for it. She had to know what I'd guess if this really was Deanna." I chew my lower lip, pacing back and forth behind his chair. Think, *think.* "She left that Nighthawks message about Nash in the same code we used as kids. She hid the note in the same place we hid. So it's got to be something we'd think of as children, but not as adults."

"Largest breed of dog," Leo says.

I stop pacing, staring at him. "Uh, what?"

"Canis Major. Greater dog. What's the largest breed of dog in the world?"

"I have no idea."

He smirks. "For once, neither do I, but that's what Mr. Google's for."

He's quick on the keys, but I'm faster on my phone, whipping it out and tapping away in a quick search. "English Mastiff! Also known as the Old English Mastiff."

"Let's give it a shot," he tells me.

He taps it in fast and lets it run—nothing on English Mastiff. Nothing on Old English Mastiff.

Just a big fat red nothing.

Crud.

I'm about to give up when something hits me. "Wait. Wait,

the constellation names are in Latin, what about the Latin name for dog?"

Leo rubs at his chin again. "Dogs don't really have individual Latin names for the breeds. They're all just *canis lupus familiaris*."

"*Try it*," I urge. There's a hunch running through me like a high-voltage current. I don't want to quit now, so I lean over him, his body heat soaking into me as I stare at the screen. "Maybe it's not about the *big dog*, maybe it's just that we needed the big dog idea to lead us on a U-turn back to this."

He looks skeptical but amused. "This shit's next level, Rissa. You and your sis should've been cryptographers," he says, typing it in. *CanisLupusFamiliaris*.

Enter.

Numbers flash by, and then...

Password Accepted.

My heart stops just long enough to hear the complete and utter silence that settles over the cabin.

I let out a triumphant squeal that startles even *me*, flinging myself at Leo in a bear hug. "Oh my *God,* we did it!"

He lets out a stunned laugh, rising to catch me, meeting me like we're on the same wavelength. His strong arms bundle around me, turning us around in a wild, sweet spin that lifts me off my feet and makes my heart soar.

"We did," he gasps, burying his face in my hair. "We figured it out. Don't know what we'll find, but I know it's going to lead us to Deanna."

Maybe it's joy.

Maybe it's his confidence.

Maybe it's the first real feeling like something might go right, and I've actually done something to help save my sister instead of just sitting back and passively waiting.

But the feeling that surges through me can't be contained.

Before I can even think, second-guess myself, I kiss him like mad.

I half expect him to push me away. Everything's been so

strange between us since the last kiss, those wounded words, the way we pulled away.

Not this time.

When my mouth crashes against his, he collides back.

If I'm kindling, he's all fire.

Leo growls, claiming my mouth, and it feels perfect and right and fantabulous in a way I haven't felt in *years.*

It's how we used to be.

Pure, scorching inferno, consuming every spare inch of skin.

We'd tear each other apart, twined into a mess of need and rolling bodies and clinging hands.

And then we'd be so soft in the afterglow.

The calm after the storm, when the night goes clear and quiet and the thunder is just a rumble on the distant horizon.

But right now, that thunder grinds out scalding hot between us, roaring and crashing in the heat of our breaths and the tangling of our bodies as we crush against each other, holding on like starving animals given the one thing we've needed for years.

And God, do I *need* Leo.

There's never been another man.

Never anyone else.

Never another beast who can sate me like he does. So thick, so hot, so wild.

Filling me until my entire world centers on his wall of a body and his cock takes me completely. I remember like it was yesterday and want it right now, even as my hands slip under his clothes to find ridged scars, hard muscle, the perfect rippling cords of his power under his animal skin.

We don't need words.

We never have.

We know each other too well, and we speak in moving hands and gasping sighs and biting teeth and twining tongues. We tuck in and tear each other to pieces.

He hoists me up with those huge arms I've missed. So

perfect, so powerful. I wrap my legs around his waist, digging my fingers into his hair, sealing his mouth to mine with a moan.

Holy Toledo.

But he's always done this to me.

Made me forget the scared, shy Clarissa who crept around like a mouse, afraid of making too much noise.

I'm not that girl anymore. I'm a woman who stands on her own two feet, made stronger by the years apart.

But he still finds something inside me, some core wildness I'd never show anyone but him.

"Fuck," he grunts into my mouth, his huge hands winding to my ass. Then his fingers push between my legs, cupping my throbbing mound, and squeeze.

Oh, he makes me *howl.*

Clothing tears away as we fumble to the bedroom together. First, it's clutched in his hands, then it's thrown to the floor as he tumbles me down on my bed in nothing but my panties and bra and slick, needy heat.

I don't even know when I tore through his shirt. Don't know how his desire gave me strength, but it hangs off him with a huge gash across it. I'm so shocked by how bad I want him I just flush.

Leo smiles darkly, rips it away, and covers my body with his.

The tight, bulky taper of his torso crushes my breasts. He's sculpted so gorgeously that the tattoos and scars stamped across his body are more like living art, a firestorm taming the skin that just accents the sensual, bestial shape of his body.

His weight is almost crushing. Hot. Frantic.

Divine.

And even if it's been years, I still *know* him.

Know this is where I've ached to be for eight flipping years, buried under this mountain of his body in a wall of protection, desire, love.

God, I've never stopped loving him.

And it's that fueling my fire so raw, making me burn so fiercely.

He looks down at me, his eyes wide and wicked. It's the gaze of a lion before it devours.

I know that look.

Just like I know what he'll do to me. My pussy aches with the anticipation tingling through me as he smiles slowly, devilishly, baring his teeth in the shadows.

And they *feel devilish* too as they descend on my body, leaving me writhing.

Soon, molten points of pleasure and painful teasing leave my whole body trembling as he leaves *marks.*

My neck. My shoulders. The upper curve of my breasts, the vulnerable crook of my elbow, the soft expanse of my belly, my calves, my inner thighs. *Oh, hell!*

There's no denying it. He knows every forbidden place because he's the one who taught me how sensitive they were in the first place.

And he knows how to make me beg for him, reminding me what it's like to be *his.*

There's possession in every love bite.

Every nip of his teeth brands me in terrible, wonderful ways, leaving behind spots that throb and burn on their own. Then his sinful mouth presses on another place, and another, and I'm just *gone.*

Lost. So wet and tingling, my nipples peaked and hot, and yet he touches me everywhere *but* there.

Everywhere but those sweet, sweet points that can hurl me over the edge.

"Leo!" I hiss, dragging my nails through his hair, over his back, his shoulders. *"Don't."*

Don't tease me, I think.

I've waited so long. Even another minute is too freaking much.

We can play later—because I already know I can't let go of

this again. Another time, we'll slowly rediscover each other's bodies and relish skin like fine wine.

Right now, I just want what I've been missing.

I want it as fast, as hard, and as savage as he'll bring it.

And understanding flickers in his violet eyes as he presses a searing, sucking kiss below my navel, making me whimper because the meaning is crystal clear.

It's so on.

Leo pushes himself up and kisses me harder. His big, rough hands engulf me, making me feel fragile and protected and so wanted as he takes control.

He knows my breasts. Every knead, every stroke, every flick of his tongue sends raw lightning through my blood. His fingertips play at my nipples, smoothing the marks he'd left earlier.

This man is too good.

Every bit of me feels riled. Then his tongue delves into my mouth in hot, rhythmic, teasing flicks. It's almost mocking as he mimics the rhythm of my want, the soft murmurs I can't hold in.

My needy body grinds against him, my pussy against his huge thigh, begging *please, please, please* with every movement. He pushes a growl down my throat, his cock rubbing hard.

Bastard.

He's a beautiful, savage bastard, keying me up until he knows I'm on the verge of losing my mind.

"Leo," I whimper. He looks at me through narrow eyes, amusement and lust fencing in his eyes. They're almost the shade of purple lightning right now.

Mercy.

He's reduced me to this. No pride, no dignity, just animal *wanting*.

And the worst part? I kinda like it.

There's never been a need for games with him. I know when I give him all of me, he'll handle it as preciously as my heart.

Maybe it's missing him that makes it more powerful.

Maybe it's how long my body's been deprived.

Maybe it's just his cock's friction coming harder, and I *swear* he feels bigger than I remember.

But when he draws my lower lip into his mouth to suck at the exact same moment when his hand slips down between us and two thick, heavy fingers part my pussy folds and dart inside with wild familiarity, I can't.

I break.

Shatter in this clutching, gasping, slick, and oh-so-spontaneous release. My cunt pinches tight around his fingers and I throw my hips into him, taking his fingers, grinding out an O that hits like a fever storm.

Coming!

And that storm has so much heat, ripping right through me, reducing me to a sizzling mess.

"Shit, Rissa," he growls against my mouth, his deep-rumbling voice doing terrible things to me, all part of that wave that crashes over me and doesn't let me go. "Still so tight, so damned ready, aren't you? Tell me since your pussy can't lie."

I almost can't answer—because he won't let me come down.

I'm just caught in this trembling high, trapped in the moment of coming undone, throbbing everywhere. Legs thrashing, toes curled, raking the sheets with my nails as my blood rushes through me in one loud sensuous *scream.*

And he pins me there with those devious fingers, strumming my clenching heat with twisted thrusts and strokes that ride the waves of an endless orgasm.

I can't flipping breathe!

He's too good, too hot, and he knows exactly *how* to drive me into ecstasy. How to leave me gushing, flooding, mindless, shrieking my pleasure to the rafters.

I hate-love every second of this.

It's torture and pleasure all at once, but it's still not what I want.

It's still not *him* in all his beastly, intimate fullness.

Just when I think I'll die, he stops.

But only long enough for the rasp of a zipper, a crinkle of a condom wrapper.

A kiss, so tender, so right, our lips wet and swollen and slick. I sink my teeth into his bottom lip, panting, *begging*.

"Leo, *please*," I whisper.

I don't know how I'm holding back from just mounting myself on him. I feel his cock pressed against me, a wickedly familiar sensation my body remembers like the sound of my own voice.

But he doesn't make me wait anymore.

His fingers dig into my hips in that rough way I love, he pins me down with a reckless strength I crave, and then—oh, *yeah* —then he fills me.

For just a second, the sensation blinds me.

His cock sinks deep, stretching me apart. All eight lonely, sexless years go up in a blaze of Leo's beast-sized glory returning home.

I'm not used to it anymore.

Not ready for how it feels to be split open by his thickness, his sheer size. My own fingers and every battery-operated play-thing I've had are a *joke* compared to his cock-head stretching me open, his flared edge rooted deep inside, the ridges of his dick branding themselves on my inner walls.

"Fuck!" he snarls, like the memory of how it used to be hits him too. "Need this, Rissa. Need every tight inch of you. Need it more than I need goddamn air."

My pussy clenches around him, one mind to our own lust.

My whimpering peaks, breaks off, turns into shuddering gasps as the initial shock of him lances through me. Then it melts in the pit of my stomach, reforges itself into a spear of the most divine pleasure *ever*.

I don't know how I hold all of him.

It's like he never ends, going deeper and deeper, conquering places inside of me no other man ever could, filling me in ways that border on *rampage*.

He's holding me the entire time, those huge, inked, roughed up hands locked on my hips.

Leo pulls me into every thrust, wringing his pleasure from my body, using me so hard and so sweet I never want him to stop.

He grunts louder, showering my face in hot kisses, his breath panting and raspy and harsh. "There's my Rissa. There's my girl. Never gonna miss you again. Never, ever gonna miss *this.*"

Then his mouth rules mine, stealing the sound of lusty, conflicted heartbreak in the back of my throat.

Rock-hard muscle falls around me, crushing my breasts, my body, the softness of me into the bed.

And I'm trying not to cry when I wrap my arms and legs around him, pulling him into me, bringing him home as deep as I can.

We're two crashing plates then. Human tectonics. Lovers prodded into the wildest, most emotional horizontal tango of our lives because we're sharing every last freaking feel in the book.

His cock comes faster, harder, pushing me past *oh my God* and into *oh hell.* It's perfect velvet on iron, rough friction building like a static charge, two hips and tongues locked and loaded.

And the pace just ticks faster, until we're frantic, wild, *crazed.*

We're burning each other down, and I know it's worth it when my first O hits on his cock.

Snarling, he buries himself deep, lifting me up and throwing me back into the mattress. His hips crash into mine so hard it almost hurts, but it's the delicious kind of ache.

My vision goes white and my mouth opens to scream, but I'm too breathless.

Coming!

His pubic bone grinds into my clit. Every stroke is a fresh new hit of this man, an avalanche of fire, a heaping slice of sweet, feral lion-man.

Before, with him, I thought I knew good sex.

But this? What he's doing to me tonight with his teeth pulling at my lip, growling with every thrust, grinding himself into me like I'm marked forever?

This is *next freaking level.*

And I can't think anymore. Can't do anything but *feel* in the maelstrom of his ink and muscle and swearing strokes, and it feels *glorious.*

Cataclysmic, maybe.

There's no question he's a beast, my lion, and he mauls me with his love. He turns me over when I'm done coming, shifts back inside me, and delivers a crisp *smack* to one side of my butt. Then those manic thrusts of his drive home, drive higher, and push me dangerously close to another sheet-clenching finish.

Frick. I want to hold out longer, but after this endless pleasure flux, after I've waited so many years to feel him again...

I don't have a chance.

Not when he owns my body this hard, teaching me how it feels to be re-broken in, used hard, loved harder.

Not when our pleasure has *teeth*, digging into me with every frantic thrust that makes me feel filthy and like I've been purified.

Not when he's everything I ever need.

And he fists my hair, pulls my face back to his, and delivers another mind-bending kiss. I only tear my mouth from his so I can scream his name, telling the whole universe I'm his, as he slams deeper and deeper to his own growly finish.

"Come with me, Rissa. Come on. Come the fuck *now!*"

Everything goes white as he plunges to the hilt, burying his swelling cock in me.

Then the best climax of my life rips through me like a bursting dam, years of tension expelled in a single moment. His cock twitches, his whole body shudders, one groaning mountain spilling his own pleasure into me.

Every part of me goes to pieces, shredded, just ashes left of my nerves.

Five minutes ago, I was utterly destroyed, but he wasn't done.

Not until that moment, as my inner walls clutch around him, locking us together in our rapture.

He's in the same moment, his whole body shuddering with this perfect intensity.

I'm breathless. He's one big snarl. Just like before, but *better.*

That's how it goes as we fuse into our own pleasure, crashing down into the deep, cool darkness.

XVIII: NEW DIRECTIONS (NINE)

I can't comprehend what the fuck just happened.

Only know I'm not upset it did.

Fuck it. I'm not even trying to play it cool. Right now, after what happened between me and Clarissa Bell, I feel like stomping around and beating my chest. Full Tarzan.

I feel like a whole new man again for the first time in a damn eternity.

What the hell it means, who knows. Us tumbling into each other's arms like this, her kissing me real sweet, touching me like my scarred, warped body somehow brings her off.

But I saw how she came like lightning. There was no faking that.

I should be royally freaked right about now. But the only thing that truly freaks me out is the thought that the hottest sex of my life is a one-hit wonder.

This can't just be a fiery trip down memory lane.

I'm not closing the door as soon as we're done.

Hell, I shouldn't even be thinking about this.

I should be looking through the data on that drive. Figuring out how it'll help us find Deanna, stop Nash, and intercept whatever Galentron plans to do that makes burying this info so important.

Not gonna beat myself up over bending to Rissa's siren call, though.

Especially when she's tucked close in my arms, our bodies cooling as sweat dries on our skin, her naked flesh so smooth against mine.

The contrast is fascinating. Her velvety skin slides against the gnarls and whorls of my scars. Her pastel white tone glows against the dark and the weathered tan that's part of me now after so many years in the wild.

Rissa tangles our legs and traces her fingers down my chest, following the patterns etched across my body. Looks like I'm not the only one fascinated.

"Have you been practicing?" she teases softly. "Because you've gotten better at that."

I snort. "So you're saying I wasn't any good before?"

"Oh, you were amazing." Laughing softly, she tilts her head to rest her chin on my shoulder and looks at me. Her hair's a wild mess, her green eyes glitter, like this Venus sent down to remind me what love feels like. "Maybe I'm just deprived."

"Maybe I was, too." I linger on her face, on her softness, the way her lips purse with repressed laughter, pink and light and lush. "Haven't had anyone since you, Clarissa. No one."

Her smile fades, leaving a wide-eyed, startled blush. "Leo..."

Whatever she'd been about to say gets cut off by the sound of the front door banging, and Zach calling out. *Shit.*

"Mom?" His footsteps carry from the living room. "Ms. Wilma wants to know if you're coming to the house for dinner?"

Muffling silent laughs, we break apart, scrambling for our clothes.

"Just a minute, baby!" she calls, grabbing her panties and yanking them on.

I can't help but reach out, snagging my fingertip in the waistband of the lacy little thing that made me go wild when I saw her half-dressed. "You dress like this all the time now?"

She bats at my hand playfully. "Behave. And let me have my indulgences. Single moms don't get to feel sexy often."

I arch a brow, hoisting up my jeans. "So were you waiting for a chance to show those off? I'm a lucky damn dude."

That wide-eyed look comes back, before she ducks her head, her hair falling forward to shade her face as she fastens her bra. "There's never been anyone else for me either, Leo," she murmurs.

Then she tugs her shirt on and slips past, almost escaping me, though I catch a glimpse of her red face, her breathless lips.

Does she even realize what she's just admitted?

What she's just confirmed, even if I had my suspicions? It knocks the breath out of me and leaves me frozen, elated, terrified, awed, and fucking confused.

Because she's just erased any and all doubts.

Zach's mine.

All the more reason I'll die before I let my family go to pieces again.

* * *

IT'S A QUIET NIGHT.

We do dinner at the main house. It's strange for me to blend in like I *belong*.

Doesn't leave me much chance to look at the data, though it's hard to care with good company. By the time we get back to the cabin, Zach's falling asleep.

He'd been riding on my shoulders. The boy's like a cat. He digs being up high and will climb the tallest thing around, whether it's a tree or me.

But once I know he's dozing, I swing him down into my arms, and hold him cradled against my chest, his little breaths tickling my neck as I follow Rissa down the trail through the trees.

Shit, he feels so right, so perfect, and I'm bleeding a little inside.

My *son*.

My son, safe in my arms, with his fingers curled tight in the front of my coat.

Like he doesn't want to let me go.

I have to pry him free when I finally settle him down in his room, tugging off his shoes before I tuck him in. His small fingers knit even tighter. I gently peel them loose one at a time, laying them against his blanket and resting my hand to his head.

"Sleep tight, little man," I whisper. "Good night."

And some deep, painful part of me wants more than anything to hear him say, *Good night, Dad*.

So I watch him sleep for a minute or two.

It's easy to see the blend of her features and mine with the last doubt erased. My stubborn jaw, her nose. My dark violet eyes, her hair.

A long time ago, we made something beautiful together.

That something made some*one* even more precious.

He stirs, turning over, and I stroke his hair back from his brow.

You'll be okay, I promise. *Never gonna let anything happen to you. Won't let the things that hurt me touch you.*

Not you, and not your mother.

Fuck. Speaking of those things...

I can't let anyone at Galentron figure out he's my son. They'd jump at the chance to study the effects of their sick conditioning and unknown drugs on my kid, passed down to the next generation.

They won't turn my son into a lab rat.

I'll kill everyone in the entire company before I let that happen.

A soft sound at the door warns me I'm not alone. I lift my

head, looking up to find Clarissa watching us with her heart in her eyes.

Tell me, I want to ask. *Tell me he's mine so we can make something out of this.*

Slowly, I stand to join her in the dark hallway.

She only smiles, her eyes pained. "You're good with him," she says softly.

"Easy. He's a good kid," I answer. "It's not hard."

I pull Zach's bedroom door closed, latching it silently. Clarissa sways closer, resting her hand on my chest.

"Stay?" she whispers, and my heart wrenches. "I just...I need you tonight, Leo."

Like hell. I don't think I've ever heard such perfect words.

And I brush my fingers under her chin, tipping her face up so I can lean down to kiss her. She rises toward me without hesitation, meeting me halfway. It's a soft thing, a chaste thing, and I can feel her shaking right down to her toes.

"Of course I'll stay, sweetheart," I growl.

We're quiet while we change for bed. She slips under the covers and holds her hands out to me.

I go to her in a breath, sliding under the sheets and pulling her into my arms, kissing her hair, pressing my forehead to hers.

She hides against me, still trembling.

That's when I realize it's not just body heat she's after. She needs me to feel safe.

Needs me to make her *feel* safe.

"I'm so scared," she whispers against my chest. "So scared for Deanna."

"I know," I answer, holding her tighter. "But we've got a fighting chance, Rissa. You made sure of it."

She says nothing.

Let her have her pride and secrets. I squeeze her gently. She rolls her shoulders and shakes against me with dry, soundless sobs till she finally drifts off. I wait for her soft, steady breathing before I set a mental alarm.

There'll be no rest for me tonight.

Not when my heart's so heavy, and I wonder how much time we've got left to save her little sis.

* * *

I FORCE myself to doze for a couple hours, but I'm awake well before Rissa.

Slipping out of the bed, I gingerly ease her down and tuck the covers around her before dressing, peeking in on Zach, and then heading into the kitchen to start breakfast.

Once the coffee's brewing and I pop open one of those cans of doughy crescent rolls and leave them to bake, I settle in front of the laptop and wake up the screen.

The application's still there, waiting to give me a window into the secrets on the drive. I start poring through everything.

A good deal of it looks like contractor agreements, financial records. Pointed highlights left in the documents by some unknown reader, outlining ambiguous language and correlations to illegal activities, financials that make no sense.

Receipts. Paper trails. Even medical charts.

I wonder if mine's in there somewhere. Either from Nighthawks, or after they blamed me for torching their lab. I spent at least a solid week in a burn ward before they shipped me off to prison as inmate 907.

Fuck, I don't even want to see it.

It's all damning, but it's not *enough*.

Not when it's all vague, dull corporate speak that can easily be denied in court as long as there's no concrete proof. And I'm not finding it here.

Proof would be photographs with enough context to link them to Galentron with no questions. Video capturing illegal activities, with perps easily identified. Emails sharing confidential info in free conversation instead of veiled terms.

What's here is suspicious, but it isn't evidence.

It's just supplementary material, useless on its own. My heart sinks.

What the hell? There's nothing here that would even tell me where to start looking for Deanna herself.

So why would Nash have kidnapped her over this?

A single Notepad file among the many folders catches my attention.

It's named COAIIG.SZ. Weird.

SZ isn't a file extension. The software recognizes it as a text file. Except SZ isn't the file type at all.

It's the last two letters of Clarissa's name, I realize, written in their sisterly code—with the period marking one letter off, turning the last two into a file extension.

CLARISSA.

And its last modified date was only two weeks ago. The rest of these Galentron files must be years old.

Before I can click to open it, though, the sound of little footsteps alerts me that I'm not alone. I lift my head as Zach comes padding down the hall, rubbing at his eyes, his hair sticking up like a chestnut cactus.

Can't help but smile. "Hey, little man," I say. "You're up early."

"I heard you typing." He nudges his glasses up to scrub his eyes even harder, then plops them back into place and climbs up on one of the chairs opposite me, watching curiously across the table. "What're you working on, Mr. Monster?"

"Typing too loud, I guess." Chuckling, I stand, heading into the kitchen to pour a glass of orange juice and fish out a plate for him. "I'm just looking at some secret documents we unlocked last night. Your ma figured out the code."

His eyes round, watching me raptly. "Are you and Mom spies?"

"Not your ma, candy's more her trade. She's just a smart lady." I fetch the crescent rolls from the oven, covering my hand with my sleeve to protect it from the heat, and then toss a few on a plate and bring it back to put them down in front of Zach.

"I wouldn't say I'm a spy, either." I grin. "I just know some things."

Zach grins back, his eyes glittering as he picks up a roll and starts plucking at it, tearing off little bites. Clarissa does that, too. "That's kinda what a spy would say if he didn't want me to know he was a spy, isn't it?"

"Then I think you just answered your own question." I reach over and ruffle his hair. "Eat your breakfast, and then you can go play for a while before your teacher comes."

He nods, bobbing his head happily, and tears in.

It's a quiet, cozy moment, eating with my son, me sipping black coffee as I browse the screen. I keep coming back to that Notepad file, though.

It almost feels sacrilegious, opening something meant for Clarissa.

Too bad it's in the interests of finding her sister.

I don't think she'll mind.

Screw it. I double-click the file, sucking in a breath.

More star designations. Those six-digit strings with *HR* followed by four numbers. Only, more appear now.

A longitude point. No latitude. Plus a time.

Seven twenty-one p.m.

And a degree, an angle.

I frown, tilting my head. What—*oh.*

I know what she's saying as clearly as if she'd whispered it in my ear.

Find the point where you can see this constellation. Right at this angle from the horizon at this exact time, along this line of longitude.

Christ.

Deanna's brain could give Fuchsia a run for her money.

So this is the game. Following the trail of clues. In order to move to the next one, it looks like we'll have to *find* it first.

Zach makes an excited sound. "Mr. Nine! Mr. Nine, Mozart's here! Can I go feed him?"

I barely glance up, frowning at the screen. "There's some

277

turkey slices in the fridge," I say. "Stay on the porch. Don't go where I can't see you."

It's almost funny, how easy I've slipped into the father role.

Luckily, Zach seems happy to listen, tumbling off the chair with crescent roll crumbs still around his mouth as he dives for the fridge, digs out some turkey, and then bounces out on the deck where that fat orange tabby waits, flicking his tail.

With a friend, apparently. I watch over the top of the laptop screen as Zach tears up little strips of turkey and feeds them to Mozart and another massive grey cat who looks like he's had his ears chewed half off.

Mean-looking bastard.

Zach offers his hand. The new cat sniffs it, and then butts its head into his palm.

Guess looks can be deceiving.

Clarissa's voice purrs behind me, sleepy and amused. "Hey, I was saving that turkey for sandwiches."

I glance over my shoulder at her. "He only stole a couple slices. Promise."

"And you let him." She smiles faintly, leaning against the wall. She looks smaller somehow, in her striped pink silk pajama pants and the thin, near-translucent white babydoll shirt clinging loosely to her slender curves. Looks younger. Sadder, too. "You've missed out on so much with him, Leo."

Those words jerk me from my thoughts, right to the present.

I twist to face her, rising to my feet. "Clarissa..."

"No—no, I need to tell you something." Her eyes glitter, going damp, her words thick as she shakes her head, holding her hand up. "I need you to know...to tell you..."

She can't get the words out.

And I can't stop myself.

"That Zach's my son," I finish.

Hell. Saying those words out loud? It's like taking a bullet of pure euphoria.

She gasps, jerking her head up, staring at me. "You...you knew?"

I smile slightly. "You know anyone else with eyes like his?"

Her lips tremble. She takes a faltering step toward me. "Leo, Leo, I—"

I'm with her in half a second, pulling her into my arms, gathering her so close. "I know, Rissa. I know. And I get why you didn't tell me."

She huddles against me, burying her face in my chest. "You do?"

"What happened that night ran you out of Heart's Edge," I whisper, running my hands down her sides. I'm fucking breaking inside, but in the best way. "How were you supposed to come back even under the best circumstances, and tell me I have a son? Not exactly an option when I've been living in the goddamn mine, roasting wild rabbits for supper."

She lets out a pained, amused sound. Her shoulders jerk as she burrows deeper into me. "You're too good to me."

"Real funny, babe. Feels like I'm not good enough." I rest my chin to the top of her head, taking in her scent, her teary-eyed smile, *every-damn-thing*.

Everything that makes her special, makes her mine.

Everything that came together in our own little melody to make Zach.

"Let me get my shit good enough to love our son right, Rissa."

She lifts her head, looking up at me with something like hope in her eyes. "But you already—"

"No. You heard me. Can't give him much of a life with a wanted man as a dad, no matter how much I want to love him."

And to love you, I want to say, but that's not something I can ask for. Not till we know everything will be all right.

I brush my fingertip under her eye, tracing the gleaming line of her lashes. "If you're up for it, I want to tell him soon, when things are better. First, I need to show you something."

Her brows knit together, and she shakes her head. "Show me what?"

"The next clue."

* * *

IT SINKS in for Rissa almost immediately.

We sit on the sofa together, just a little too close, thigh to thigh, the laptop propped between us as we plan, keeping an eye out for Zach as he's in and out with his tutor. Today's lessons take them into the trees to identify plants.

Later, we decide we can ask Ms. Wilma to take Zach for the night, and then head out together to find the point marked by the coordinates and the stars. With any luck, whatever we find there will make all the difference.

Or at least give us solid leverage to flush Nash out of hiding and get him to reveal where he's keeping her.

I have a few ideas, but hell.

He wouldn't take her there, not after everything was shut down.

Would he?

I'm torn from my drifting thoughts by Zach crying out. Not playfully.

Clarissa and I are both on our feet in an instant, fighting each other to get out the door.

She beats me to it, but I'm hot on her heels, my heart pounding. Derek comes through the woods with a sniffling Zach in his arms, and I see the kid's jeans torn at the knee, stained in blood.

"Oh my God, Zach!" Clarissa cries, stumbling down the steps and reaching for him.

Derek offers a reassuring, apologetic smile as he moves him into Rissa's arms. "Just had a little tumble," he says. "Zach tried to climb too high."

"I told you," Rissa scolds gently, while Zach clings to her with his arms around her neck. She rubs his back soothingly and turns to mount the steps. "Let's go get you cleaned up, ZZ."

I watch her go for a few moments, trying to calm my racing pulse.

So this is what it's like to have a kid you'd *die* to protect.

Derek catches my eye and winces. "I'm sorry. I should've kept a closer eye on him."

"It's all right." I shake my head, offering a smile. "Kids will always find ways to get themselves in trouble, and Zach's more precocious than most. Why don't you take the rest of the day off? I doubt she'll let him out of her sight today."

"Might be a good idea. Give him a hug for me, okay, Papa Bear?"

Shit. Even Derek sees it.

That connection between me and my boy, between father and son, existing without words.

I join Rissa inside and help her get Zach cleaned, bandaged up, and placated with a cinnamon roll. The scolding he gets is halfhearted. We're both just relieved he's okay.

But as we all settle on the couch, Zach sandwiched between us and cuddled up tight, Rissa looks at me over his head.

"It's scary being back here with him," she says softly. "After what happened with all those missing kids years ago...it's easy to assume the worst."

I shudder, something powerful gripping my balls like ice.

It's fucking revulsion.

Revulsion at the idea of Zach being taken, just like I was.

Broken until he no longer remembers who he is. Or who loves him.

Whoever *could* love him, once he'd become a beast.

* * *

Twenty Years Ago

281

ONE DAY, I think they'll kill me.

But maybe death would be better than living in here.

I feel like my insides just burst. Exploded, bit by bit, every time the ring of whipcord-muscled teenage boys around me kicked me again and again. Their brute strength matches mine too well.

They're like pack animals, controlled by a single Alpha.

And every time he tells them to take me down, they do.

Because if they don't, they might be up next.

I'm the latest example. What happens to any Nighthawk who steps out of line.

I lie on the cold, dirty stone floor in this dark hell-chamber, staring dully at the polished shoe that steps into my line of sight. My reflection in the patent leather is swollen, purple, bloody, barely even human.

Ha.

Barely even human.

Dr. Maximilian Ross looks down at me with his cultured, bearded face twisted with disgust, his voice thick with condemnation.

"You tried to escape again," Ross says matter-of-factly. "You know it's futile, L-9."

His voice is hypnotic. There's a part of me that wants to agree with him just because he said it. Because that's how my mind was trained.

That man's voice is law, certain words tripping off actions that make my body move on its own, even when I don't want to do what he says.

But he hasn't managed to brainwash me enough to destroy the burning urge to run.

I'll find my freedom again, or die trying.

Sometimes, I still think of a girl in a pretty sundress, twirling flowers, and wonder if she'll hear me through layers and layers of stone if I scream.

"I won't..." I can barely talk around the blood in my mouth. "I won't give in."

"Excuse me?" Ross says, calm and confident, then flicks his fingers. "You will, Agent L-9. Everybody out!"

He claps his hands, then pauses, pointing at one of the other kids. "Ah-ah—not you. Stay."

I know who it is without even seeing him.

The boy with the silvery eyes, shining like gunmetal.

The boy who does everything Ross says without question.

With pleasure.

The boy who strokes my cheek and tells me I have such lovely hair.

Right before he tears me up with his fists and his kicks and leaves me bleeding some more.

The sound of the door closes, locks, leaving me alone with him.

It's a dark and final thing like a coffin slamming shut. A promise, hateful and hard and awful.

As sinister as Nash's smile. He grips a handful of my hair and jerks my head back, staring into my eyes with his own wide and mad. His lips slink to my ear, and his breath pours out real hot and thick and disgusting.

"Now, Lion-boy, listen good," he says. "Listen to what I say like you do with the Doc, and let's get that cool fucking mane off you..."

* * *

Present

I COME BACK to the present gasping.

Holy shit.

Up till now, I'd managed to keep the memories at a distance. Half-forgotten things, but now I feel them sick and dark and real inside me. They're heavy, weighing on my heart like a damn boulder.

The room focuses around me in a sudden sharpness, and I realize Zach is staring at me with wide, worried eyes. Rissa's hand is on my arm, gripping tight.

"Leo? Hey," she whispers, giving me a little shake. "Are you all right? Are you with us?"

"Yeah," I answer raggedly, covering her hand with my own and squeezing it tight. "I'm okay, but I need you to stay here with Zach." I take a deep breath. "You can't come with me tonight, sweetheart."

Her brows knit, and she shakes her head fiercely. "Huh? No, I—"

"*No.* Just listen." I can't help how my voice turns harsh. I can't argue over this, even with the wounded look she gives me. "I remembered more. Remembered things I won't say right now, but I'll tell you later. Trust me, woman."

She's staring at me, almost betrayed, but I hold my ground.

Because I *know* some things are worse than Nash killing Deanna.

Nash knows exactly how to pull my leash. Ross taught him.

I can't fucking let him make me hurt Rissa. Make me hurt Zach. Make me hurt my own family.

"Leo?" Rissa whispers again, looking up at me as I stand.

"It's too dangerous," I finish. "*I'm* too dangerous. I can't explain right now. Just need you to stay put."

XIX: OFF THE BEATEN PATH
(CLARISSA)

I'm so flipping mad at Leo I could *pop*.
  I have been for *days*.
Because he just had to go and pull that macho crap on me, didn't he?

Because he went tearing off into the night and left me here alone to mind the house like a good little girl. I don't understand.

He wouldn't even know where to look next if I hadn't gone digging at the old house. And then he tells me he's *dangerous*, but won't say why?

Nope. He just disappears, leaving me to put Zach to bed and pace all night, sleepless and worried.

He came back hours later covered in dirt, holding a dirty Sweeter Things box.

It had a drive inside plus another piece of paper in Deedee's handwriting.

I saw what was on the first drive.

All those documents, but what's here...it's worse.

Photographs and videos of people bound to tables, hooked up to strange devices, screaming in pain, the Galentron logo clear on much of the equipment and on the walls. People in white masks and coats, moving clinically, jotting down notes like nothing was happening.

It makes me feel sick.

But what's worse is when Leo says it's not the end.

He won't tell me much. Not where he found the cache, not what it means or how he knows there's more.

There's also another set of coordinates in star-numbers and degrees and time. Deanna left me messages Leo's been intercepting.

He heads out into the night again and again, while I sit here staring at the laptop, trying to do something useful cataloging the data. I wish I could piece together a timeline.

Something we could use to present a clear case in court and completely destroy them.

Whatever else happens, I won't give this up. It's even bigger than my sister now.

Not after seeing what's being done to the people on these videos.

Not when, in one of the still photos, old and clearly scanned from film to digital, I see his face.

A teenage Leo, maybe a couple years before we met again at my house and he came stumbling into my kitchen.

He's bound to a table, veins bulging in his neck, a roar of pain on his face as they pump something into his body from an IV pouch. I also see that horrid man I remember skulking around the house, Dr. Ross, standing over him like the grim reaper in a lab coat.

God. What did they *do* to him?

What would they have done to all of us, if Leo hadn't given up everything to stop my father and his friends?

I can't even look at this stuff when Zach's awake.

I'm not risking my son's innocence.

It's bad enough that every night I pass out in the morning darkness, I keep seeing those awful photos in my head. And it's even worse that I'm alone.

Was it just *one* blissful night?

That's all we had before Leo pulled away.

He's just that firelight out in the dark again, so close and yet so far.

How could he be *dangerous?*

How could he tell me that and shut down on me, not even hours after saying he wants to be a father to Zach?

Maybe it's the price to pay for being stupid.

I thought there was hope. Thought we could start over.

But I don't know if that's even possible as long as Leo's keeping his secrets.

I sigh, pressing my fingers to my temples—only to rocket up in my seat as something crashes against the glass front door of the house.

My heart thuds, slamming up and down and back and forth like my chest is shaking and rattling it around. Opening my eyes, rising warily to my feet, reaching for something I can use as a weapon.

I come up with a stick of French bread. *Awesome.*

Still, I hold that stupid baguette like a baseball bat, creeping toward the door.

Only to drop it with a silent scream caught in my throat.

I see Leo slumped there in a hulking mess, covered in blood.

"Oh my God!" I whisper, ripping the door open.

He tumbles inside, collapsing with the full force of his heavy weight across the threshold. Panting in little panicked breaths, I drop to my knees, reaching for him, then jerking back.

His clothes are tattered, but there's so much blood *everywhere* that I don't even know where he's been hurt, where to find the wound.

"Leo!" I gasp. "Leo, are you—"

"Breathe." Despite the raw, gritty edge in his voice, he's surprisingly steady, calm. "It's not all my blood. It's not as bad as it looks."

I bite my lip, clutching my hands together. "Where?"

"My thigh." He hauls himself up, wincing, squinting one eye open as he props himself in the doorframe and lets his left leg sprawl out. His jeans were sliced open by something that made jagged tears, something serrated, and there's a deep gash in the muscle underneath. "Fucker used a hook knife."

Gasping, I clap my hands over my mouth. "Oh *God*, we need to get you to a hospital—"

"*No hospital!*" He grinds out. "I'm still a wanted man, Clarissa. They'd handcuff me to the bed."

"Shit." My head is spinning.

He lets out a bitter laugh, huge shoulders shaking. "Yeah. Just help me in and I can stitch it up. Wouldn't be the first time." When I don't move, he offers me a tired smile. "Don't worry. You'd be amazed how fast I heal."

"I'm *going* to worry." But I shift around, kneeling against his side, draping one of his thick arms over my shoulder. "You weigh as much as a Mack Truck, you know. But come on."

"I'll try not to crush you."

That sardonic humor, nearly groaned against my ear, gives me sweet relief. If he's teasing me, he's going to be fine.

But I still don't breathe until I get him standing, staggering, limping and trying to carry all his weight on one foot as I guide him inside and kick the door shut behind us. He steers toward the couch, but I shake my head firmly and pull him along.

"Let me take care of you," I say.

He gives me an odd look from the corner of his eye, but he says nothing.

He just lets me drag him deeper into the cabin, lurching one step at a time.

I'm about to collapse under his weight by the time I get him slumped into the bathtub, his legs hanging out the side.

"Rissa—"

"Don't," I say, my voice thick, hurting, as I fumble with his shoelaces. "I need to do this. I need to take care of you. You asshole, you left me here worrying about you every freaking night, and then you come back like *this.*"

He catches my hand, stops my fussing, looking at me intently. "Better me than you, babe. And it could've been you."

"No." I shake my head firmly. "You'd never let that happen to me..."

"I might be the one to do it," he says urgently, staring at me, amethyst eyes sharp-edged as cut gems.

What does he mean? My heart skips a beat.

"You don't get what I am, Rissa. You don't get *me.*"

My jaw tightens. I stare right back at him, then jerk my hand away and pull his boots off firmly before dragging at his clothing, starting to strip him down.

"So tell me," I demand. "What happened tonight? What did you think you were protecting me *from?*"

So he tells me while I wrestle him out of his clothes and start filling the bath with hot water.

He tells me in unflinching terms, nothing spared, one word at a time.

I feel like I'm *there*, living his memory through those bright, determined violet eyes.

* * *

Hours Ago

IT'S LATE.

Almost nine o'clock, to be precise, because the note on the second cache pointed Leo to the constellation Capricorn as seen from a spot in the valley at nine fourteen p.m., and he's almost there. He consults his compass and stops to use his telescope, checking the constellation against the horizon, the North Star.

Maybe this will be the one.

The one that has not just evidence of Galentron's crimes, but the incriminating stuff that just might exonerate Leo.

Might let him go back to having a life in the light, a life with me, with Zach.

That's what he's truly been looking for all this time. *A way to be with us.*

It's an oddly warm October night. Leo swelters in his layers, his own sweat masking scents around him, the scents of brush and dry earth and old, faint chemicals that remind him this used to be Galentron's playground.

Too many memories, he says.

Too many terrible things.

He can't wait to find this cache and haul ass back to us.

He crests a pile of tumbled rocks, checks the angles again, then slides down to a spot that looks innocuous, but he can already tell something's off.

It's too loose.

A little depression against the rocks, with more tumbled in it, small pebbles with a few tough plants growing out.

He brushes them aside to dig, planning to push everything back in place to make it look like no one was ever here.

It's so dusty.

He's trying not to cough, breathing shallowly through his mask. He searches deeper in the ground...only for his fingers to feel cardboard.

A feeling he recognizes now, after finding it twice before.

Another box from my shop. Inside, there'll be another cache Deanna hid.

He's figured out by now that the caches are a combination of unique and redundant stuff.

It's impossible to get the complete picture without every-thing, however many there might be in this strange wild goose chase of star charts and codes and coordinates.

He manages to scrape the ground aside enough to get a grip on the sides of the box.

Only for a sixth sense to hit hard, warning him that some-one's close.

He thrusts himself to the side.

Something bright and silvery goes whizzing past him. It clatters off the rock where his head was a second ago in a shower of blinding sparks.

Holy hell.

A knife.

And as he rolls to one knee, poised in a crouch, he finds himself face-to-face with a tall shadow of a man. Nash, moving smooth and cool and confident with his powerful build like a prowling panther, those horrible gunmetal eyes locked on Leo with excitement.

Greed.

Hunger.

He remembers how he used to hurt him. There's a sick, creepy fondness that forges a screwed-up bond between them.

Leo bares his teeth.

Nash stops several yards away, spreads his hands, and smiles. "Lion-boy. You beat me here again, but looks like you lost your lead."

Leo narrows his eyes. "Eat shit. I don't want to think about what you did to her to get these coordinates."

"You already know, L-9. She's gonna run out of that pretty, pretty hair real soon, though. And I don't know what I'll start cutting next." It's chilling, his calm. "But I need this cache, you see. Can't let you have it."

Leo barks out a harsh laugh. "So you think I'll hand it over if you just ask nicely?"

"No, but I had to try. I think you'll let me have it when you know what I do."

"Enlighten me."

Nash sinks into a crouch, resting on one knee in Leo's mirror image, mocking him. "Deanna doesn't know where everything is."

"Bull. It's not possible."

"Wrong. That old bitch she was working with...I guess I killed her too soon." Nash's smile is still so terribly, hatefully pleasant even as he talks about murdering an old woman, Marianne, my father's former secretary.

"Deanna buried half the caches. Marianne buried the others." He holds up a finger. "They thought they were being real clever without telling each other. They left coordinates instead. A little game of connect the dots. It was supposed to be their insurance policy, but the dumb bitches didn't think about one thing." He leans forward, his eyes too wide, staring at Leo. "It doesn't keep them alive if the only ones who know about their little insurance policy is them."

Leo realizes what he means instantly.

All Nash needs is one more set of coordinates to not need Deanna anymore.

And the only leverage we'll have is the few we've already recovered. He might just decide that following the caches to the final end and gathering what he can find will be enough.

Then Deanna will be useless.

Then my sister dies.

Leo positions himself with his body blocking off the half-buried box at his back, shaking his head. "I don't think that's what you need to say to convince me, Nash."

"No?" Nash shrugs and smiles. "How about if I tell you I'll kill that low-functioning whore if you don't move your burned up carcass?"

"Sounds like you'll kill her anyway, so I might as well do whatever I can to fuck you up."

"So the data's more important to you than the girl? *Interesting.*"

It's not.

Leo knows it's not, but he also knows how Nash works.

He still needs Deanna. She's still a source of information,

when there are countless caches they haven't found yet, and Deanna knows where at least half of them are.

Nash can't risk losing that information if it means getting to them before Leo does.

So Leo's just got to keep him away.

He shifts his weight, ready to lunge, fists clenched in preparation.

But Nash only stands, smiling slowly as he flicks his fingers at Leo.

"Bad little mutt," Nash says calmly.

Pain hits between Leo's eyes, blinding him.

He *knows* those words.

That phrase, that tone, it's carved into his brain, a programmed response he can't deny.

Leo lets out a harsh, hurting roar as he drops down to his hands and knees, slamming against the earth.

Oh, he tries to fight it.

Tries to tell himself he's not that creature anymore, that slave, and the words have no power over him. It's not even Dr. Ross' voice.

It's Nash.

Another trained monster like him, a beast warped and broken and reshaped, the chemical switches in his brain programmed to respond to the simplest triggers.

No!

Leo won't give in. He won't.

Gritting his teeth, fighting muscles that just want to obey, he shoves himself up.

He flings himself at Nash with screaming fury, tearing at him with all the rage and frustration and pain it takes to break that simple bit of conditioning.

They crash together in a storm of fists, but Nash doesn't fight fair.

Leo hits him again and again as they roll.

Then Nash catches a handful of Leo's hair, dragging his head back, and snarls in his ear.

"Red-blue-yellow-green switch off," he hisses.

And Leo feels paralyzed.

He locks up, unable to even close his mouth mid-snarl, trapped inside the unmoving shell of his own body.

Fuck. Fuck, fuck, but he's only got ten seconds to suffer.

The off switch—it only ever worked for ten seconds on resistant subjects, fifteen on passive subjects.

It was usually enough in the Nighthawks to get a sedative in the offender and put them out until they calmed down.

He doesn't think Nash has a sedative.

He does, however, have a knife, one with a wicked curve and a jagged hook on the tip.

And while Leo lies in the dirt, trapped, motionless, counting *five-six-seven-eight-nine*, Nash moves.

Nash slashes the knife down. Rips into his thigh.

Pain explodes everywhere, but he's still counting.

Ten.

And despite the pain, despite the dizziness, Leo gathers himself into a ball of muscle and slams himself up at Nash just as the man turns away to retrieve the box.

He doesn't know how he gets his hands on the knife.

He only knows he manages to snare it in Nash's clothing, ripping through his shirt, and the Kevlar underneath. He gets a foothold above his ribs and carves a trench in his flesh.

Then a fist slams into his face, and he sees stars.

Nash stumbles, clutching the box to his chest, the cardboard flimsy and popping open as he fights to keep a hold on it while Leo tries to tear it away.

But one last boot to his skull, and he can't hold anything at all anymore.

He's lost too much blood, too fast.

And the last thing he sees is Nash swearing, reeling, staggering away before blackness comes crashing down.

* * *

Present

I DON'T KNOW what to say when he's finished.

Everything inside me just hurts. The pain. The sickness. The *horror* of being dragged back into that awful place he left by that man messing with his mind.

"That's what you were scared of," I whisper, staring down at the man turning the bathwater muddy pink with his blood. He's sprawled out there, closing his eyes as he tilts his head against the tub. "You were afraid if Nash caught us out together, looking for clues, he'd use your trigger words to control you. And make you hurt me."

His lips crease grimly. "Yeah. It's as fucked up as it sounds. And even if I can't control my reaction...it'd still be my fault. Won't do that to you, Rissa. Never fucking ever."

I'm about to break my no-crying rule. We'll just pretend I haven't already.

My body tenses, trying to hold back, and I force myself to focus on gently dabbing a wet towel around Leo's thigh to try to get a better look at the wound. I gently wipe away the blood, trying not to hurt him.

"I...I saw you," I say. "When I was looking at the data on the drives." My breath shudders. "There's a photo of you. Hooked up to something and in so much pain, I...Leo, what did Galentron *do* to you?"

"Kidnapped me," he answers flatly. "Tortured me till I forgot my family. Forgot where I came from. They made me a Nighthawk. Just like Nash."

I shake my head. "I don't know what that means. What are Nighthawks supposed to be?"

"Supersoldiers. Secret agents. Assassins for hire." It's harsh, but oddly toneless, like he's trying to divorce himself from the words. "The ultimate killers. Physically enhanced to do more than ordinary men. Trained to perfection. Brainwashed to obey. You could drop a Nighthawk in a village full of families, turn around, and turn back thirty seconds later to find them all dead without a moment's hesitation."

Oh, God. I can't stand picturing it.

I can't stand thinking that's what they tried turning this sweet, brave, gorgeous man into.

What they might've succeeded at, if not for the gentle heart inside his giant bones.

"I'm sorry, Leo. I'm so sorry." I want to hug him, hold him, soothe him, but I have to do something about that wound. Still, I reach up with my clean hand and gently touch his cheek.

"It's okay," I tell him. "It's okay that you couldn't stop him. He still needs Deanna, so he won't kill her...and you could've gotten yourself killed. You don't have to be superhuman for me, Leo. Just be *you*."

Those violet eyes darken and he curls one damp hand against my wrist, turning his head to kiss my palm. "Check the left pocket of my coat."

I frown, confusion ringing through me. But I drape the towel against the edge of the tub and fish through the pile of clothes I'd stripped off him and tossed on the floor. I dig in the pocket until I feel the dry crinkle of paper.

I pull it out.

Stationery.

Deanna's handwriting.

Another mix of coordinates again, that strange code that's a little bit me and a little bit her and a little bit something else.

I stare down at it. "What?"

"The box popped open," Leo says with a touch of dark, vicious satisfaction. "Bastard got the data, but he didn't even notice me stealing the coordinates. So he has no idea where to go next."

"Meaning we still have a chance to catch him while he looks," I whisper, heavy realization dawning on me.

"I know what he'll do next." Leo sinks back against the edge of the tub again with a tired groan. I'd be lingering on the beautiful contrast his huge, naked, and glistening body makes if everything weren't so serious. "He might take Deanna out in the open. Use her to hunt down a scent. Force her to show him so she won't send him on a wild goose chase. If he brings her out, we might be able to steal her first."

Hope flares inside me. "You really think so?"

"Maybe. But if I'm wrong...still might have an ace up my sleeve, if we get to that point. I'll need to leave town for a few days if it comes to that, though."

I frown. "Leave town? For what?"

"Dr. Ross."

The name comes out like a curse. "You mean, what, he's still alive?"

"Retired in Missoula, of all places. I looked the fucker up." Leo's eyes close. "Nash was his pride and joy. His pet attack dog. The rest of us were just shadows when Nash took so well to his training. And Ross might know a way to stop him."

My lungs won't work. I don't know why I feel such a dread chill at the words that come next.

Maybe it's the guarantee that something could go very wrong, very fast, and I won't want to see the horror that'll come.

"Ross is the only one who knows Nash's trigger words," Leo growls.

Hello, worst fears. Confirmed.

Yeah, I think to myself, but my tongue goes dry, this tangled knot in my mouth. *But he also knows yours.*

THERE'S NOT MUCH ELSE to say.

Not when Leo's dog-tired, close to passing out, even if he's too stubborn to admit it.

I put my Girl Scout merit badges to good use, sealing up his wound while he guides me. I'm a whirlwind, trying to quietly sterilize a needle and thread in boiling water without making enough noise to wake Zach.

It takes all my willpower and a bit of bullheaded arguing to bully Leo off to bed. He bites down on a rolled-up towel and rips up handfuls of the sheets while I swab antiseptic salve and iodine into his wound, then finish stitching it together.

I faintly remember how from first aid. Never sew up a wound like you're sewing a shirt. One popped stitch will unravel the entire thing.

And knowing Leo, he'll have popped something by morning.

He watches me calmly as I tie off the last bit, completely unfazed by the sight of a needle piercing his flesh. I'm clammy and shaky after having to do it again and again and again.

"You're good at that," he says, rumbling amusement in his voice. "You spend a lot of time stitching guys up, or what?"

"First time," I say, my voice trembling a little, though I manage a smile as I wipe my hands off on a wet towel. "Last time was years ago on a rubber dummy. Real flesh pierces a lot easier than rubber."

"You're telling me." He shifts, drawing his good leg up to push himself against the headboard. "Don't think I can make it out to my camp right now, but I'll be out of your hair by morning. Sorry for stealing your bed."

"You're *staying* in this bed until you're better," I bite off. "You'll just end up bleeding and passed out somewhere if I let you go."

He scowls at me. "I've got to start tracking Nash. Trying to anticipate his next move."

"Warren and Blake can help with that. They volunteered, remember? But you keep trying to do everything yourself, Hercules." I fold my arms over my chest, mock-glaring at him

when I'm just ready to pass out. "*I* can look. I need to do something for my sister again and you just need to—"

"*No*," he snarls. "Not resting. You stay here. Stay here out of
Nash's sight, because the next person he's chasing down is you—
and I can't guard you if you're running through the hills."

"You can't guard me if your leg rots off, either," I fling back.
"I'm not a doctor, Leo. I don't know if I helped or made things
worse. Until you actually start to *heal*, you're staying in this bed,
and the least you'll do is get that thing looked at by your
buddy, Doc."

He opens his mouth, eyes flashing, ready to argue.

So I do the only thing I know to make him stop.

I push myself across the bed, mold myself against his body,
and kiss him.

He goes stiff—and I wonder if he'll continue arguing, but I
know him too well.

I know exactly how to get him going.

I know how to distract him, even if we can't be quite as wild
as we usually are.

I won't *let* him.

I won't let him hurt himself, even if I have to use my own
body against him to do it.

His mouth comes hot against mine, questioning, searching,
and I shudder with a sweet, sighing need as his hands fall to my
hips. He holds me tenderly, like I'm fragile, as I slide carefully
across his lap—hips to hips, still holding myself away from his
injured thigh.

I realize something then.

In all our years together, we've never made slow,
sweet love.

We've always been violent, two forces of nature coming
together.

It's wild animal rutting, mating, and while there's always
been passion to fit the raging need...

We've never gone slow and gentle.

Never taken the time to savor each other's bodies until we're melting together and sighing in slow, perfect tandem.

But there's no other way to be right now. He's lost so much blood. I can't stand to hurt him even more.

For the first time, I'm the one who leads.

I'd never known anything could be totally *new* between us, when everything so far feels like reigniting old memories into a fresh flame.

But this?

This is different enough to make me hesitate as I pull back from the slick lock of our lips and look down at him.

His eyes are smoldering, but he's quiet. Watching me.

Waiting to see what I'll do.

It's heady, realizing this beast-man is at my mercy, in my hands.

All that raw power caged by little old me.

And it makes me feel mischievous as I bend to kiss his neck, tracing my lips over his pulse, his scars.

Even inked, even marked, he still tastes the same.

Salty manliness and that perfect, weathered skin that's so freaking *Leo*.

I tease him with my teeth. He groans.

Then I make my way down his body, pulling the last of his clothing away, leaving him free to my exploring hands, my mouth.

I know him, but I *don't*.

Now I want to know every change, every new sensation of his flesh under my hands, my lips.

And, of course, I want more of his soft, growling surrender as he thumps his head back against the headboard and lets me have my way. "Take it, baby. Take every fucking inch," he whispers.

Oh, sir, yessir.

I taste him all over.

Every beautiful sculpted ridge of scars.

Every hard slab of muscle underneath.

Every thud of his heart through his skin.

Everything I can stand until I'm drunk on him.

Then it hits in force. I'm tearing my shirt off, rubbing my nipples against his body.

The texture of the scars on his chest, oh *God*, I've never felt anything like it against my skin. His tiniest indents make me sensitive and needy all over, gasping and desperate.

I'm trying to be slow, to be careful, to make love like in the movies but...

Like I could even *try* to stay away from his cock.

It's pressing so hard against his boxers, leaving a wet stain of pre-come.

Inhaling sharply, I drag the fabric down, baring its thickness.

Leo smells musky, earthy, hot, and tastes the same. I brush my lips over the head, opening wide to take him in. He snarls, holding still, grinding out a warning.

"Rissa!"

And I feel like a vixen.

I only smile, and murmur, "Be good for me."

Right before I take him into my mouth again.

Oh, he's too big for me. He's always *too big.*

I've always known it, too, but I can't resist trying anyway, working my mouth over the head until it's slick, and my lips stretch a little more with every attempt.

More slow thunder builds in his throat. He snaps his hands out, gripping the headboard behind him, his entire body going rock-hard with the effort to stay still.

"Babe...babe, fuck, I'm gonna—"

I know. And that's why I suck him harder, until he starts to bend.

I shouldn't love torturing him like this.

But I love knowing he still *responds* to me, and that I can still make him grit his teeth and clench his jaw in *just that way* as his cock bucks, spurting against my lips.

His seed floods out, hotter than magma, thick ropes over-flowing my mouth.

One seething inch at a time, I force myself to swallow him.

My mouth hurts, but I don't care. I love his taste, his throbbing on my tongue, his growl getting harder, thicker, meaner by the second.

I love how he's always ready for me.

All it ever takes is one touch, and I can get him so hard he's raging, ready in seconds.

Like I'm any better.

Tonight, he hasn't even laid a hand on me, and I'm already so wet my panties are film against my skin, slipping into my folds.

I almost want to touch myself.

But waiting makes it better, the pulsing want louder, aching deeper and deeper.

I devote myself completely to worshiping his cock. I don't think he ever even goes soft before he's rock-hard again.

Those little sounds I love in the back of his throat come faster, hotter. Again and again, I let him pump my mouth. He tosses his head back, straining, breaths coming fast as he whispers in a sharp snarl.

"*Rissa.*"

I know that urgency. I know that heat, and I pull back quickly, shaking my head.

"Not yet," I say. "Not without me."

I push myself up on my knees, stripping away the rest of my clothes.

Then I mount him for all I'm worth.

Just like that, I hold myself above him, poised with his cock almost touching me, spearing up and ready to impale me.

Our eyes lock.

I press my fingers to his lips.

He kisses them, watching me so I feel like a thing of beauty, a work of art, something fairy-tale perfect like nothing he's ever seen before.

It's flipping glorious.

And it makes me wild as I slowly shift down.

My pussy's so ready for him I hardly feel the shock that comes from his size—but I savor it anyway, drawing it out, hanging on to that heady feeling this awareness of every last sensation that's so different from the wild storms we've had in the past.

This is something *more.*

Something intense.

Something captured in one crystal clear second after another.

Something meant to savor.

So I take my sweet time bringing us together, stretching my body, accepting every inch of him one at a time as he pulls me open, fills me, buries so deep.

The entire time, our eyes never part.

It's like we're joined by the same invisible thread that's kept us together across miles and years, unbreakable and bright.

My breath hitches tight in my throat as our bodies press flush, the fullness inside me so heavy as I seat him fully inside me.

Capturing his face in my palms, I kiss him, a soft *I love you* on my lips that I can't say.

But it feels like the same thing is in his growly tone as he wraps his arms around my waist, arching my spine against him, crushing my breasts between us, and kisses me like madness.

"You're so fucking *beautiful*," he says against my mouth. "All these years, and you've never stopped being beautiful."

I want to tell him he's beautiful, too.

That who he is now is the same as what he's always been.

Now he just wears his wild and passion and animalism on the outside.

But I'm too tangled up for words.

Too caught up in him as I begin to *move.*

It's slow, deep, almost like I'm following the rhythm of our hearts, rocking my hips to the beat of some unseen drum that's always guided us.

It's pleasure. It's passion. It's beauty. It's pain.

It's perfection, every single time that thick, steely cock grinds so deep inside me. He sets off a thousand tiny explosions, endless cascading sparks.

How did I ever live so long without this?

How'd I survive without *him?*

Right now, he's everything I need to stay sane.

Everything I need to keep me strong while I fight to save my sister's life.

Me and Leo.

Together.

Just like old times.

Just like we'll be again.

And just like the moment, as that slow, steady collision of thrusts and gliding strokes and raw pleasure sweeps us up together, takes its hold, and drops us on our heads.

We're tearing at each other when we find our release. We meet and mate and explode together in some mystic place, lips tangled together in teeth and tongue and steaming breath.

We've been strangers for too long.

Tonight, we're just two stars in our very own universe, combusting and collapsing together.

* * *

LEO LOOKS downright pale by the time we sink down on the bed.

I won't lie.

I'm a little proud of myself.

But also embarrassed as hell, considering I just jumped a man who's half-dead from blood loss. I'm only exaggerating a little.

He collapses against the sheets, staring up at the ceiling before letting out an exhausted laugh.

"Okay, you win, babe," he grunts out. "I'll stay the hell in bed."

"Good." I burrow under the covers, snuggling against him. "Don't try to get out again."

"Shit, I don't know...*that* gonna happen every time I try?"

"*Leo.*" I slap his chest, and he chuckles, draping one tired arm around me.

"Okay. I was being unreasonable. Let's blame the blood loss."

"I don't think any of us are being reasonable right now. Or sane. There's just...so much." I shake my head, nuzzling at his shoulder. "All the bad memories, new fears, worries. We're having to count time in minutes and hours and days while Deanna lives by the second because we're so helpless."

"I know." He lets out a soothing rumble, his fingers trailing over my back in soft caresses. "But we know now he's desperate. Nash will throw down his cards in the open. We'll find a way to use that to our advantage, Rissa. I promise."

"I believe you," I whisper, kissing his shoulder.

And I do.

Other people make false promises. Other people lie, change their minds, double back, cheat, pretend. Other people pretend to be good, hiding the demons under their skin.

Not my Leo.

This unbreakable beast might have his secrets and a short fuse, but the only promise he couldn't keep wasn't under his control. I know that now. He'll keep the new ones he's making as well as he keeps his secrets.

There's more happening under the surface as I lay my cheek against his shoulder, breathing him in, wondering how I'll ever get a hold on my love for him. Because he's giving me faith, more reason to believe, every single day.

There's no question.

I trust Leo Regis with my life, with my sister's, and with our son's.

XX: SWITCHBACK (NINE)

I think she's trying to kill me.

Honestly, if I'm gonna go like this, balls deep in my Rissa, I wouldn't mind an early grave.

It's hard enough staying buckled down for a few days to rest. Can't even get up to take a goddamn piss on my own without her yelling at me to get *back in bed.*

If I don't?

I end up on my back with her gorgeous legs straddled over me, moving in sweet, sexy ripples that make her flesh flow like honey.

Her body's different now.

I'd heard having a kid changes a woman, but I'd never seen it till I took her in the light, watched her moving over me, her tits heavy and full with a weight that makes my gut tighten as I sink my fingers into her flesh and knead them.

Her hips are just as lush, just as thick, her hourglass thighs gripping me with all her softness. Her belly has a delicious rounded swell that strokes my hard muscle every time she grinds her hips over my cock and loses herself in the frenzy, gasping as she practically uses my dick to pleasure herself.

Fuck.

It's real damn hard to recover my red blood cells when she's draining me dry of certain white cells every chance she gets.

But she's found one way to make me stay in bed, all right.

I'm not in any real danger, frolicking with her like this. Don't know how to make her get how easy I can heal.

It's what I was made for.

To be dropped in a combat zone and keep taking hits no matter how hard they come, this unstoppable juggernaut who could keep killing like an angry bear even while he's bleeding out.

When my adrenaline's up, I don't even feel the pain.

But she's not wrong, either. Rest helps any man who's been stabbed, even a human freak like me.

Hell, at this rate, she's gonna spoil me.

By day four, though, she's finally let me up—and lets me put on more besides my boxers.

Mainly because we've got company bringing word.

The news isn't good.

I can tell even before Warren opens his mouth.

I limp out to the kitchen and drop down at the table, favoring my bad leg. We've sent Zach over with Derek to the big house, giving us freedom to talk. Clarissa, Blake, Warren, and fucking *Fuchsia* are gathered around, everyone but the witch at the table. Fuchsia has pulled herself up to sit on the kitchen island like some kind of goth demon pixie, looking down on us from her perch.

God, I really hate that woman.

Warren makes a frustrated growl under his breath, then runs a hand through his thick crop of dark hair. "We found the marker," he says. "But it was empty. Freshly dug up."

I look at him. "Shit. He must've forced her to give it up."

"That means she's still alive," Blake says.

"For now," Fuchsia throws in merrily, and I snarl in the back of my throat.

307

"You're not fucking helping." Under the table, I reach for Rissa's hand and squeeze it tight.

She's pale, lifting her head to look at me, her eyes a little too wide. "Would Nash be able to figure out the code?"

"If I can figure it out, so can he," I tell her reluctantly. "Assume that anything I can do, he can do just as well. Maybe better, considering he's willing to go to extremes I won't."

She clutches my fingers. "Then what reason does he have to keep her alive, now that he can follow the trail on his own?"

"That's where I come in," Fuchsia says. "We already *have* enough information to make things very, very uncomfortable for Galentron. Maybe not to prosecute, but we can completely eviscerate their stock value and make their shareholders jump ship. They'd lose so much money they'd have no choice but to fold into chaos." She shrugs, almost chirpy. "I don't care if they rot in jail or in a cardboard box in an alley, as long as they *rot*."

Warren stares at her oddly. "Lady, what did they *do* to get you so mad?"

"Fired her without her 401K," I mutter, and Fuchsia flings me a deadly look.

"Yours isn't the only life they ruined," she hisses. "You have no *idea* what they took from me."

"Didn't know you had enough heart to care about losing anything. Do you mean that lump of coal in your chest actually feels something?"

The stare Fuchsia gives me is seething, dark.

Human.

And I realize she's serious.

Underneath that cold, murderous, flippant exterior is a woman in agony.

I doubt she'll ever tell me what Galentron took from her.

What part of her life they ripped to shreds and left in tatters at her feet because that's what they do to everyone.

But now I get her determination to thrash them by any means. Her hunger for *payback.*

It's not so different from mine, even if I'd like to think my mission's more noble.

I look away. No use in prodding her anymore. "Okay, Fuchsia. Talk. What's your ace in the hole?"

"Public access radio," she answers simply, with a heavy look for Blake.

Blake goes pale.

"Why are you all looking at me like that?" He darts me a nervous look. "Buddy, why's she looking at me like that?"

"Because that's how cats look at mice before they eat them," I mutter. "Fuchsia, you'll have to clarify."

"It turns out your little Podunk radio station actually gets quite a bit of air coverage. It gets picked up by larger stations and their towers a few miles away, and then beamed not just across the Pacific Northwest, but straight through the Dakotas into a good-sized chunk of the Midwest." She arches a brow. "Enough coverage that if we do a radio tell-all show...too many people would hear it to sweep everything under the rug. Plus, every boring shock-jock with a mic in his teeth gets archived everywhere online these days. There'd be no stopping it."

Rissa scowls. "You really won't be happy until you get to put on your song and dance, will you?"

Fuchsia points a manicured finger at her. "Watch your tone, little girl, or no candy for you." She sniffs. "Don't you get it? We let a few things slip so burning little ears carry it back to Nash. Let him know we're preparing for something. Something that would mean his mission failed, and his handlers won't be happy with him."

I'm there almost before she finishes speaking. "Meaning he has to keep Deanna alive longer because she's his leverage over us."

"Look at you, using that super-brain!" Fuchsia smirks. "And we'll lure him out. He'll be more open, more direct. No more sniper fire. Whatever he does will be big, drastic...and it'll leave him totally exposed."

"And possibly a lot of people dead," Warren says slowly. "From what you've said, he's not above causing a hell of a lot of collateral damage to get his damn objective."

"Then it's a good thing we've got our own Nighthawk to play superhero to the people, isn't it?" Fuchsia purrs.

Blake frowns. "Nighthawk?"

"It's a long story." I sigh, curling my fist against the table. "Look, it's a crazy goddamn plan, but it's the best we've got. The only other option is staying hot on his trail, and since we don't know how many cache sites there are, that might give us twenty more chances or it might give us two. We *need* to head this off at the pass. Before he has time to do something wild or call in reinforcements."

Fuchsia shivers her shoulders mockingly. "Imagine a strike team storming this tiny little town and wiping it off the face of the earth."

Clarissa fixes her with a venomous look. "I swear, I'll make you eat your own ludicrously expensive heels."

"Try it, candy girl. I'll snap your neck before you can blink."

"*Enough*," I snarl. "We'll try Fuchsia's plan. Blake, can you get her on the radio?"

Blake looks uncomfortable but nods. "Yeah. Maybe even do a few promo spots, you know, promising a big show on Halloween with an explosive ending, so everybody and their dog tunes in."

"I do love a flair for the dramatic," Fuchsia interjects, pursing her lips.

Warren, though, has been oddly quiet, a strange expression on his face.

I study him for a minute, tilting my head. "Warren? Something on your mind?"

He shakes his head. "Something about this doesn't add up. If they can put all this to bed by sweeping the town and killing everyone, why haven't they yet?"

"Because there's still something here that they want," Fuchsia says, her flat-grey eyes fixed knowingly on me.

I recoil. "No. *No*. What do they need me for? They had that fucking cat for their vaccine—"

"And feline antibodies aren't human antibodies." She's firm, that lilting edge still there but no longer toying with me. "I'm fairly certain Nash's secondary mission here is to capture you, Leo. You're still the only known carrier of SP-73 viral antibodies. You could be very useful in the wrong hands."

"Any hands are the wrong hands," I growl. "Don't want anyone else using my blood to cook up vaccines for their soldiers any more than I want Galentron doing it."

Now it's Clarissa's turn to squeeze my hand, but it's only some small comfort. I can't help but think if Nash is also after me, he might just see Rissa as extra leverage.

"How do we make sure they can't use SP-73 anywhere ever again?" I ask. "We got it out of Heart's Edge, but fuck. Who knows where they're scheming it up now."

Fuchsia shrugs. It's oddly listless. Her mask is slipping, letting the human being out.

"We make them accountable," she says. "Expose them to the light like the vampires they are and watch them shrivel up and die."

"But couldn't the virus just fall into someone else's hands?" Clarissa asks softly. "Couldn't it just disappear into some government agency until they find another contractor willing to do their dirty work?"

The entire table goes silent, full of grim possibilities.

Then I say, "Doing nothing when we could do something isn't an option. Doesn't matter what might happen down the road. We have to do whatever we can *now*."

Fuchsia smiles sadly. "Aren't we the plucky band of ragtag heroes."

I arch a brow, eyeing her. "You're including yourself in 'we?'"

She wrinkles her nose at me. "You were the one who told me I wasn't allowed in the do-gooders club. I've been *trying*."

Yeah, shit, and I really wonder why, but now's not the time to drag her secrets out.

Stick to business.

I sweep the table with a look. "So we've got a game plan. Blake, I want you shadowing Fuchsia when you can to prevent any assassination attempts while you get her set up. Work together to get the word out. Set the bait, and Warren and I will set the trap."

Clarissa looks worried. "Leo, your leg..."

"It's fine," I promise, squeezing her hand. "You heard Doc say it's on the mend. He's a good doctor, trained in people, even if he's mostly mixed up with animals these days."

"You're still limping."

"It's just a twinge."

It really is. The stitches are half-embedded in my healing flesh. I'm going to have fun picking them out later when they're fabric thread and not the degradable stuff doctors use.

I'm not a hundred percent, but I'm good enough to protect the people I love.

I can't stand just sitting here and doing nothing.

I've spent my life being pushed around, dragged into the riptide of Galentron and pulled under deeper and deeper.

The first time I tried to come up for air, I caused a catastrophe so great I've been on the run ever since.

Time to stop running.

Now we stand and fight.

Right now, though, it's time to get everybody moving, and I lift my head. Only to realize Blake and Warren are watching me and Rissa with cheesy, indulgent smirks. I scowl.

"*What?*"

"Nothing," Warren says mildly. "I just remember when we used to play down by the creek. You'd be mooning at each other."

Blake's smirk turns into a grin. "They were awful cute even back then."

Clarissa's face flames, but she laughs. "Oh my God, *shut up*. I hate you both."

"They're just being assholes." I glower at them. "And assholes don't get to stay for breakfast."

"Hey! Warren started it!" Blake yells.

"Don't you throw me under the bus!" War barks back.

With a chuckle, Clarissa stands, curling her hand against my shoulder. "We can at least feed them if they're going to be part of the Scooby Gang." She pauses as she heads toward the kitchen, though, looking back at Fuchsia. "Do you even eat human food, or do you live on a diet of iron filings and eye of newt?"

Fuchsia curls her upper lip, mouthing her lips and mocking Rissa, then she sniffs and stands, tossing her hair. "As if I'd eat *your* food." She saunters to the door, her heels clicking, and flicks her fingers at Blake. "Eat quickly. I want to get started ASAP."

She steps outside, into the dapples of morning light coming down through the trees. Everyone stares after her silently before Blake lets out a whimper like a kicked puppy.

"Dammit, guys. It's gotta be me, huh?"

I shake my head. "You're the one with the radio station side gig, man."

Groaning, Blake drags a hand over his face. "Aw, hell. I should've listened to Andrea about that show being a stupid idea."

"Smart girl, your little Violet," Warren says, smiling at the nickname she's got from the purple streaks in her hair.

"Smarter than you think, Blake," I tell him. "Your show might help us save this town."

BREAKFAST FEELS LIKE OLD TIMES.

Most of the old crew from childhood eating together, like I'd never vanished into the woods and Rissa never fled town.

We're just missing Deanna and Blake's brother, Holt.

That absence is in the air, in momentary pauses, in a voice that doesn't fill in the laughs as we tease each other.

We're coming.

I promise, Deanna, we're coming.

After everyone's gone, though, I join Rissa washing dishes. Me scrubbing, her drying and stacking them on a towel. She leans her shoulder into my arm, resting her head against me, her fingers still working at drying the plates.

"I don't like it," she says. "This waiting around while you do everything. The big damned hero."

"It's for the best." I turn my head, looking down at her. "We've got Zach to think about. Nash can't figure out he's mine. He'll use him to get to us both."

"I know." She bites her lip. "I won't let them take him and do whatever they did to you. But Leo..."

"Yeah, Rissa?"

"...he needs you," she whispers, her lashes lowering. "He's so *different*. The same way you're different. He's smart in ways that scare me sometimes. These light-speed leaps of logic, that gift he has with numbers or even just sensing how I'm feeling. He might grow up to be just like you."

"He might," I admit, my heart rising in my throat. "What're you saying, sweetheart?"

"I don't know. I don't." She shakes her head briskly. "I'm just worried."

I set down the plate I'd been scrubbing, wipe my hands off on a towel, then capture her face in my palms.

She looks so distressed, so worried, it kills me.

This whole ordeal has frayed my girl so much. Her emotions are raw on the surface, waiting to be crushed, and all I want is to protect them.

Not tear them apart more with my fuckery.

"We'll figure it out," I promise. "If you don't run, I won't either, Rissa. I want to be part of Zach's life. I want to be *Dad*. He's gonna have a lot of struggles as he grows up. I'll be there. Every damn day."

There's more I want to say, even if I don't know how.

About not just staying for Zach, but for *us*.

If it's what she wants, I can be her friend and Zach's father, but I'm a greedy man.

I want *more*.

I want us to be a family.

I want to make up for the last eight years of missing them both.

I want her back, in my bed every night, wearing my ring.

But I can't promise her everything till we bring Deanna home.

She searches my eyes, looking for something to hold on to. Then she smiles faintly, even if there's a tremor to it, unsure and hurting.

"I'd like that," she whispers. "We have to tell him soon. I never told him much about his dad, and he's just about the right age where he'll start asking."

"We will." I lean in and kiss her forehead, promising her silently that *I'll* tell *her* soon, too.

Every square inch of me hopes we can try for something better.

"We'll work it out." I tuck her hair back gently, grazing over the delicate shell of her ear, before I trace my fingertip down the line of the scar on her cheek. "But I need to go take care of this first."

"I know." She sighs, lightly thumping a curled fist to my chest. "Go on. Go be the big damned superhero."

"Don't get nervous if you see Warren skulking around," I say. "If I'm not here, he will be to check in on things. I'm not leaving you and Zach alone."

"Right. I just wish it was you. But I get why it can't always be that way."

It should be, I think, swallowing a growl.

But there's unfinished business waiting.

I lean down and claim her lips one more time, stealing a taste of her to tide me over. Trying to coax that wavering, sad line of hers into warmth, teasing at her lips till she goes soft for me and sways into my arms with a sigh.

"Wait for me," I tell her. "I'll be home soon, Rissa, and then we'll fix everything."

* * *

THAT MIGHT'VE BEEN my biggest promise ever.

Damn if I didn't mean it, though.

Now I just need to make sure my insurance is in place. And that means making sure more folks Nash can't easily escape can get the data saved from the drives we've recovered.

Nash might be able to track down the rest of the caches now, but his mission isn't complete till he recovers it all —and me.

What if Zach's immune, too?

What if he has the same antibodies to SP-73 in his blood?

I don't even want to know if the reason that stuff didn't kill me during the lab breach years ago was due to some genetic freak effect or something they did to me in Nighthawks.

More important, they can't ever know.

Ever.

So I leave copies of the data with Ms. Wilma, with Haley, and with Gray.

I save my old friend for last because he's step two in my insurance plan, and I can't pull this off without him.

Ember's fussing and worrying over tea at their place, trying to get me to drink some when I'm too tense to even think about it. Gray checks the files on his laptop, reviewing them with his face set grim, the horrible images on the screen reflected back in his glasses.

"Brings back memories, doesn't it?" I say darkly.

"Unfortunately."

He sighs and pushes his glasses up his nose. I always found it a little funny when he does that. Makes him look like a neat ninja-assassin preparing to kill someone and hoping they won't *bleed* in too big a mess.

It's not that funny now.

He gives me a discerning look over his glasses. "Are you sure this plan is our best bet?"

"Yeah. Nash listens to Ross. He's vulnerable," I say. "And when we hit him, he won't be expecting the old man there."

"The problem," Gray says, "is that you're *vulnerable* to him as well, Leo."

"That's why I need you there. To keep me grounded."

"Fine. I do love being useful."

As he says it, though, he turns his head to watch Ember almost absently. Gray's always been so reserved and withdrawn, so it's almost strange to see the love there so clearly as he watches his wife.

His *pregnant* wife.

Fuck. That's what gets me.

I'm peeling Gray away from his wife and unborn kid, Warren away from Haley and their son, Blake away from Andrea—all to clean up my messes.

I want to promise I'll bring them all home safe, but I can't.

I'll just have to make sure if anyone takes the fall, if anyone gets hurt, it's me.

Even if that means taking a father away from Zach before he even knows he has one.

Gray's watching me just as keenly, though, his green eyes sharp. "Will you be able to hold it together? That night at the facility, years ago..."

"I froze up. I know. I was out of my wits." The shame of that shit still burns inside me. "But I wasn't ready then. I thought I knew the ugliness of Galentron, only to find out it was worse. I'm ready now." I offer a faint smile. "And I'll have you with me, won't I? Just like old times."

"You will," Gray says firmly, and in those two words are a promise.

He was there for me then.

He'll be there for me now.

I can trust him the way I've always trusted him.

Because for him, this is just as personal as it is for me.

* * *

Eight Years Ago

I DON'T WANT to believe the worst.

Goddammit, I don't.

But after finding out the kind of man the mayor is, it scares me that I haven't heard from Rissa in *hours.*

I told her not to go back to the house.

Once Edgar Bell realizes she has damning stuff on him and she's looking for more, trying to capture the abuse her and Deanna have been suffering for years under his thumb, there's no predicting what's next.

I'm afraid of what he might do to her.

I don't have much time. Not if I'm gonna put a stop to this, and I need to get to the lab *tonight.*

Before they realize I've gone AWOL and revoke my security clearance, making it impossible for me to get to the SP-73 cache and obliterate it.

But I can't do what I have to do unless I know Clarissa's safe.

So I park my Galentron-issued Jeep outside the mansion, looking up at its tall spires.

It's always looked like something out of a Gothic novel to me, maybe a horror movie. It never quite fit in this homey little town, but it's somehow just right for the mayor's overblown ego and the terrible shit Dr. Ross did in its lower halls.

It's the opposite of what it's supposed to represent.

Any notion of dignity gets left at the door.

I mount the steps, start to knock, then realize the door's open.

Instantly, I hear the rush of loud, clipped shouts echoing down the halls. Followed by a crash that makes me picture too many things I can't stand to imagine.

I'm on the move before I even realize it, shouldering through the half-open door, racing toward the sound of Edgar Bell's voice.

It's not hard to miss when he's shouting to the rafters.

"You'd *dare* betray me?" he demands, and I can just barely hear Rissa protesting, her voice drowned out as his shouts climb higher. "I tried to spare you. I would've sent you away! And yet you—you selfish little bitch, you little ingrate—you're going to ruin *everything* I've worked for the last fifteen years!"

Oh.

Fuck.

He must've figured out Rissa was recording him.

That she caught damning evidence of his scheming, and she has every intention of reporting him to the authorities.

I pick up speed, crashing through the house, fear and anger building up inside me into an explosive cocktail.

The study.

The noise is coming from the study, and I go charging in, hitting the door hard enough to nearly rip it off its hinges.

Just in time to see Edgar Bell pick up a huge Ming vase off a pedestal and smash it across Clarissa's face.

The vase shatters.

Clarissa screams, crumpling to the floor.

And the red of the blood on her cheek becomes the red of my vision.

I charge headlong at that motherfucking mayor with murder on my mind.

For an older man, he's fast.

He sees me coming and darts over Rissa, leaving her a crumpled, shivering barrier between us.

It's the only thing that draws me up short. I won't trample over her—but I'm not letting this asshole get away.

He retreats behind his desk. It won't save him.

I'm between him and the door.

He's not getting through me.

"How could you, you fucking maniac?" I snarl. "How could you sell out all these people? Was it worth it?"

"Don't you dare judge me," he snarls. "I don't speak grunt. You're acting out above your pay grade, Agent."

Anything I might say gets cut off by Rissa at my feet.

"Leo..." she whispers brokenly, reaching for my leg with one weak, shaking hand.

I sink down to one knee next to her, clasping her hand.

"I'm here, sweetheart," I whisper. "You're safe. It'll be all right."

I'm torn between calling her an ambulance and disemboweling her old man first.

But Mayor Bell seals his fate when he snarls again, realization thick in his voice.

"*You*," he bites off, shaking his head. "Now, I see. I knew she'd gotten reckless, but you've been the one putting these...these asinine ideas in her head! You've corrupted my daughter."

Oh, hell no.

I don't even realize it the instant I snap.

Maybe it's his tone.

Maybe it's his fingerprints I can see bruising her throat, smeared in her blood.

But everything goes black, and next thing I know, I'm on top of Edgar Bell, smashing his head into the floor again and again and again, timed to the violent mantra in my mind.

Die, die, die, you piece of shit!

There's a satisfying *crack* and his eyes roll back. He goes limp.

My hands shake, bloody as I pull them back from his crushed-in throat, staring down at him.

Shit. He's not breathing.

He's *definitely* not breathing.

I didn't—did I?

I've never killed a man who wasn't pointing a gun at me in a war zone before.

I don't even remember moving. I don't know what I did. Reality just blurs, adrenaline scorching my veins.

I'm on full berserker mode, this fury rising up inside me, this wild animal thing with only one thought.

Protect Clarissa.

And to save the woman I love, I just murdered her asshole of a dad.

"Oh, God!" A voice shouts from the doorway, strangled, shocked.

I lift my head sharply, adrenaline pulsing through me in a wild rush. One of the maids stands there, her hand pressed to her mouth, her face pale as she stares at me and the body beneath me.

I stand quickly, holding out a hand. "It's not—he was going to—"

She shakes her head, cutting me off, and takes a shaky breath.

"Don't...don't tell me," she says numbly, already bustling to Rissa's side. "If you don't tell me, I can't repeat it to anyone. Just *go.*"

I stand there stunned while she helps Clarissa sit up and gently touches her cheek.

And that's when I realize the maid doesn't blame me for killing Edgar Bell.

I wonder what she's seen under this roof, why she'd look at

his dead body with relief and tell me to run, tell me she's willing to cover.

But I can't fucking go. Not till I know they'll be safe.

I throw my arms around Rissa, hot panic ripping through me like a current, holding her together. She sways so gently in my arms while I push my forehead to hers, wiping her blood, muttering words back and forth. I wish I could stay here and keep her talking.

I'm scared that sick fuck gave her a concussion. She's mumbling, barely able to stand, but the maid gives me a knowing, promising look. My baby girl's in good hands.

"Get her out of town," I say. "Out of Heart's Edge. You, too. Get as far away as you can."

Both the maid and Rissa lift their heads, staring at me.

Rissa looks wounded, wretched. "Leo, Leo, come with us..."

"I can't." I retreat toward the door, scrubbing my hands on my thighs like I can still feel the chicken-skin stubble of Bell's neck scratching me. "There's something I need to do."

"Leo!" she calls, but I'm already turning, running from the question, the plea in her lovely, sad voice.

She's begging me not to go.

But I don't have a choice.

So I shift back a few steps and gather her up and cradle her in my arms one more time.

"I'm already damned," I tell her. "Already going to jail. Let me do one last thing right before they find me and throw away the key. I have to, Rissa. For the town. But if you'll wait for me, I'll come back. Somehow, some fucking way, I swear I will. I'll *always* come back for you, woman, no matter how much hell it takes."

That was my promise.

And I had no earthly clue it was a lie.

Or was it?

Maybe it's just a promise delayed, one I have a chance to finally fulfill.

* * *

Present

I'm still reliving that nightmare when Doc and I pull into the parking lot of Sweeter Things.

I just want to do one last check.

One final chance to see her before we head to Missoula and hope we can get the drop on Ross.

The radio's playing in the car, and in between some garbled country-rap song blaring over the speakers, there's an ad spot. Fuschia's voice.

Smart.

I know Nash will recognize it and what it means.

She lets out a sultry purr, like she's advertising for one of those late-night sexy radio call-ins. "Hiya, Heart's Edge, do you love *scandal?*" she lilts, and I roll my eyes. "Then tune in tonight! Midnight sharp. You'll find out secrets about this town that will blow your mind. Open your eyes. Learn the truth, and join me for the ride of your life."

As the sound trips over to some jingle for toothpaste, Gray snorts from the driver's seat. "Well, at least it'll get people curious."

"For all the wrong reasons. But if it does the trick..."

I trail off as Doc throws the truck in park, and I catch sight of Rissa.

For a moment, I can only sit there and watch her. She's speaking animatedly with one of the contractors.

The sun shines through the storefront, shimmering over her. Rissa almost glows, and every time she moves, it's a thing of grace and beauty that makes her seem to flow in rhythm with the music of her curves. Her hair trails around her in a sweep as she turns, surveying the interior of the shop.

323

Her shop.

Even if Deanna ran it, this was her dream. I'm proud of her for making it come true.

"You," Gray says, "are so damned obvious."

I snap a look at him. "Obvious?"

"Yeah. The fact that you're head over heels in love with the mother of your boy."

I grin halfheartedly. "Sounds like a pretty normal thing to be."

"Leo." Gray's hand grips my shoulder, grounding me. "Don't do anything reckless. We're in public."

"You don't get it," I say. "There's nothing I *wouldn't* do for her."

No matter what it costs.

Warren's truck is parked in front of the shop, and he's leaning against the hood of the car, nursing a coffee and looking bored as hell. He catches my eye and nods, though, giving me the all clear.

I'm trusting him not to let anything happen to my family while we're gone.

When Clarissa turns and sees me, she lights up and practically comes dancing out to the truck.

I roll the window down. She drapes her arms over the door and leans in. "Hey. I wasn't expecting to see you before you headed out again."

Gray clears his throat, and I'm suddenly self-conscious, knowing he's watching and trying not to smirk—but I ignore him, brushing my knuckles to her cheek.

She leans in so naturally, angel face glowing in the sweetest way.

Damn, I feel wrong right now, even if I can't pin down why. Then her gaze flicks over my face, and I figure it out.

I'm actually *uncomfortable* under my hood.

I've been so used to hiding myself for so long. But around the cabin with her and Zach, up at the big house with Ms. Wilma and Warren and our friends, something changed.

I've come to feel natural in my own messed up skin.

It's just me. And these people see the real me, accept me for what I am.

That's some heavy shit.

Glancing over my shoulder, I make sure there's nobody around who might catch a glimpse of me and recognize the legendary Nine. Then I flick my hood down, making my hair stick up everywhere. The mask goes next, dragging it down around my neck.

Clarissa absolutely beams. She reaches in to cup her palm to my cheek.

"There. Happy?" I grin, turning my head to press my lips to her palm. "Just wanted to check in with you before we hit the road. Everything's going down tonight. With any luck, we'll have Deanna back by morning."

Her eyes widen, and her smile fades. There's trouble in her eyes.

Like she's scared to hope, after all this time.

Like she's scared I'll fail her.

"That soon?" she asks, trying a shaky laugh. "Wow, that's going to be quite a Halloween."

Oh, hell. I'd forgotten it was almost Halloween.

That worries me.

There'll be tons of people on the streets. If Nash wants to make a major move, it'll be easier tonight, when he can blend in with people in costumes and won't draw any attention to his weird, creepy self.

Then again, his advantage could be mine, too.

Because this is the one night of the year where no one would look twice at a burned man dripping wild ink.

I quit pondering and focus on Rissa.

"Babe," I murmur, stroking my thumb to her cheek. "What's with that look? You okay?"

She takes a deep breath. "All this time, as long as I didn't know for sure, I could believe she was alive. But what if she's not, Leo? What if you find her and she's...she's..."

Her voice hitches, thick, cracking around the unspeakable.

I'm out of the truck in a flash, careful with the door so I don't shove her, wrapping her in my arms like no tomorrow.

"That's not gonna happen," I soothe, as she presses into me with her shoulders hunched and shaking, her head hidden against my chest. "Nash needs her as leverage. She's safe as long as we've got something he wants."

"But we don't *know* that," she whispers. "We're guessing. He could've killed her before we even saw that video. She could be dead, and he's just playing us to get what he wants."

My stomach sinks.

This is my fault.

I brought this mess to Heart's Edge. Even if we get rid of Nash, Galentron will always follow me, unless they're destroyed.

I'm starting to wonder if those hopes about having a family, about being a father, about being there for Clarissa and Zach are all in fucking vain.

How can I protect them, when I couldn't even keep Deanna safe? But I hold those thoughts in like venom.

She needs me to be strong.

So I kiss her forehead, stroking that rich mahogany-brown hair back.

"*She's* too important to die," I remind her. "Whatever we know, she's got intel we don't. The full picture. She's her own damn bargaining chip. And we know Deanna, Rissa. She's smart. Crafty. She'll hold out and string Nash along to buy us time. She knows we're coming. She *has* to know."

Clarissa lets out a shaky laugh. "Yeah, maybe. That brat would toy with him like that."

"Exactly." I curl her hair around my fingers, brushing the tip of those gleaming locks to her cheek, and smile my best for her.

"So tonight, just try to stay safe. I wish you could take Zach trick-or-treating."

"Next year," she says, and there's a promise in those words, soft and heartfelt.

I hope there'll be a next year.

For all of us.

"Next year," I agree, pulling her closer one more time.

I just hope it's not the last time.

I'm going to bring that bastard Ross back and stop the demon he created.

This time, it's different.

I have too many promises to keep, come hell or high water.

XXI: HAIRPIN TURN (CLARISSA)

I should've gone with him.

That's the only thought in my head while I'm pacing the cabin.

I should've insisted. To get Dr. Ross. To confront Nash.

To bring my sister back.

If I'd offered, though, if I'd tried, I just know what he'd have said.

Too bad right now, I feel like a prisoner, cooped up in this cabin with Warren sprawled out on the front deck, pretending to be nursing a beer when he's actually keeping Zach and me safe.

I hate that we're targets, leverage for Galentron.

And I hate that it leaves me trapped, unable to help my sister or the man I love.

Zach's curled up on the couch with a book. I envy his ability to be so calm right now. He takes so many things in stride it's kind of scary.

I sink down next to him, leaning over to watch him focusing intently on his book.

"Hey," I say. "Did you want to be an Animorph for Halloween?"

He pushes his glasses up his nose. "Maybe," he says distract-edly, turning a page. "I kind of like Abe Sapiens, too."

I have no idea who that is.

He's a little sponge, picking up everything from pop culture characters to politics.

But I smile, slipping an arm around his shoulders. "Maybe next year. I'm sorry you couldn't go trick-or-treating this year."

"It's okay, Mom. I know you're going to give me a lot of candy later anyway." He tilts his head back, grinning up at me, reading my mind. "And I know you'd be sad and worried if I went this year. So it's okay. I don't want you to be sad, Mom."

God, this boy.

I pull him close, feeling tears trying so hard to break free, and squeeze him tight, burying my face in his hair.

"I'm so lucky to have you, ZZ," I whisper. "Don't know what I'd do without you."

He hugs me without reservation. That makes me smile even more.

Some little boys his age have already started their "Ew, Mom has cooties" phase, but not my Zach.

He wraps his arms around me and snuggles in close, my little bug-bear, sweet and warm.

"It'll be okay, Mom," he says. "Auntie Deanna's okay, too."

Damn it.

I've tried so hard to keep him from really understanding what's at stake here, but it's been impossible to keep him from overhearing everything.

I just hate it.

Just want my little boy to *stay* a little boy a while longer.

Please.

I curl my fingers into his hair, looking down at him with a wavering smile. "Baby, how much do you know about what's going on?"

Zach looks up at me, solemn, thoughtful, considering. He looks so much like Leo my heart could pop.

Leo has that same way of carefully considering every word, choosing what he's going to say so it's as gentle as possible.

Finally, Zach speaks, clear and crisp, "That man you're after, the weirdo at the museum who liked your hair, he took Auntie Deanna somewhere, didn't he? Because she knows stuff he needs to know. You're scared he'll hurt her, so you're trying to find a way to get her back. And Mr. Nine's out there helping you."

"Yeah, baby," I say, kissing the top of his head through my blurry tears. "That's pretty much it."

He tucks into me closer. "It's okay, Mom. I know you can do it. That creep's a monster, but we've got one too."

With a choked sound, half laugh, half sob, I just squeeze him tighter.

If only I could have as much faith in myself as my little boy has in me.

But I glance up at the sound of Warren's voice from outside. He's talking into his phone. Something about the way he speaks sets me on edge.

His shoulders are tense, his neck stiff, even his short beard seems to be standing on end.

His words are short, clipped.

Everything in his tone says *trouble*.

And I'm scared that trouble is coming for me, when he pockets his phone and stands, pushing the door open with his jaw set in a grim line.

"Clarissa? There's something you need to hear," he says, his gaze locking with mine. "Bring Zach. I'll take you down to the radio station."

* * *

I DON'T KNOW what I'm expecting to hear.

The station is a small brick building on the outskirts of town, a ways off from the last few buildings and houses, a tall network tower with its red blinking light protruding from the roof like a unicorn's horn.

There's not much room inside the studio. We cram in with Zach's small hand clutched in mine. Especially when Rex Natchez, the station owner, is already in there with Blake.

And with Fuchsia Delaney.

That wretched woman looks at home surrounded by a lot of weird equipment. I can't figure out what's what, all these black boxes with hundreds of buttons and dials and little glowing screens.

I just know everything doesn't look like radio equipment.

It definitely doesn't belong here, considering it's piled up with all the other stuff that's been built into the walls.

She looks so out of place, surrounded by so much machinery in one of her sleek dresses, a headset clutched in one hand and held up to her ear instead of looped over her head. But she's focused in a way I've never seen her.

It's weird.

I don't know Fuchsia that well, but I *know* her. She's a bogey-woman from my childhood.

I know her oily, cloying slickness. I know her false face. I wish I didn't know her wicked witch smile.

What's new is this look of dead set determination as she listens with her mouth pursed in a thin line, her brows drawn together, steely eyes distant but dark.

She's serious about this.

I only wish I knew what caused it.

Part of me hates that I actually feel some kind of pity for her. She's been the face of so much death, so much loss. But maybe some leopards can change their spots.

Maybe some leopards have their reasons.

She looks up at me, her eyes grave. "Finally. You need to hear this."

Blake looks pale, his face drawn. Warren still seems so grim, it's scaring me.

My heart just patters away, almost breaking.

I reach into my pocket.

Call me crazy, but I needed a good luck charm today. So I grabbed that old ring box and shook the band out and hid it in my pocket, but it's comforting now to run my finger over metal that's absorbing my body heat.

It's a reminder.

Leo will come back.

Everything will be okay.

And I'm strong enough to handle this, to steel myself for whatever it is. I pull my hands up and cover Zach's ears.

"Okay, ready," I say, my voice catching. "Play it back."

Fuchsia looks at me soberly, then tugs the cable from a box at her elbow, unhooking the headphones.

A jittery crackle leaps out of the speaker at the front of the device. She pushes a button, and I hear the sound of an old-fashioned tape playback, before a voice comes growling out of the speaker.

"—athetic. They're trying another expose."

Is that...Nash?

My teeth pinch together. I don't know him well, but I can't forget that serpentine edge to his voice, hissy and malicious. But the voice that comes next, rising from my past, strikes chills through me like a reverberating bell. It has to be Dr. Ross.

"Don't let that happen, my boy. You know what you have to do."

"I'll get the communications shut down before they try their little stunt." Nash pauses. "This looks like a dead-end operation. They tried to be clever. I'm not sure cleanup's an option."

"Recommendations?"

"You know what my recommendation always is. What I wanted to do instead of this stupid goose chase," Nash sneers.

That's when another voice cuts in.

Feminine.

Familiar, heart-chillingly so.

"You fucker!" Deanna cries in the background—rasping, broken, but furious, her spirit still strong, and I catch my breath, my entire body forming a painful knot of hope and fear and longing. *"You think hurting people will stop this from getting out? I've—"*

A sharp *crack* sounds, flesh on flesh, followed by my sister yelling in pain.

Then silence.

Tears prick my eyes. I grind my knuckles against my lips.

Dear God. Even if he hasn't heard more than muffled noise, Zach presses against me like a puppy offering comfort.

Warren and Blake watch me worriedly, but it's Fuchsia who speaks, pausing the playback.

"That's her, isn't it?" she says. "Deanna."

I nod slowly, sucking in sharp gasps. "No question. When...when was this?"

"Half an hour ago," she answers. "So half an hour ago, Deanna was still alive."

Ouch. Hope has never hurt more than it does now.

I don't have to wonder.

I *know.*

I know, with very little doubt, my sister's probably alive for now.

Hurt, scared, but alive.

There's a *chance.*

I swallow hard, trying to keep myself together. "Is there more?"

"Not much," Fuchsia says. "Nothing really relevant."

"Play it anyway," I say.

She eyes me, then nods and pushes the playback button again.

Ross' voice floats out, mocking and gravelly. *"I see she's a feisty one. You've not been having fun with her?"*

"Just the hair, Doc. I need her to be able to walk," Nash says with an almost sulky sigh. *"It's so boring."*

For the first time in my life, I feel very capable of murdering someone.

Especially when I can hear Deanna sniffling in the background.

But I hear something else, too.

A dripping sound, slow, familiar.

It's so rhythmic it's almost like a metronome, the sound of water striking against...stone?

Wait.

I *know* that sound.

But I'm distracted as Ross drones on in his icy, hypnotic tone. *"You're under orders to complete Operation Black Forest. Authorization code Cellar Door."* He stops and then repeats it again, very slowly, precisely, *"Cellar. Door."*

When Nash speaks again, it's eerie. Empty. This numb, toneless hush, repeating it back. *"Cellar...Door. Understood."*

I don't understand. Cellar door?

Cellar door.

Oh.

Holy effing hell.

A memory hits me right between the eyes, so fast and furious I have to put my hand on Blake's shoulder to keep from toppling over.

I know where Deanna is.

* * *

Many Years Ago

I ALWAYS LOVE GOING out in the woods with Mommy.

But it's not as fun this time because Mommy can't hold my hand. She's got to hold on to my new baby sister.

Deanna's okay, I guess. She's kinda cute, but she cries a lot, and right now I want Mommy to pay attention to *me* and hold my hand instead of holding my dumb baby sister.

I run through the trees. The leaves are so green and bright. They look all sparkly, and I spread my arms and dash ahead, then pick up a bright-pink flower and run back.

"Look, Mommy!"

I hold the flower up, and she smiles, her green eyes crinkling.

"It's beautiful, baby. Do you want me to braid it through your hair?"

I hesitate, then look at Deanna, sucking her thumb. Her hair is all curly wisps stuck to her face, and she's watching me with wide eyes like she's scared of me.

I think sometimes she's scared I don't love her, just 'cause I get mad that she takes Mommy away from me sometimes.

I do love her. I really do.

So I reach up and tuck the flower into her hair and smile. "I like it better in Deedee's hair."

Deanna stares at me with big eyes, then lets out a happy burble and turns her head, hiding her face in Mommy's shoulder.

Mommy smiles at me, her eyes so warm, and strokes her hand over my hair.

"That was a nice thing to do for your sister, my little bell," she says, then takes my hand, keeping a tight hold on Deanna with the other. "Come on. I want to show you something."

I stare up at her. The sun makes pretty halos around her head.

Mommy always looks like an angel, even when she's sad and her smile hides her crying.

"What are we gonna see?" I ask.

"Walk with me," she says, "and you'll find out."

So we walk some more. I skip sometimes, kicking up leaves. Deanna falls asleep. I'm starting to get tired. My legs hurt a little and my tennis shoes are pinching my feet, but then we stumble out of the trees and into a clearing.

There's a door.

Double doors that look like they're buried in the ground.

They're wood, very old, and they have a big wood bar across them.

Thick plants are growing all over them, vines and honeysuckles, like they haven't been touched in a long time.

Mommy leads me to the door, then leans down and puts Deanna in my arms. She's heavy, but I've got her, and I hold on tight while Mommy smiles at me and says, "Do you remember how to get here, Rissa?"

I bite my lip and nod, looking back toward the trail.

Two big trees loom to the sides of it, and one of them is weird. It looks like it's split into five different trees at the bottom. Almost like a big tree hand. I know how to find that tree again.

"Yes, Mommy," I say.

"Good girl."

She smiles and picks up that big board and drags it up, before pulling the doors open.

The hinges make a loud metal squeaking sound. When they open up, it's like a big black mouth, and there are stone stairs leading down inside. There's dust, so much dust, and it smells all wet and muddy and weird and old.

It's *spooky.*

I stare down inside. The walls are stone, too, and there's green stuff growing on them.

There's water trickling down them like a stream, and it makes a steady dripping sound.

I'm holding my breath, holding Deanna tighter.

Mommy looks at me and says, "Do you know what this is?"

I struggle for the words. I've seen something like it before, but I can't remember.

Then it clicks, and I nod quickly.

"Storm cellar! Just like the old one at school."

"Exactly." I love the way Mommy smiles when I get the

answer right. "Only this is a special one. It goes all the way to our house."

My eyes widen. "But we're so far away from home!"

"We're not as far away as it seems. We came in a big circle." Mommy crouches down to look at me at eye level. "You know where you like to play in the basement?"

Uh-oh.

I'm not supposed to go down there.

Mommy's not supposed to know about that.

But I don't want to lie, so I admit it. "Um, yeah..."

But Mommy's not mad.

She just smiles more, tucking my hair back. "Well, this tunnel leads to a very special door there. If you're ever out playing in the woods and a bad storm like a tornado comes, you come here. You take your sister here, and you go under the house. Just like the storm drills at school." She hesitates, her smile fading. "And if you ever need to get out of the house without being caught, for any reason..." She shakes her head. "Find that special door, baby. Find it and run."

She seems so sad.

I don't like it when Mommy's sad, but sometimes...

Sometimes I hear Papa screaming, and that's when Mommy comes to our room looking sad, and she pulls us close and holds us until we all fall asleep together.

Maybe that'll help now, so I move in close to her and snuggle me and Deanna into her. Her arms clasp around me, and I rest my head on her shoulder. "I will, Mommy."

I don't get what's going on.

But she holds us both so tight and kisses my hair, and even if she's sad she sounds like she's happy with me anyway when she says, "That's my little bell. That's my good girl."

No, I don't understand.

I won't for many more years.

By then, it's too late, and the memory of that day in the woods and the special door are almost long gone.

* * *

Present

I NEVER KNEW REMEMBERING COULD *HURT*.

Guess I'd just buried so many memories of our mother. Like after she died, after the cancer took her away from us, all the good in our life was gone, too. My father's humanity died with her, leaving him falling farther and farther down into his own hell of bourbon and bad business.

I'd forgotten that day.

Her hand in mine, Deanna on her hip, and that weird door way out in the woods.

I'd been around five.

And I don't know if I can trust memories from when I was five years old.

I'm not Zach with his freaky photographic memory.

Still, I can't ignore it, either.

"I have to go," I gasp, looking desperately at Warren. "Keep Zach with you—*please*," I say, gently nudging my son toward him.

Warren looks at me, confused, but holds out his hand for Zach, who goes to him like the good kid he is. "Mind telling me what's going on?"

"I think I know where Deanna is. I have a hunch," I say, already backing toward the exit. "Cellar door."

He frowns, stepping forward. "Hold up. Let me go with you—"

"*No.*" I shake my head fiercely.

I don't know why, but I can't stand the idea of someone else being there if I'm wrong.

"If I'm right, I'll call for backup. It'll draw less attention if I go alone. Besides, you're all needed here if this whole thing tonight

338

is going to work, right? And I need someone to stay with Zach. He can't come with me." I look between them all.

Fuchsia watches me with a hard dose of skepticism, Blake just looks confused. Warren's still scowling, scratching at his beard, clearly worried. "I'll be right back, I promise. I just want to check something out."

Warren shakes his head. "I don't like this. What if Nash comes after you?"

I smile faintly. "Sounds like Nash has his hands full with bigger things. Just try to figure out what Operation Black Forest is. Call Leo once you know. Let me handle the rest."

I'm backing out before they can say anything else. Before they can stop me.

I'm still reeling.

Now I know exactly how Leo would disappear and reappear when we were kids.

I know where to find Deanna.

I know how to save the town. To find out what Nash intends to do and stop him.

Heart in my throat, lungs nearly bursting, I flee from the radio station, running like I've never run before, straight into the woods a mile or so away.

Sis, hang on. I'm coming.

XXII: SUDDEN CRASH (NINE)

*W*ho the hell knows if I'm ready for this.

It's not like I've got any choice.

I haven't seen Maximilian Asshole Ross in years. Not since the mansion.

Once the Nighthawks were ready for deployment, we were assigned to different units, rented to different government contracts, different locations overseas. Sometimes Kabul, Djibouti, Mosul, Tripoli...effectively rented to Uncle Sam for black ops, highly dangerous missions they didn't want to risk with regulars.

Dr. Ross never saw us after our teens until Galentron brought us home to protect their own turf. He was there in the mansion, quietly observing the men we'd become.

Even before, his voice was always there over radio, our hellish, abusive father guiding us. Whenever one of us went off programming, Ross was brought in to bring us back on track.

I'll never forget that bastard.

I remember the table. The syringe. The *pain.*

Him leaning over me, looking down with his frigid, empty gaze. A mechanic gives a faulty engine more affection than this monster gave us.

My lip curls in a fit, remembering the sick, fucked up feeling of his wrinkled hand stroking my brow, winding my hair back.

Pretending to care about me.

Less than he'd care about a pet.

All he ever cared about was if I'd obey, just like the others.

"Leo," Gray says, trying to ground me back to earth. "Are you with me?"

"I'm here," I say, tearing my gaze off the passing miles through the window. "Don't worry. My head's in the game."

Gray pulls his truck to an idling halt at the beginning of a small lane that branches off the highway and into the woods just outside Missoula.

Up that path is the house Dr. Ross retired to after he took his pension. That's what the personnel files said, the ones I'm not supposed to have.

He doesn't know we're coming.

He sure as hell doesn't know he's about to make up for every shit he ever took, whether he wants to or not.

We've been driving for hours, past sunset, and well into the night.

It's dark except for Gray's headlights, which he dims now, easing the truck onto the shoulder. He kills the engine.

But instead of getting out, he just turns to look at me, draping his arm along the back of the seat, green eyes solemn behind the glint of his glasses.

"Look, man, I'm serious," he says. "I need to *know* you can do this. Tell me I'm not leading you into something that could destroy you."

I smile grimly. "Little late for that, huh? I've already destroyed myself seven ways from Sunday."

"Ross can still hurt you." He's sharp-edged, fierce, but I know Gray. And I know his icy brand of concern is how he shows he cares. "I don't know everything about the Nighthawks program. Active biowarfare agents were my area of expertise, not mind control and child abuse." He snorts. "But if we're here for Ross because he knows Nash's control words, then it's safe to say he knows yours, too."

After the brush with Nash and taking a knife to the thigh, he has no clue how right he is.

Still, I can't seem to shake this cynical smile. "What makes you think I have control words?"

Gray sighs. "Leo."

I close my eyes.

Bad idea. Bad joke.

Can't blame a man for trying. Being here with Gray, in the dark, tension vibrating between us, so many of the old horrors coming home to roost...it's too damn much.

It reminds me of that night I snapped, killed Edgar Bell, and burned down the entire facility and the Paradise Hotel to destroy SP-73 before it could get loose.

Reminds me of the screams, too. Employees who may not have been innocent, not really, but then none of us are.

Not me. Not Gray. We were complicit.

The fact that we tried to change something after the fact?

It's atonement, not salvation.

I don't know if I can ever atone for the lives lost because I tried to do the right thing, and it all went so horribly wrong. But I can at least try to stop anyone else from dying. I can try to save my family.

"I have to do this," I say, looking at Gray. "There's no other option. If I start going weird..." I take a deep breath. "Just knock me out, Gray. Knock me on my ass before I get dangerous."

"Me?" Gray smirks dryly. "Knock *you* out?"

"You're fast and strong and tricky. You'll find a way." I take a deep breath and push the truck door open, stepping outside. "Let's go trap a snake."

Gray follows me as we slip into the woods, taking cover under darkness and following parallel to the road, moving up to the house unseen.

The lights inside start flickering through the trees, and his voice drifts through the darkness quietly. "Leo?"

"Yeah?"

"How do you intend to make him cooperate?"

I don't like the smile that spreads over my lips. It makes me feel like the monster Ross tried to make me, capable of anything.

"I'm not giving him a choice," I growl. "Not if he wants to live."

"And if he doesn't?"

Then I'll make sure he suffers so much he wishes he could die.

Anything to put an end to this. But I don't say that.

I only shake my head, forging on through the trees.

We creep closer till we can see the tall brick house, constructed in a rustic mountain style but accented with huge windows and many modern touches.

It's comfortable. Cozy. Hidden.

Probably complacent, unless there's a security system with features I can't make out in the dark.

No guards, though.

Not even motion sensors. I scan the grounds, searching for even the smallest oddly-shaped rock that might be a disguised sensor, a defense system.

Nothing.

I guess Dr. Ross really trusts they've eliminated anyone who might want him dead.

The broad front window gives me a clear look inside the wood-paneled interior, all lit up in soft gold light. That light shines off the rims of Ross' glasses. He's moving through his kitchen, chopping vegetables, pouring red wine into a glass.

It's so idyllic. So peaceful. Just an old man going about his evening.

And all I can think about is how easy it'd be to take a sniper shot from here. A monster like Ross doesn't *deserve* this kind of peace.

It's disgusting how the worst people, the cruelest people, hide behind the mundane.

How they sleep so easily at night.

All because they don't have enough of a human soul left to care who they hurt.

A snarl curdles my lips, and I rise from my crouch—only for Gray's hand to smack my chest.

He gives me a warning look. "Go easy," he says.

He's right. I nod and rein myself in.

I can't fly out of control. Not here.

Taking a deep breath, I stealth-creep, slipping across the lawn with Gray in my wake. We keep low, out of the line of sight, only standing once we've reached the front door.

Just to keep things simple, I knock.

There's the sound of the wine bottle clinking down inside, a momentary pause.

Bastard barely even hesitates. He feels *that* safe, and it makes my blood boil.

My eyes flick to the squeak of the lock turning, the click, the door unlatching.

Then he pulls it open, a quizzical look on his face.

It's the face of my nightmares, just a decade older, more seamed, more wrinkled, the flesh a little less firm, his eyes not quite so wickedly bright.

He was an older man when he destroyed me.

He's an *old* man now.

That doesn't hold me back even in the slightest when he looks between me and Gray, his eyes widening in recognition, his lips parting on—

We'll never find out.

Because I draw back, clench my fist, and mutter, "Long time no see, Doctor."

My fist crashes into his face.

Ross goes staggering back with a garbled sound as his nose explodes with red, his glasses cracking.

I'm on him in a flash, crossing the threshold, fists raised. One more hit and I'll knock him out cold. I need him incapacitated. Helpless.

"The blue wharf," he gasps out, even as he staggers out of my reach. "The. Blue. Wharf."

Shit.

Just like that, my entire body locks up.

It's like a charge rushes through me, changing my whole polarity. Everything feels turned inside out.

My brain doesn't even feel connected. It's disembodied.

I just fucking *blank*.

Nothing in my head except the roar of white noise, and *I can't move.*

I can barely even breathe.

Gray's voice seems to spiral down a distant tunnel as he yells my name.

"Leo? Leo!"

I watch him shouldering around me, crashing into Ross before that asshole can turn and run. They go down together, Ross hissing and clawing like an angry cat.

The old doctor's no match for the vet.

Gray grips him by the shoulders and slams him down *hard*, his head bouncing against the wood flooring.

I still can't fucking move. I'm just raging inside, beating against the cages of my own damn mind.

Then Ross, straining against Gray, snarls out another word. "Boudica!"

It's like a hot-burning rage flashes through me in an instant, painting everything jagged red.

Gray looks brightest, like he's on fire, glowing. I can see the blood in his veins, waiting to be squeezed out until he *pops*.

The only thing soft-colored is Ross, a passive target, not to be touched, but my body wants to kill, to rend, to destroy, to—and it damn sure wants to stop the source of this hot red knife in my mind. Right now, that seems to be my friend.

345

"*No!*" I roar, even as my hands clench into fists and my muscles bunch to launch myself at Gray.

I won't.

And suddenly it takes everything in me to *stay* still, but I refuse to move.

I won't hurt my friend.

I refuse to obey my conditioning, those words that act like implanted commands I'm meant to follow without thinking, even as my body screams.

My legs strain, wanting to lunge forward. Only for me to pull back with all my will and all my strength. It feels like my muscle fibers are about to *snap* with the tug of war between my free will and my conditioning.

"Boudica!" Ross roars again, loud and demanding, but I snap my head to one side, closing my eyes, clenching my teeth.

"*No!*" I snap back again, holding on to that word as a lifeline, my entire body in flames.

Fuck. You.

I. Will. Not. Give. In.

There's a violent crash of flesh on wood. I can just piece the sound together even if I won't look. Gray slams Ross against the floor again, and I hear my tormentor grunting in pain.

"Say it," Gray roars. "Say the release word. Let him go."

"I'll do no such thing," Ross spits back. "That savage will kill me if I release him."

"Shame. I'll kill you if you don't," Gray fires back, and Ross makes a sneering sound.

"You won't. You obviously need me for something, or I—*hnngh!*"

This time the sound is a crashing fist on flesh. Ross belts out a howl.

Gray growls. "You remember how good I am with a scalpel, Ross. I can do a lot of things to you without killing you, believe me. You won't like a single one of them."

There's silence.

346

Then another crash, another grunt from Ross, while my body coils tighter. The mental leash I've got on myself stretches.

There's a scream in my mind that I can't and won't succumb to.

This howling banshee in my head wants to eat my free will alive and leave me mindless and broken and full of regret and—

"The cool green day," Ross gasps. It's not quite right, missing that hypnotic cadence I'm conditioned to listen for, but it's the *words* that matter right now. "L-9, come back to *the cool green day.*"

I'm a puppet with its strings cut.

That rage bleeds out like a dam breaking, leaving me empty, loose, and I collapse, falling to my hands and knees, sucking in desperate breaths.

"Fuck," I gasp. "Fuck."

"You all right?" Gray asks.

"Yeah." I push myself up on my knees, dragging my hood back so I can *breathe*, looking at them.

Gray still has Ross pinned, one hand curled in his shirt in a tight and straining lock, the other hand up with his bloodied knuckles clenched.

Ross' face is a mess. His nose is smashed in, blood down his beard and cheeks and mouth. His lips are swollen and split, and I don't think that was me.

It was Gray.

I smile. This is why I trusted him to have my back.

I stagger to my feet, striding closer, looking down at the demon who made me what I am.

He's just a pathetic old bastard now, but he still looks up at me like he's in control, his red-smeared mouth spreading in a bloody smirk.

"You don't look well, L-9."

I don't bother answering the fuck.

Just slam my boot into the side of his head, watching with

347

grim satisfaction as his eyes widen before he slumps unconscious.

"Come on," I mutter, reaching down to hook a hand under one of his arms. "Let's get him back to town."

* * *

WE'RE MORE than halfway to Heart's Edge when Gray's phone rings on the dash, cutting off the GPS.

It's Warren's name on the caller ID.

We've got Ross tied up in the back seat. He's gagged, just in case he wakes up before we get back and tries to pull anything.

Gray gives me a worried look, then leans over and taps the screen, putting Warren on speaker. "Here."

Warren's voice comes out haggard, dark. "Put Leo on!"

"I'm here." I lean forward, instantly tense, alert. "You're on speaker. What's going on?"

"You need to get back here," Warren says. "And I'm talkin' *now*. Fuchsia was fucking around with the transmission gear while we were gearing up to broadcast. She intercepted a communication between that creepy fucker and somebody with the company."

"Shit." I check the time; we're still probably half an hour out. "What's it say?"

"Move over," I hear Fuchsia suddenly, impatient, interrupting. "Have a listen, Lion-boy."

I bite back my retort, even if a snarl bubbles up inside me, as crackly recorded audio starts playing over the line.

Nash's voice, and another one I don't recognize—dry, deadpan, sounds like it's been mechanized through a filter.

One of the higher-ups at Galentron, then.

"—*not answering*," Nash says in that clipped, cool tone that comes with an official report, the same tone drilled into us. "*Ross may have been compromised. The entire mission is compromised. He gave me the order to enact Black Forest.*"

I go pale.

Black Forest?

Black fucking Forest means a controlled release of SP-73 from the air over Heart's Edge.

No.

No, Nash, he wouldn't have brought a sample of the virus here? Not enough to infect the whole town...would he?

But that sick feeling inside me turns into pure horror, dread, as a mechanized voice answers.

"No. We can't risk Black Forest spreading into the wild," the voice says. *"Not in the current climate. We'll have to forget subtlety and take the brute force method. Your orders have changed. Enact Black Phoenix."*

There's something almost eager in Nash's voice when he says, *"Black Phoenix? That's a lot of explosives, but I know the perfect place to stage them."*

For a moment everything goes blurry.

The road in front of me, the night sky, the dashboard of Gray's truck.

Black Phoenix.

"Leo?" Gray says sharply. "Translate. I wasn't in that deep with security. What's Black Phoenix?"

"Whatever it is," Warren interjects, "I can guess it involves a lot of fire."

"Highly flammable payload," I grunt out. The words feel robotic, dredged up from inside me. "Pick a central target and use a highly flammable payload to make sure it goes up hard, goes up fast, and takes out as many structures around it as possible before the flames jump to take care of everything else."

There's a dead silence.

Finally, Warren swears softly, and I hear Fuchsia's disgust on the other end of the line.

But when someone speaks; it's Blake cutting in. "Everyone's out tonight. *Everyone.* It's the Halloween event at the museum, and people are trick-or-treating, they—*damn*. Leo, fuck, they could kill half this town in a matter of minutes."

"Not if we have anything to say about it. Gray, drive faster. Fuck the speed limit."

"You get to explain why we're speeding with an unconscious man trussed up in the back of my truck if we get pulled over," Gray says, charging the truck forward in a hard, growling leap.

I glance over my shoulder.

In the small cargo area between the front seats and the back of the truck, Ross lies unconscious, hog-tied, mostly out of sight.

He won't be a problem.

I hope.

Turning my attention forward again, I focus on the phone. "Listen. Forget broadcasting the Galentron announcement. That can wait. We made a bad move. We baited Nash too far. Use the radio system, hook it into the town emergency PA, tell everyone to evacuate. Get into the storm shelters. It'll be the safest place in the event of an explosion. Whatever you do, get those kids off the streets."

Blake pipes in. "I'll get my volunteer firefighter crew on it, too. Start an ordered evacuation procedure."

"Good," I start to say, until Warren interrupts, oddly quiet.

"Hold up. There's more."

But before he can say anything else, I hear another voice that makes my blood go cold.

Zach.

"Mr. Warren?" he says. "Is my mom gonna get hurt?"

I clench my fists, straining into the phone. "Clarissa's not there?"

Fuck. I hadn't heard her voice, but I'd been so preoccupied with everything else.

No one answers at first, until Fuchsia cuts in. "She took off. Left the kid with us so no one could really chase her down. We've all got our hands full. She thinks she knows where

Deanna is, because Ross said 'cellar door.'" She pauses. "You know what that means, don't you, Leo?"

I do.

And it makes my stomach drop down to the soles of my feet as a memory hits full force. Just a scene.

Cellar door.

That door in the woods.

That memory of trauma and pain I've blocked out.

That room buried deep underground, so deep it's barely connected to the mansion.

Shit.

The damn museum is a perfect central location. Especially if Nash has been working out of the subterranean spaces all along. I see his plan.

Stage the explosives there. Kill as many people as possible during the Halloween bash. Watch the fire consume the whole town.

He could even make it easy to cover up. The museum's an old building, after all. Blame it on a gas main exploding, and while the flames are on a tear, he'll move through the chaos, picking off people who manage to escape so nobody talks.

But as much as I should care about that, there's only one thing I can think of.

Clarissa's going to be in that building when it explodes.

Fuck!

There's no other word. No way to describe the flood of panic and rage that rushes through me.

"We're on our way back now. Blake, get that evac crew going, find Clarissa—"

"I'll do my best," Blake promises. "I'll get your girl, Tiger."

"Warren—"

"Zach's safe with me," War says firmly. "No one's going to hurt him. No matter what happens."

"Thank you."

I want to feel relief, but there's this sickness inside me that says I need to be there to handle it all myself. I'm the only one besides Gray who knows the full extent of what Galentron and Nash can do.

And we're still closing in on the town.

I can't lose everything. My woman. My son.

Not because I let my shadows become too safe and didn't step into the light soon enough.

My chest crushes up like a fist, and I can't breathe.

I take in several deep, rough breaths, then force myself to calm down, to talk. "Let me talk to Zach for a second."

There's a silence, then Zach speaks. His voice has that clear, quiet calm he always has, but it's hushed, soft, and I can tell he's afraid. "Hi, Mr. Nine," he whispers.

"Hey. Hey, kiddo," I say. Fuck.

There's a lump in my throat, my eyes stinging. "Listen, little man. You're gonna be okay. I'm gonna find your mom, and fix this mess."

"But..." The hesitation in his voice kills me. Fucking *kills* me. "But you're not here? You're far away."

"Not as far as you think. I'm on my way back. I'll get there in time." I clench my fists against my thighs so hard I nearly draw blood. "There's something we need to talk about, Zach."

I shouldn't tell him now.

I shouldn't.

But if something happens to one of us tonight...

"What's w—" His voice cuts off in a crackle. "—ng, Mr. N—" More crackles. "—ne?"

"Zach? Zach, you still there?'

Nothing.

"Zach!" I lean forward hard, clutching at the phone, tearing it from the dash holder. "Zach! Zach, I need to tell you—I'm...fuck, I'm your dad. Can you hear me?"

There's no answer.

Nothing but that empty static.

After a long pause, Gray says gently, "Nash probably put in

signal jammers to prevent the broadcast from reaching past town and block anyone from calling help."

I swear, curling forward, hugging Gray's phone close to my chest like that wonderful little boy is somehow inside, close to my heart.

"Go," I snarl, my mouth dry. "Just *go*. Get us there."

Gray's only answer is to change gears, sending the truck leaping forward into the night at breakneck speed.

At this rate, as long as we don't get caught by some do-gooder cop, it's twenty minutes.

Maybe less.

We'll get there in time, I tell myself.

We *will*.

That's what I hope, right before a dark, slick voice that's haunted my nightmares for so long rises behind us, biting off one clipped word.

"Homunculus."

Before I know what's happening, my entire body spasms.

My heart turns to stone.

I jackknife straight like I'm trying to stand up in the seat.

My arms fling out from my sides.

One busts out the passenger window. The shock is instant, the pain biting and harsh as glass slices through my glove and sleeve, the impact bruising my knuckles, the cuts hot teeth against my skin.

My other arm crashes right into Gray, smashing against the side of his skull.

I don't mean to do it, but I can't fucking help it.

It's a trigger pulling my puppet strings. Ross must've gotten his gag off somehow and waited for just the right second to use it against me.

And all it takes is a split second.

Gray's head snaps to the side, blood erupting from the corner of his mouth.

His hands wrench the steering wheel.

The truck jerks, spins, fishtails. The whole thing bucks as the tires bite the road.

We're leaping.

Flipping.

And suddenly the world goes into a somersault, and we're flying.

It happens in slow motion, everything moving one inch at a time while my body feels paralyzed.

There're just sparks whizzing by, axles scraping the road, then the wheel covers as the truck rolls.

The hood scrapes asphalt, ripping up fire, and the ground becomes the sky.

Then the windshield folds in and fragments into a million beads, and I can't see anything at all.

But I *feel* it as the truck goes careening, screaming off the road, and smashes past the safety barrier.

There's a whiplash pain in my neck as we go skidding down the hill. A *slamming* in my skull, a blur, a sound of crunching metal.

There's the faint smell of gasoline. Then nothing but dull pain.

Everything goes dark.

* * *

I DON'T THINK I'm out that long.

Not much can knock me out short of a tank, but at least the brief unconsciousness is enough to release that trigger hold on me and let my body go limp in the seat belt.

I'm hanging there before I feel hands on me, dragging me back to the real world, and a voice hissing my name.

"Leo..."

Gray. Thank fuck, he's all right.

I swim through my brain fog, shaking myself, opening my eyes. He's practically crouched over me, his feet braced against the seat, the truck's cab upended and me pressed against the door.

He's bloody, but his eyes are emerald-sharp, focused, as he fights the buckle on my seat belt.

The *warped* buckle. It won't come loose.

I shake myself again, breathing in the smell of gas, and something else burning, sparky, rubbery?

Electrical wires.

Something must've ripped loose, and with gas leaking...fuck.

"Let me," I say, shoving his hands away with a gasp.

Then I curl my fingers in the strap of the seat belt and *rip*.

The woven nylon bites my hands, yanking at the cuts on the right, but it tears, shredding apart with one vicious pull.

They made me to be a brute. Sometimes, it saves our lives.

"Go," I say, shoving at Gray, pushing him up to the only way out, the broken driver's side window hanging over our heads like a sunroof. "We've got to get clear."

He lets me nudge him, reaching up over his head, gripping the door and hauling himself out.

I push myself up to follow, too, ignoring the ache in my body, bruises and cuts throbbing everywhere.

I can barely squeeze my bulk through the window.

But I'm free—free and dropping down from the upended truck into the dry scrub grass that's about to catch like tinder. It'll go up in a blaze if the sparks flicking from the undercarriage hit just right.

"Ross," I snarl, turning quickly back to the truck. "He's—"

"Not in the truck. Damn," Gray confirms, dusting himself off as neatly as ever, adjusting his shirt cuffs like he isn't covered in dirt and grime and blood. "Bastard slipped away like the eel he is."

"He couldn't have gotten far," I growl under my breath, scanning.

I'm not letting him off this easy.

Not letting him escape without facing payback for what he just tried to do.

Stop me from getting to my woman and my son.

There's got to be a trail. It's only been minutes. He can't be far.

But the truck's skid down the rocky slope into the dry roadside scrub has torn up the grass and the earth, obscuring the trail.

I circle around the truck, stalking, nostrils flared like I can catch his scent.

I'm not quite that much an animal. I'm looking for the one bent blade of grass that could only be left by a human foot, not thousands of tons of crashing steel.

I'm so preoccupied I don't hear the spark.

The hiss.

The crackle.

Not till Gray shouts *"Leo!"* and crashes into me, knocking me away from the truck and into the thick stands of trees just past the base of the hill.

The night lights up orange, and the remnants of Gray's truck go up in flames.

The fire shoots out in a *whoosh*, gasoline and sparks catching on the grass, sending them up in a blaze. Heat rolls over the night in a choking wave, torching the trees, burning the leaves till they glow like these fucked up skeletons.

For a second, I'm back in that night eight years ago.

The fire everywhere.

The screams.

Then the sight of a silhouette darting across the flames slaps me back to reality. I fumble away from Gray to go charging into the wall of fire.

I'm *not* letting this bastard escape.

Ross is busy throwing himself into a crop of trees that hasn't caught fire yet when I find him. I don't even hesitate, just tackle him to the ground.

He's still bound. He'd managed to get his legs free and his gag out somehow, but his arms are still tied behind his back, and there's nothing he can do to stop me as I crush down with the full force of my weight.

He cries out in pain, a sound that satisfies my dark side far more than it should.

But before he can open his mouth to make another peep, I slam my fist into his face.

He won't get another chance to fuck with me and mine.

Time to end this.

Standing, surrounded by the trembling flames, I look up, watching Gray stagger through the field of leaping orange and gold.

The determination in his eyes reflects the rage pooling in my gut.

Hard-focused. Ready for anything. We don't have much time.

Not when, even if Nash doesn't set off the explosives, this blaze could consume the entire countryside, and with the phones jammed, we can't even call it in.

We've got to get moving *now*.

Bending, I catch Ross by his collar, scuffing him up like the mangy animal he is.

"Come on," I say, turning to trudge toward the hill, dragging Ross away from the flames. "Let's go finish this shit."

XXIII: THROUGH THE WOODS
(CLARISSA)

*I*t's like something out of a slasher flick.

A lone woman on Halloween night, creeping through the dark woods with her palms sweating, her breaths racing, everything turned freaky orange by the distant lights of the town through the trees. Somehow it just makes the darkness around her that much thicker, colder, scarier.

Only her phone lights the way.

And every small step sounds like a terrible crash, the crunch of leaves and twigs echoing through the night.

But nothing's louder than the thump of my heart.

It's like a gong ringing inside me as I make my way through the woods, looking for that storm door set deep in the earth.

I've been gone for years, but I still know these woods like the back of my hand.

This is my home.

The one thing it never stopped being.

And right now, I cherish the thought that when this is over, maybe I could make Heart's Edge *home* again.

If I can just find my sister.

If I can just talk to Leo about the quiet, beautiful thing building between us.

That's what's holding me together as I edge through the darkness.

No, I'm not a horror movie heroine.

I'm not going to die in a splash of blood, taken off guard by the killer because I made one stupid move and didn't run when I should have.

I'm the girl who lives.

I'm the girl who survives and saves the people she loves.

That gives me a steel backbone as I step out into the clearing and finally see it. The door almost seems buried under so much autumn-shriveled ivy that it looks like it hasn't been opened in years.

I hesitate, wondering if I'm wrong.

Maybe she's not down there, and I'm just chasing dead ends.

But I have to *know*.

I can't walk away without trying.

Taking a deep breath, scrubbing my free hand against my thigh, I step forward.

The chilly night slices at my throat with every nervous breath. My phone's beam of light passes over the door, illuminating the leaves, the weathered wood. I brush away the vines, clearing off the heavy coverage, ignoring the skittering bugs coming out of their hiding places.

In seconds, I've ripped away enough to expose the crossbeam barring the door.

I stuff my phone into my pocket, plunging me into darkness, but leaving both hands free to shove that heavy wood up.

It fights me. It fights me *hard*, the wood almost swollen and stuck in place, absorbing moisture and expanding. I grunt under my breath as I shove and drag and *strain*.

I can't give up.

I can't.

Not when something—some intuition—tells me everything I've been desperately looking for is on the other side of these doors.

So I give it my all.

And even though my hands scrape against the wood, even though my shoulders protest, there's finally a shriek of hinges and creaking wood. The crossbar sealing the doors shut breaks free. My grip slips and I go tumbling down against the doors.

Oops.

If there was a serial killer out here, I might as well have just screamed HERE I AM, flapping my arms around like a maniac.

No time to worry about that, though.

I feel around in the dark for the rusty metal handle on the right-hand door, then grab on and give another *heave* with all my strength.

The door feels like it weighs a ton, but it comes open surprisingly easy. I almost stumble back as it swings wide, before I grip the edge and catch myself. It falls to one side with a *clang*.

I take a few deep breaths, rubbing my stinging hands together, then fish my phone out again.

The light illuminates a dusty stone stairwell leading down.

I remember this now.

The wet, earthy smell. The dust, the cobwebs. The gleam of dampness down the walls.

It's all just like Mom showed me years ago.

What's different are fresh footsteps on the dirty stone steps. They're left behind in watery prints drying against the surface. *Hmmm.*

My chest goes tight.

They're faint. It's hard to tell if the steps were going in...or coming out.

But *someone's been down here.*

In the last hour, maybe less.

Oh, *crap.*

Maybe I shouldn't be doing this alone.

I should call Leo. He's got to be back by now, right?

I fumble with my phone, killing the light and digging up the number for that weird burner phone he uses.

But when I try to call him, lifting the phone to my ear, I don't even get the sound of the phone dialing. Just an odd static crackle, loud and harsh.

Dead air.

I try it again and again—but the call just won't *connect*. It's less like no signal and more like the whole system's gone down.

Great timing.

Heart in my throat, I take several heaving breaths, staring down at the darkness beckoning me into the tunnel.

I can't wait any longer. Every minute makes a difference in Deanna's life, especially if that radio broadcast urges Nash into doing something drastic.

Looks like it's just me, myself, and I.

Biting my lip, I step down onto the stone staircase carefully, sweeping my light in front of me. I should probably turn it off. It might tip off anyone down here that I'm *here*...but I'd rather have light to show me the way than creep around in the dark with no idea which way's which.

My boots scuff too loud, even though I try to keep quiet.

Everything seems too loud, ratcheting up my nerves. I creep down the stairs slowly, bracing one hand against the damp wall so I don't slip on the slimy floor.

The air down here tastes dusty and thick with moss. But weirdly *fresher* than it should.

Like this tunnel was opened many times.

And I remember, all those years ago, when I was just a little girl, the shadow-men from Galentron.

They'd come into the house, and then disappear somewhere.

I always told myself they just left, but something never seemed quite right.

I never saw them. Deanna and I hid in the lower levels and crawl spaces.

Maybe I never saw them because I never looked deep enough.

This whole place feels claustrophobic. The last faint speck of night deserts me as I reach the bottom of the stairs and move deeper, following it deeper beneath the earth.

That constant trickle of water shadows me, makes me feel less alone down here.

I don't know if it's comforting, or terrifying.

I feel like I've been walking forever, the ghostly white light of my phone's flashlight sweeping out in front of me, highlighting cobwebs, less than I'd expect.

Someone's *definitely* been down here.

And my breaths pick up as I creep a little farther in.

There's a light another few hundred yards down the tunnel.

I shut off my phone quickly.

Darkness plunges down around me, but that only makes the small golden square ahead jump out.

So I'm not imagining it.

There's something down here.

Someone had to have left that light burning.

I stuff my phone back in my pocket and let the light guide me forward, struggling to move quickly and silently, keeping my body low to the ground.

If Nash is there, I can't let him hear me coming. But if he's *not*, I can't waste time if my sister's cooped up there alone.

Closing in, I finally make out another door. It's wood, an old-style cellar door with a square peephole crisscrossed by iron bars.

I slip to one side of the tunnel, hopefully out of sight from inside the room, and creep up a few more inches.

Now I'm flattened on one side of the door, leaning over to peer through the window.

Whatever I expected to see...it's not *this*.

The room is massive, larger than anything I could ever imagine under my old house. Against one wall, there's what looks like old bunk beds, military style, just steel framing and thin mattresses, all dusty and mildewed.

Remnants of old equipment rotting away here and there.

Everything from what looks like a dilapidated fridge and stove to a stainless steel table that makes me nervous because it looks like an operating table.

The straps don't make it any better.

That photo of Leo flashes in my mind. He's captured and lashed to the table, his mouth open on a roar.

God. I feel sick.

And I don't have time to take in the rest of it—what looks like worktables, and even a few classroom-style desks, old chairs scattered around, large storage crates filled with who even knows.

Because there's only one light on in the room.

A portable lantern, one of those bright Colemans that can turn night into day. It's set up in the center of the floor, illuminating a little campsite. There's a tent, supplies scattered everywhere, a backpack.

And tied up on a dirty pallet outside the tent, a figure.

Deanna!

I don't know how I don't die then and there, when my heart stops beating.

She's alive.

Bruised, bloody, her hair a ragged mess. It's chopped down almost to her scalp and sprayed around her face in sad brown wisps, her ankles and thighs tied together, arms bound behind her back, duct tape over her mouth, the wet tracks of fresh tears cutting through the grime on her cheeks.

But she's alive.

I stop thinking. Stop *anything*.

"Deanna," I breathe, wrenching the door open.

It squeals open harshly, dust and debris shedding down. The weight nearly rips my arms from their sockets, but I don't care. I dive in, scrambling across the floor.

She comes to sharply, tensing, opening her eyes, jerking like she's afraid she'll be hit.

I so want to kill Nash for everything he's done to her.

I can't *believe* he's turned my sister into this small, scared thing, flinching at the idea he might be coming back.

I tumble to my knees next to her, catching her face in my palms, nearly sobbing as I look down into wide, blank green eyes that don't quite recognize me.

"Deanna?" I whisper. "Deedee, it's okay. It's *me*. It's Rissa, your sister. I've come to get you, baby girl."

She trembles, frozen in my hold, only for her eyes to clear in a heartbeat and her entire body to relax. Her eyes well bright with tears, and she slumps, making muffled, sobbing sounds against the tape over her mouth.

I can hardly see for the tears blurring my vision as I scrape at the edges of the tape with my nails, catch it, then pull it away, wincing at her cry of pain. Her head falls. I catch it, cradling it in my lap, curling over her.

This hot, hurting, wretched sob just bursts out of me.

I said I wouldn't cry.

Told myself I wouldn't cry until I *found* her, but now she's here, and I hate that I've been so *close* to her so many times and never freaking knew I was *standing* right over her, searching and searching and searching but never quite knowing where to look.

"It's okay," I whisper again and again, and I don't know if I'm trying to tell her or trying to tell myself. "It's okay, Deedee. You're safe now..."

She weeps against my thighs, deep and hoarse and rasping, mirroring my own sobs.

I've got to get her untied.

I've got to get her to a hospital.

But for a moment, sheer relief leaves me too weak to do anything but *cry*.

After several shaky moments, though, I make myself focus.

I pull back, gently stroking my fingers through the dirty, matted spikes of her hair, trying not to break down crying again when the short tufts slip through my hands too fast.

"Give me a second," I say, reaching behind her, feeling for the knots in the ropes binding her arms and wrists. She's been hog-tied, practically, and the knots are *tight.* "Here, let me get started on this."

But then Deanna goes stiff against me, her breath catching.

Her head lifts, her eyes widening in dread.

She's not looking at me.

She's looking *past* me.

And trembling with fear, she barely whimpers out, "Clarissa!"

A black shadow falls over me. Pain erupts in my skull as a hand snares my hair, wrapping a handful around a cruel fist, peeling me backward.

Away from my sister, even as I stretch a hand out, grasping at her, screaming.

Then a cold, nasty voice purrs against my ear, and my blood turns to ice.

"Well, well," Nash whispers, his numb voice coiling against my eardrums. "What'll we do with *this* lovely head of hair?"

It's the last thing I hear.

Fear, the last thing I feel, thick and terrible and scalding hot in my veins.

A second later, my head explodes again, and everything goes completely black.

XXIV: THE RIGHT WAY OUT (NINE)

I thought I knew what chaos was.

Swore I'd lived out every aspect, every damn way anything could be terrible and frightening and consumed by uncertainty.

But it's all been nothing compared to the moment when Gray and I crest the hill just outside of the highway barrier along the road leading into town. The distant glowing flame at our backs follows us into town, now lit up with what seems like a thousand flashes.

The entire night is painted in red and gold and orange and specks of blue.

It's too much like that night at the lab, eight damn years ago, when everything was flame.

—fire everywhere, beams dropping, everything crashing down, I'm going to die, I'm going to die, but it doesn't matter as long as everyone's safe, as long as she's safe—

That last hellish incident did one good thing.

Ever since the Paradise Hotel went down, Heart's Edge has loudspeakers mounted to the outside of the school and several other public places.

Blake's voice blares out of them now. "Please follow all emergency evacuation routes to the outskirts of town. If you've been separated from loved ones, do not attempt to search for them; reconvene at the Charming Inn. Do not return to your homes for your belongings. Proceed on foot, do not create traffic stalls. This is not a drill. Please follow *all* proper evac procedures."

It's almost strange remembering that underneath that goofy Labrador, Blake Silverton is a trained volunteer fire chief, an ex-military man, a radio jock, and a father.

The authority in his voice keeps people moving.

Good thing, too, the streets are a mess of noise and scared townspeople.

Parents clutch their kids and run. Gaggles of teenagers tumble through alleyways, half running, half treating it like some kind of exciting adventure, laughing and shoving at each other.

Langley's in the street like a glorified crossing guard, directing traffic. I catch hints of shouted questions, people wanting to know what's wrong, why they're evacuating, what's the threat, is this a joke?

It'd be almost comical against the Halloween backdrop of orange string lights, paper cutout ghosts, hanging plastic skeletons, pumpkins everywhere.

If only I didn't know just how real the danger is.

Worse, the only key to stopping it dangles from my arms, battered and beaten and unconscious.

Or pretending to be, if Ross knows what's good for him.

I can't promise I won't cut his throat to keep him from triggering me again, trying to turn me into a weapon against everyone I love.

Gray stands tall, looking through the chaos, then nods firmly. "We'll start at the radio station."

"Yeah." I shift Ross' weight, hoisting him up over my shoulder so I don't literally drag him to death by asphalt. "Let's haul some ass."

Still feels like it's not quick enough.

Not even with the Missoula police and fire department on the way to reinforce the town.

I called it in while I was dragging Ross' half-dead carcass up the road. Nearly a dozen more calls in to multiple numbers in Heart's Edge wouldn't work, but I could reach Missoula, let them know about the fire on the highway and a potential terrorism situation in town. They were already dispatching people by the time I hung up.

Shame Missoula's almost a couple hours away.

It won't be enough.

They'll get here just in time to clean up the corpses.

Gray and I set out at a sharp jog, Ross' head bouncing against my shoulder, and soon we collide with the wall of confusion flowing the other way, forging through the people toward the radio station with Blake's voice still echoing around us.

I've got to get to the museum.

Got to get to Rissa.

Just can't let the entire countryside burn down, either. Not again.

Trying to do the right thing costs me precious time, though. I hate like hell that's playing right into Nash's hands.

Finally, we're bursting into the station. Everyone freezes—Fuchsia, Warren, Blake, Zach.

"Cut the mic!" I yell.

I don't want to cause a panic. People will stop running *out* of the town if they realize a fire's heading toward us.

Blake slams the button, lifting his head, looking at us, staring at Ross. "What's with the—"

"No time," I snarl. "We crashed. Sparks caught on a gas leak. There's a fire burning about a mile and a half south, currently dry brush and trees, but it's gonna spread. We've got Missoula fire and police on the way, but they're a good hour out, maybe more."

Ready tension goes through Blake instantly. He nods, sharp

and businesslike, heading for the door. "I'll get the crew moving. Split half here, half for the road. Why didn't you call?"

"Lines are dead."

"Jammers," Fuchsia cuts in. "I've been trying to get some kind of signal out, but there's nothing but static. Nothing's going any farther than the town limits now."

"Yeah." My gaze shifts to Warren. "You're sure she said 'cellar door?'"

Warren nods. He's got my son's hand held tight in his, and later I'm going to thank him for that and be goddamn glad I've got friends like him. "Yes. Leo, I can—"

"No. Stay with Zach," I growl.

Precious seconds are slipping by. "Gray and I got this. You stay, War."

But I can't stand the fear in my boy's eyes.

The way he looks at me, so wide-eyed, like I'm the only one who can make things better.

It's like he knows I am.

And without a second's hesitation, I shove Ross' limp body at Gray, leaving him stumbling to catch him, while I drop to my knees in front of my son, pulling him into a tight bear hug.

He clutches at me, little fingers grasping, and I hug him so close I'm afraid I'll break him, then pull back and cup his face in my hands.

"Hey," I say. "Listen to me, Zach. You call me Mr. Monster sometimes, right?"

Zach smiles faintly, trembling. He's like his mom, barely ever cries when things get bad.

He cries when it's over and it's safe. But his eyes are wet now, his voice thick.

"I know your name's really Leo," he says.

"But I'll be Mr. Nine for you, and Mr. Monster." *And Dad*, I want to say, but that impulse I had before goes quiet on my tongue.

The other things I need to say are so much more important.

"Listen, some bad people turned me into a monster a long time ago, little guy...but being one made me strong. Strong enough to save your mom and make everything okay. Do you believe that? Can you believe in me?"

Zach hesitates, then nods slowly, taking a calming breath.

"I believe in you, Mr. Nine," he whispers.

"Good." I smile like the sun. "Hold tight. I'll be back with your ma real soon."

I stand and pin Warren with a look.

"Take him," I say. "All of you get out of here. Get to the inn. It's far enough to be safe if I can't stop this, and it really goes sideways, but keep away from any windows."

A dark, somber silence fills the room.

Everyone knows what we're not saying.

If I can't fix this, there might be nothing left of Heart's Edge to save by morning.

It's Fuchsia who breaks the silence.

She slams her hands on the table and stands, eyes snapping, as she flings her headset off. "Well, we're not going to fucking stand here, are we?"

I stare at her as she stalks toward me. "Where are you going?"

"To call in the cavalry," she hisses, then shoves past me and out the door, making Ross flop against me as Gray passes him back.

Gray stares after her. "What's gotten into her?"

"No clue, but for once I trust she's on our side. Now let's move."

My last sight of my son is his wide eyes as Warren picks him up, bundling him close.

Takes everything in me to force myself to turn my back on him.

Fuck. It feels like my entire life I've been walking away from the people I love to save them.

Only this time, it's different.

This time, I'm walking away from them to do something real, something final, instead of just running away.

I'll always *come back for you, woman,* I'd told her, *no matter how much hell it takes.*

Eight years later, I'm about to make that true.

* * *

GRAY and I cut out into the parking lot of the radio station. Something about the emergency lights mixed with the Halloween decorations makes the town look like it's already burning.

I feel like I'm standing at the entrance to hell in *Dante's Inferno.*

Abandon all hope, ye who enter here.

It's hard to make anything out in the chaos. But at least I won't stand out with my hood back, my face exposed, my hands a bare, scarred, tattooed mess.

No one even looks twice when we're fighting the current of skeletons and Frankensteins and vampires and zombies. The only thing that makes us stand out is that we're moving counter to the crowd.

Humans are herd animals. They swarm.

Whether they realize it or not, they run on patterns, and some sort of hive mind makes it all too easy to pick out those who don't fit.

While we press on to the museum, breathing gasps of adrenaline-scented air thick with the musk of October, I see him. Someone who doesn't fit.

Someone tall, gargantuan like me.

Someone far too calm in the middle of this shit.

Nash.

He's strolling merrily down the sidewalk in the panic, a pleasant smirk on his lips, his eyes bright and thoughtful.

371

He's watching people run past like he's seeing trained zoo animals.

Like he's *enjoying* their horror, and it doesn't bother him at all that we've intercepted his plans. Just as long as this fucking vampire gets to see people scared, running wild.

He's *sick*.

He's the kind of monster Ross tried to make me.

I stare him down till he lifts his head and catches sight of me. Then our eyes lock, his smile widens, and all I see is a human shark.

Vicious teeth and dead, empty, killing eyes.

Right before he turns away and vanishes, disappearing between two buildings.

Like hell!

Snarling, I push forward, using my bulk to clear a path as I break into a jog, Ross' limp body bouncing against me. "Come on!"

Gray hangs close on my heels as we sprint across the street, fighting through the crowd. There's nowhere else Nash could've gone except between the laundromat and Felicity's bakery, but by the time we break free from the throng—it's like moving through mud—he's nowhere in sight.

I stand at the mouth of a hell-lit alley, panting, my lungs on fire.

Fuck.

No. He wasn't moving fast. He's taunting me. He couldn't have gotten far.

Without stopping to wait for Gray, I charge forward, sprinting down the alley to the next narrow cross street. I don't even feel Ross' weight on me now. He's been the albatross around my neck my entire life, but now he's a weapon and I carry him with ease.

There's nothing, not even evacuating people, when I hit the cross street.

I scan left, right, and see only emptiness.

A silence that's almost eerie for the chaos engulfing this town.

At my back, Gray pants, "Leo—"

"Quiet." I snap one hand up.

I can *feel* Nash here. His eyes on me. Almost jealous.

It's like he remembers when he used to drink my pain like booze, and he's a drunk who wants just one more taste.

There.

A flicker of motion on the roof of the building in front of me.

Just a glimpse of steel eyes, black clothing, a smirk.

He's turning away. I catch one very deliberate scuff of a boot before he takes off running.

Baiting me again, the asshole.

Only, I won't let myself be hooked.

Not like this.

He doesn't realize he's not the tricky hunter.

He's the prey.

And I've got the scent, my blood running hot and high and ripping through my veins, making me a machine charging through the streets, unstoppable, following every flirting hint of color and sound Nash uses to tease me onward. I don't even know if Gray is still with me anymore.

I don't care.

Don't have time for games.

For now, I'm every bit the beast Galentron made me, using every strength they forced on me to run this fucker to the ground.

For Rissa, my future wife.

For Zach, my son.

For my *home.* This town means more to me than it's ever known, and I've been its silent, punished guardian in the shadows for too long.

* * *

WE'RE ALMOST to the edge of town when Nash breaks cover.

Right in the parking lot of Sweeter Things.

It's almost poetic fucking justice when he goes vaulting through the broken-out front window. He hurls himself toward the freshly cleaned storefront where I'm waiting.

Then I smash through the door, crashing right into him.

Guess he'd expected me to follow him through the window. I'm done being subtle.

We hit the floor together—me, Nash, Ross, all crashing down in a tangle of limbs.

The sicko just laughs. His high, wild, crazy laughter echoes through the dark shop.

My blood boils.

So I grab him by the shirt, straddling him, lifting him up, then slamming him down against the tile.

His head bounces off the floor with a loud *crack*.

And the jackass just *laughs* some more.

"What's so damn funny?" I growl. "*You fuck*. I know about Black Phoenix. Where is it? Where'd you plant the bombs? What's the code to disarm them?"

Nash only grins up at me, his eyes narrowed, his silver gaze glinting like a snake.

Pain *is* his pleasure.

"Wouldn't *you* like to know, Lion-boy." He lets out a harsh, grating cackle, reaching up toward me. "Ah shit, you aren't such a pretty lion anymore, are you? But your *mane's* still nice."

He actually reaches for my hair—and I flinch back. My instinct recoils from his touch.

That's when he slams his head up and smashes his forehead right between my eyes, ramming into me with such violence I see hot red stars exploding in my skull.

"Leo!" Gray yells.

I don't know when he got here, when he caught up, but even if I'm blind, I can *feel* him there, and when I reel back and then snap forward again, there's a *crunch* of bone on bone. I open my eyes just in time to watch Gray plow his fist straight down into Nash's face.

Good man.

Another friend, another brother I'll have to thank after this is over. Now, I want a piece of this turd.

Leaning forward, I grasp Nash's shoulders, digging my fingers in like daggers, fighting through the pain and blinking away the star-shot blindness to shove him down. Gray falls, kneels at his head, dragging a handful of his hair back to slam his bloodied skull down against the tile.

Nash blinks up at me, fuzzy through the haze in his expression.

He's not smiling anymore.

"I'm gonna ask you one more time, fuckwit," I say. "Where are the explosives, and what's the code?"

"And what if I don't tell you?" he mocks. "Kill me, and leave this entire town and your precious beloved Clarissa to burn? You're in a pickle, L-9."

"You know damn well what I can do to you," I grind out. "And you *know* who I brought with me."

"Yeah," he sneers, his gaze rolling to the side toward the limp bundle of Dr. Ross. "An unconscious old man who can't do a thing and wouldn't help you if you paid him. Genius."

"Wrong."

I trust Gray to keep his hold on Nash while I let go with one hand, reach over, and yank at Ross, dragging him across my lap and making him another weight holding Nash down.

There's a pressure point on both sides of the neck that inflicts incredible pain.

Pinch it, and you'll make a man scream. The jolt to his system even overrides the inhibitors keeping his brain subdued, forcing him awake to react to an imminent threat.

I spread my thumb and forefinger to the nape of Ross' neck. Find that pressure point. And *squeeze*.

I've never heard a grown man howl like him: high, pitiful, terrible.

I actually fucking wince, but I don't stop as the doctor bucks and strains in my arms, paralyzed by the pain ripping up his vertebrae.

This is what he taught me.

This is why I have no qualms using it on him.

Snarling, I relax my grip just enough to let him stop screaming. He lies there staring up at me, this pathetic old man who's been reduced to nothing after he fucked me up for life.

I'd almost feel sorry for him. *Almost.*

"You awake?" I ask coldly. "Can you understand me?"

Ross' lips tremble. "Y-yes," he manages, his voice thick.

"You understand that if you try anything besides what I tell you, Gray here kills you and none of your tricks will stop him?"

Ross says nothing, swallowing hard.

So I squeeze down again. *Enough.*

And he lets out that high, sickening scream again.

Just a quick burst in a few seconds before he cries out, "*Yes, yes!* Anything!"

"Weak," Nash spits, prideful to the end. "Pathetic, old man. I thought you were better than this. I thought you were in *control!*"

"Quiet, you whelp," Ross bites back in a gasping voice as I relax my hold. He slumps. Even trembling with pain, that familiar authority enters his voice. "You blew this entire mission."

"And *you—*"

"Shut up. You can have your lovers' quarrel from inside your cell," I snarl, cutting them off, pinching down on Ross' neck just enough to make him tense, bracing for more torture. "Give Nash the command phrase. Tell him to tell me *everything.*"

"Don't do it," Nash hisses. "Don't you *dare* betray us."

I almost laugh.

Us? They think they're fighting for a *cause?*

It makes a sick kind of sense.

When an evil company becomes your cult, doing its bidding becomes your religion.

"*Do it*," I say.

My fingers pinch Ross' neck harder, applying enough force that he can't even scream—he just arches into an almost perfect curve, his entire body stiff, his heels clacking against the floor.

I want to be a better man and say I don't enjoy this.

But after everything he did to me? Everything he did to every Nighthawk, turning kids into monsters?

There's a grim satisfaction I'll savor later when this is over and my family's safe.

I hold till I'm sure I won't have to get my message across again, then let go.

Ross slumps, choking, his eyes closing, his lips slack.

"Say it," I repeat slowly, growling. "Say the command phrase!"

Ross takes several shaky breaths, then nods slowly. "The...the small red truck spins its wheels."

Bingo.

I often wonder what makes him choose the phrases he does, individualizing them to each of us so we're all triggered by different things and can be controlled by these gibberish phrases people would hardly ever say in real conversation.

But whatever made him choose that phrase for Nash, it works.

The fuck suddenly goes limp under me.

His sadistic eyes blank out, vacant, dull, his lips open but not moving.

It's like he's a doll—a semblance of a living thing.

I shove Ross off me, onto Gray. My friend lets go of Nash's hair and drags a weak, beaten Ross out of the way.

Leaning forward, bracing my hands to either side of Nash's head, I look down at him steadily.

"Talk," I say. "What's the deactivation code? Where'd you put the explosives? In the museum? What's the exact location?"

Nash doesn't answer.

Cruel seconds blur by like my heavy pulse, imagining Clarissa's life blood slipping away. I'm terrified she went to the museum looking for Deanna, and Nash chose the same spot for his fuckery.

Maybe she was lucky.

Maybe even now she's staggering out of that cellar door with her sister in tow, getting safely away.

But I need to hear it from Nash's mouth.

After a few empty seconds, he speaks mechanically. "Four-oh-seven-alpha-six-zeta-niner-four-eagle," he says, pronouncing the words carefully.

Okay, 407A6Z94E. That's our code.

That'll kill the bomb, if I can find it first.

But he smiles in his slow, eerie way, struggling past the blankness. It's like I can *see* him fighting through his conditioning, just like I did, trying to find the willpower to defy me.

"Not much ti-*iiime*, my cowardly Lion-boy," he sings.

"How much?" I roar, clasping his face in my hands, digging my fingers into his temples. "How much time left? *Where the fuck is it?*"

His creepy-ass smile widens. His eyes roll back like he sees something else, something far away.

His own sick version of heaven, maybe, waiting for him.

"Sixteen minutes now," he whispers happily. "And you just wasted so much precious time chasing me. Following me away from *her*. Can you get to the museum in sixteen minutes, Leo-Leo-Lion-boy? Can you find her deep in its bowels? Are you ready to go home?"

Home.

That room, with its steel bunks and thin mattresses and terrible metal table with the bands I can still feel biting my wrists.

Shit.

Clarissa's there.

And so are the bombs.

White-hot rage rushes through me so fast I feel like I've gone nuclear. My fingers gouge in, threatening to crush Nash's skull, lines of strain over his temples and his face going red.

"What did you do to her?" I spit, shouting, my damaged vocal cords struggling to lift my voice, turning it into an animal's hateful cry. "If you hurt her, I swear to fuck I'll—"

"You won't do anything," Nash answers with a strange serenity. "Because you won't get to her in time."

It happens in a flash.

His hand snaps up.

I go to block it just as I catch the glinting edge of silvery steel, razor-sharp.

A military utility knife, heading for my face.

I'm roaring as I grab his wrist, swing it around, and plunge the damn thing straight into his throat. Nash's body jerks on impact.

In a single swift slash, his skin opens up. Seething, cherry-dark blood pools on the tile. I finish him with a vicious relief surging through my veins.

The psycho goes limp a second later, the life draining from his eyes.

I realize too late that he wasn't really going for me.

It was too reckless. Too soon. He wanted this to happen.

The worst part is, he's still fucking smiling.

Like he's won something in the end.

Ice runs up my spine, wondering if it's true. He made me kill him before he could give up the answer I truly needed—the exact location of the bomb in a sprawling house with a bunker under it and endless rooms and hallways and closets.

There's no time to triangulate the most efficient location.

I just have to get the hell in, get Clarissa out, and *run* before total disaster happens.

Jumping to my feet, I leave Nash's body behind. I'll deal with Ross later.

I know what that fucker did. He gave Nash the wrong trigger, the command that would let him mimic compliance till he found a chance to die, rather than compromise the mission.

It makes sense because I've got the same trigger buried in me.

But he'll never get the chance to pull it.

Gray starts to rise. "Leo, we can—"

"*Stay here*," I snarl, pointing at Ross. "Make sure he doesn't get away. He's evidence now, and he's gonna pay for this. Everything!"

Gray stares at me with sharp, worried eyes. "Damn it, man, you can't do this alone."

"I have to." I shake my head. "Sorry, Gray. I can't wait for anyone else. There's no time. I have to do this next part alone."

Then I'm stepping out into the night, leaving one of the last hellish fragments of my past in the grip of one of the only men in this world I trust. One of the only people who truly knows who and what I am.

All of this, it's on me.

I set these wheels in motion years ago.

It's high past time to grind them to a halt, before they plow anyone else under them.

* * *

THE STREETS ARE ALMOST EERILY empty.

I take off at a ground-eating sprint toward the town center. It's desolate, forlorn, decorations torn down and trampled in tatters on the streets, lights knocked loose and coiling in dead strings along the sidewalks, trash and bits of paper blowing everywhere, a few of the volunteer firefighters still herding along the last stragglers.

Heart's Edge looks like a ghost town.

I have to hope everyone's safe for now at Charming Inn, over a mile away.

At least empty streets means no one to see me.

No one to slow me down, either, as I let myself off my leash and *fly*.

I've never fully tested my limits like this.

Nighthawks made me faster, stronger, better than a normal man. But I learn to push everything to breaking point now, pouring every bit of strength in my body into *running*.

Sixteen minutes, he said.

Fifteen, now.

I'll get there in time.

I *will*.

Hell, I don't even remember tearing through the city streets.

It's like the time passes in a rush of adrenaline, and deep down, this crazy sense of *hope*.

I know I can save her. There's no other choice.

I won't leave our son to grow up without a mother.

Just like I won't live a day longer without the woman I love.

Four minutes and twenty-seven seconds.

That's how long it takes me to cover over a mile between the shop and the museum.

It feels like forever and like nothing at all, the seconds counted out in the pounding of my boots against the pavement and the drumming of my heart.

I burst against the museum door like a battering ram.

It doesn't budge. Heavy oak, locked.

Not gonna stop me.

I gather my strength, bunching every muscle in my body. Then I throw myself at it again like a human cannonball.

The wood splinters, the hinges squealing, and the door bursts inward, ripping clean off its frame.

I tumble inside, surrounded by shadowy halls and bad memories, half truths under the faint light gleaming off the glass of the display cases.

"Clarissa!" I roar, then fall silent except for my heaving breaths, listening.

I don't hear anything.

Nothing but my own voice echoing from the high rafters.

Ten minutes now.

Counting down faster to the frantic drumming of my pulse.

I head deeper into the museum, pausing to call out again.

"Clarissa!" Nothing. "Rissa, baby girl, if you can hear me—it's Leo, I've got to get you out of here—"

Nothing, nothing, *nothing.*

Damn.

Fuck, fuck, double *fuck.*

I have to hope Nash wouldn't be twisted enough to hide her on the upper floors when he knows exactly where I'm going to look.

In the chambers down below.

I find the stairs leading down to the subterranean levels on the second floor, barred off by an *Employees Only* sign with a safety sticker plastered underneath it.

It's unlocked.

Pushing the door open on a gate to my nightmares, I descend.

There's no time to be delicate on the rotting steps.

I race down, crunching boards in half, nearly getting my damn ankle stuck but moving so fast nothing can collapse beneath me before I'm moving on. Feeling my way around in the dark, I go by sound and memory. My hearing making the echoes of my own movements bounce back like sonar to tell me how far away the walls are.

And the whole time I'm calling her name.

Clarissa. Clarissa. Clarissa!

And she's not answering.

First comes the level with old servants' quarters, then down —and the stairs nearly drop me this time, crashing under my weight as I hit the fourth step. Suddenly it's just me and tumbling wood falling everywhere, splinters and boards jabbing me, the stabbing feeling of sharp wood in my skin.

It's got nothing on the dagger in my heart that says I won't find her in time to do anything but die with her.

Eight minutes.

I hit the floor from a dozen feet up, pain slamming into me as I crash against the stone.

For a moment, I lie there groaning. "Fucking hell."

Feels like I've got a fractured rib, a red-hot sensation so livid against my side it's practically glowing in the dark with pain.

Shit.

No.

I can't let pain slow me down.

Seven minutes, two seconds.

Hissing in pain, I drag myself up to my feet. I don't need to feel my way in the dark to find that one corridor, that one damn door.

Six inches of thick, impassable wood.

Seemingly locked.

It leads down to the storm cellar they converted into a torture chamber, into my worst nightmare, and whose only other entrance is a cellar door buried deep in the woods near a creek where I used to play with my friends.

It hurts to breathe, and not just thanks to my ribs.

I haven't been down here since I was officially "graduated" from the Nighthawks program, after I pretended they'd tamed me long enough to make them believe they'd shaped me into everything they wanted.

Six minutes, thirty seconds.

I don't have time to waste on trauma. On memories. On pain.

I feel along the wall till I find the hidden catch, a single stone that moves where the others don't, and punch it.

It grinds into a depression under my palm. Then I hear the *click* as it hits the disguised locking mechanism.

There's a loud creaking and groaning as the door comes loose in its frame, the latch coming undone.

In the dark I grasp at the handle, pull it wide, and *finally* see light.

It's coming from deep down the stone steps.

"Clarissa?" I call, listening as my voice bounces down the walls to sink into the cellar.

Nothing.

Then a split second later, it floats back.

"Leo?" It's faint, worn, and I can hear the hurt in her voice. If Nash wasn't already dead, I'd fucking kill him. "Is...is that you?"

Six damn minutes.

I don't even think. Just bolt down the stairs at breakneck speed, nearly tripping over myself, my heart leaping. "Hold on, Rissa! Hold on, I'm coming, we'll—"

The tremor cuts me off.

A warning like a building earthquake, right before the colossal crash hits.

It's like being at the heart of a nuclear blast, raw vibrating force and shockwaves everywhere, stone raining down, the heat practically searing my skin off a second time as the explosion slams into me from behind and hurls me down the stairs.

Shit!

The explosives must've been set one floor above. The servants' quarters—all wood and old stucco, highly flammable.

The perfect floor to start a blaze that'll spread fast, spread easy, and collapse the entire building. Ground fucking zero if you wanted to start an inferno that'd jump to the rest of the town.

Meaning Nash *lied* to me, deliberately set me up to die down here with my girl so he could go to his happy place flipping me the bird one last time.

Even as I crash down into the cellar and hit the bottom of the stairs like a fist smashing my body into the earth, even as the flames rush down through the passageway of the stairwell, I don't care.

I won't let it happen.

I won't let that killing fire burn us down *again*.

* * *

Eight Years Ago

THE LAB IS A HOLLOWED-OUT TORCH, and I've never felt pain like this in my life.

If this is hell, I've earned it.

Letting myself be consumed by the fire I caused, trapped and crushed to death under the beam that came crashing down as the entire facility went up in smoke.

I can still hear the screams of the others.

Scientists, guards, anyone unlucky enough to be down here when I broke into the lab and went berserk.

Gray, he tried to talk me down, but I wasn't in my right mind. I wasn't thinking.

This shit is on me.

The broken vial. The containment system activating.

Then malfunction, the blast, the panic, the *fire*.

The shrieking rush of the people who couldn't get out in time.

Maybe some of them deserve it, if they knowingly aided and abetted and profited off Galentron's plan to use Heart's Edge as a testing ground for bringing agent SP-73 into the wild.

If they were willing to let this entire town die for their cushy corporate bonus, fuck 'em.

But some of those people are just like me.

Trapped by something powerful, unsure how to fight it, afraid.

And it's for those people that I deserve this punishment.

I'll die here, burned by the flames. Just as long as that virus and Galentron's plans for Heart's Edge die with me.

It's what I deserve.

If I were a better man, I'd have found a way to save all of them.

But I guess in the end, I failed after all.

Those thoughts move sluggishly through my mind as I stare hazy-eyed through the smoke, through the flames, through the darkness. Past the debris crashed down on me, I sense moving feet. Voices.

Good.

That means people are getting out.

I'm ready to let go, I think.

The darkness is closing in. My eyes are too heavy to keep open.

I'm sorry, Clarissa. I know I said I'd come back, but now I can't.

"You asshole," an acerbic voice bites off over my head, sardonic and dry even in the crackling flame, everything crashing down around us. "Of course you'd leave yourself buried under a metric ton of rubble. Of course."

Gray.

My only friend.

The one who tried to stop me from creating this mess.

The only person I don't blame for his hand in creating it, when he was lied to, fooled the same way I was.

Fuck.

I can't let him die down here with me.

So when I open my eyes and find him setting his broad shoulders to the thick crossbeam crushing down on me, I find the strength.

This body is cursed. Burned. Scorched and twisted by Galentron into a beast.

My friend gives me strength. I know he's brave enough and cares enough underneath that icy façade. He'd kill himself trying to save me. To help me keep my damn promises.

I can't let him down.

So I brace my raw, aching hands against the floor, flex my shoulders, and heave, putting all my strength into fighting the rubble on top of me till it slides away. Gray rips the heap of debris off me piece by piece.

Maybe I don't deserve to live.

But he does.

And one way or another, I swear to everything holy I'll keep my promise to Rissa.

Even if it means living this cursed life so far away from *her*.

* * *

Present

THE MEMORY WHACKS me so hard that for a minute I'm back there, caught in the hellfire branded on my skin forever. But it's not eight years ago.

That flickering urge I had then to just give up and die after murdering her old man and being torched to a crisp, it's not in me anymore.

If anything, these new flames wash it away.

A baptism by fire that leaves nothing but resolve.

I haul myself up. The first thing I see is *her*.

Not the shadow of my past, burning all around us, the steel bunk rails and the lab tables with the empty vials and beakers that once held horrific things that made my body burn like acid was devouring me from the inside out.

Just her. Just Rissa. Just *us*.

She's huddled in front of a tent that was set up in the middle of the room. It's halfway collapsed, the nylon on fire in little patches.

And Deanna's next to her, unconscious but breathing. Rissa looks at her wide-eyed, conscious, grimy, sobbing.

Then she stares at me with those beautiful green eyes like I'm her only hope.

"Leo," she gasps, and I start toward her—only for a sudden rush of flame to warn me an instant before a beam in the ceiling gives way.

I thrust myself back. A fireball of decaying wood smashes down where I'd stood, spraying sparks at me in stinging bites of heat.

I'd say the heat seems unbearable, but fuck.

I was made for this.

She wasn't.

"Fuck," I gasp, holding a hand up over my eyes to shield against the heatwave, peering through the flames at her. "This place is too old. It's gonna come down on us any second."

"I know," she gulps. I can barely hear her over the crackling flames. "He was gloating. Saying the whole building was going to collapse into the storm cellar and we'd probably be crushed to death before we burned, and it's a far kinder end than we deserved."

Goddamn. Again, I'd fucking kill Nash a second time if I could.

"He's dead, babe," I say, even as I search for a way past the wall of flame in front of me—the damn beam ran the length of the room, and now it's a barrier screaming *you shall not pass.* "He's not gonna hurt you again. Give me a second. Stay low, breathe shallow. Smoke's far more dangerous than the fire."

She lets out a shaky laugh, and I love her for that, for her bravery in the middle of this. "Oh, sure. Say that when it's *your* hair on the verge of catching fire."

"Been there. Not fun."

That gets another giggle out of her, but it's more like a sob.

Shit.

We don't have time for me to figure out some safe way around the blaze.

You ever heard the saying *I'd walk through fire for you?*

Well, here the hell we go.

Holding my breath, I brace my arms in front of my face to guard it, and *leap*.

It's like jumping into water, only this water's made of boiling-hot air trying to swallow me up in one stinging bite. But just a second of pain, of that horrible sinking feeling taking me back to that night my entire body screamed in agony—

No, I'm *through* it, tumbling to the ground and rolling to put out the sparks, then nearly throwing myself at Clarissa.

I crash into her, pulling her into me, and God, she's so perfect and wonderful and warm and *alive.* I'm supposed to be untying her, but for just a split second, she's mine.

I *hold* her, pressing my lips into her hair.

"I love you," I whisper. "And I'm here to make up for years of not being able to tell you that to your face, just as soon as we're out of here."

I'm already fighting at her ropes, searching for knots tied tight by someone who's just as horribly strong as I am. She lets out that sobbing sound again, only this time I can hear the joy in it. The sweetness.

"I love you too," she says. "And Leo, if you'll...if you'll stay..."

"*If* I'll stay?" I echo back, hope as thick in my throat as the smoke gathering in the room and blurring my vision grey, my fingers raging at the knots. "It's not even a question."

"I won't run," she says, burying her face in my neck, her tears against my skin. "I won't run again. I'll never run from you, from this. Only back *to* you."

"That's a promise I'm going to fucking hold you to," I choke out.

Right before I grip my fingers in the ropes and *riiip*.

Fuck this pussyfooting around.

I feel when the nylon scrapes my palms in a single burning rush and leaves them bleeding.

I don't care anymore.

I'll bleed, I'll die, but most of all, I'll *live* for this woman.

It takes three swift, sharp jerks, and she's free. I'm dragging her to her feet as she wraps her arms around me with a desperate cry.

One kiss.

That's all we have time for.

One kiss that sears us like the fire roaring around us, a crackling high that builds through me at the taste of her lips and the feeling of her body crushed tight, unharmed and totally *mine*.

Before we break back, looking at each other with a quiet understanding.

I know her mind. She knows mine.

We're *together* again for good.

And without a single word, we drop down, gathering her unconscious sister together. I tear through the ropes again—and then Clarissa helps me lift her up, nudging her against my chest and settling her in my arms. Then it's Rissa, not me, who turns to lead the way out.

There's no going back the way I came. Not with the fire so focused up there, burning every which way, and not with the stairs collapsed under my weight.

But Rissa knows the way. She knows it as well as I do.

Together, we rush toward the tunnel leading out, diving from the sweltering, simmering heat of our own personal hell and into cool stone walls dripping with running water.

The sudden plunge into damp shadows feels like cold kisses soothing my overheated skin.

We're not out of the woods yet, though.

Not when another explosion rocks above us, and everything shakes like an earthquake back with a vengeance. *Fuck.*

Must've hit a gas main. We both hunker low, I throw myself over her, freezing and peering up at the ceiling as bits of gravelly rock shower down. I hold her and Deanna closer, shielding them with my body, praying I'm big enough to keep whatever falls from hitting them.

The shaking doesn't stop.

It gets worse.

We stare at each other, wide-eyed and tense.

"Run," I breathe.

She only hesitates for a second.

Then my girl takes off, ducking low and sprinting to the exit, pelting along the stone tunnel floors.

It's like she knows I'm right behind her.

I'll *always* be behind her.

She can trust that, now and forever, and so can I.

We make a run for our future.

XXV: END OF THE LINE (CLARISSA)

*T*here was only one other time I've ever been more afraid.

One time worse than being strapped down, waiting for a bomb to go off, and my childhood home to crush me to death alongside Deedee just as I'd found her.

It was the night my father smashed me in the face with a vase, leaving a mark that would scar more than my face for life.

And both times—both flipping times—Leo Regis saved me just in time.

This time, unlike before, there's zero chance he'll vanish after tonight.

After the way he's been tortured, after he threw himself into the flames just to get to me?

No question.

I've never known a man more beautiful, more brave, and more right.

His scars prove how much he loves me, body art revealing what's inside his big, beastly heart. They exist so the whole freaking world can *see* how beautiful he is, inside and out.

I don't care if we've got crap to work out.

I don't care if he goes back to prison.

I don't care how if it takes ages to clear his name and really, truly put this nightmare behind us.

He's with me now, and I feel that beautiful shield of a man at my back, his footsteps pounding behind me. He's so gentle carrying Deanna as I sprint for the steps, following the sliver of moonlight from the doors I'd left open.

Finally, we're bursting free.

Then we're erupting into the forest, the creek bubbling close by, all the memories of then and now and oh *God* the taste of sweet, sweet air that's so fresh and clear. Not clogged with the smoke of all the ruins in my life burning down.

We tumble onto the grass and collapse together. Leo lays Deanna down first, and we're both quick to check her over, her pulse, her limbs. She's bruised, nothing broken, breathing. *Thank God.*

"He hit her," I whisper, choking a little, touching a fresh bruise on her jaw. "Right before he knocked me out again. I guess it's harder for her."

"She'll be weak after being chained up for so long," Leo says, reaching across her to clasp my hand. "But she'll be all right. Let's get her somewhere safe. She needs a doctor."

I nod, standing, helping him gather her up, but I can't help but stop. The little town shines through the trees.

Everything is lit like one big phantom jack-o-lantern in Heart's Edge, this orange splash against the night, plumes of white smoke rising in awful flickers.

The mansion is a fiery spear, stabbing at the sky, and I'm worried the rest of the town is next. Blazes that big can destroy cities, especially ones so small and fragile.

Oh, crap.

"Leo—Zach, I left him at the station with Warren and—"

"He's safe," Leo growls softly. "I had Warren take him to the inn. Wouldn't dream of letting anything happen to our son."

Okay.

I'm about to cry with how much I love this man.

393

I'm about to cry, period.

I have to turn away from him for a second, from the sight of this beloved beast-man with my broken, battered sister cradled so gently in his arms. I watch the flames devouring what was once my childhood home.

"I don't want it to take Heart's Edge with it," I whisper. "But I'm glad it's gone. There was so much evil there. Let's hope they don't rebuild it."

"We'll make sure they don't," Leo says. When I look back he's gazing down at me with such tenderness in his amethyst eyes. "And we'll make damn sure they save the town, babe."

"Yeah?" I say, smiling up at him. I finally feel a pinch of relief.

Suddenly, I just know...everything's going to be all right.

He nods firmly, then nudges me with his elbow. "Let's go. Pretty sure half the folks in medicine in this town are at the inn. We can find her a bed there."

But as we turn to that trail in the trees leading back to civilization, I go still, hearing the sound of something whirring far off in the distance.

No, more like *beating*.

A rhythmic *whup-whup-whup* that I feel like I should recognize, but I can't quite place.

"What's that?" I ask, turning, looking up at the sky through the canopy of the trees.

A dark shape streaks by so fast I can barely catch it, blending into the night.

But I make out the reflective USAF logo on the tail, right above the shape of a cross that's a universal sign for *help*.

"Military aid and evac choppers," Leo says right before several more whiz past. "Gonna have to thank Blake later. He got through."

I stare at the weird sight of a helicopter with a *bucket* dangling from it and can't help but laugh as it starts dousing the forest.

"Know what I hate the most about this?" Leo growls, smirking to himself.

"What?"

"We're gonna have to thank Fuchsia goddamn Delaney, too. She must've deactivated whatever was blocking signals and called in a little backup that can scramble faster than the locals."

Wow.

Fuchsia, coming to the rescue?

If you'd said it a couple weeks ago, I'd have never believed it.

I watch a few more helicopters dash past, their tail strobe lights winking red against the stars, and smile faintly. "I don't get that woman."

"Doubt we ever will," Leo mutters. "She's probably already on her way out of town with tickets to the Maldives in her pocket. But if the authorities are here, we're good." He lets out a heaving sigh that seems like it lifts the weight of the world off his shoulders. "It's over."

"Hard to believe," I answer, but no words have ever tasted sweeter. I lean against Leo's arm as we turn, making our way through the woods again, my hand curled close against my sister's dangling legs. "Is it that easy? Everything's okay?"

"In time," he promises. "This town's strong. We'll rebuild."

"You mean we-we?" I ask.

"You, me, and Zach," he says firmly. "Can't think of anything else we'll ever need, Rissa."

Smiling, I follow him into the dark.

* * *

WE'RE PICKED up by a fire truck just a block past the woods, on our way to the inn that's now officially been labeled a "reunification center" by military people who need to slap names like that on everything to make it official.

Other fire trucks whoosh down the road in the opposite direction, toward town, helicopters circling, and it's so strange to watch buckets of water come raining down from the sky, eclipsing the smoke in fast hissing bursts.

At least they're *here*.

At least the town's going to be okay.

I'm so exhausted I can hardly keep my eyes open. But I can't rest until I see my son, so I keep myself awake watching the paramedic assigned to the truck do first aid on Deanna. Even as the fire truck rocks back and forth on the road, the paramedic works like he's standing on solid ground.

Leo holds my hand so tight the whole time.

And for just a second, Deanna opens her eyes, right as the paramedic slips an IV with glucose into her arm. Her gaze drifts to me, and then slips around, taking in the truck, the sky, before her eyes clear.

The fear that was there when I found her vanishes.

"You *came*," she whispers, her voice a dry creak, but it's *there*. It sounds so lovely to hear her conscious again, thick with tears but free from fear. Her fingers twitch weakly, and I immediately clasp them with my free hand. "Sis, how—"

"I did, and I had some help. That's all that matters." I nod quickly, squeezing her fingers tight, sucking in breaths. "I'll always come for you, baby sister. Isn't that how it's been since forever?"

"Yeah," she says, though I can already tell she's fading fast. But her eyes flick to Leo, studying him, and she manages an exhausted smile. "Hey, you. It's really good to...to see you again. It's been so long."

Leo chuckles, flashing her a gentle look. "Yeah, been busy. We've got plenty of time to catch up. I'm not going anywhere, and neither is Rissa."

That gets a smile from her—and one from me.

Deanna dozes off with a soft sigh.

My heart skips with panic, but the paramedic looks up at me with a smile, wiping his hands. "She'll make a full recovery. Don't you worry. She's just exhausted, traumatized, dehydrated, and malnourished. She hasn't lost much blood, and the bruises are mostly surface trauma."

It's the best news I've heard in ages, which is really kinda sad.

So I just smile back, lean my head on Leo's shoulder, and let myself breathe.

After a few minutes, the fire truck pulls up outside the inn. Several ambulances and military medical supply vehicles are parked outside, and my sister gets offloaded onto a stretcher and ushered inside while a couple of EMTs look me and Leo over.

They say we're fine except for a few minor surface burns, then they give me something in case that blow to the head gave me a concussion, and usher us inside to be assigned a room.

I don't have the energy to tell them we'll be heading back to our own cabin, assuming it's still free, especially when I'm not going anywhere without Zach.

Ms. Wilma is at the heart of things, as usual.

Charming is overcrowded with frightened, worried people and total confusion. She's there calming them down and making sure people have a cup of hot tea, a bed to lie down on, things to distract scared children.

But I don't see *my* scared baby anywhere, and the second I notice Warren rushing past with a stack of towels, I grab his arm. "Zach. Where is he?"

He freezes, blinking down at me before smiling tiredly. "Atrium. With the cat. *Again.*" His eyes soften. "I saw Deanna; we're getting her bedded down now. I'm so damn glad you're both all right, Rissa." His gaze rises to Leo. "And you."

Leo looks like he's drooping himself, but he manages a smile.

"Thanks, man," he says. "For everything."

Warren just shakes his head. "No need. That's what friends do." He nudges me with his elbow. "Go on. Zach's been worried sick. He needs to see you both. I've gotta help Hay figure stuff out so she's not running around like a hen on fire."

I don't need to be told twice.

397

With another look at Leo, I catch his hand and nearly drag him through the house to the atrium.

It's the only quiet place in the entire inn.

Surprisingly, we find our son alone, sitting stone-still on the bench. He's holding that huge orange cat they call Mozart like it's some kind of prayer doll, his eyes closed and head bowed as if he's focusing with all his might on bringing us back.

Heart in my throat, I step forward. "Zach?"

His head comes up sharply. His eyes light up, wild and sweet and wide, catching the wild moonlight through the atrium roof and turning the same soft violet color as his father's.

"Mom. *Dad!*" he cries, scaring the cat off him with a yowling screech as he launches himself into us both.

I don't know who's even hugging who at this point, or who started bawling first, only that we're a mess of tears and clinging and Zach holding on so, so *tight*, sobbing. "I was scared. I was *so* scared, Mom..."

"It's okay, baby." I stroke his hair back, hugging him fiercely to me. He's sandwiched between me and Leo with my man's ginormous arms around us both. "We're all okay. Your Auntie Deanna's okay, too. She's home. She's safe."

There's just silence as we cling together.

For the first time in forever, my family feels whole.

Then my mind flicks back to sixty seconds ago.

I blink sharply, staring at Zach. "Wait. Did...did you just call Leo *Dad?*"

Zach looks up at me, lifting his glasses up to scrub at his eyes, sniffling, then peeks sheepishly between me and Leo. "I...sorry, I wasn't 'sposed to know, huh?"

This freaking kid.

Smart enough to figure that out, young enough to still say *sposed*.

Leo lets out a rumbling, heartfelt laugh. "Can't keep anything from this one."

He ruffles Zach's hair, and it warms my heart to see the feels in every glance, the love of a father for a son he seems to have accepted so wholeheartedly it's like there's a hundred years of built-up affection in every touch.

"We were just trying to figure out the right way to tell you. I'm glad you know." He hesitates, then adds, "If you're okay with me being your old man, anyway."

My face lights up.

That sweet *dork*.

So much sensitivity under his snarly, beastly façade.

And Zach lights up, too, twisting in my arms. He throws his little hands around Leo's neck and answers the question with one sweet, simple word.

"Dad!"

I swear I see tears in Leo's eyes as his arms come around Zach, and I let our son's weight ease from my arms to his. He's got this stunned look on his face like he's just seen a miracle.

Beautiful isn't even half of it.

And I don't even try to stop the happy tears welling in my eyes as I watch our son accept his father with such sweet, unreserved trust.

Leo meets my eyes over Zach's head, and the smile he gives me, wondering and soft...

It's *everything.*

After a few moments of silent, exhausted warmth, though, Zach asks. "So are we gonna be a family now? Is Dad gonna come home with us?"

I flush. I've been wondering that too, but I didn't know how to ask.

The fact that Langley and his boys saw us several times tonight making the rounds and didn't arrest him on the spot seems like a good sign, at least. But any awkwardness fades when Leo just grins at me, beaming wide like it's the most natural question in the world.

I duck my head, tucking my hair behind my ear. "Well, ZZ, I

was thinking we could stay in Heart's Edge. Would you like it here, Zach?"

"Only if Dad's here," Zach says firmly, and Leo laughs.

"I'd never dream of going anywhere else. I'm the local legend. In Spokane, I'd just be Leo." His grin turns downright cocky. "So what do you say, sweetheart? Feel like playing house?"

"Oh, you ass—" I cut myself off in front of twitchy little ears, and mock-scowl at him, face burning, and prop my hands on my hips. "You're going to ask me like *that?*"

"Well..." He gently jostles Zach, and our boy giggles. "My hands are a little full to get down on one knee."

Now I'm blushing for a whole different reason.

Honestly, I think the next bomb that goes off in Heart's Edge just might be *me.*

"Yeah, um, about that." My face burns brighter than the night.

Biting my lip, I slip my hand into my pocket to retrieve the ring—that slender silver band with its diamond, the same not-so-lucky charm I've held on to all these years.

Leo's eyes widen as he sees the little circle in my palm, gleaming in the moonlight. I think there might actually be a blush fit to match my own under his beard and scars.

"I never forgot," I whisper. "And I never really let you go."

"Clarissa." My name growls out of him so hot with emotion. Suddenly, he's got his arm around me, pulling me in until I'm crushed tight with him and Zach. "Let me, babe. Let me give you that promise we made years ago. Will you wear that ring for me, Rissa?"

"I..." My voice is breaking, and I hide my face against his shoulder. Zach pats my shoulder sweetly, and Leo just holds me tighter. "I've never wanted anything else all these years."

There are no words, then.

No freaking words needed.

Our hands clasp behind Zach's back, resting against our son, the ring trapped between our palms until Leo works it free.

Then I just feel cool, delicate silver against my skin, sliding down my ring finger like it's always belonged there. Because it *has.*

Our fingers lace, twine, holding Zach so close.

It's an amazing thing when I realize my heart's complete. This gorgeous man, stolen away for so long, has found his way home.

Tonight, we're together again.

We're whole.

And we're so done with suffering for our tomorrow.

* * *

Three Weeks Later

AFTER SO MANY YEARS APART, you'd think we could wait a little longer to get married.

But once the idea takes life, we just couldn't stand *more* waiting. We've been denied for far too long.

There was barely enough time to invite our closest friends. Somehow, though, a good chunk of Heart's Edge shows up, too.

I guess everybody wants to celebrate the town hero's redemption with the hometown girl back in her natural habitat. They're filling the entire field now leading from the back of Charming Inn up to the famous cliff.

Yep, our wedding is standing room only.

There are news crews here, too, hoping to get a word with the groom.

Galentron's downfall has been plastered all over every twenty-four seven national babble network ever since the night I said *yes.* A girl can be a little jealous when she's got to fight reporters for a little time with the man she's been missing for eight freaking years.

Honestly? I couldn't be happier. It didn't take long at all to exonerate Leo once Langley stepped in and helped relay everything to the FBI. And with Maximilian Ross as a broken, busted-up material witness who'll never see a free day again, the company's goose is thoroughly cooked.

Leo tells me he's already flipped, spilled so much. Someone tried to kill him three times in his cell, but the info's out there, enough to convict several very high and mighty evil senior execs for high crimes and misdemeanors

Only, in this case, the misdemeanors are *more* atrocities.

Nope.

Not today.

The journalists can buzz off with their drama.

This is our day, and today, I get to be *his.* Mrs. Leo Regis.

Holy hell, he looks so handsome in his tux, waiting up near the altar with his hands clasped behind him.

So, maybe it's a little like putting a bear in a tux, as big as he is. We had to have the thing custom-tailored, and they just barely finished it this morning.

My dress was a little easier.

I like simple things.

A sheath dress, white and trailing over the little strip of white silk carpet running up the aisle. The strapless design hugs my bodice, leaving my shoulders bare to the nippy November air, my veil pinned to my hair, streaking in a gauzy banner down to mingle with my train.

I feel beautiful today.

Like I've been taken back in time to how things *should* have been. Maybe our happy ending was delayed, but it's finally here.

It's the one we've always *deserved*.

Happiness is finally ours.

And I can't stop smiling with pure, wild joy, looping my hand in Deanna's arm. She escorts me up the aisle to the tune of soft music and the hush of people turning to watch as I approach.

It's nerve-racking, wonderful, and I'm eternally grateful for my sister here. There's no one else I'd want to give me away and play maid of honor.

She's crying like a baby as she leads me to the aisle, then turns to face me and grips my shoulders.

"You look so beautiful, Riss!" she whispers. She's styled her close-cropped hair into an adorable bob that frames her face in a lovely way and highlights her cheekbones, and for a moment I see that faint, distant memory of Mom in her sculpted face. "You look so *happy*." She pulls me close into a ferocious hug. "Be happy, sis. Be happy so something good can come from the mess I made."

"Hey, hey. No blaming yourself again." I hug her back just as tight, whispering so any straggler reporters here for Leo can't hear. "You wanted to do the right thing. Thanks to you, those people will have a hell of a time ever trying to hurt anyone again."

She pulls back with a sweet smile. It tells me no matter what trauma she's been through, she'll be okay.

We'll *all* be okay.

And for a moment she turns that sweet smile on Leo, looking up at him with the warmth and love and acceptance of a sister who already considers him family. Then she withdraws, leaving me and Leo and the altar and this moment we've waited for since we were young and impulsive and full of so much passion.

Maybe we're not so young anymore.

But our love is ten times stronger, this palpable, vibrating emotion that's so bright I swear it's like something *everyone* must see. All of our guests, from the grinning men lined up behind Leo as his groomsmen to the crowd of breathless townsfolk, as we take our places and look at each other.

We might never look away. The priest starts his sermon and our vows. Gray nods at our side like he was made to play best man.

I don't even know what the guy marrying us is saying.

I really don't care. The words are just a beautiful formality to a promise already etched in blood and tears with my husband.

Here, today, forever, there's just Leo and me.

Oh, plus one rambunctious son, adorable in his tiny tux, holding the little black velvet cushion with our rings.

They're hand-carved wood.

Beautiful.

Delicate works of art so detailed it's almost impossible they were made by a human hand, and yet...I *know* who made them. He's standing right in front of me.

Leo himself crafted our story in every tiny, ornate curl of starlight and flower petals and flame.

He spent whole nights hunkered over his desk and a lamp, drawing on his talents as artist, as beast, as new dad, as soulmate. When I asked why, he said it was so we'd remember in the years ahead.

There'd be no need to ever doubt on the curvy, twisty roads of life up ahead. Not when we can feel our story on our skin, or look down and see its scenes unfolding in the intricate, indescribable beauty that reminds me why *I. Love. This. Man.*

So very flipping much I just might die.

But that'd be a shame.

Because the cool, glossy wood of my ring slips perfectly over my finger. Leo slides it on slowly and whispers, his gravelly voice rough and husky, "...with this ring, I thee wed."

My turn. I look down with the ring in my fingers.

His hand feels so calloused, thick knuckles so coarse compared to the delicate wood. "With this ring, I thee wed," I whisper around the happiest tears I've ever cried in my life.

There's an *I do*, and another.

Then the peanut gallery goes wild.

We're told we can kiss, and it's almost a joke thinking we need permission.

For just a flicker, as I fling my arms around Leo's neck, something catches my attention, a darkness from the corner of my eye.

There's a woman in a long black coat and black glasses in the back of the crowd. Her coat's hood is drawn up, covering her face like some stereotypical Russian spy chick. There's nothing but a hint of short black hair, and a lipsticked mouth like a crimson gash.

I only glimpse her for a moment.

Just a hint of a smile, and a nod, and then she pops a neon pink candy ball into her mouth and chews approvingly. If this is Fuchsia's freaky way of saying *congratulations,* I guess I accept.

I nod back, turning back to Leo, but when I look her way again...

She's gone.

And now I know everything will be all right.

I smile up at Leo, leaning into him, my fingers buried in his hair.

"You know, we kinda have the most screwed up fairy godmother in the world," I whisper, and he chuckles, his arms sliding around my waist.

"Yeah, yeah, but that's how I like our love, babe. Screwed up, scarred, and beautiful. Wouldn't have it any other way," he growls, and his mouth descends on mine.

I kiss him for what seems like forever, giving his chest a playful swat. "Let's try for a little *less* messed up and a little more beautiful, okay? You know I'm good with the scars."

He chuckles. Then I show him just *how* good I am, moaning a soft kiss against his skin, right where his wild ink and untamed scars start around his throat.

"Hell, woman, no argument here. Everything turned out okay in the end, didn't it?" His huge hands cup my face, the safest harbor in the world for my smile.

"More than okay," I tell him.

And that's all the truth we need as I kiss my *husband* some more for the first time, while the cameras flash around us, while the town cheers, while I toss my bouquet blindly over the edge of the cliff, while our son giggles "ew, *gross*" playfully, and while our mouths mate and meld in a shameless heat and passion and love that's survived being torn apart.

Surely, it'll thrive in the decades to come.

Just as long as it's me and my unbroken beast against the world, everything will always be *right*.

EPILOGUE: FINDING EDEN (NINE)

*W*ho knew life in the light would be so blinding?

Maybe because it's not just my own little beam anymore.

It's the full, blaring spotlight, an entire nation suddenly looking at me, at Heart's Edge, at the truth of my story.

At the truth of one fateful night that changed so many lives and set so many things in motion the wheels keep turning at a hundred damn miles an hour. Until I say, *enough.*

Now *I* can finally rest.

Even if it hasn't felt like it for the past few weeks.

When you spend so long in the darkness, sometimes the light sears the world open.

Did I mention how I'm *so fucking tired* of being on TV? There's a reason fame makes some people snap.

Lucky me, I'd already gone half-crazy before I became a hot shot freak of nature hero.

I'm still in the back of the mobile dressing room I've been shoved into by a news team from Seattle, here on location to film the drama I lived. I scrub at my face with a wet towel. The towel comes away beige.

Makeup.

Unreal. They'd slathered makeup on me not to hide my scars and tattoos, but to *emphasize* them. All for sensationalism.

I don't really know what angle they're going for.

Pity for the disfigured beast? Fascination with the monster who always had a heart of gold? Cry-your-eyes-out empathy for the punished hometown hero?

It all feels so fake, but hell.

At the heart of it, I hope I help people learn what Galentron did. If we can prevent a few more evil empires from cropping up, so be it.

If the news needs a mascot to do that, let it be me.

My fists are sick of war. I've had enough hell, enough death and destruction for one lifetime. I wouldn't dream of picking up a gun or going back into security unless there's a damn good reason.

Guess haunting the screen, getting a small cut of the profits with that fancy-schmancy agent I signed with doesn't seem half bad. It eases me back into civilian life, and it's about all I want to do with these hands besides using 'em on wood to make something beautiful.

If this is my job now, there's a reason.

As long as it does somebody somewhere some good.

Thinking about that makes me think of Fuchsia damn Delaney.

Nah, I shouldn't care.

Shouldn't wonder where she is right now. What she lost to boomerang her back into our lives in the first place.

During that whole mess, she put herself at risk, and in the end she got nothing out of it but slapped in handcuffs. Then she scampered off like the black cat she is.

She was off into the wild with her tail in the air before they could even properly book her at the little drunk tank in town. Nobody's seen her since her low-key pop-in at our wedding.

Sure, she's forever part of my worst memories, but there's something else that eats at me.

Wherever she is now, after she put everything on the line to keep Galentron from silencing me, the woman I love, and our son?

I hope she's okay.

I scrub the last film of sticky makeup away, then toss the towel aside and stare at my reflection. It's strange to see my face so bare, my hair and beard neatly trimmed.

I almost don't recognize the man looking back at me.

I'm so used to not looking at myself.

Can't help but smile. The deep-violet eyes beaming back at me are clearer than I'd ever expect them to be. Hard to believe what I'm seeing.

A man I can respect. After everything I've been through, I can finally respect myself.

I smile wider at my reflection and wink.

Helps a whole lot, too, to have the love and respect of the two most amazing people in my world. And I can't take any more of this nonsense today, keeping me from my family.

There'll be more interviews later. A few major morning shows want to fly me out to New York City for the talk show circuit. A couple literary agents have contacted me about writing a tell-all book.

I'm not much for words, but I've heard Doc say a few times it's a lot like carving wood. Not that he's got much experience with art besides helping Ember write those sappy love songs they sing together sometimes at Brody's.

Right now, I want to steal my wife and son, and run away for our long-delayed honeymoon. We've spent weeks dealing with the news vans and Feds swarming Heart's Edge like hornets, keeping the entire town hopping for *weeks*.

I actually have to take a moment to peek outside the trailer.

But the film crews are all busy packing up their things.

No one's gonna look my way.

I *hope*.

NICOLE SNOW

It feels almost like old times as I sneak out, closing the trailer door, careful with the squeaky hinges.

I slip around the side of the trailer, out of direct line of sight, listening for a moment to make sure no one's calling my name, asking me to stay just for *one more interview.*

There's nothing left that matters to me now except my Rissa and my boy.

* * *

SWEETER THINGS DOESN'T RESEMBLE a war zone anymore.

I can't help but have a touch of pride as I pull up to the shop in my shiny new pickup truck. Yeah, I've had to actually get wheels, now that I'm moving around in broad daylight like a normal human being again.

Affording it wasn't hard. Speaking fees have already covered it.

The rest of the fees went to helping Rissa with her shop's grand re-opening, rather than waiting for the insurer to stop being dicks and cut a damn check.

The wait was worth it. It's never looked better.

The glass in the front window shines with the curling Sweeter Things painted across in gold letters. The floors have been retiled, this time in candy-colored mosaic tiles instead of bone white.

All the fresh display cases sanctify my wife's work. Truffles and bonbons and other delights sit real pretty, works of art fit for a museum—and not the kind that blew to kingdom come.

Behind the register, I see her.

Rissa's glowing today.

She'd been uncertain about taking over the shop at first, but with Deanna wanting to get out of Heart's Edge for some inner peace, it was a perfect swap. They traded places.

My sister-in-law took over the main franchise in Spokane, while my wife settled in to call this town home once more.

I know Heart's Edge has a dark history.

Terrible secrets.

So many hidden pains, losses that never should've happened.

But it feels like the clouds are clearing. The town's already busy rebuilding everything that burned down, minus the twisted shadow of the old mayor's mansion.

Hell, maybe we're all due for a fresh start.

All I know is, we're definitely overdue for that honeymoon.

I watch as she boxes up an order, then step out of my truck as the customer walks out. There's a moment where the woman stops and stares at me, strange expressions playing on her face as she recognizes me and does a double take.

Fuck it, I've gotten used to it now.

Little by little, their shocked instincts are replaced by something I've never seen from the townsfolk before, not toward me.

Warmth.

Relief.

Respect.

And the lady nods at me. "Afternoon, Mr. Regis!" she says before ducking around me to her car, leaving me standing there startled and still a bit shell-shocked myself.

Mr. Regis. Not Nine. Not *monster.* Not *outlaw.* Not *freak.*

Shit. This is going to take some getting used to.

The late afternoon light makes the silver fixtures in the shop shine gold, drawing my eyes to that wood wedding band I carved for my girl as I step inside. Looks sexy as hell perched next to the engagement ring she's kept for so long.

My eyes linger, my chest nearly bursting, before that feeling turns into an outburst as she lifts her head, catches sight of me, and smiles with her green eyes so bright it's like she's spring in December.

We lock eyes for a split second.

Then she ducks her head with a breathless laugh, flushing and reaching up to tuck back a strand of mahogany hair that's escaped its twist. *Fuck, this girl. This wife.*

Her blush highlights the scar down her cheek, a reminder we match in more ways than one.

That's my Rissa. My brave girl, who I'm so proud to love I still want to hop up during one of those studio interviews and scream it to the world.

She's around the counter in a second, tumbling into my arms.

I kiss her cheek, only for her to catch my mouth instead. We savor each other slow and soft with a heat that makes my blood turn into dark molasses, sweet in my veins.

If we weren't in public...

Growling, I nip at her upper lip, wrapping my arms tight around her.

Those lush curves make her more delicious than anything in those cases, pressed against me so hard I almost forget where we are, too busy claiming her mouth, taking her tongue.

She buries her fingers in my hair, moaning softly as her mouth flares hot against mine.

"Hi," she says softly, her voice thick and husky.

"Hey, sweetheart," I answer, sliding my palms down her back to cup the firm, addicting curve of her ass before relaxing. "Good day?"

"Things are still slow while the town settles down, but...it wasn't bad." Her eyes glitter as she drapes herself against me. "All done with filming for the day?"

"Hopefully for good, till whenever they fly me out to NYC. They want to put me on stage with Galentron's defense attorney so the fuck can try to make me look crazy. Anything for ratings," I growl.

She rolls her eyes. "Ugh, good luck. There's too much evidence between Ross and Deanna's files. And too many people willing to testify."

"I don't like it. You on the stand." I grimace. "Hell, I just wanted to protect you from all of this. It's never-ending."

"And *I* want to protect *you*." She rubs her nose on mine. "And

I can do that best by testifying, telling the whole truth about what happened. Then and now. It's time for this town to come clean. It's time to end the secrets."

She's right. I know she's right.

And I remember what Gray said that fateful night I set foot back in town.

It won't be over until you don't have to hide anymore.

I'm not hiding now.

Not from the truth.

Not from my family's love.

Not from the light.

And I feel like, finally, I can start a new chapter in our lives.

"Let's worry about that later," I say, lifting her off her feet in a little whirl. "Where's the munchkin?"

"Playing Fortnite on the office computer." Groaning, she slumps against me, letting me hold her up fully, her weight so wonderful in my arms. "He's started doing this weird thing called 'flossing' he learned in the game. It's harmless, but he's going to break something flailing his arms around like that!"

"Stuff can be replaced." I set her down gently and tangle my hand in hers, tugging her toward the back and the office. "Think you can close the shop up for the weekend without hurting anything?"

Rissa blinks at me quizzically. "Probably. I don't have any open catering orders, and word's still getting out that we're open again, and most of my recent stock is still at The Nest. Why?"

"Because we never had ourselves a proper honeymoon," I say, tossing back a wicked grin. "And I think it's time for a family getaway."

She gasps, but anything she says is drowned out by a sudden shout.

"Daaaaaad!" echoes from the office.

Zach must've heard my voice. I'd be lying if I said it didn't feel like the sweetest goddamn heartbreak every time I hear my son call me *Dad*.

He comes rocketing out of the office, and suddenly I've got my arms full with both of them, Zach swept up against my chest, and Clarissa hugging me close.

I never imagined having this.

Never dared imagine this could be mine.

It's like I've just come out of purgatory on the other side of Eden. I've *earned* my way in.

I squeeze them both tight, while Clarissa makes a soft, hitched sound and curls her fingers in my shirt, resting her head on my shoulder.

"Leo," she whispers, rubbing her cheek against me. "I'll close up and we'll pack. Anywhere you want to go, we're there."

* * *

So MAYBE IT's not some grand romantic getaway to Italy.

Fine by me, I don't even want to think what the paparazzi would do if they got their hands on me.

But the snow at the ski resort in Squaw Valley is beautiful, blanketing everything in white silence.

We're surrounded by other people—vacationers, honeymooners, athletes—but the snow makes everything peaceful and perfect, cutting us off from others, leaving us isolated in our own little world.

Our cabin's set back in the woods, a spectacular view over rocky, snow-strewn slopes.

No reporters here.

No curious townsfolk wanting to be part of a new legend.

No friends who, no matter how well-meaning, can sometimes be a little too protective.

Just us.

Just right.

It's been an exhausting day, teaching Zach how to ski, then carrying him on my shoulders when he turns out to be a little too clumsy for it right now.

Can't say I was much better.

While Clarissa skied circles around us, we floundered down the mountain again and again, laughing, exhausting ourselves till it was time to head back in, clean up, and make some dinner.

Clarissa's inside now, putting our very tired son to bed in his own room, while I hunker down on the porch and take in the evening.

It's just stars over treetops, and snow turned blue by evening light.

Perfection.

I've got a fresh bit of wood in my hand, slowly shaving it away to match the shape in my head. I'm not sure what I'm making just yet.

Maybe a little wooden kitten for Zach. He's been hinting at wanting a cat like Mozart, but we're not sure he's ready for the responsibility yet.

I know because Zach's not like other little boys.

He'll be different, but at least now I'll be able to be there for him, so he won't have to deal with that shit alone.

Rissa's soft footsteps warn me before the door opens and she steps outside. I'm in a thick coat against the cold, but she shivers as she steps out in nothing but jeans and a light sweater, her face warming in a lovely smile as she looks down at me.

"Hey," she murmurs, and I tilt my head back against my chair and smile up at her.

"How's Zach?"

"Out like a light. Good job letting him tire himself out." She giggles, leaning her hip against my chair, her thigh warm on my arm. "He tried to stay awake to ask for a story but didn't even get the words out before he was gone."

"It's been a busy day." I flick my knife closed and slip it into my coat, the bit of carved wood following, and slide one arm around her waist. "Seems like we could use a bed, too."

Clarissa's so pliant when she sways against me. Turns my dick hard instantly.

I love how she tumbles into my lap. The way she wants me, makes it so clear.

Sweet fuckery.

It ignites my blood till there's no earthly way I could be cold.

"I have a feeling," she murmurs, faking a yawn, slipping her arms around my neck, "you have something *else* in mind besides sleep, if we go to bed."

"Damn good hunch," I say, sweeping her up in my arms, against my chest as I stand.

There's barely any hesitation. We're on each other—needy, insatiable, this hunger that feels like it's taken me over and swallowed up my soul.

We've always been like this.

Combustive. Consuming. Crazy.

Always with the passion of a thing that could burn out at any moment.

Almost like we knew, deep down in the dream we'd made for ourselves all those years ago, that these moments could be torn away from us by the darkness.

But the dark's gone now.

And there's only light left between us, light and heat and love everlasting.

Nothing's *ever* taking it away from us again.

And tonight, miles and memories away from Heart's Edge, it feels like the first time all over again as I lay her down in our bed beneath a skylight full of stars.

Cold seeps through the glass, but I can't feel it with this wildcat under me.

"Yeah, fuck, just like that," I growl, grinding my hips into hers, loving how she moans against my tongue.

I can only feel raw heat as I look down at her against the sheets, remembering the first time she laid beneath the stars and looked up at me with that little smile the sky reflected in her eyes and her hair spread around her in a pool of rich, gleaming brown.

She's older now. The sweetness of her features aged into an elegance that makes her beauty even deeper.

That scar of hers isn't so fresh, slashing down her cheek, but it's a muted accent. It highlights the smoothness of her skin, the crests of her cheekbones, the kiss I want to bite and taste and own like fire.

My hands explore her body, savoring every bit of it, every way it's changed too. Her tits sway heavier, her hips and thighs thicker, a legacy of the first time I knocked her up, making me want to do it all over again.

Biggest change is, she's stronger.

I sense it in every line of her, and it makes me burst with pride, knowing everything she's fought through to get where we are now. Here and absolutely *mine.*

Usually, I feel the need to tell her how much I love her. Not tonight.

I need to fucking *show* her.

So I do.

I give it in the way I touch her, reverently pulling her out of her clothes, peeling everything down her arms and legs, trailing my lips over every naked bit of pale, soft skin.

"Fuck, Rissa," I snarl, stamping my hot, wandering mouth against her skin.

"Leo!" she whimpers, tangling her feet around my calves.

This woman might just kill me. But if she does, I'm fucking her off this sweet earth with me.

She's all sighs and moonlight and saucy purrs, offering her curves, savoring my fingers.

Once, long ago, I might've felt like I was defiling her beauty with my coarse, battered hands.

But she's made me realize I'm not ugly at all.

If I'm a monster, a beast, a dick with a one-track mind, I'm *hers.*

Wild and fierce and made to protect her, protect our family, and always, always guard what matters to us most.

Once she's naked, I take in her full glory.

My Rissa.

My *wife*, the ring on her finger etched like my body, set above the diamond that represents a promise made so long ago.

She's never looked more perfect than she does now.

She smiles shyly up at me and reaches to run her finger down the front buttons of my coat. "Bad news. You're staring," she whispers, green eyes on fire with emotion. "And still dressed."

Smiling, I catch her hand and kiss her palm. "You want me that bad?"

She nods eagerly.

"Rules are rules. It's totally not fair if only *you* get to stare." Her fingers curl against my cheek, roughing at my stubble. "Let's see my sexy beast."

One thing I've learned: I can't deny this woman anything when she asks in the buff.

I peel off my clothing in a frantic snarl, baring myself to her.

To her gaze.

To her touch.

I have nothing I need to hide anymore.

No shame in who I am, exposing myself to the sleek touch of her greedy fingers as she strokes them over my chest, curls her fingers against the back of my neck, draws me down, and engulfs my tongue.

Fuck!

The feeling of skin on skin as I sink down makes me delirious. It's electrifying.

I fit between her thighs, groaning like a bull. We lock together like somebody made us that way—our mouths, our flesh, her legs spreading around me and ankles digging into my ass.

Naked as the day we were born, in flesh, in heart, in soul.

Screw secrets. I've got no more. Not from her.

And I give myself over to the raw, seething honesty of our

kiss, feeling my heart overflow as this minx accepts me with such total horny faith.

Her love always makes me whole. Her pussy makes me *crave* deep, wicked things.

There's just the soft flick of her tongue and the warm curl of her breath and the sweet caress of her palms.

Her plush tits slide against my chest, and the way her flesh yields burns me right down.

Her inner thighs hug my hips like she's clay.

We move as one, total opposites and kindred spirits. We fuck like we're still making up for yesterday and for tomorrow too, but damn if we're not in the present.

Heat becomes passion, then desire.

Then the shivering, sweet friction along my flesh gathers in my cock. I feel like I'm harder for her tonight than I've ever been, the rampant emotion of taking her hotter and sexier than even the wildest lust.

You don't know desire till you *know* the feeling of a woman in full surrender.

You don't know need till you've got her in your arms, and you know she belongs, she's yours, rousing that animal instinct that needs to claim and mark and rut and mate.

It's a slow burn, thrusting together, teasing each other with every stroke, with a rhythm that entices and pushes us toward what I know we both want.

Slow, but undeniable.

Hot as a desert sun, ready as hell to burn right through the winter night.

It's like we're white-hot pistols as those teasing ruts turn into real, deep strokes. She opens herself to me, lifts her hips, meshes our bodies together and on the next sway, I slip inside her, finding home.

No matter how tight she is, how small, it's always the same.

She opens for every inch of me.

She accepts my dick to the hilt, even as I push my balls against her ass, all her warmth driving me insane.

We share one rhythm as my hips go to work, pounding into her.

Yeah, call me crazy, but we even fuck with one pulse.

And as her heat surrounds me, as I snarl at her mouth and sink my teeth in her lip, bringing her off for the first of many Os, I'm undone.

Complete.

Once a shell of a man, broken into fragments, this half life of mine hidden out in the hills and my forgotten cave, nothing more than a holding pattern.

With her, I can finally move forward.

With her, I can finally stand in the light.

With her, I can fuck myself into the stone age and love every second.

And with her, I sink myself into the purest pleasure I've ever known.

She gives it back just as good, every bit of her writhing under me, soft peaks and sweet cunt stroking my cock something fierce.

Fuck! We tumble together, locking ourselves in gasps and the wet, slick sound of flesh sliding together in sharp, searing bursts. Rissa clutches so tight at my shoulders, at my cock, at my *everything.*

She won't let me go.

I won't lose her again.

We won't lose *this.*

That's my vow, branded in the flesh, my hips working hers so hard they might bruise.

I kiss it into her lips, her throat, lacing our fingers together, ring to ring, and whisper the words that matter to me more than anything.

"Love you," I growl, and I know I'll say it a thousand more

times so she'll never forget. "I always have, Rissa, and I always will."

Her eyes flutter open big, and I surge a little deeper, making her arch, but she still, *still* holds me so tight.

"Leo," she gasps, her voice ragged with desire "God, *Leo*, I've always loved you. I always knew who you were."

"The only one who ever did. The only one who ever *will*," I promise, and kiss her again and again and again.

No denying it.

Can't deny what she does to me either as I fuck us both home, my whole body working, driving her into the bed so hard I think we'll shake the damn thing apart. She senses it a split second ahead of my whole body tensing, swelling, erupting.

Then we're just coming so hard together.

Her *you* tangled in my *I,* this heap of Mr. and Mrs. Regis so lovely I can't tell where either of us begins or ends.

And hell, after tonight, I don't think I want to.

* * *

OUR FATES WERE TANGLED up since the first day I stood on the edge of a creek and watched a pretty little girl twirling a flower between her fingers, the sun so bright in her hair and the wind blowing through her dress.

Since the first second our eyes met, she smiled at me with a sweetness that's never changed through the years.

We were always meant to find each other.

I was meant to come back for her.

Always.

And now that I have, we'll never be apart.

That's a promise I know I can keep.

ABOUT NICOLE SNOW

Nicole Snow is a *Wall Street Journal* and *USA Today* bestselling author. She found her love of writing by hashing out love scenes on lunch breaks and plotting her great escape from boardrooms. Her work roared onto the indie romance scene in 2014 with her Grizzlies MC series.

Since then Snow aims for the very best in growly, heart-of-gold alpha heroes, unbelievable suspense, and swoon storms aplenty.

Already hooked on her stuff? Visit nicolesnowbooks.com to sign up for her newsletter and connect on social media.

Got a question or comment on her work? Reach her anytime at nicole@nicolesnowbooks.com

Thanks for reading. And please remember to leave an honest review! Nothing helps an author more.

Still Not Love

Baby Fever Books

Baby Fever Bride

Baby Fever Promise

Baby Fever Secrets

Only Pretend Books

Fiance on Paper

One Night Bride

Grizzlies MC Books

Outlaw's Kiss

Outlaw's Obsession

Outlaw's Bride

Outlaw's Vow

Deadly Pistols MC Books

Never Love an Outlaw

Never Kiss an Outlaw

Never Have an Outlaw's Baby

Never Wed an Outlaw

Prairie Devils MC Books

Outlaw Kind of Love

Nomad Kind of Love

Savage Kind of Love

Wicked Kind of Love

Bitter Kind of Love